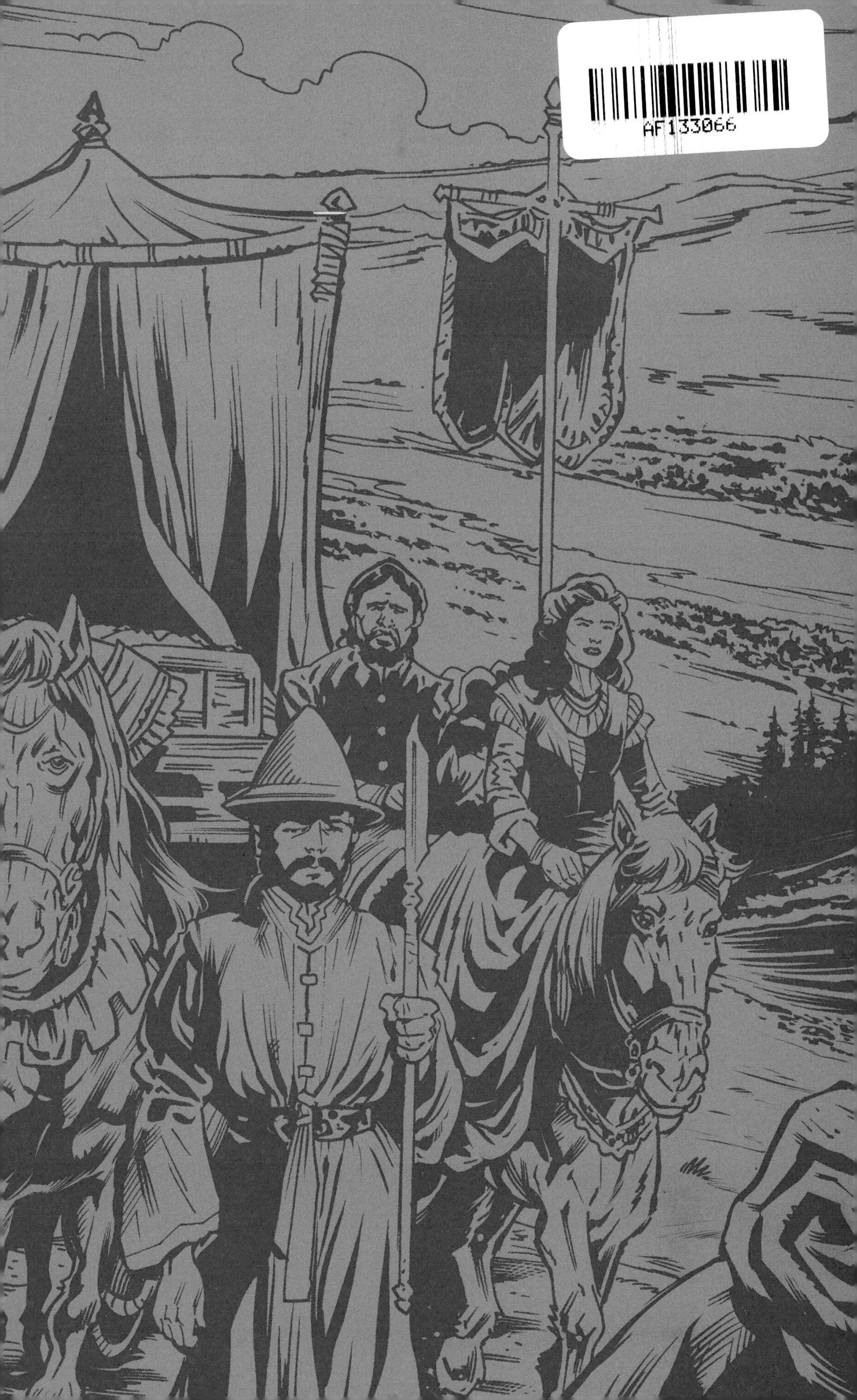

Assassin's Apprentice

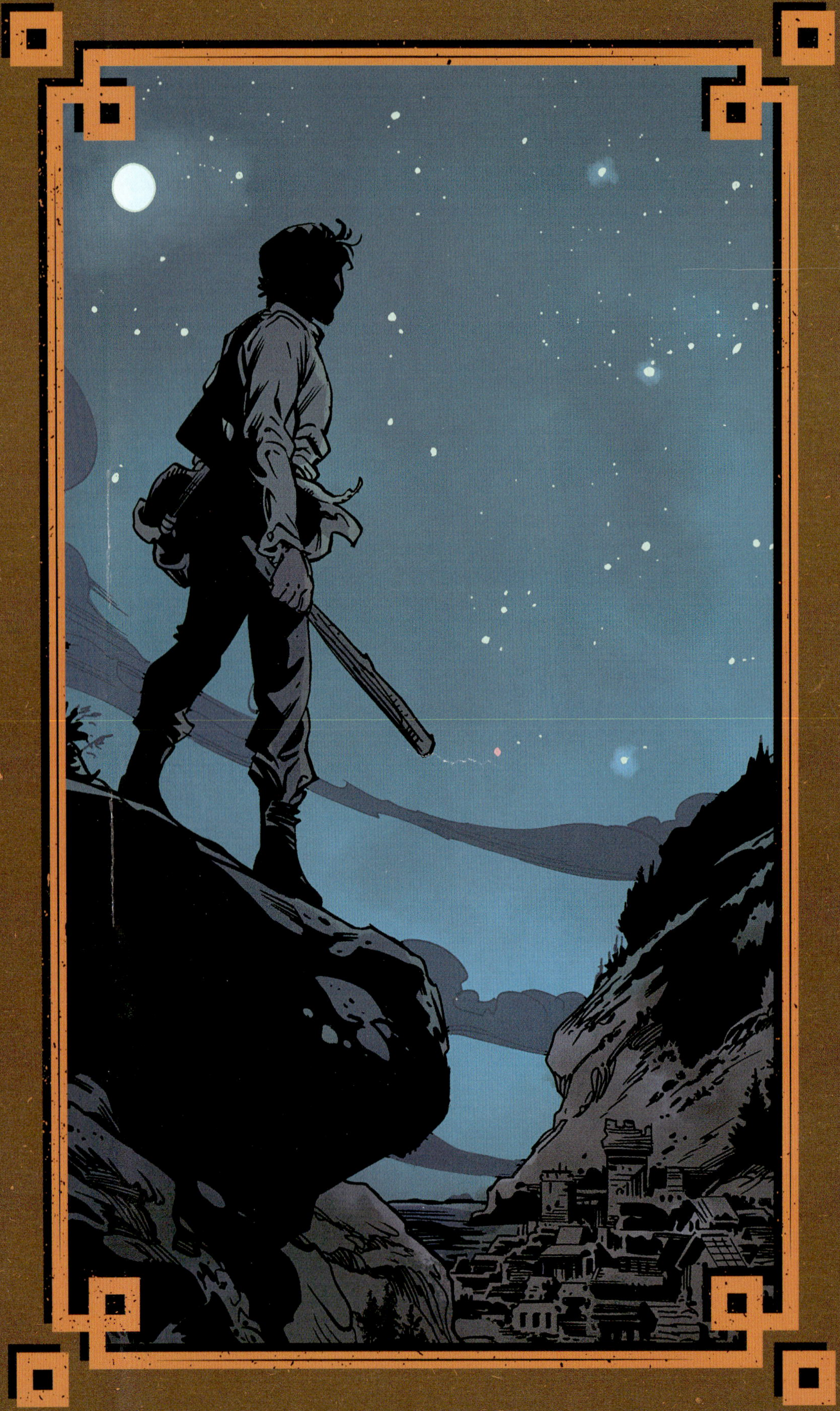

Assassin's Apprentice

Volume 3

Written by
Robin Hobb and Jody Houser

Script by
Jody Houser

Illustrated by
Ryan Kelly

Color Art by
Jordie Bellaire

Letters by
Hassan Otsmane-Elhaou

Cover Art by
Anna Steinbauer

Assassin's Apprentice Created by Robin Hobb

HARPER
Voyager

President and Publisher
Mike Richardson

Editor
Brett Israel

Assistant Editor
Tara McCarron

Collection Designers
Kristofer McRae and **Lia Ribacchi**

Digital Art Technician
Betsy Howitt

Prepress
Maureen Heaster

ASSASSIN'S APPRENTICE VOLUME 3

Copyright © 2024, 2025 by Robin Hobb. Based on the novel *Assassin's Apprentice*, copyright © 1995 by Robin Hobb. All characters featured in this book, and the distinctive names and likenesses thereof, and all related indicia, are trademarks of Robin Hobb, and are used by permission. Dark Horse Books® and the Dark Horse logo are registered trademarks of Dark Horse Comics LLC, registered in various categories and countries. All rights reserved. Dark Horse is part of Embracer Group.
Published in the US in 2025 by Dark Horse Books.

Harper*Voyager* an imprint of HarperCollins*Publishers* Ltd
1 London Bridge Street, London, SE1 9GF

www.harpercollins.co.uk

HarperCollins*Publishers*,
Macken House, 39/40 Mayor Street Upper,
Dublin 1, DO1 C9W8, Ireland

First published in Great Britain by HarperCollinsPublishers 2026
1

Written by Robin Hobb and Jody Houser; script by Jody Houser; illustrated by Ryan Kelly; color art by Jordie Bellaire; letters by Hassan Otsmane-Elhaou; cover art by Anna Steinbauer.

A catalogue record for this book is available from the British Library.

ISBN: 978-0-00-868252-1

This novel is entirely a work of fiction.

The names, characters and incidents portrayed in it are the work of the author's imagination. Any resemblance to actual persons, living or dead, events or localities is entirely coincidental.

Printed and bound in India by Replika Press Pvt. Ltd.

All rights reserved. No part of this publication may be reproduced, stored in a retrieval system, or transmitted, in any form or by any means, electronic, mechanical, photocopying, recording or otherwise, without the prior written permission of the publishers.

Without limiting the exclusive rights of any author, contributor or the publisher of this publication, any unauthorised use of this publication to train generative artificial intelligence (AI) technologies is expressly prohibited. HarperCollins also exercise their rights under Article 4(3) of the Digital Single Market Directive 2019/790 and expressly reserve this publication from the text and data mining exception.

MIX
Paper | Supporting responsible forestry
FSC™ C007454

This book contains FSC™ certified paper and other controlled sources to ensure responsible forest management.

For more information visit: www.harpercollins.co.uk/green

Chapter One

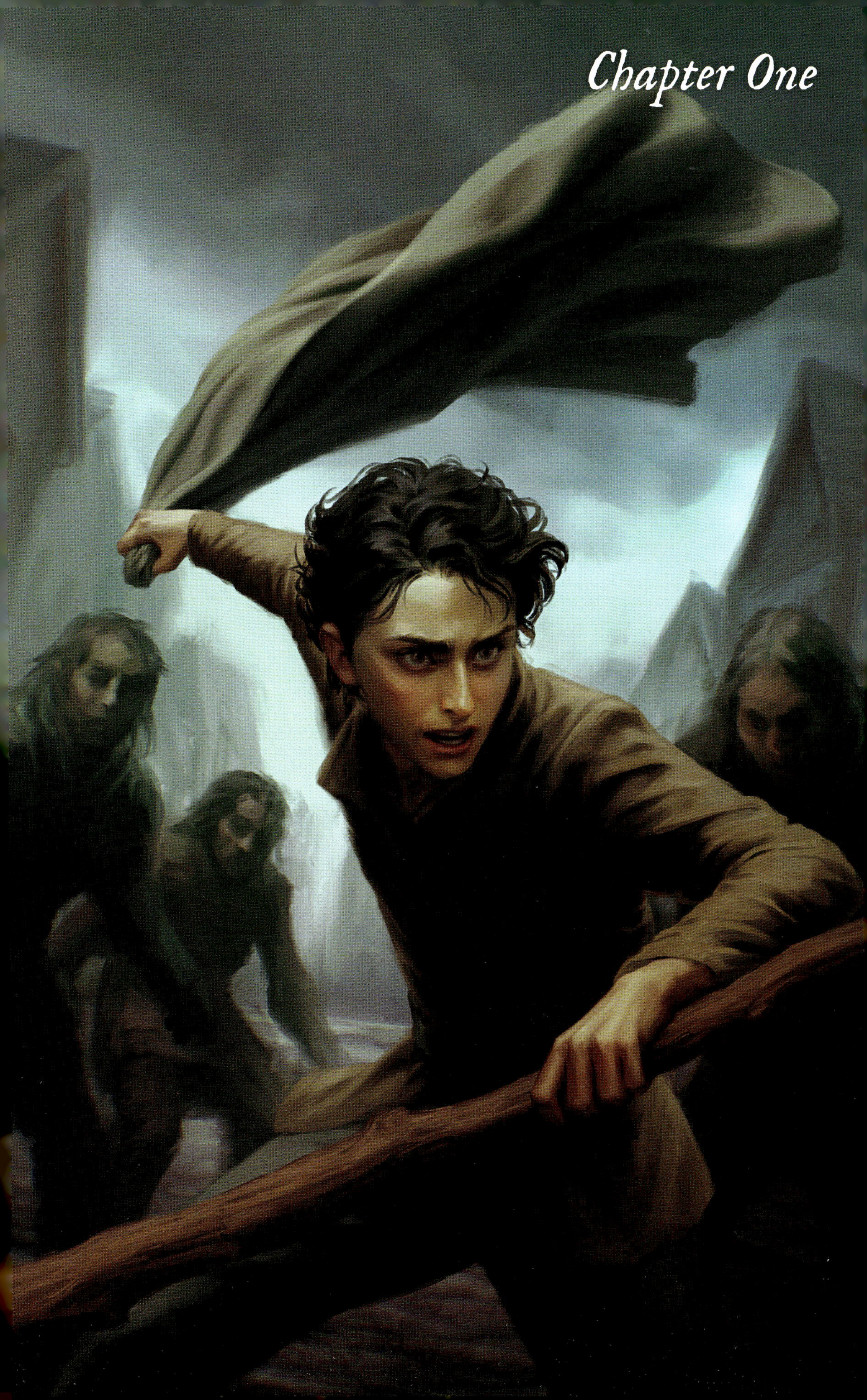

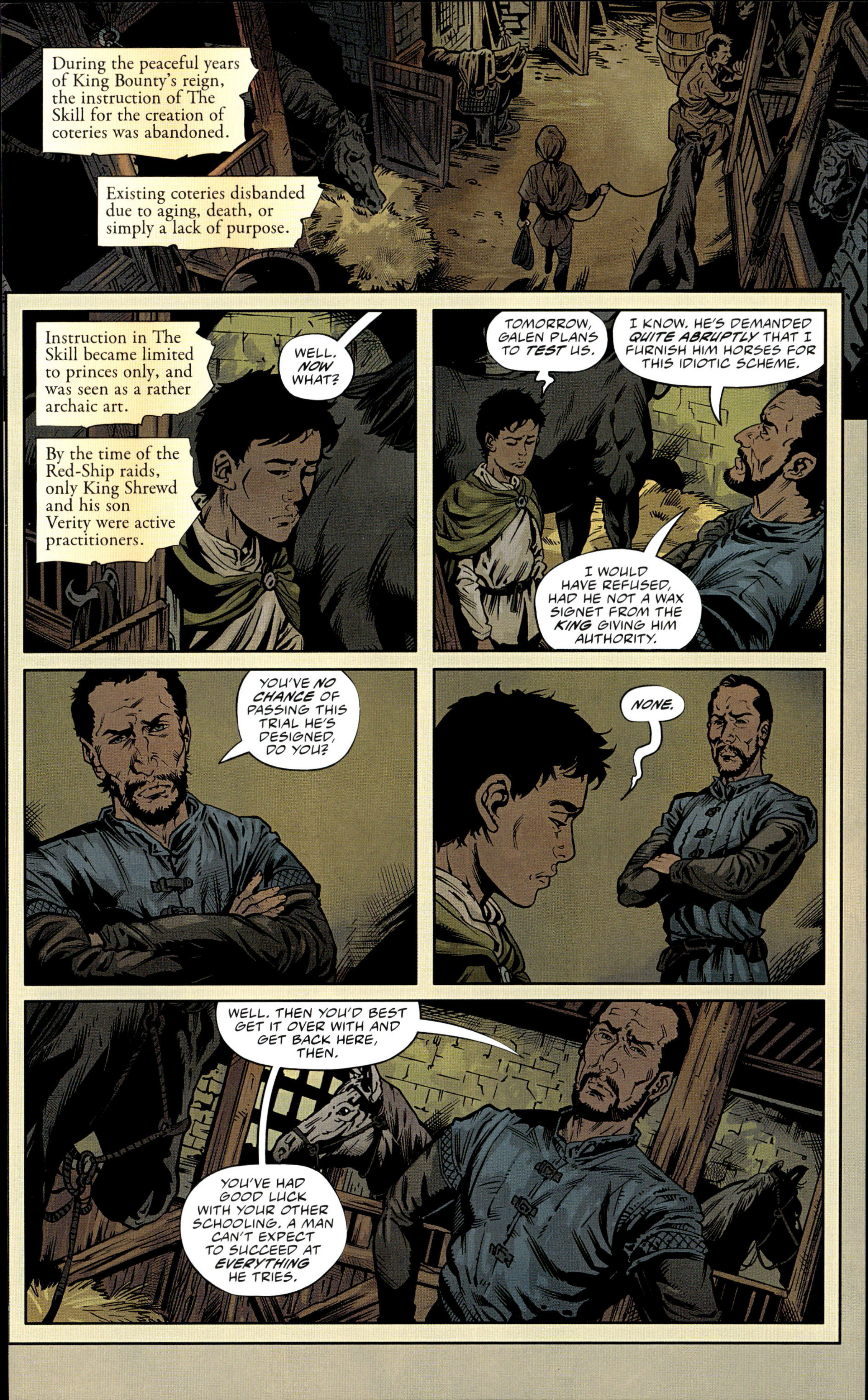
During the peaceful years of King Bounty's reign, the instruction of The Skill for the creation of coteries was abandoned.
Existing coteries disbanded due to aging, death, or simply a lack of purpose.
Instruction in The Skill became limited to princes only, and was seen as a rather archaic art.
By the time of the Red-Ship raids, only King Shrewd and his son Verity were active practitioners.
WELL. *NOW* WHAT?
TOMORROW, GALEN PLANS TO *TEST* US.
I KNOW. HE'S DEMANDED *QUITE ABRUPTLY* THAT I FURNISH HIM HORSES FOR THIS IDIOTIC SCHEME.
I WOULD HAVE REFUSED, HAD HE NOT A WAX SIGNET FROM THE *KING* GIVING HIM AUTHORITY.
YOU'VE *NO CHANCE* OF PASSING THIS TRIAL HE'S DESIGNED, DO YOU?
NONE.
WELL. THEN YOU'D BEST GET IT OVER WITH AND GET BACK HERE, THEN.
YOU'VE HAD GOOD LUCK WITH YOUR OTHER SCHOOLING. A MAN CAN'T EXPECT TO SUCCEED AT *EVERYTHING* HE TRIES.

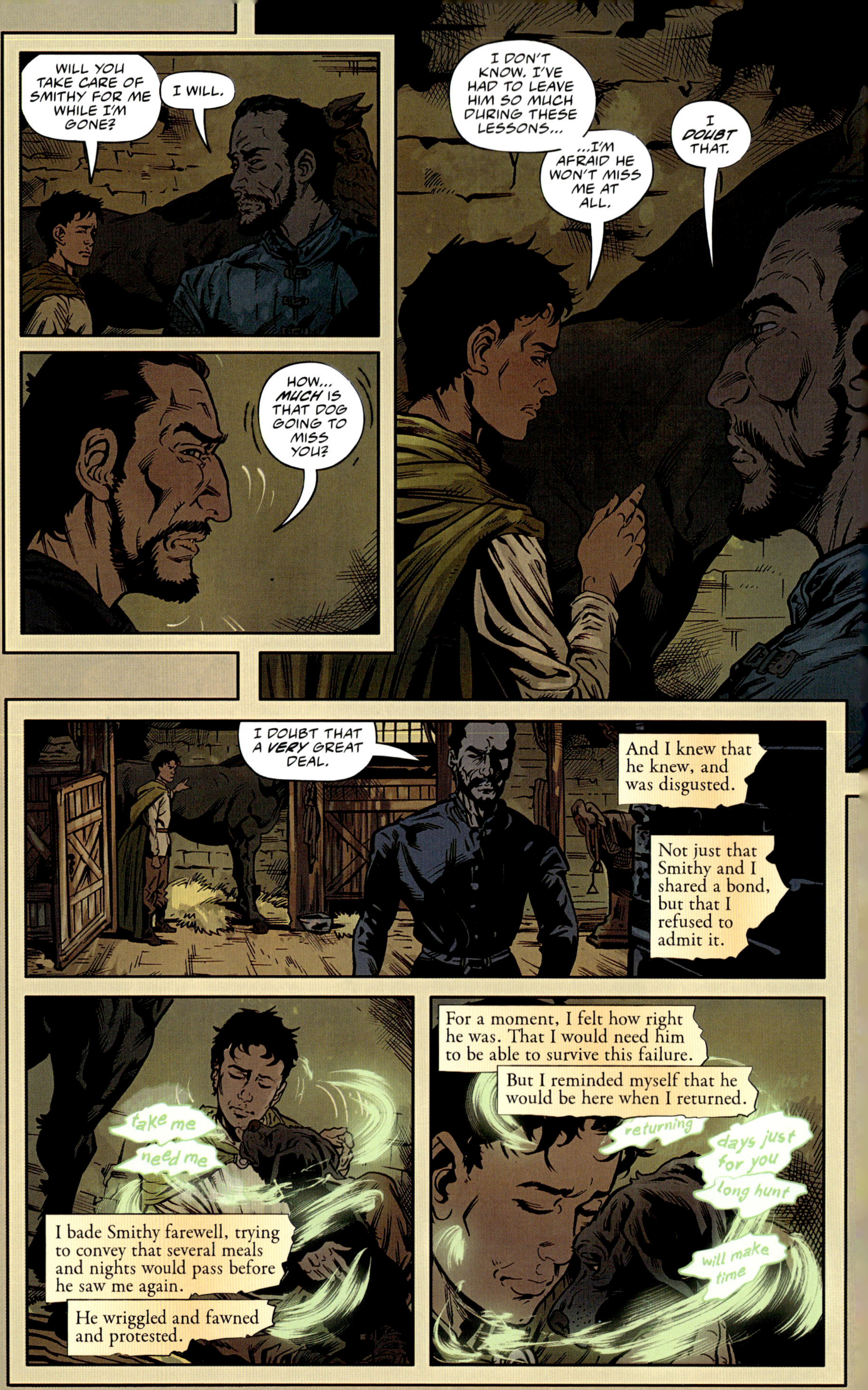
WILL YOU TAKE CARE OF SMITHY FOR ME WHILE I'M GONE?
I WILL.
HOW... MUCH IS THAT DOG GOING TO MISS YOU?
I DON'T KNOW. I'VE HAD TO LEAVE HIM SO MUCH DURING THESE LESSONS...
...I'M AFRAID HE WON'T MISS ME AT ALL.
I DOUBT THAT.
I DOUBT THAT A VERY GREAT DEAL.
And I knew that he knew, and was disgusted.
Not just that Smithy and I shared a bond, but that I refused to admit it.
take me
need me
I bade Smithy farewell, trying to convey that several meals and nights would pass before he saw me again.
He wriggled and fawned and protested.
For a moment, I felt how right he was. That I would need him to be able to survive this failure.
But I reminded myself that he would be here when I returned.
returning
days just for you
long hunt
will make time

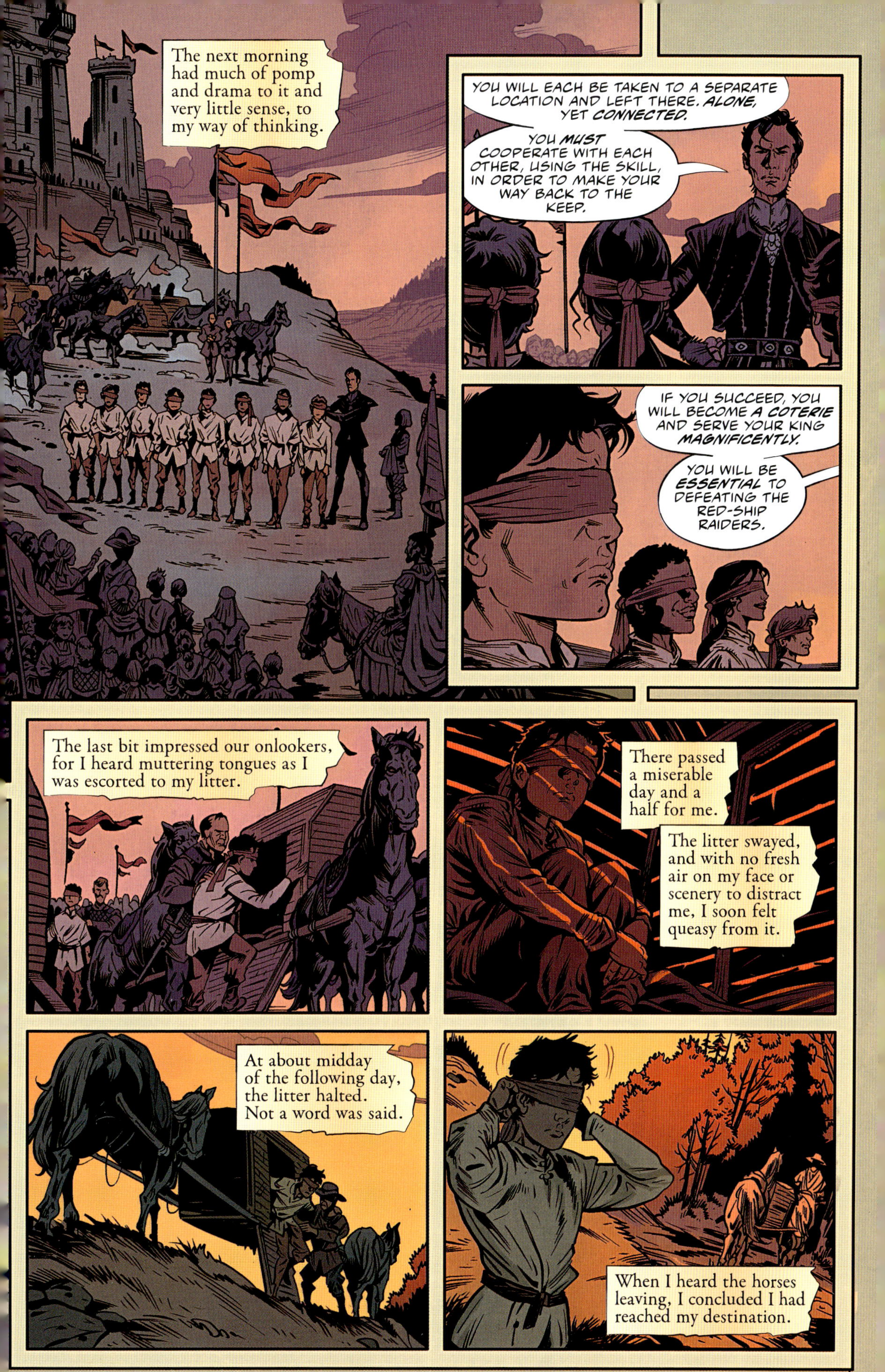
The next morning had much of pomp and drama to it and very little sense, to my way of thinking.
YOU WILL EACH BE TAKEN TO A SEPARATE LOCATION AND LEFT THERE. ALONE, YET CONNECTED.
YOU MUST COOPERATE WITH EACH OTHER, USING THE SKILL, IN ORDER TO MAKE YOUR WAY BACK TO THE KEEP.
IF YOU SUCCEED, YOU WILL BECOME A COTERIE AND SERVE YOUR KING MAGNIFICENTLY.
YOU WILL BE ESSENTIAL TO DEFEATING THE RED-SHIP RAIDERS.
The last bit impressed our onlookers, for I heard muttering tongues as I was escorted to my litter.
There passed a miserable day and a half for me.
The litter swayed, and with no fresh air on my face or scenery to distract me, I soon felt queasy from it.
At about midday of the following day, the litter halted. Not a word was said.
When I heard the horses leaving, I concluded I had reached my destination.

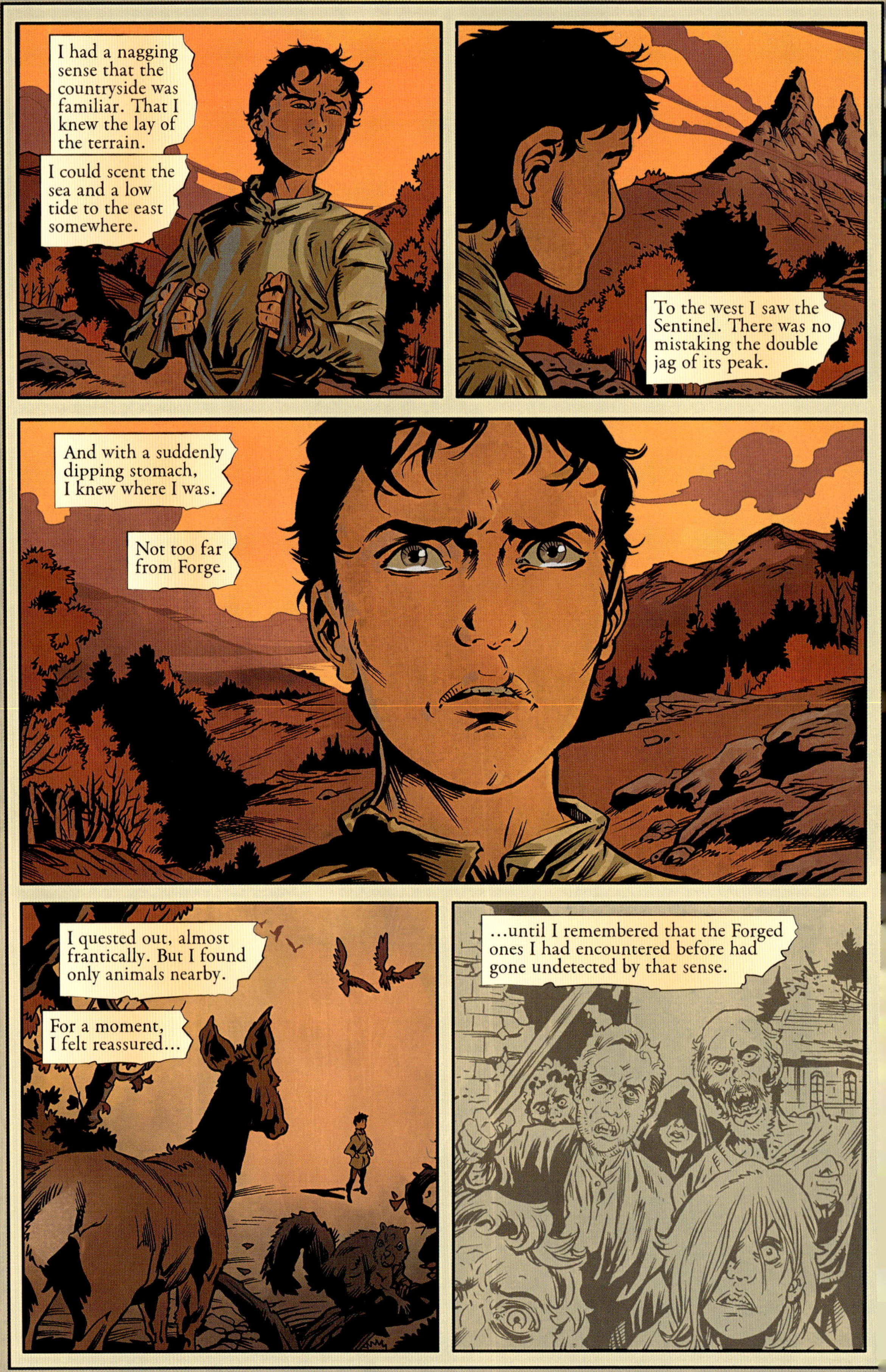
I had a nagging sense that the countryside was familiar. That I knew the lay of the terrain.
I could scent the sea and a low tide to the east somewhere.
To the west I saw the Sentinel. There was no mistaking the double jag of its peak.
And with a suddenly dipping stomach, I knew where I was.
Not too far from Forge.
I quested out, almost frantically. But I found only animals nearby.
For a moment, I felt reassured…
…until I remembered that the Forged ones I had encountered before had gone undetected by that sense.

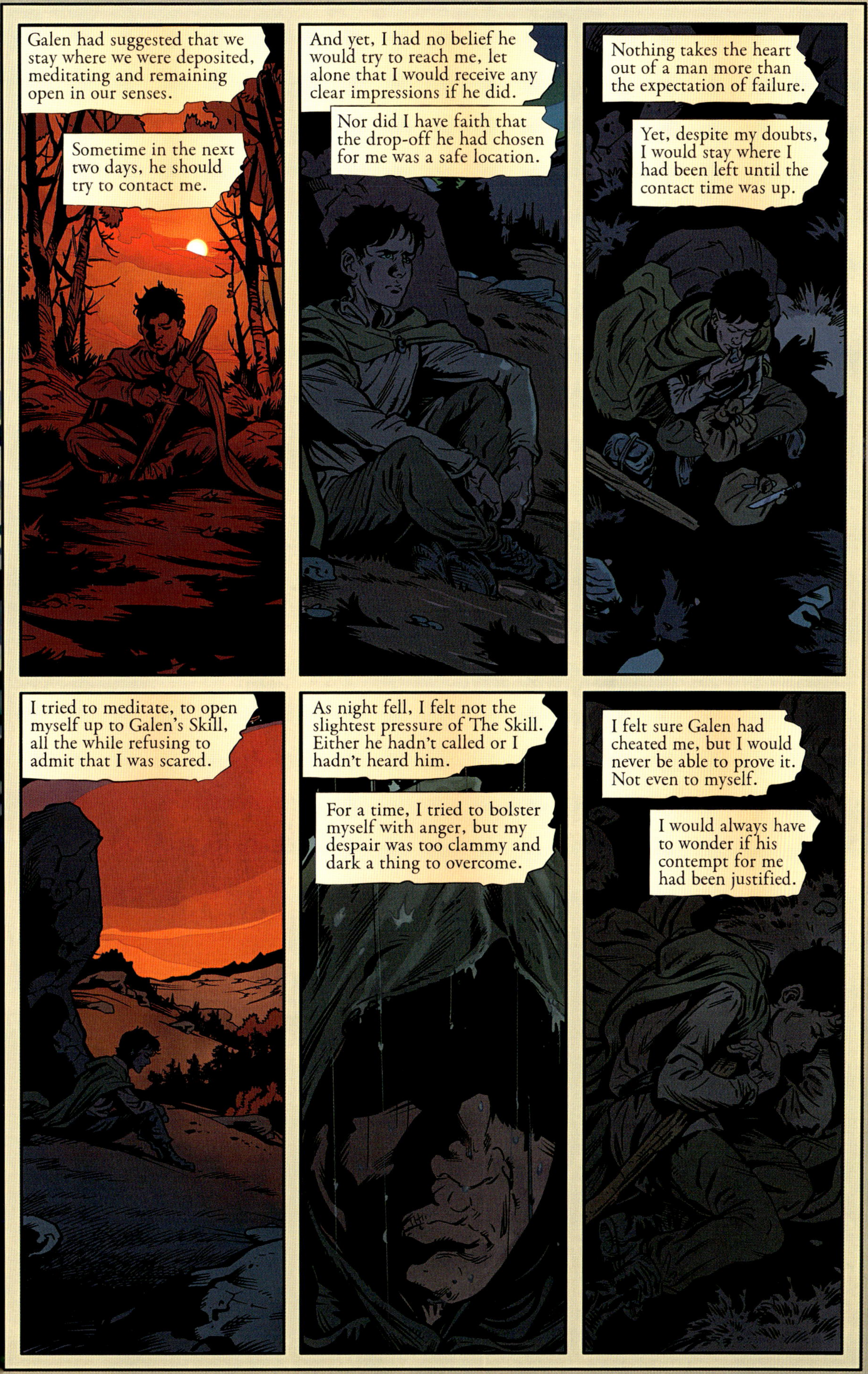
Galen had suggested that we stay where we were deposited, meditating and remaining open in our senses.
Sometime in the next two days, he should try to contact me.
And yet, I had no belief he would try to reach me, let alone that I would receive any clear impressions if he did.
Nor did I have faith that the drop-off he had chosen for me was a safe location.
Nothing takes the heart out of a man more than the expectation of failure.
Yet, despite my doubts, I would stay where I had been left until the contact time was up.
I tried to meditate, to open myself up to Galen's Skill, all the while refusing to admit that I was scared.
As night fell, I felt not the slightest pressure of The Skill. Either he hadn't called or I hadn't heard him.
For a time, I tried to bolster myself with anger, but my despair was too clammy and dark a thing to overcome.
I felt sure Galen had cheated me, but I would never be able to prove it. Not even to myself.
I would always have to wonder if his contempt for me had been justified.

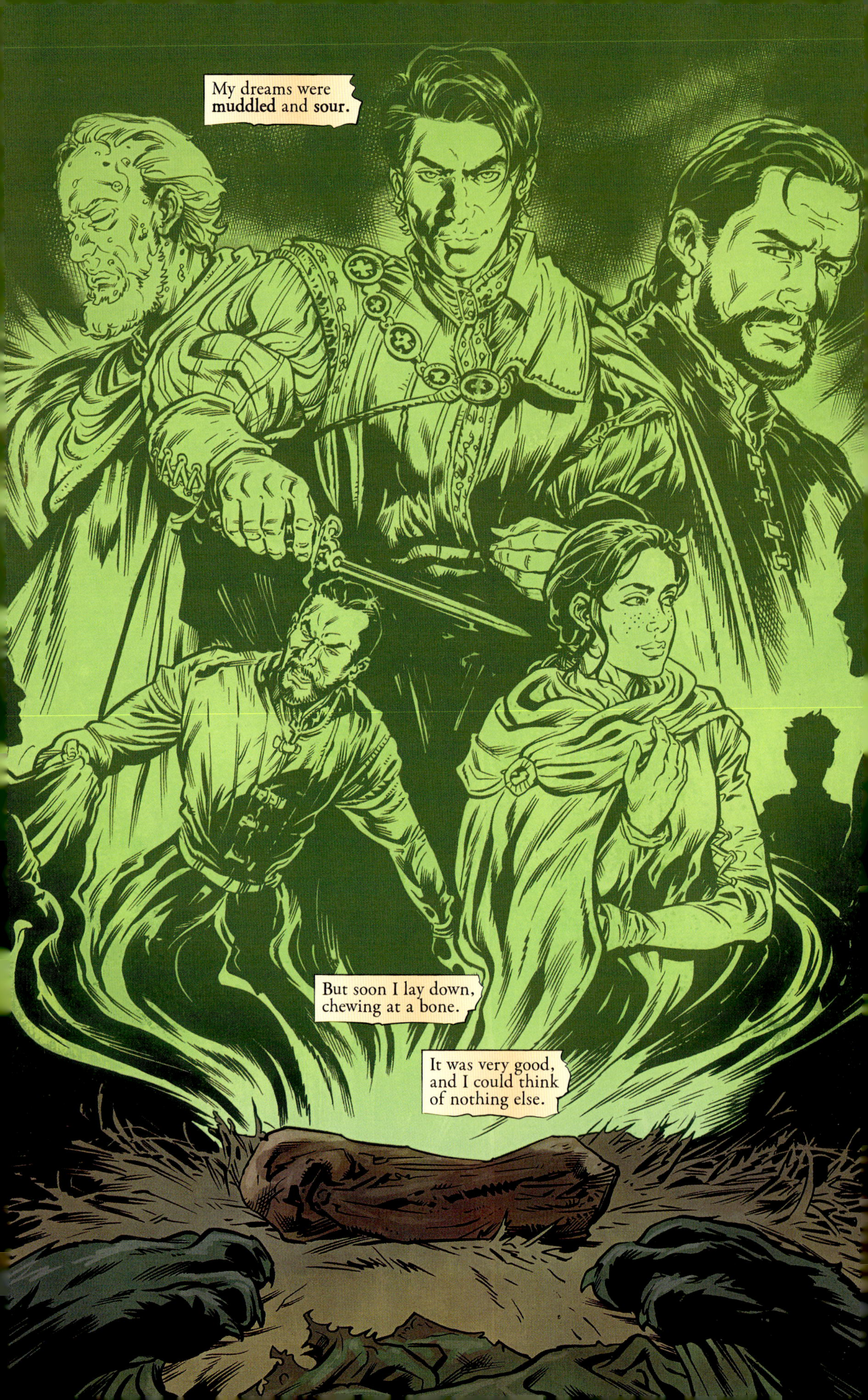
My dreams were **muddled** and **sour.**
But soon I lay down, chewing at a bone.
It was very good, and I could think of nothing else.

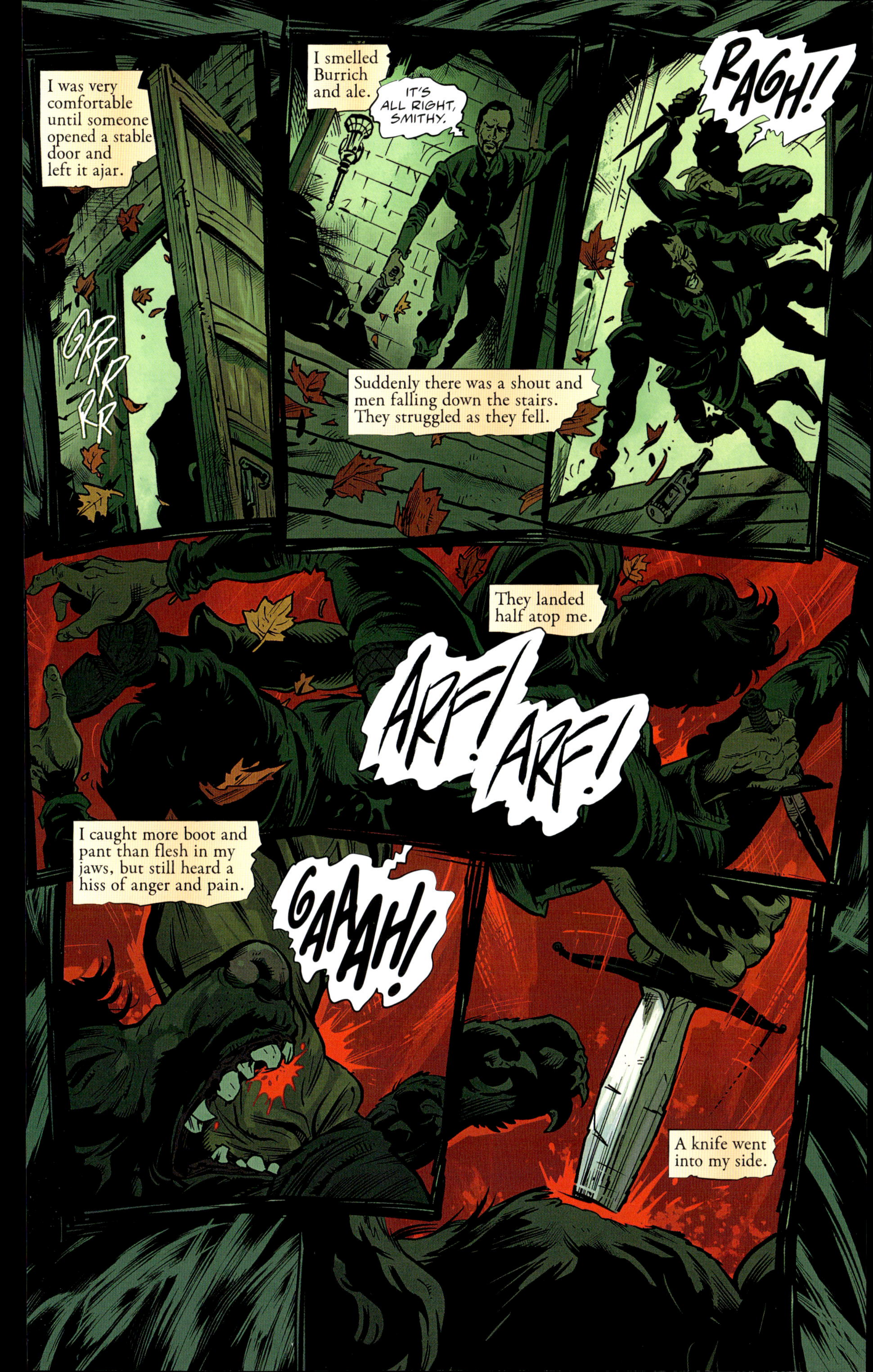
I was very comfortable until someone opened a stable door and left it ajar.
GRRRRR
I smelled Burrich and ale.
IT'S ALL RIGHT, SMITHY.
Suddenly there was a shout and men falling down the stairs. They struggled as they fell.
RAGH!
They landed half atop me.
ARF! ARF!
I caught more boot and pant than flesh in my jaws, but still heard a hiss of anger and pain.
GAAAH!
A knife went into my side.

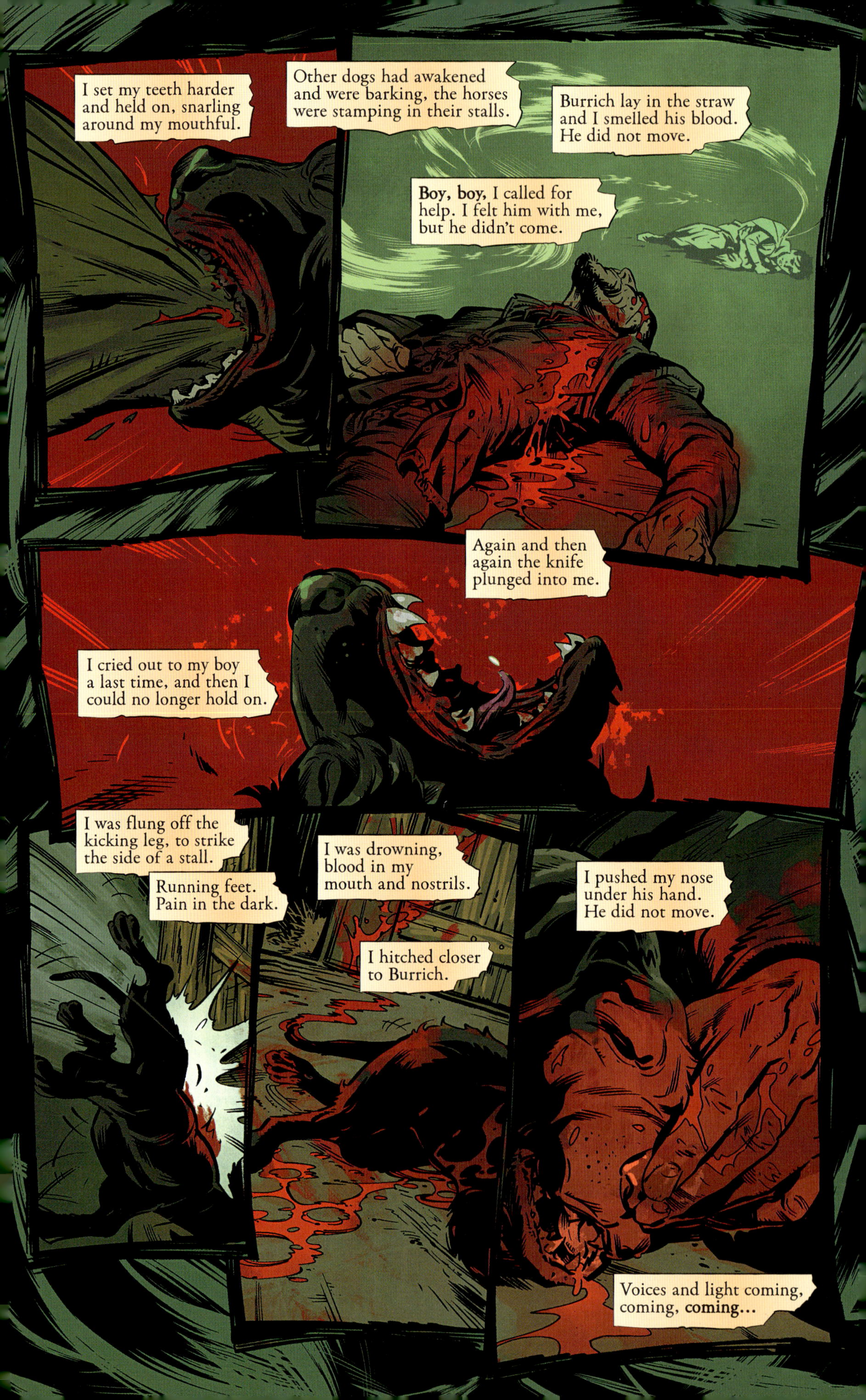
I set my teeth harder and held on, snarling around my mouthful.
Other dogs had awakened and were barking, the horses were stamping in their stalls.
Burrich lay in the straw and I smelled his blood. He did not move.
Boy, boy, I called for help. I felt him with me, but he didn't come.
Again and then again the knife plunged into me.
I cried out to my boy a last time, and then I could no longer hold on.
I was flung off the kicking leg, to strike the side of a stall.
Running feet. Pain in the dark.
I was drowning, blood in my mouth and nostrils.
I hitched closer to Burrich.
I pushed my nose under his hand. He did not move.
Voices and light coming, coming, **coming...**

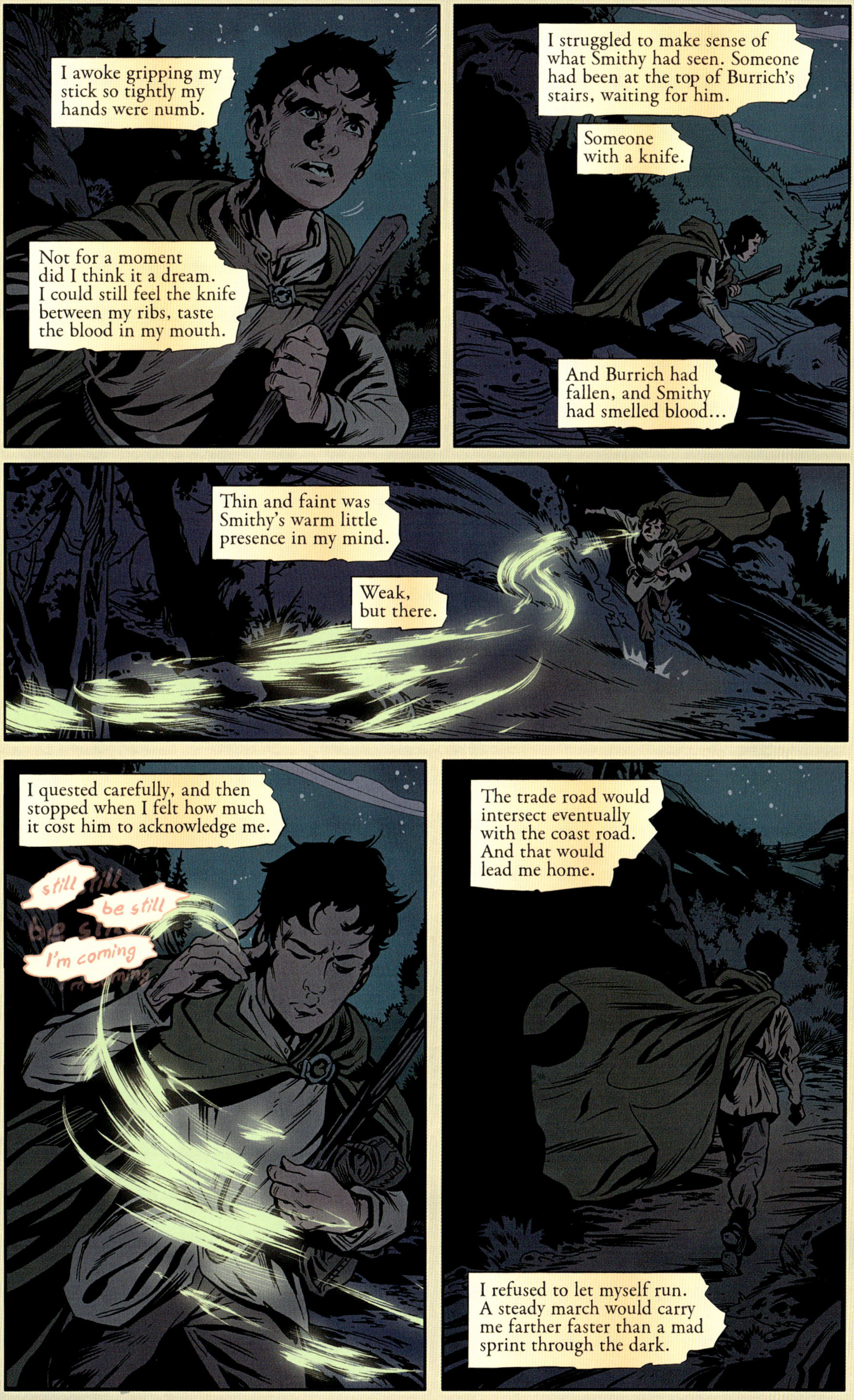
I awoke gripping my stick so tightly my hands were numb.
Not for a moment did I think it a dream. I could still feel the knife between my ribs, taste the blood in my mouth.
I struggled to make sense of what Smithy had seen. Someone had been at the top of Burrich's stairs, waiting for him.
Someone with a knife.
And Burrich had fallen, and Smithy had smelled blood...
Thin and faint was Smithy's warm little presence in my mind.
Weak, but there.
I quested carefully, and then stopped when I felt how much it cost him to acknowledge me.
still
be still
I'm coming
The trade road would intersect eventually with the coast road. And that would lead me home.
I refused to let myself run. A steady march would carry me farther faster than a mad sprint through the dark.

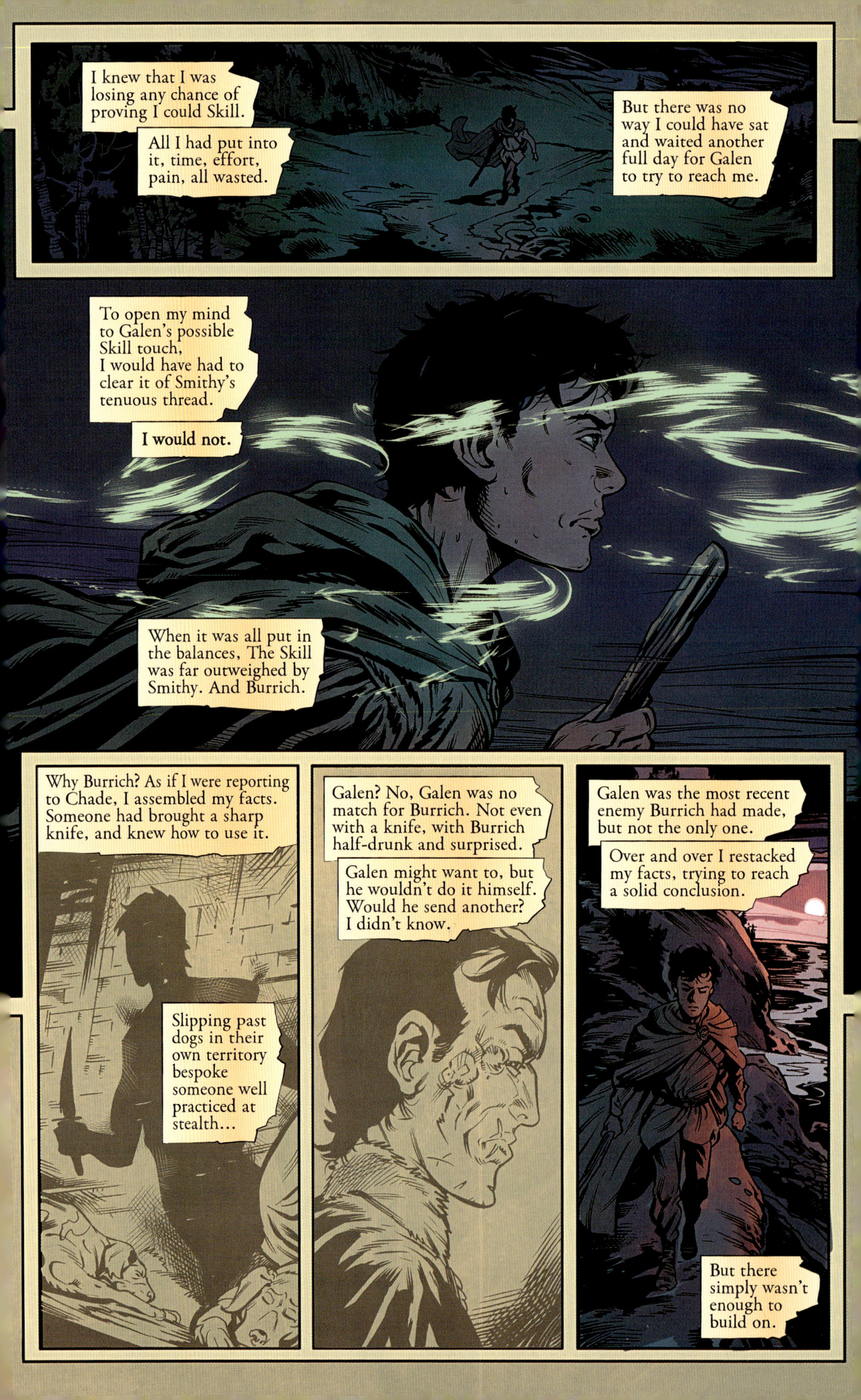
I knew that I was losing any chance of proving I could Skill.
All I had put into it, time, effort, pain, all wasted.
But there was no way I could have sat and waited another full day for Galen to try to reach me.
To open my mind to Galen's possible Skill touch, I would have had to clear it of Smithy's tenuous thread.
I would not.
When it was all put in the balances, The Skill was far outweighed by Smithy. And Burrich.
Why Burrich? As if I were reporting to Chade, I assembled my facts. Someone had brought a sharp knife, and knew how to use it.
Slipping past dogs in their own territory bespoke someone well practiced at stealth...
Galen? No, Galen was no match for Burrich. Not even with a knife, with Burrich half-drunk and surprised.
Galen might want to, but he wouldn't do it himself. Would he send another? I didn't know.
Galen was the most recent enemy Burrich had made, but not the only one.
Over and over I restacked my facts, trying to reach a solid conclusion.
But there simply wasn't enough to build on.

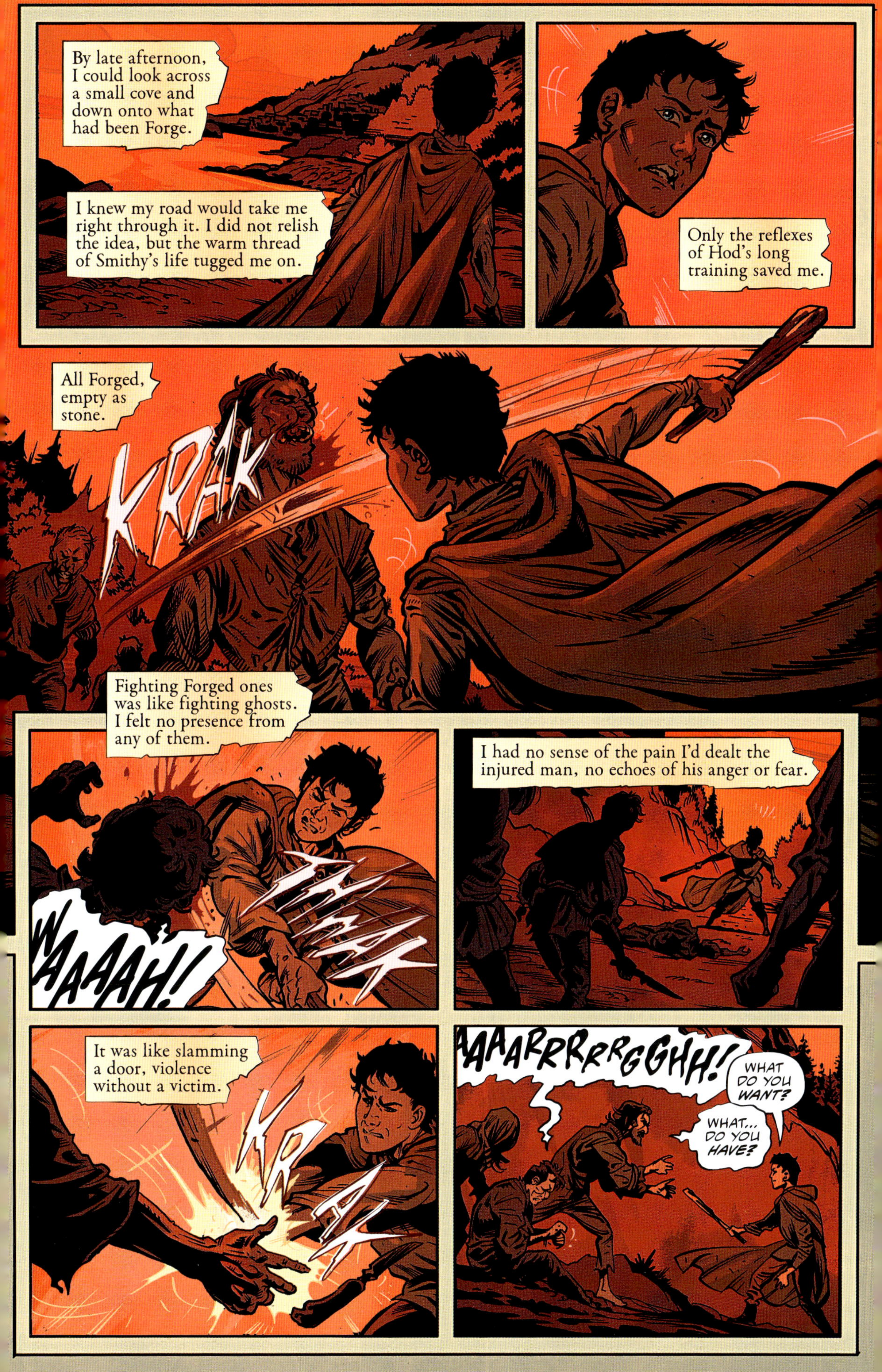
By late afternoon, I could look across a small cove and down onto what had been Forge.
I knew my road would take me right through it. I did not relish the idea, but the warm thread of Smithy's life tugged me on.
Only the reflexes of Hod's long training saved me.
All Forged, empty as stone.
KRAK
Fighting Forged ones was like fighting ghosts. I felt no presence from any of them.
WAAAAH!
THWAK
I had no sense of the pain I'd dealt the injured man, no echoes of his anger or fear.
It was like slamming a door, violence without a victim.
KRAK
AAAARRRRRGGHH!
WHAT DO YOU WANT?
WHAT... DO YOU HAVE?

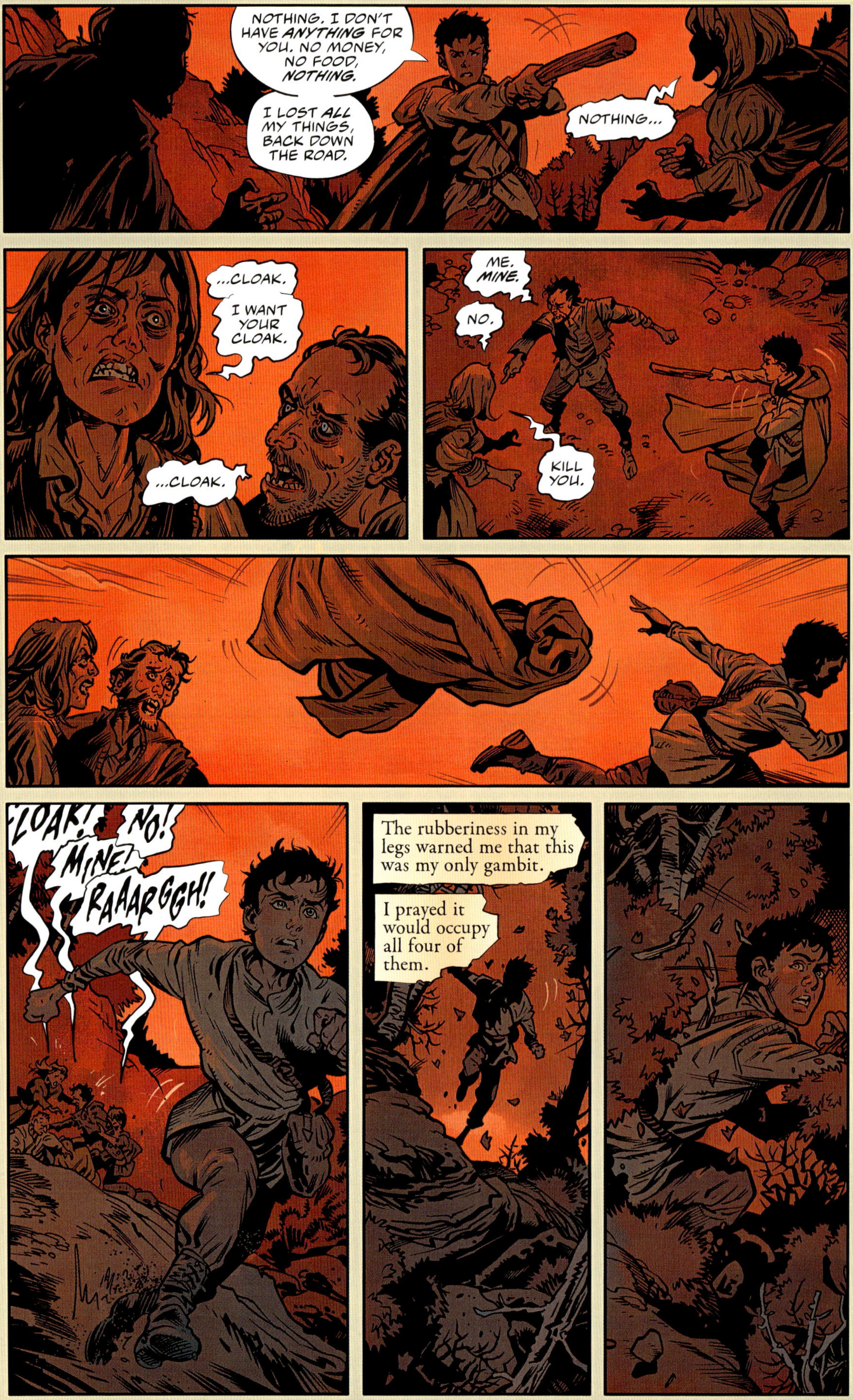
NOTHING. I DON'T HAVE ANYTHING FOR YOU. NO MONEY, NO FOOD, NOTHING.
I LOST ALL MY THINGS, BACK DOWN THE ROAD.
NOTHING...
...CLOAK.
I WANT YOUR CLOAK.
...CLOAK.
ME. MINE.
NO.
KILL YOU.
CLOAK! NO!
MINE!
RAAARGGH!
The rubberiness in my legs warned me that this was my only gambit.
I prayed it would occupy all four of them.

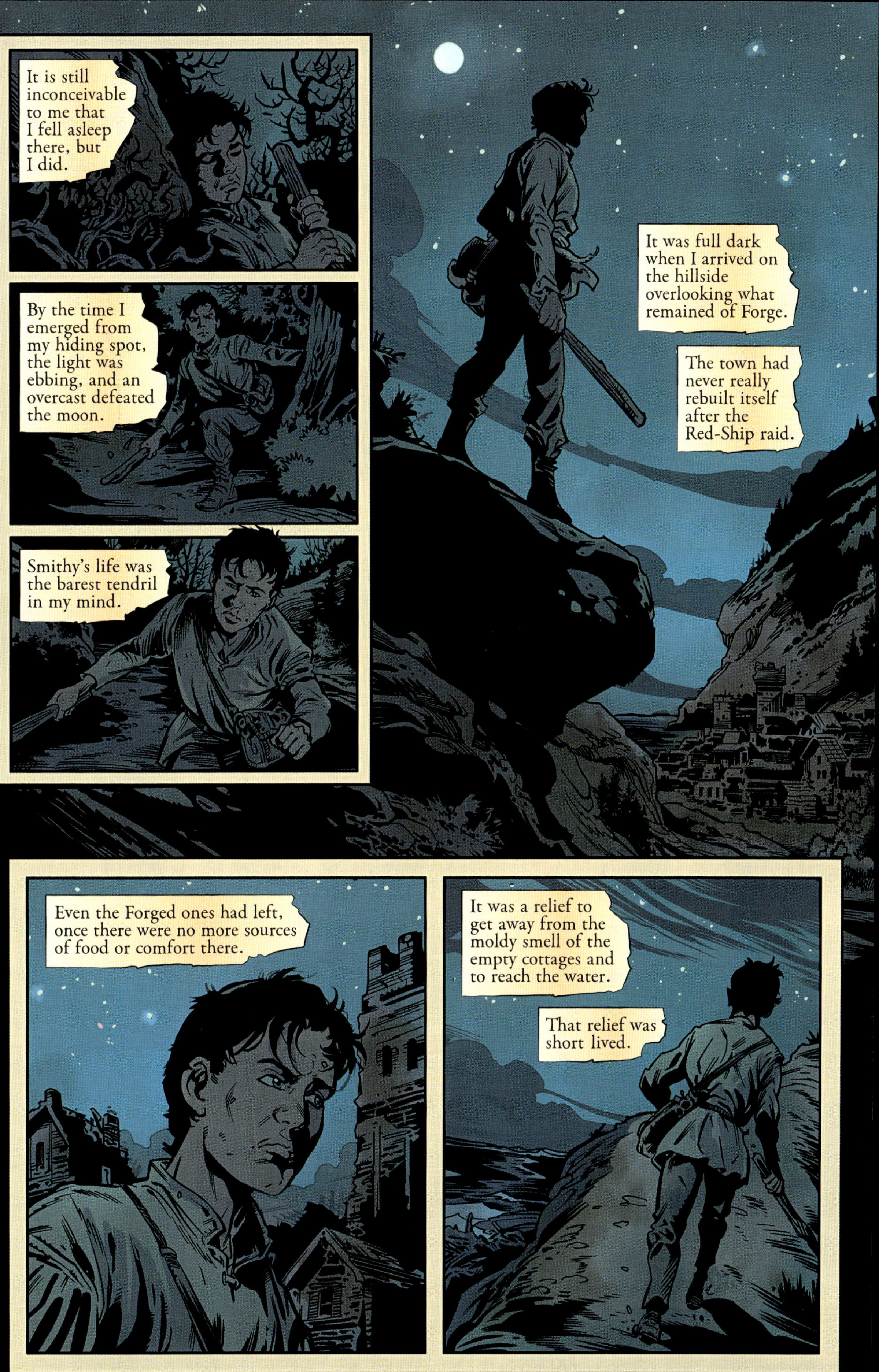
It is still inconceivable to me that I fell asleep there, but I did.
By the time I emerged from my hiding spot, the light was ebbing, and an overcast defeated the moon.
Smithy's life was the barest tendril in my mind.
It was full dark when I arrived on the hillside overlooking what remained of Forge.
The town had never really rebuilt itself after the Red-Ship raid.
Even the Forged ones had left, once there were no more sources of food or comfort there.
It was a relief to get away from the moldy smell of the empty cottages and to reach the water.
That relief was short lived.

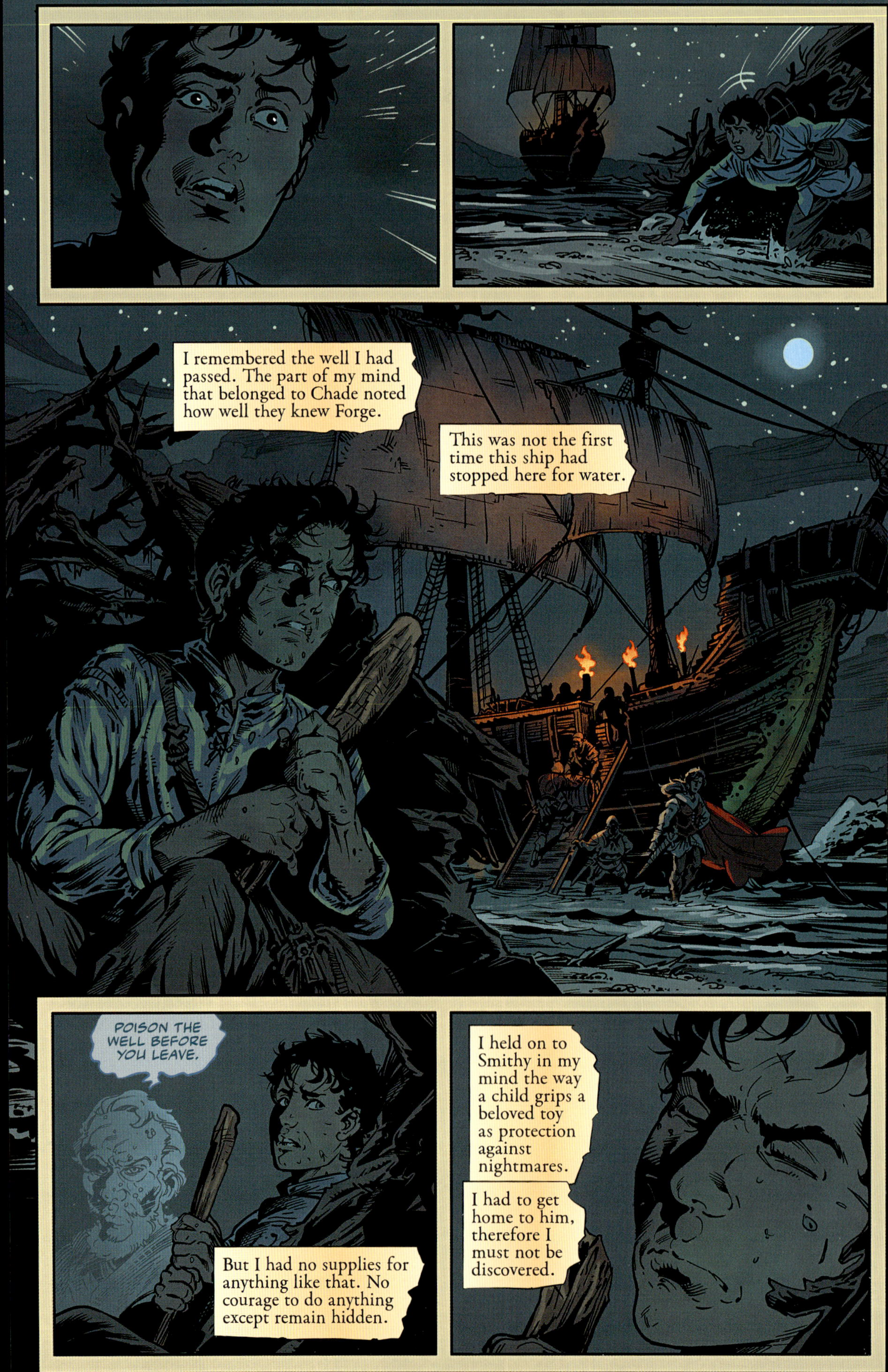

I remembered the well I had passed. The part of my mind that belonged to Chade noted how well they knew Forge.
This was not the first time this ship had stopped here for water.
POISON THE WELL BEFORE YOU LEAVE.
But I had no supplies for anything like that. No courage to do anything except remain hidden.
I held on to Smithy in my mind the way a child grips a beloved toy as protection against nightmares.
I had to get home to him, therefore I must not be discovered.

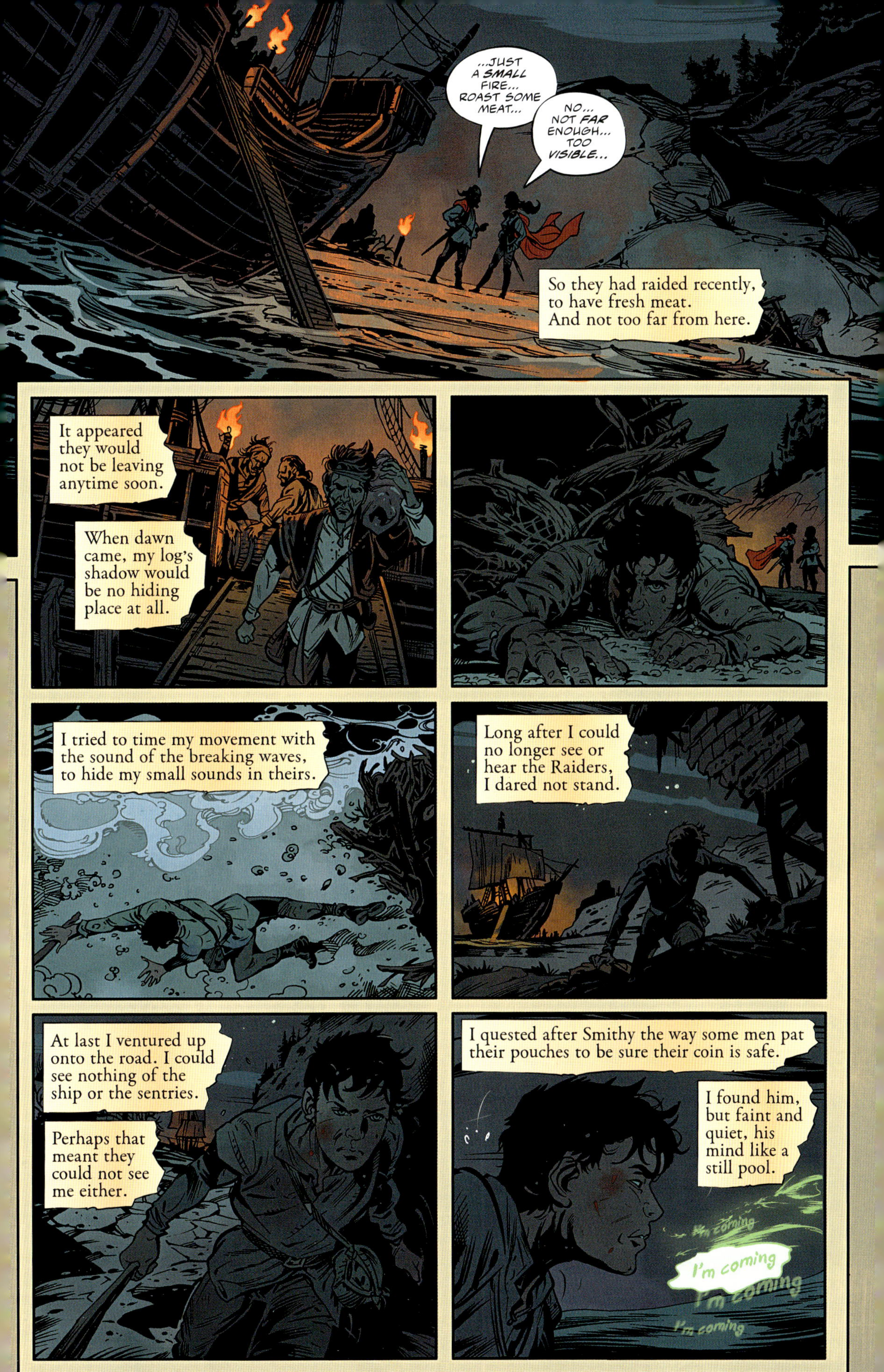

...JUST A SMALL FIRE... ROAST SOME MEAT...
NO... NOT FAR ENOUGH... TOO VISIBLE...
So they had raided recently, to have fresh meat. And not too far from here.
It appeared they would not be leaving anytime soon.
When dawn came, my log's shadow would be no hiding place at all.
I tried to time my movement with the sound of the breaking waves, to hide my small sounds in theirs.
Long after I could no longer see or hear the Raiders, I dared not stand.
At last I ventured up onto the road. I could see nothing of the ship or the sentries.
Perhaps that meant they could not see me either.
I quested after Smithy the way some men pat their pouches to be sure their coin is safe.
I found him, but faint and quiet, his mind like a still pool.
I'm coming
I'm coming
I'm coming
I'm coming

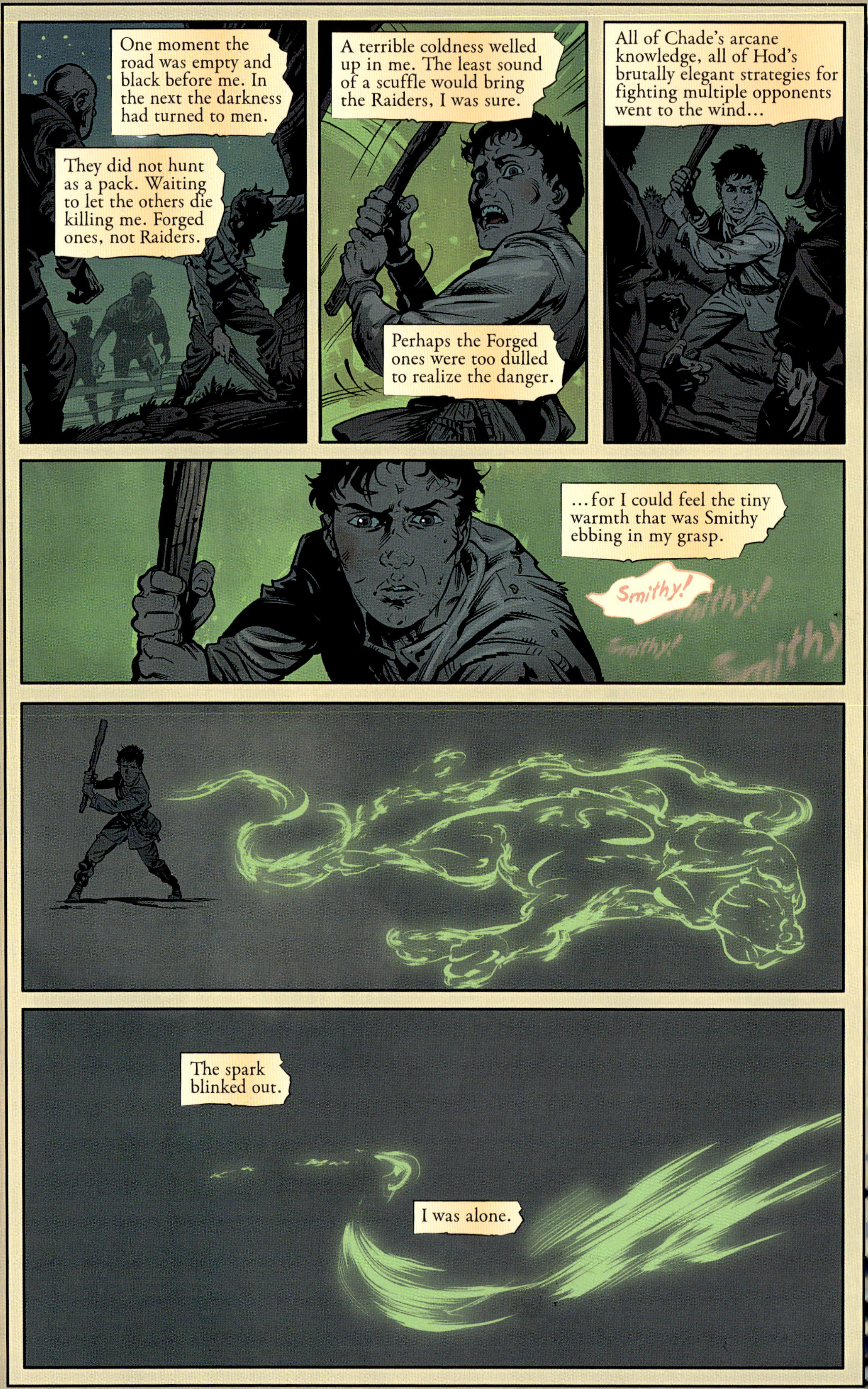
One moment the road was empty and black before me. In the next the darkness had turned to men.
They did not hunt as a pack. Waiting to let the others die killing me. Forged ones, not Raiders.
A terrible coldness welled up in me. The least sound of a scuffle would bring the Raiders, I was sure.
Perhaps the Forged ones were too dulled to realize the danger.
All of Chade's arcane knowledge, all of Hod's brutally elegant strategies for fighting multiple opponents went to the wind...
...for I could feel the tiny warmth that was Smithy ebbing in my grasp.
Smithy!
Smithy!
The spark blinked out.
I was alone.

A black flood of strength surged through me like a madness.

They had kept me from Smithy as he was dying.

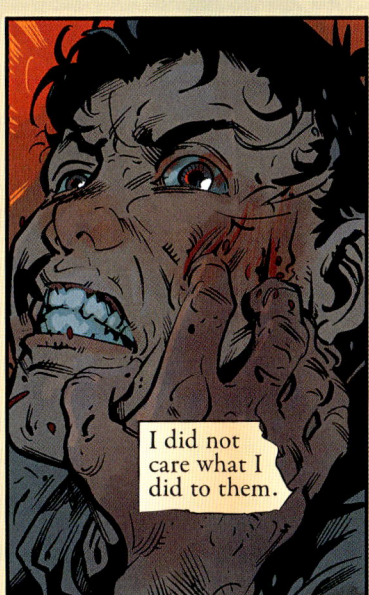

I did not care what I did to them.

So long as it **hurt** them.

I waited in the wind for someone to care enough to come and kill me. But the night was still.

I had felt nothing from them when I killed them. No fear, no anger, no pain, not even despair.

They had been **things**.

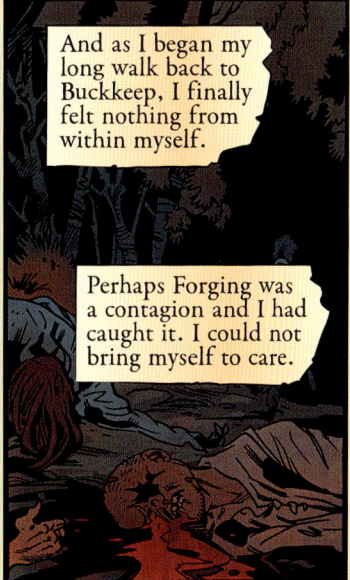

And as I began my long walk back to Buckkeep, I finally felt nothing from within myself.

Perhaps Forging was a contagion and I had caught it. I could not bring myself to care.

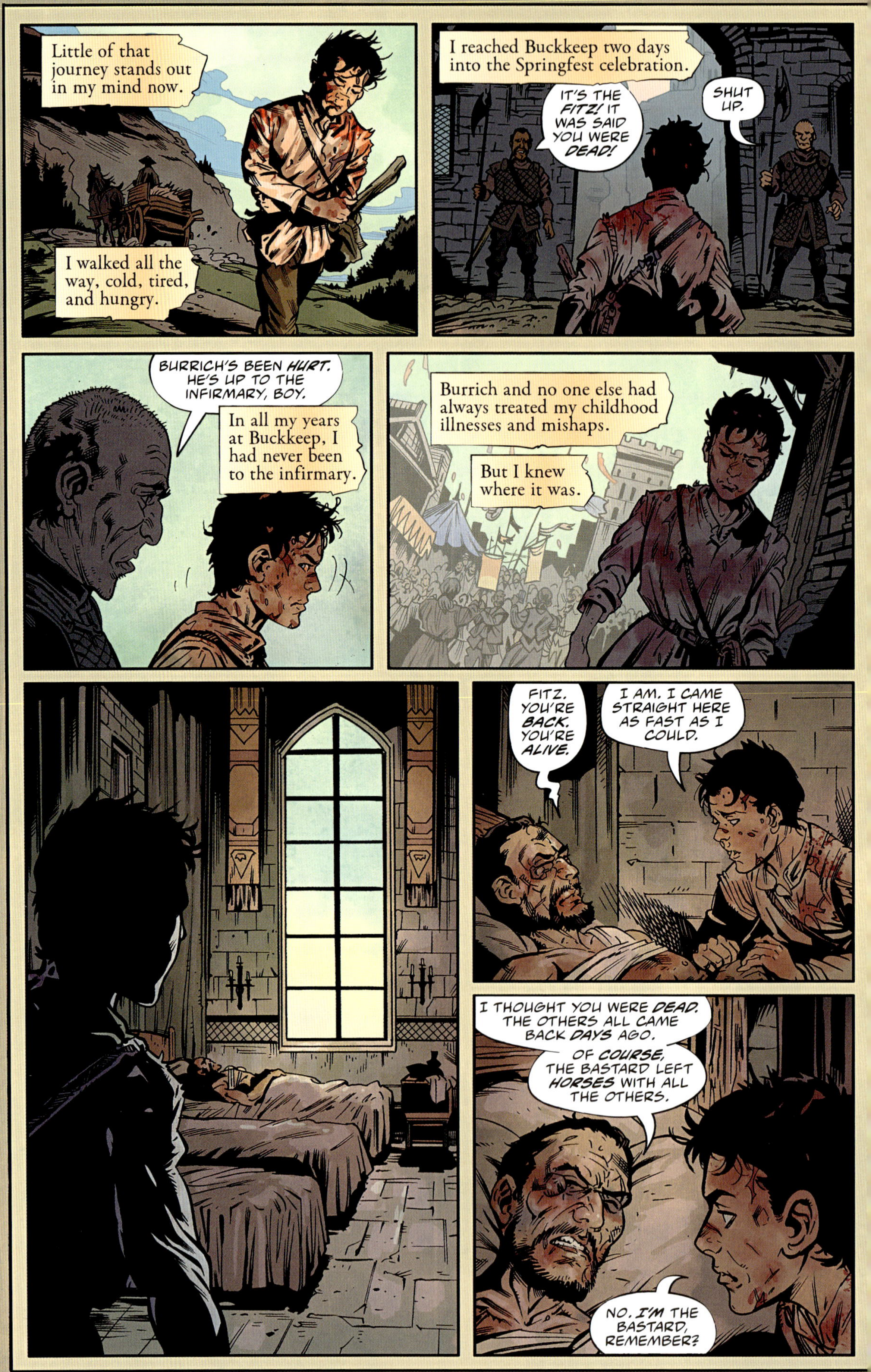
Little of that journey stands out in my mind now.
I walked all the way, cold, tired, and hungry.
I reached Buckkeep two days into the Springfest celebration.
IT'S THE FITZ! IT WAS SAID YOU WERE DEAD!
SHUT UP.
BURRICH'S BEEN HURT. HE'S UP TO THE INFIRMARY, BOY.
In all my years at Buckkeep, I had never been to the infirmary.
Burrich and no one else had always treated my childhood illnesses and mishaps.
But I knew where it was.
FITZ. YOU'RE BACK. YOU'RE ALIVE.
I AM. I CAME STRAIGHT HERE AS FAST AS I COULD.
I THOUGHT YOU WERE DEAD. THE OTHERS ALL CAME BACK DAYS AGO.
OF COURSE, THE BASTARD LEFT HORSES WITH ALL THE OTHERS.
NO. I'M THE BASTARD, REMEMBER?

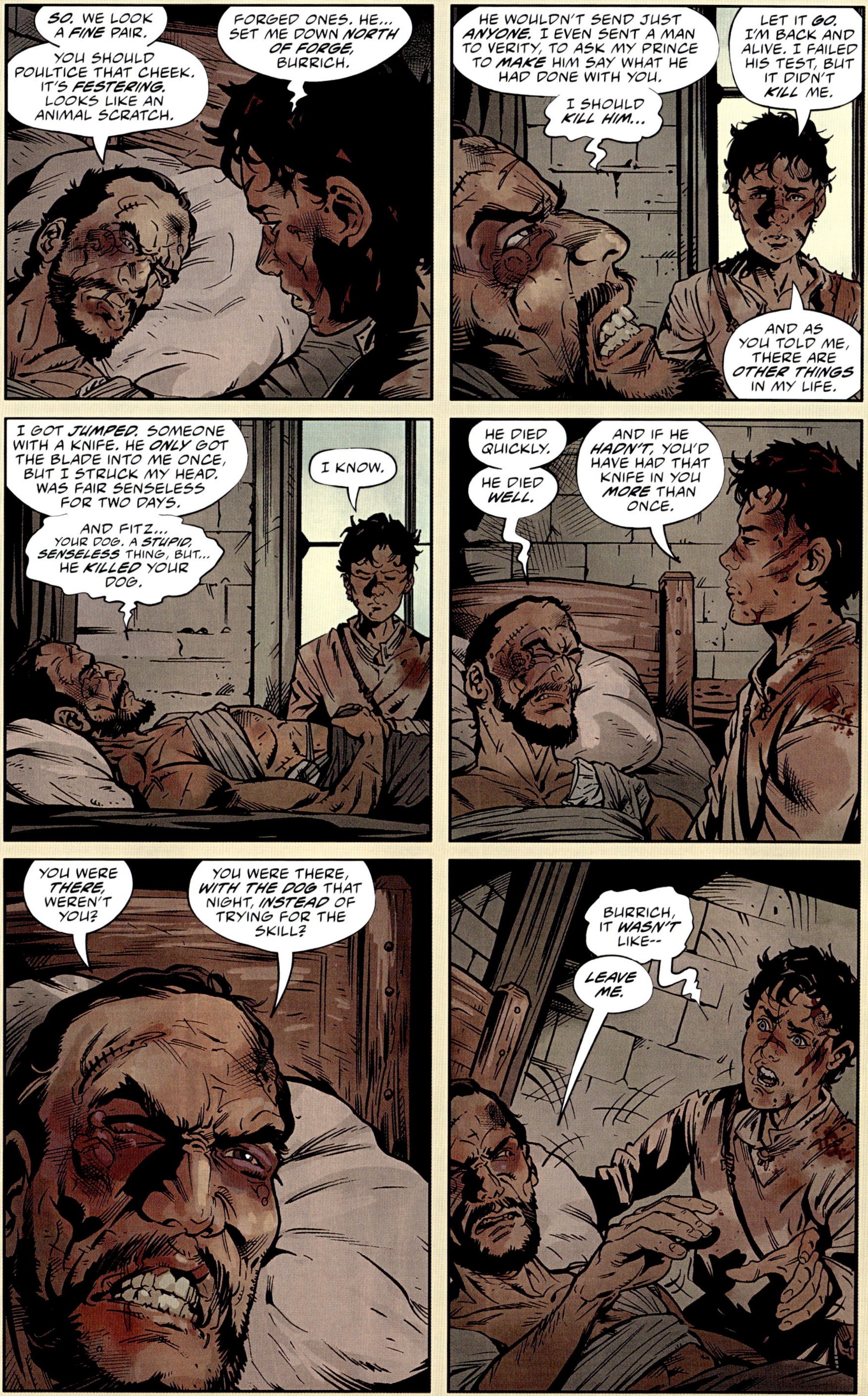

SO. WE LOOK A FINE PAIR.
YOU SHOULD POULTICE THAT CHEEK. IT'S FESTERING. LOOKS LIKE AN ANIMAL SCRATCH.
FORGED ONES. HE... SET ME DOWN NORTH OF FORGE, BURRICH.
HE WOULDN'T SEND JUST ANYONE. I EVEN SENT A MAN TO VERITY, TO ASK MY PRINCE TO MAKE HIM SAY WHAT HE HAD DONE WITH YOU.
I SHOULD KILL HIM...
LET IT GO. I'M BACK AND ALIVE. I FAILED HIS TEST, BUT IT DIDN'T KILL ME.
AND AS YOU TOLD ME, THERE ARE OTHER THINGS IN MY LIFE.
I GOT JUMPED. SOMEONE WITH A KNIFE. HE ONLY GOT THE BLADE INTO ME ONCE, BUT I STRUCK MY HEAD. WAS FAIR SENSELESS FOR TWO DAYS.
AND FITZ... YOUR DOG. A STUPID, SENSELESS THING, BUT... HE KILLED YOUR DOG.
I KNOW.
HE DIED QUICKLY.
HE DIED WELL.
AND IF HE HADN'T, YOU'D HAVE HAD THAT KNIFE IN YOU MORE THAN ONCE.
YOU WERE THERE, WEREN'T YOU?
YOU WERE THERE, WITH THE DOG THAT NIGHT, INSTEAD OF TRYING FOR THE SKILL?
BURRICH, IT WASN'T LIKE--
LEAVE ME.

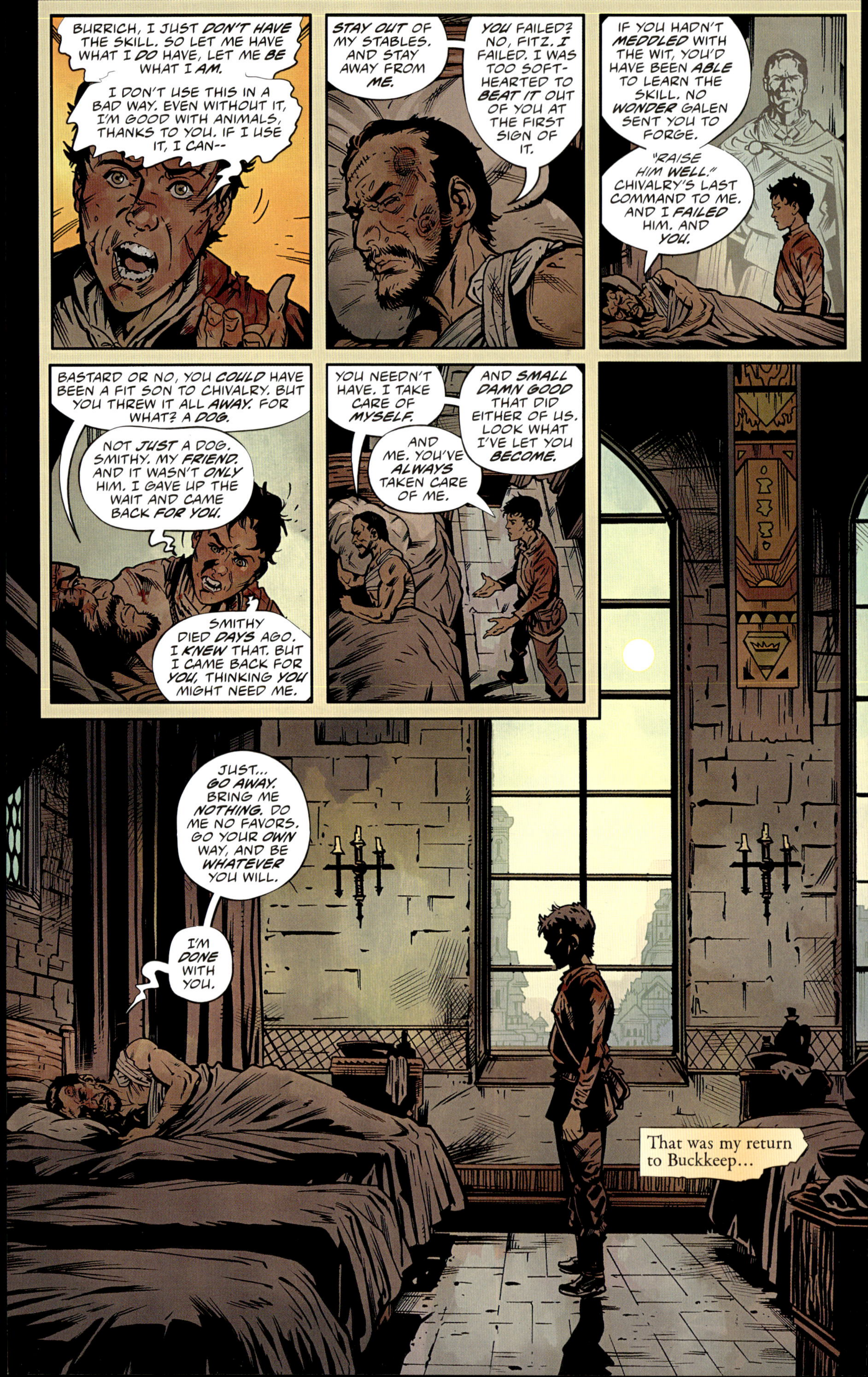

BURRICH, I JUST DON'T HAVE THE SKILL. SO LET ME HAVE WHAT I DO HAVE, LET ME BE WHAT I AM.
I DON'T USE THIS IN A BAD WAY. EVEN WITHOUT IT, I'M GOOD WITH ANIMALS, THANKS TO YOU. IF I USE IT, I CAN--
STAY OUT OF MY STABLES, AND STAY AWAY FROM ME.
YOU FAILED? NO, FITZ. I FAILED. I WAS TOO SOFT-HEARTED TO BEAT IT OUT OF YOU AT THE FIRST SIGN OF IT.
IF YOU HADN'T MEDDLED WITH THE WIT, YOU'D HAVE BEEN ABLE TO LEARN THE SKILL. NO WONDER GALEN SENT YOU TO FORGE.
"RAISE HIM WELL." CHIVALRY'S LAST COMMAND TO ME. AND I FAILED HIM. AND YOU.
BASTARD OR NO, YOU COULD HAVE BEEN A FIT SON TO CHIVALRY. BUT YOU THREW IT ALL AWAY. FOR WHAT? A DOG.
NOT JUST A DOG. SMITHY. MY FRIEND. AND IT WASN'T ONLY HIM. I GAVE UP THE WAIT AND CAME BACK FOR YOU.
SMITHY DIED DAYS AGO. I KNEW THAT. BUT I CAME BACK FOR YOU, THINKING YOU MIGHT NEED ME.
YOU NEEDN'T HAVE. I TAKE CARE OF MYSELF.
AND ME. YOU'VE ALWAYS TAKEN CARE OF ME.
AND SMALL DAMN GOOD THAT DID EITHER OF US. LOOK WHAT I'VE LET YOU BECOME.
JUST... GO AWAY. BRING ME NOTHING. DO ME NO FAVORS. GO YOUR OWN WAY, AND BE WHATEVER YOU WILL.
I'M DONE WITH YOU.
That was my return to Buckkeep...

Chapter Two

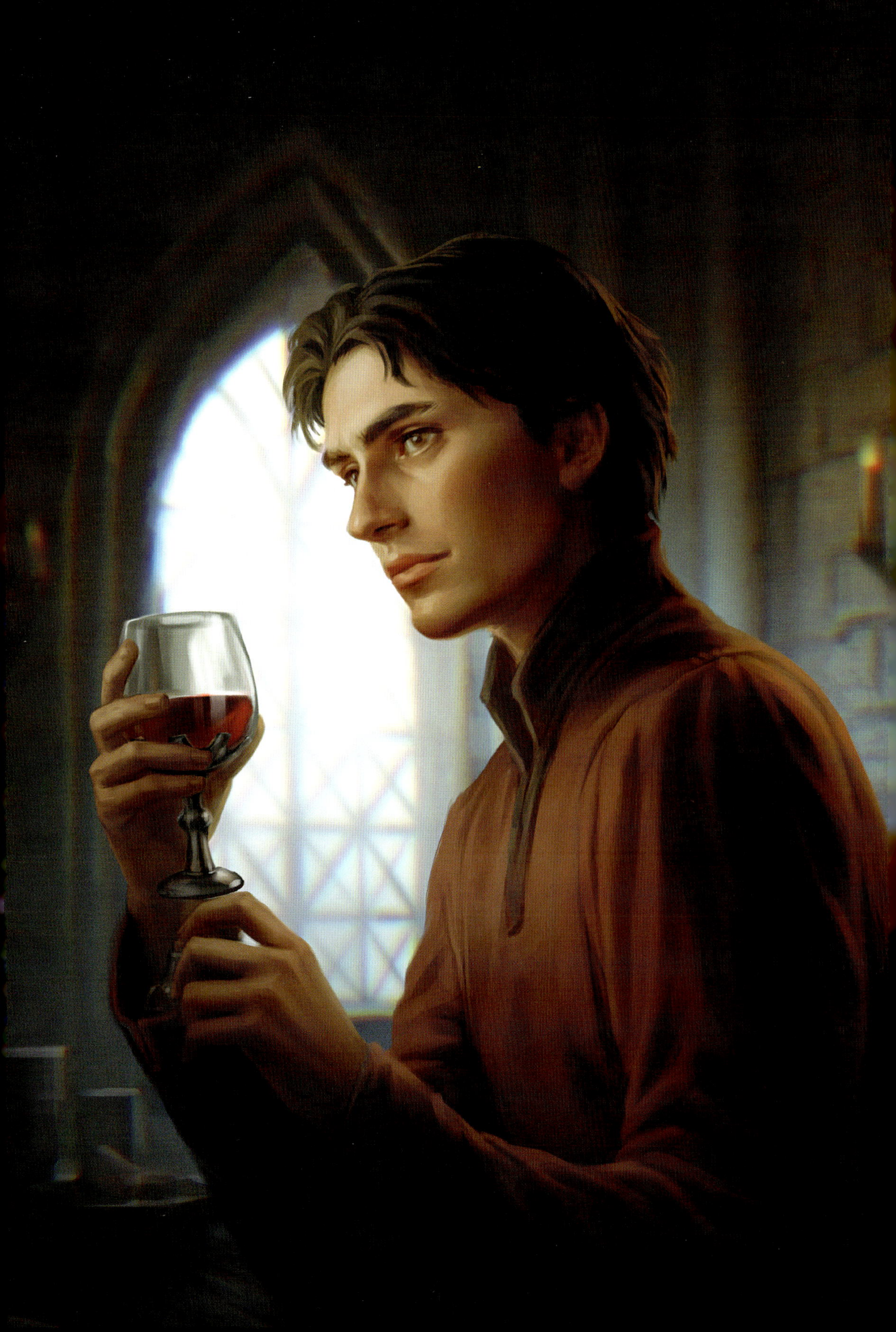

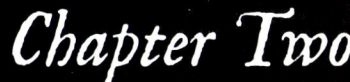

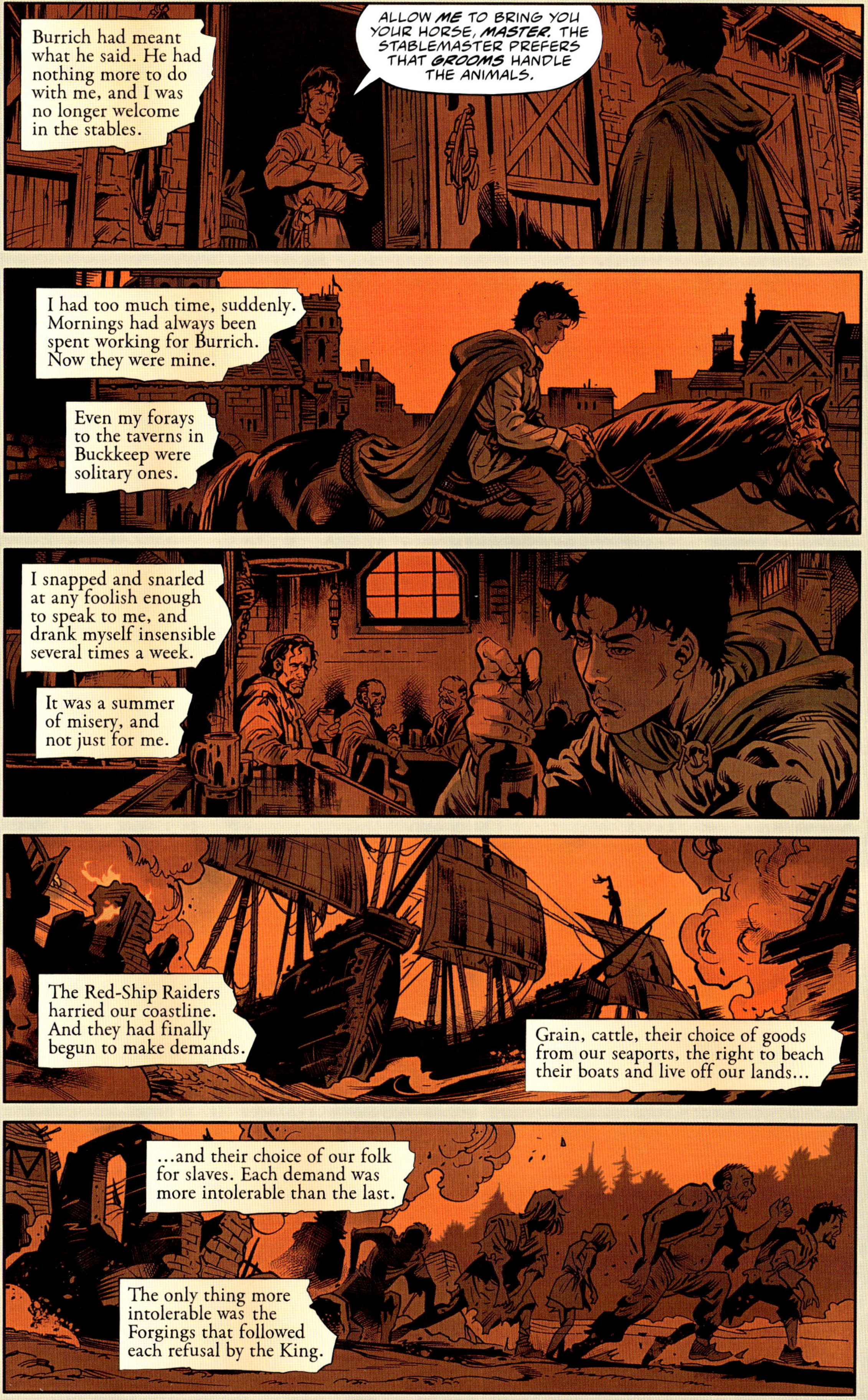

Burrich had meant what he said. He had nothing more to do with me, and I was no longer welcome in the stables.
ALLOW ME TO BRING YOU YOUR HORSE, MASTER. THE STABLEMASTER PREFERS THAT GROOMS HANDLE THE ANIMALS.
I had too much time, suddenly. Mornings had always been spent working for Burrich. Now they were mine.
Even my forays to the taverns in Buckkeep were solitary ones.
I snapped and snarled at any foolish enough to speak to me, and drank myself insensible several times a week.
It was a summer of misery, and not just for me.
The Red-Ship Raiders harried our coastline. And they had finally begun to make demands.
Grain, cattle, their choice of goods from our seaports, the right to beach their boats and live off our lands...
...and their choice of our folk for slaves. Each demand was more intolerable than the last.
The only thing more intolerable was the Forgings that followed each refusal by the King.

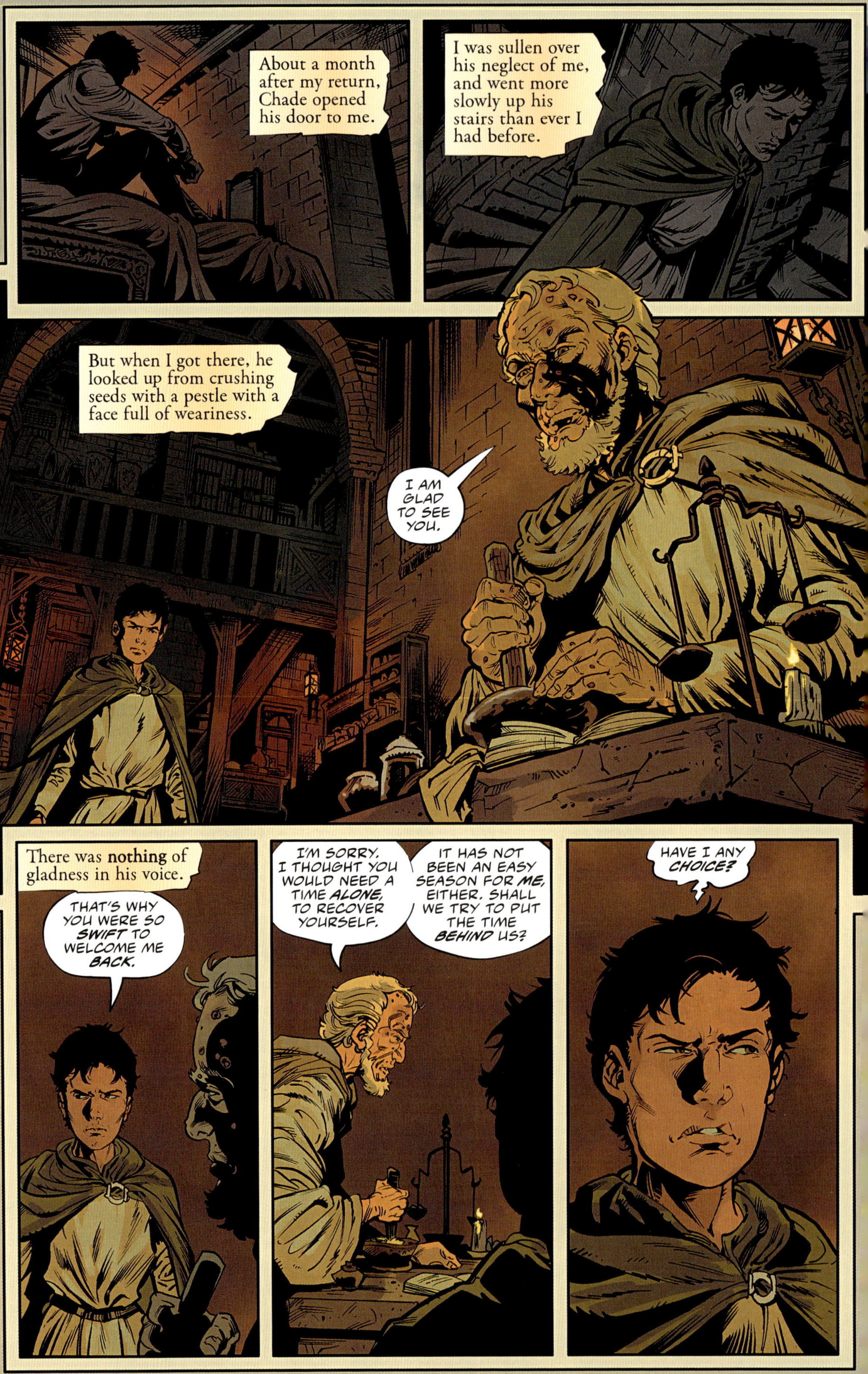
About a month after my return, Chade opened his door to me.
I was sullen over his neglect of me, and went more slowly up his stairs than ever I had before.
But when I got there, he looked up from crushing seeds with a pestle with a face full of weariness.
I AM GLAD TO SEE YOU.
There was **nothing** of gladness in his voice.
THAT'S WHY YOU WERE SO *SWIFT* TO WELCOME ME *BACK*.
I'M SORRY. I THOUGHT YOU WOULD NEED A TIME *ALONE*, TO RECOVER YOURSELF.
IT HAS NOT BEEN AN EASY SEASON FOR *ME*, EITHER. SHALL WE TRY TO PUT THE TIME *BEHIND* US?
HAVE I ANY *CHOICE?*

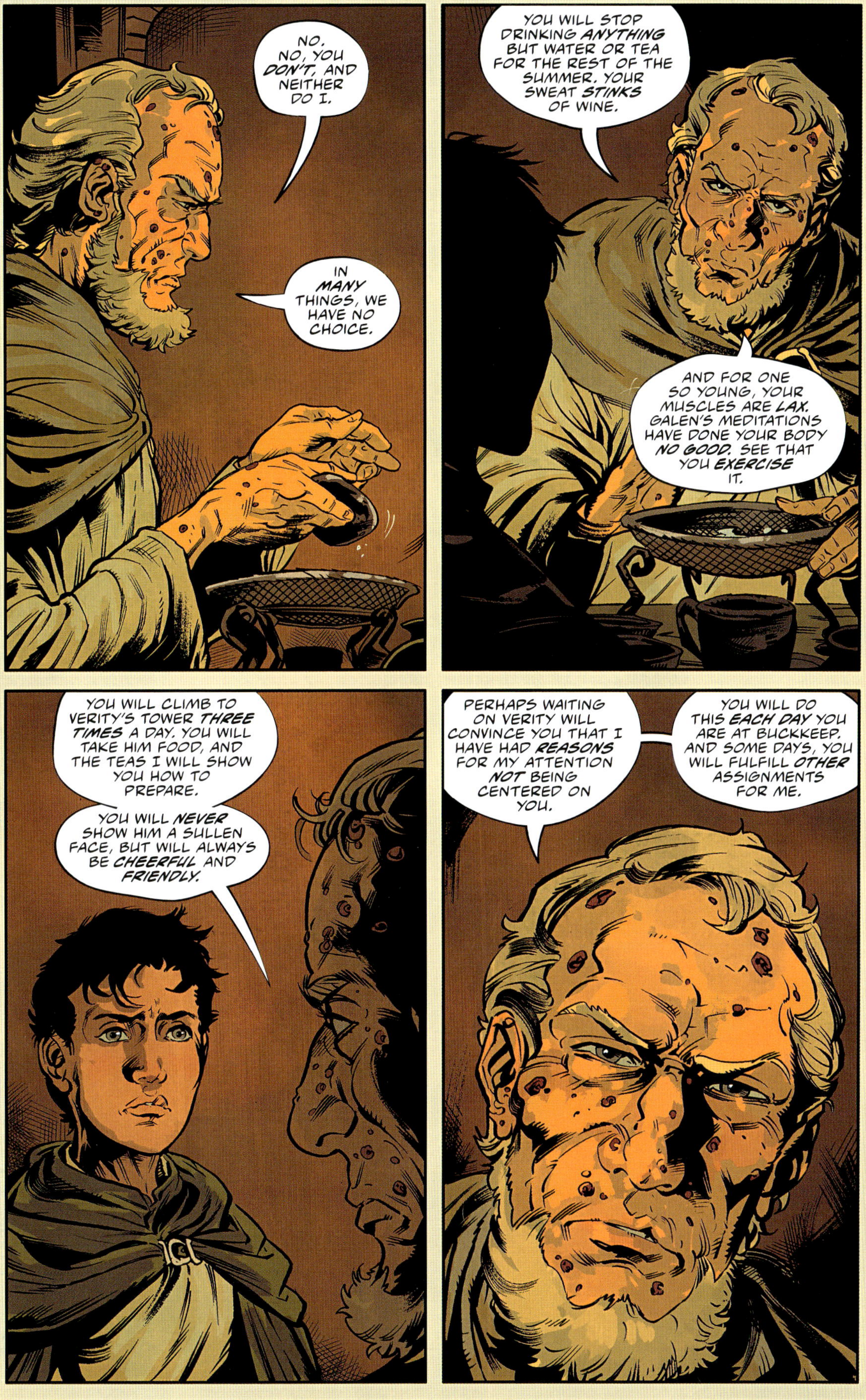
NO. NO, YOU *DON'T*, AND NEITHER DO I.
IN *MANY* THINGS, WE HAVE NO CHOICE.
YOU WILL STOP DRINKING *ANYTHING* BUT WATER OR TEA FOR THE REST OF THE SUMMER. YOUR SWEAT *STINKS* OF WINE.
AND FOR ONE SO YOUNG, YOUR MUSCLES ARE *LAX*. GALEN'S MEDITATIONS HAVE DONE YOUR BODY *NO GOOD*. SEE THAT YOU *EXERCISE* IT.
YOU WILL CLIMB TO VERITY'S TOWER *THREE TIMES* A DAY. YOU WILL TAKE HIM FOOD, AND THE TEAS I WILL SHOW YOU HOW TO PREPARE.
YOU WILL *NEVER* SHOW HIM A SULLEN FACE, BUT WILL ALWAYS BE *CHEERFUL* AND *FRIENDLY*.
PERHAPS WAITING ON VERITY WILL CONVINCE YOU THAT I HAVE HAD *REASONS* FOR MY ATTENTION *NOT* BEING CENTERED ON YOU.
YOU WILL DO THIS *EACH DAY* YOU ARE AT BUCKKEEP. AND SOME DAYS, YOU WILL FULFILL *OTHER* ASSIGNMENTS FOR ME.

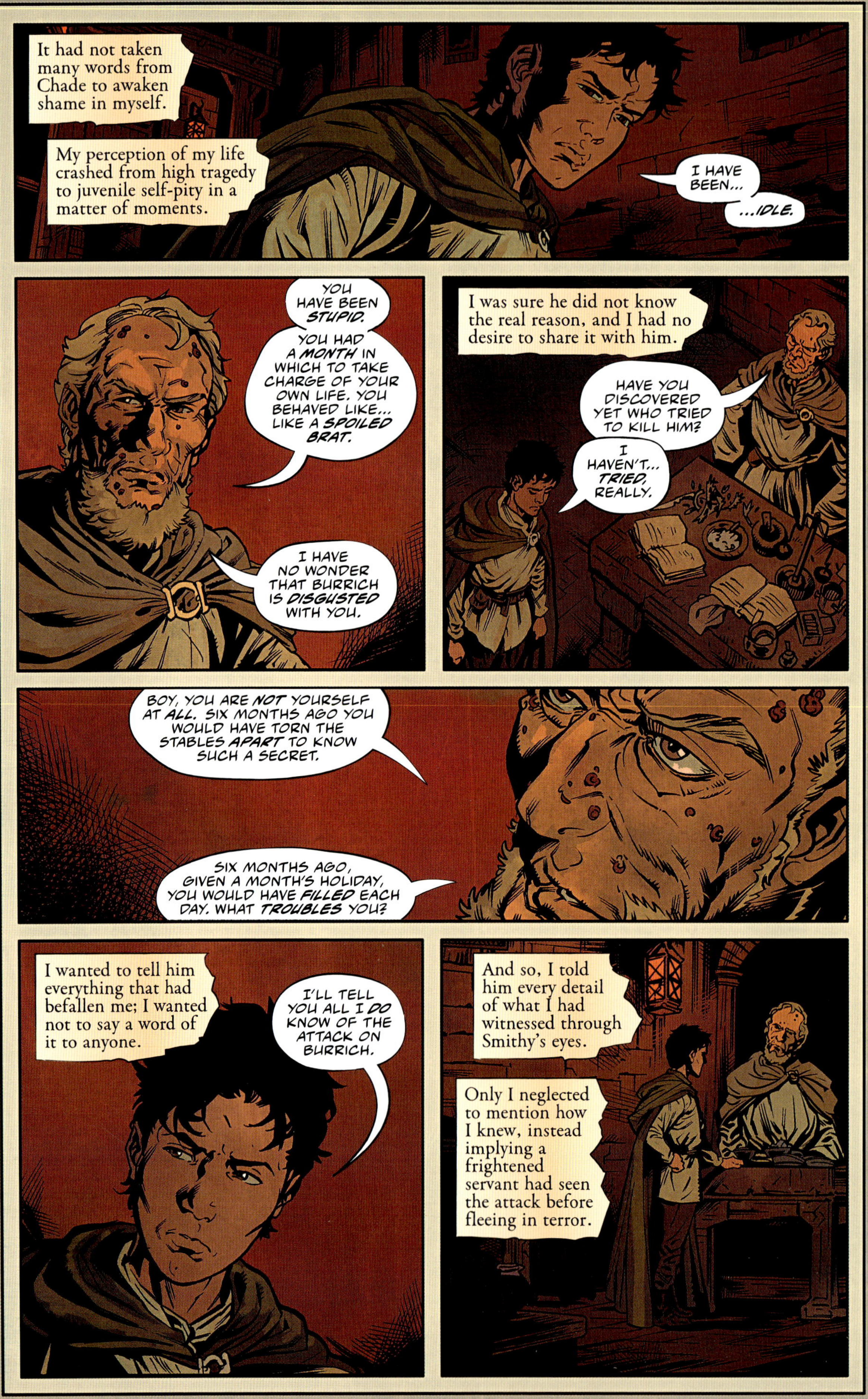

It had not taken many words from Chade to awaken shame in myself.
My perception of my life crashed from high tragedy to juvenile self-pity in a matter of moments.
I HAVE BEEN...
...IDLE.
YOU HAVE BEEN STUPID.
YOU HAD A MONTH IN WHICH TO TAKE CHARGE OF YOUR OWN LIFE. YOU BEHAVED LIKE... LIKE A SPOILED BRAT.
I HAVE NO WONDER THAT BURRICH IS DISGUSTED WITH YOU.
I was sure he did not know the real reason, and I had no desire to share it with him.
HAVE YOU DISCOVERED YET WHO TRIED TO KILL HIM?
I HAVEN'T... TRIED, REALLY.
BOY, YOU ARE NOT YOURSELF AT ALL. SIX MONTHS AGO YOU WOULD HAVE TORN THE STABLES APART TO KNOW SUCH A SECRET.
SIX MONTHS AGO, GIVEN A MONTH'S HOLIDAY, YOU WOULD HAVE FILLED EACH DAY. WHAT TROUBLES YOU?
I wanted to tell him everything that had befallen me; I wanted not to say a word of it to anyone.
I'LL TELL YOU ALL I DO KNOW OF THE ATTACK ON BURRICH.
And so, I told him every detail of what I had witnessed through Smithy's eyes.
Only I neglected to mention how I knew, instead implying a frightened servant had seen the attack before fleeing in terror.

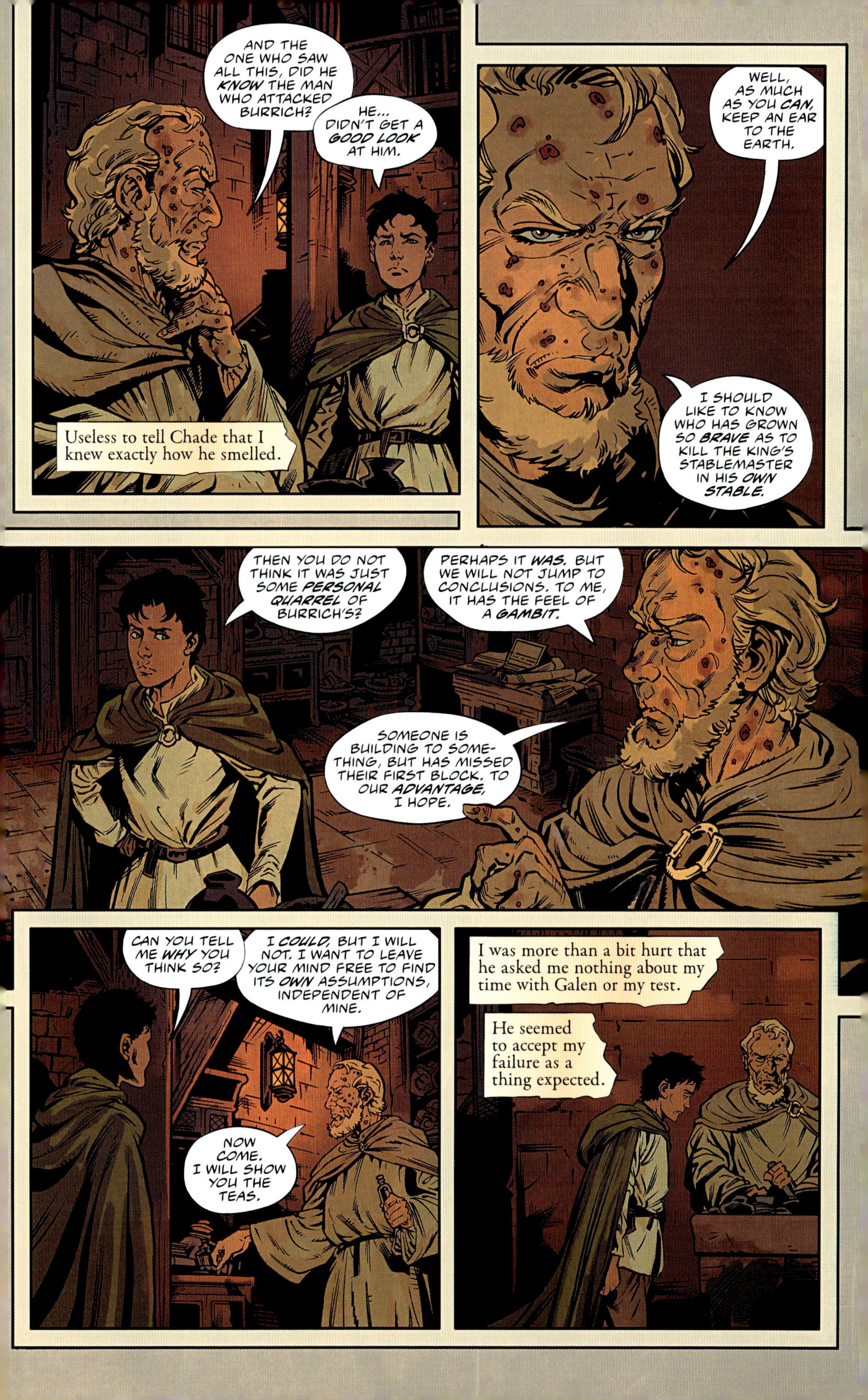
AND THE ONE WHO SAW ALL THIS, DID HE KNOW THE MAN WHO ATTACKED BURRICH?
HE... DIDN'T GET A GOOD LOOK AT HIM.
Useless to tell Chade that I knew exactly how he smelled.
WELL, AS MUCH AS YOU CAN, KEEP AN EAR TO THE EARTH.
I SHOULD LIKE TO KNOW WHO HAS GROWN SO BRAVE AS TO KILL THE KING'S STABLEMASTER IN HIS OWN STABLE.
THEN YOU DO NOT THINK IT WAS JUST SOME PERSONAL QUARREL OF BURRICH'S?
PERHAPS IT WAS. BUT WE WILL NOT JUMP TO CONCLUSIONS. TO ME, IT HAS THE FEEL OF A GAMBIT.
SOMEONE IS BUILDING TO SOME-THING, BUT HAS MISSED THEIR FIRST BLOCK. TO OUR ADVANTAGE, I HOPE.
CAN YOU TELL ME WHY YOU THINK SO?
I COULD, BUT I WILL NOT. I WANT TO LEAVE YOUR MIND FREE TO FIND ITS OWN ASSUMPTIONS, INDEPENDENT OF MINE.
NOW COME. I WILL SHOW YOU THE TEAS.
I was more than a bit hurt that he asked me nothing about my time with Galen or my test.
He seemed to accept my failure as a thing expected.

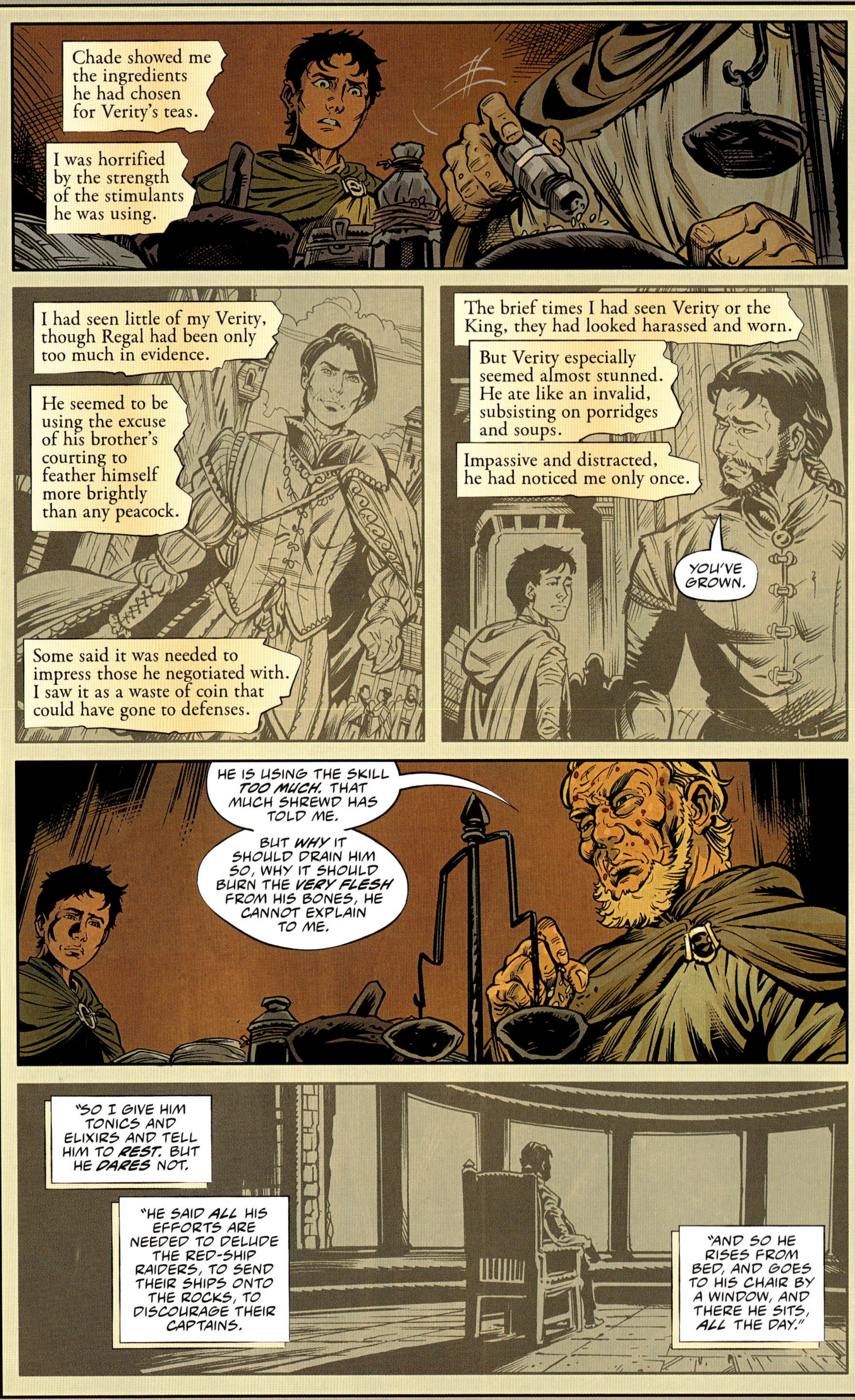
Chade showed me the ingredients he had chosen for Verity's teas.
I was horrified by the strength of the stimulants he was using.
I had seen little of my Verity, though Regal had been only too much in evidence.
He seemed to be using the excuse of his brother's courting to feather himself more brightly than any peacock.
Some said it was needed to impress those he negotiated with. I saw it as a waste of coin that could have gone to defenses.
The brief times I had seen Verity or the King, they had looked harassed and worn.
But Verity especially seemed almost stunned. He ate like an invalid, subsisting on porridges and soups.
Impassive and distracted, he had noticed me only once.
YOU'VE GROWN.
HE IS USING THE SKILL TOO MUCH. THAT MUCH SHREWD HAS TOLD ME.
BUT WHY IT SHOULD DRAIN HIM SO, WHY IT SHOULD BURN THE VERY FLESH FROM HIS BONES, HE CANNOT EXPLAIN TO ME.
"SO I GIVE HIM TONICS AND ELIXIRS AND TELL HIM TO REST. BUT HE DARES NOT.
"HE SAID ALL HIS EFFORTS ARE NEEDED TO DELUDE THE RED-SHIP RAIDERS, TO SEND THEIR SHIPS ONTO THE ROCKS, TO DISCOURAGE THEIR CAPTAINS.
"AND SO HE RISES FROM BED, AND GOES TO HIS CHAIR BY A WINDOW, AND THERE HE SITS, ALL THE DAY."

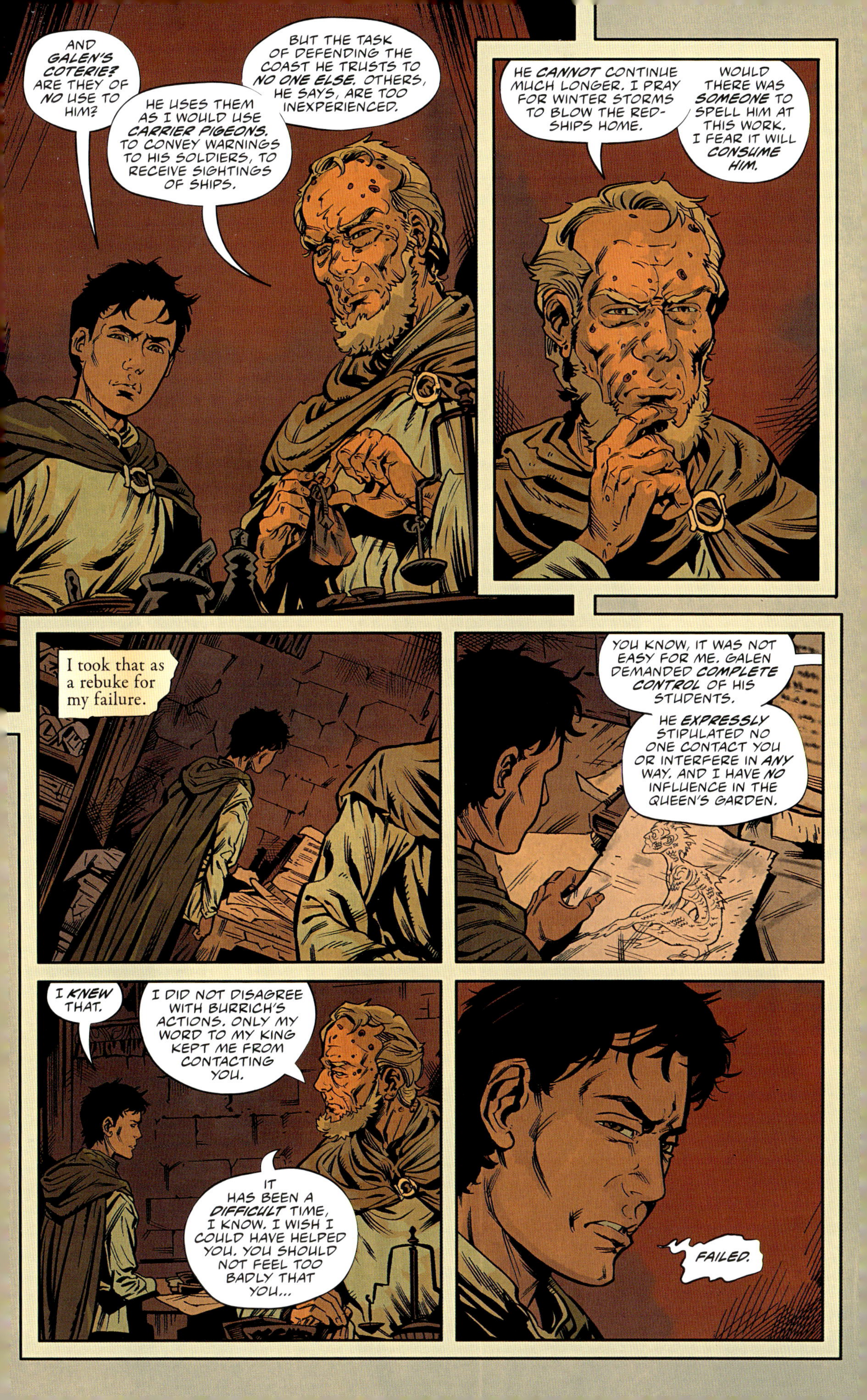
AND GALEN'S COTERIE? ARE THEY OF NO USE TO HIM?
HE USES THEM AS I WOULD USE CARRIER PIGEONS. TO CONVEY WARNINGS TO HIS SOLDIERS, TO RECEIVE SIGHTINGS OF SHIPS.
BUT THE TASK OF DEFENDING THE COAST HE TRUSTS TO NO ONE ELSE. OTHERS, HE SAYS, ARE TOO INEXPERIENCED.
HE CANNOT CONTINUE MUCH LONGER. I PRAY FOR WINTER STORMS TO BLOW THE RED-SHIPS HOME.
WOULD THERE WAS SOMEONE TO SPELL HIM AT THIS WORK. I FEAR IT WILL CONSUME HIM.
I took that as a rebuke for my failure.
YOU KNOW, IT WAS NOT EASY FOR ME. GALEN DEMANDED COMPLETE CONTROL OF HIS STUDENTS.
HE EXPRESSLY STIPULATED NO ONE CONTACT YOU OR INTERFERE IN ANY WAY. AND I HAVE NO INFLUENCE IN THE QUEEN'S GARDEN.
I KNEW THAT.
I DID NOT DISAGREE WITH BURRICH'S ACTIONS. ONLY MY WORD TO MY KING KEPT ME FROM CONTACTING YOU.
IT HAS BEEN A DIFFICULT TIME, I KNOW. I WISH I COULD HAVE HELPED YOU. YOU SHOULD NOT FEEL TOO BADLY THAT YOU...
FAILED.

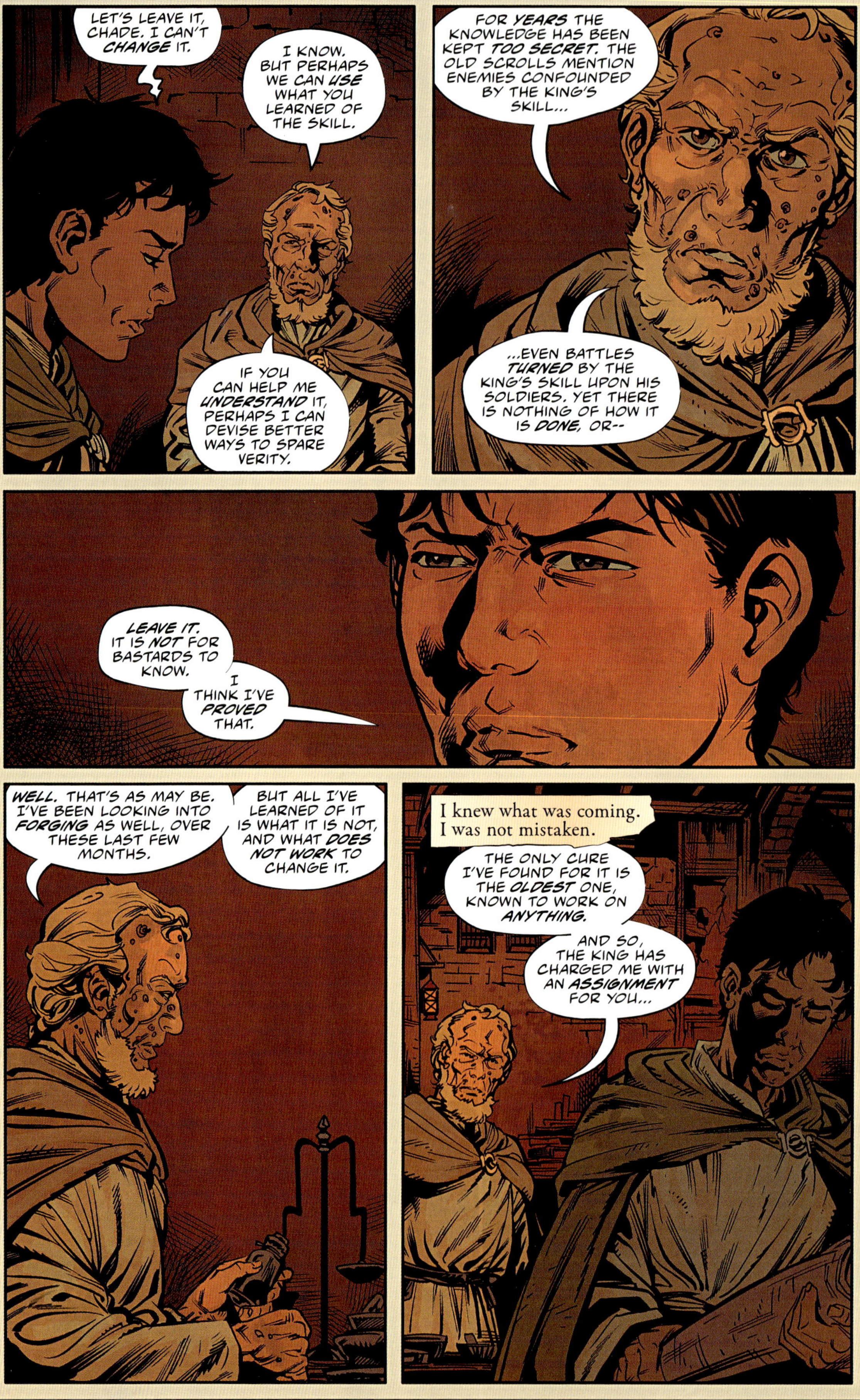
LET'S LEAVE IT, CHADE. I CAN'T CHANGE IT.
I KNOW. BUT PERHAPS WE CAN USE WHAT YOU LEARNED OF THE SKILL.
IF YOU CAN HELP ME UNDERSTAND IT, PERHAPS I CAN DEVISE BETTER WAYS TO SPARE VERITY.
FOR YEARS THE KNOWLEDGE HAS BEEN KEPT TOO SECRET. THE OLD SCROLLS MENTION ENEMIES CONFOUNDED BY THE KING'S SKILL...
...EVEN BATTLES TURNED BY THE KING'S SKILL UPON HIS SOLDIERS. YET THERE IS NOTHING OF HOW IT IS DONE, OR--
LEAVE IT. IT IS NOT FOR BASTARDS TO KNOW.
I THINK I'VE PROVED THAT.
WELL. THAT'S AS MAY BE. I'VE BEEN LOOKING INTO FORGING AS WELL, OVER THESE LAST FEW MONTHS.
BUT ALL I'VE LEARNED OF IT IS WHAT IT IS NOT, AND WHAT DOES NOT WORK TO CHANGE IT.
I knew what was coming. I was not mistaken.
THE ONLY CURE I'VE FOUND FOR IT IS THE OLDEST ONE, KNOWN TO WORK ON ANYTHING.
AND SO, THE KING HAS CHARGED ME WITH AN ASSIGNMENT FOR YOU...

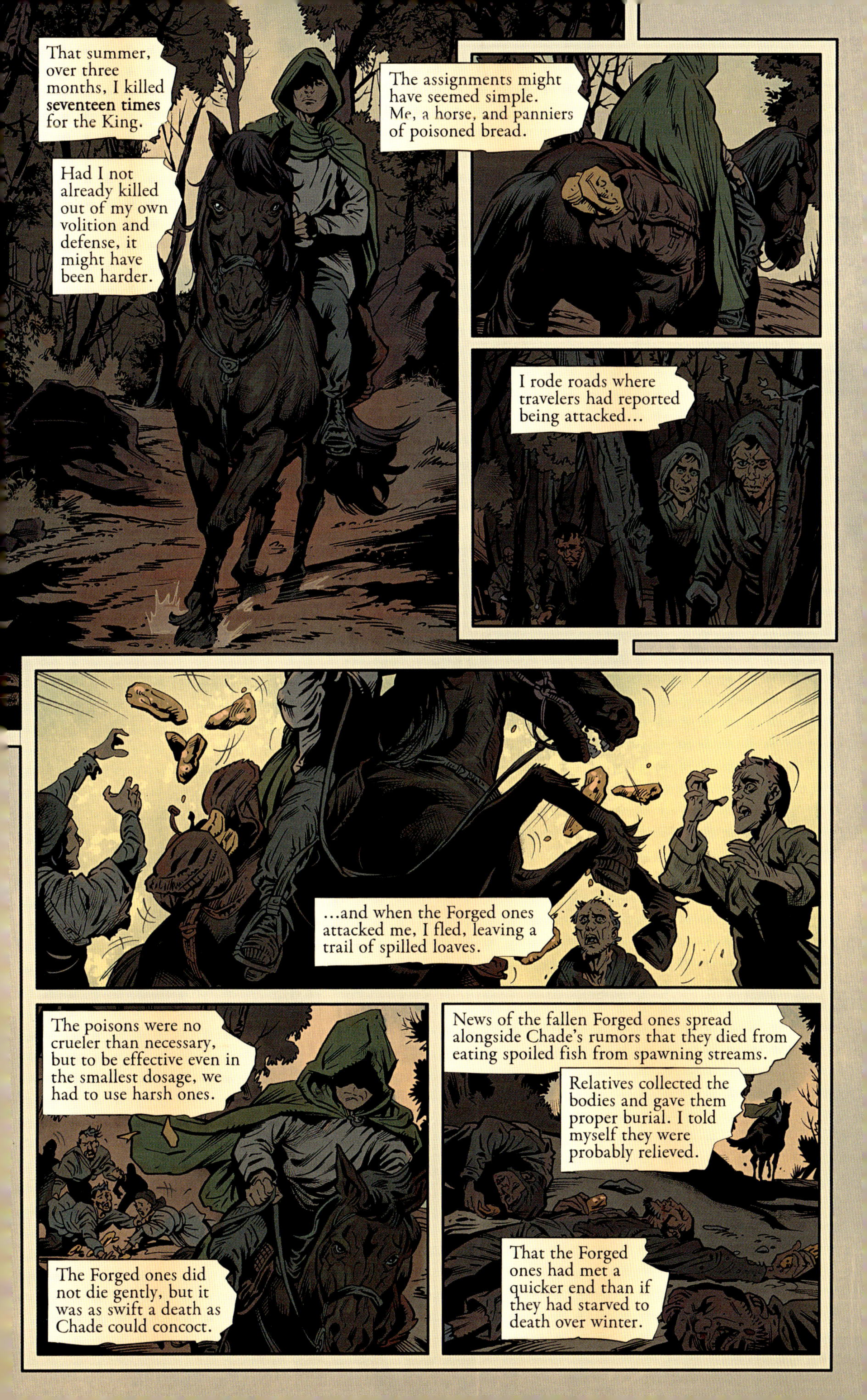
That summer, over three months, I killed **seventeen times** for the King.
Had I not already killed out of my own volition and defense, it might have been harder.
The assignments might have seemed simple. Me, a horse, and panniers of poisoned bread.
I rode roads where travelers had reported being attacked...
...and when the Forged ones attacked me, I fled, leaving a trail of spilled loaves.
The poisons were no crueler than necessary, but to be effective even in the smallest dosage, we had to use harsh ones.
The Forged ones did not die gently, but it was as swift a death as Chade could concoct.
News of the fallen Forged ones spread alongside Chade's rumors that they died from eating spoiled fish from spawning streams.
Relatives collected the bodies and gave them proper burial. I told myself they were probably relieved.
That the Forged ones had met a quicker end than if they had starved to death over winter.

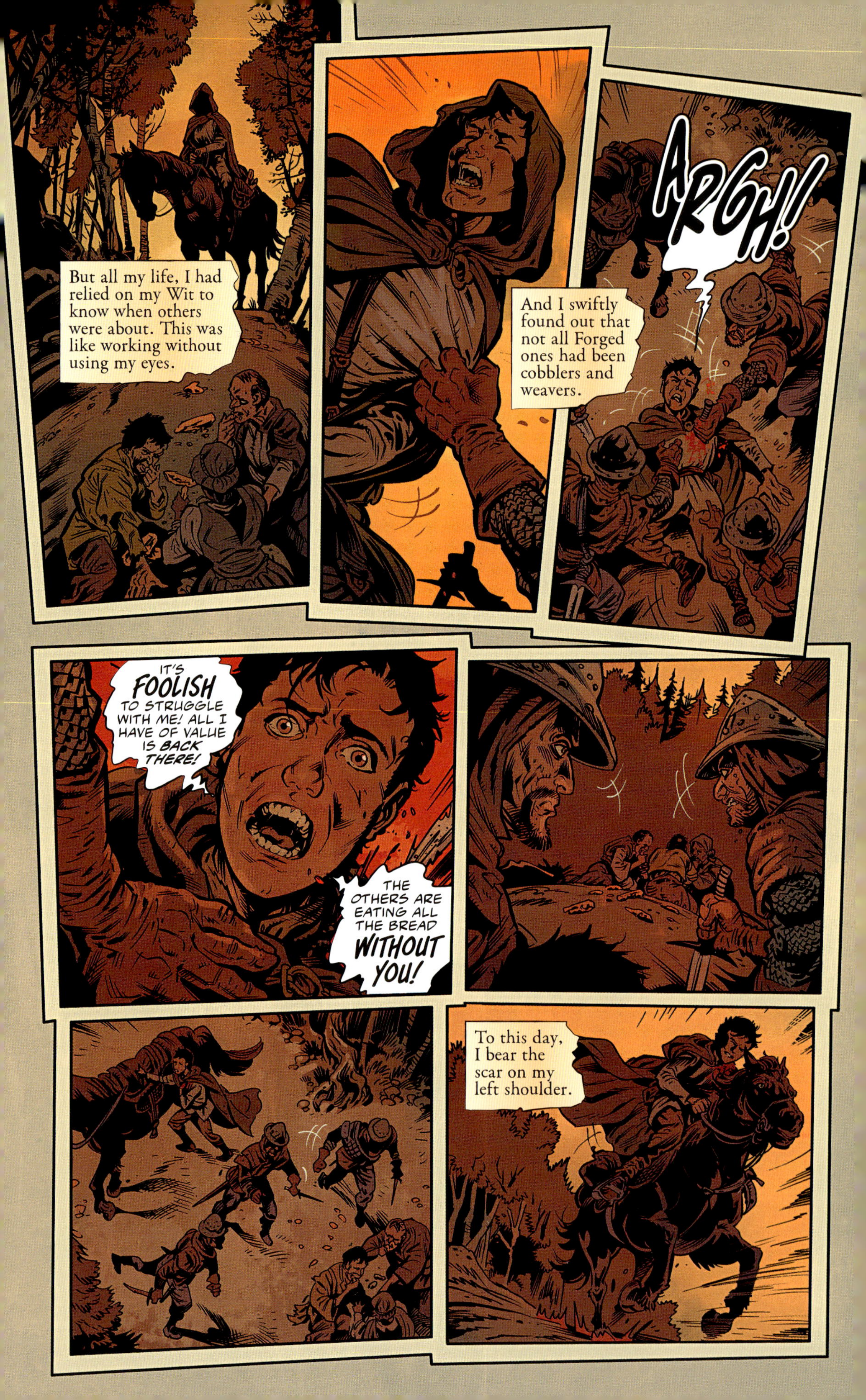
But all my life, I had relied on my Wit to know when others were about. This was like working without using my eyes.
And I swiftly found out that not all Forged ones had been cobblers and weavers.
ARGH!
IT'S FOOLISH TO STRUGGLE WITH ME! ALL I HAVE OF VALUE IS BACK THERE!
THE OTHERS ARE EATING ALL THE BREAD WITHOUT YOU!
To this day, I bear the scar on my left shoulder.

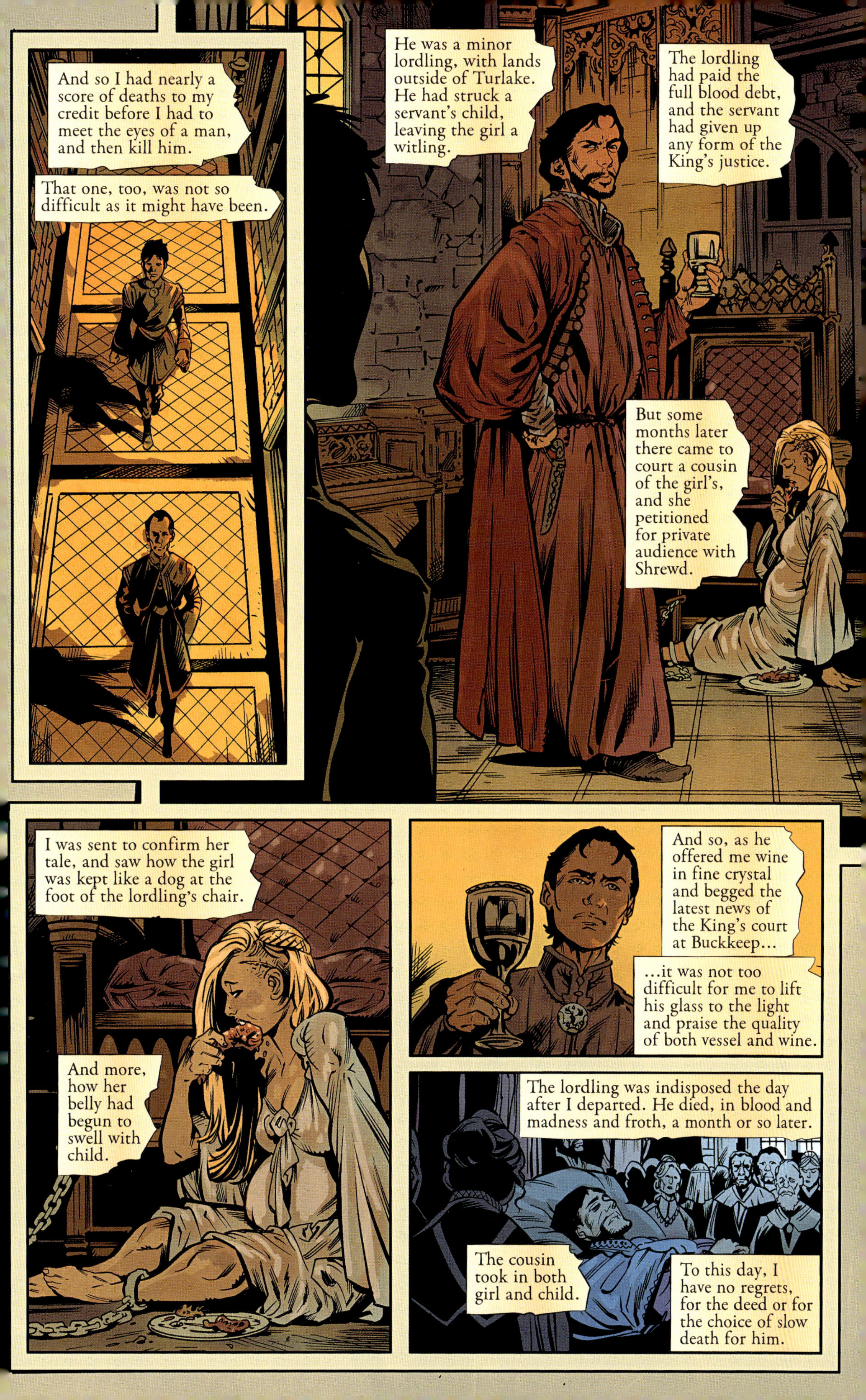

And so I had nearly a score of deaths to my credit before I had to meet the eyes of a man, and then kill him.
That one, too, was not so difficult as it might have been.
He was a minor lordling, with lands outside of Turlake. He had struck a servant's child, leaving the girl a witling.
The lordling had paid the full blood debt, and the servant had given up any form of the King's justice.
But some months later there came to court a cousin of the girl's, and she petitioned for private audience with Shrewd.
I was sent to confirm her tale, and saw how the girl was kept like a dog at the foot of the lordling's chair.
And more, how her belly had begun to swell with child.
And so, as he offered me wine in fine crystal and begged the latest news of the King's court at Buckkeep...
...it was not too difficult for me to lift his glass to the light and praise the quality of both vessel and wine.
The lordling was indisposed the day after I departed. He died, in blood and madness and froth, a month or so later.
The cousin took in both girl and child.
To this day, I have no regrets, for the deed or for the choice of slow death for him.

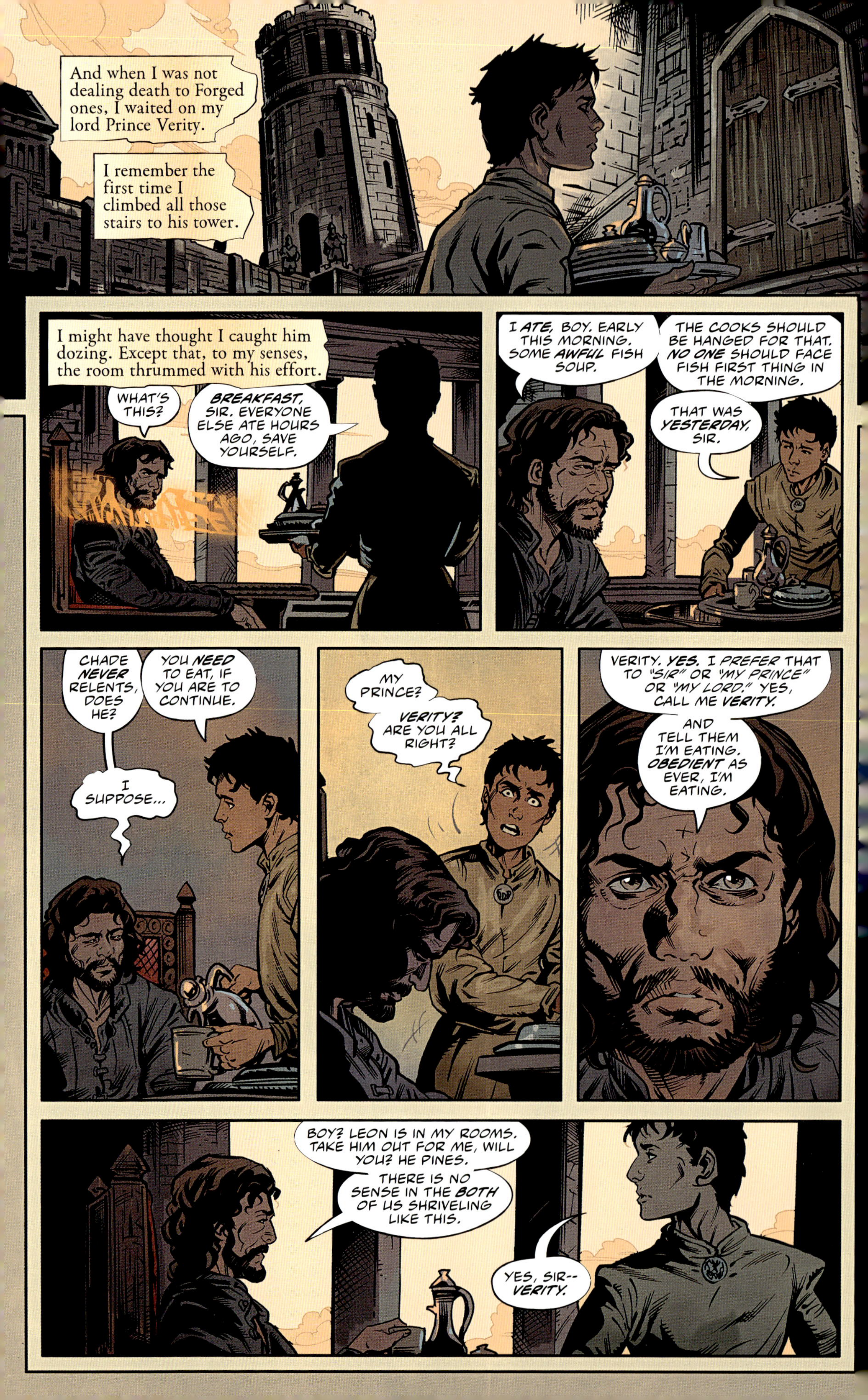
And when I was not dealing death to Forged ones, I waited on my lord Prince Verity.
I remember the first time I climbed all those stairs to his tower.
I might have thought I caught him dozing. Except that, to my senses, the room thrummed with his effort.
WHAT'S THIS?
BREAKFAST, SIR. EVERYONE ELSE ATE HOURS AGO, SAVE YOURSELF.
I ATE, BOY. EARLY THIS MORNING. SOME AWFUL FISH SOUP.
THE COOKS SHOULD BE HANGED FOR THAT. NO ONE SHOULD FACE FISH FIRST THING IN THE MORNING.
THAT WAS YESTERDAY, SIR.
CHADE NEVER RELENTS, DOES HE?
YOU NEED TO EAT, IF YOU ARE TO CONTINUE.
I SUPPOSE...
MY PRINCE?
VERITY? ARE YOU ALL RIGHT?
VERITY. YES. I PREFER THAT TO "SIR" OR "MY PRINCE" OR "MY LORD." YES, CALL ME VERITY.
AND TELL THEM I'M EATING. OBEDIENT AS EVER, I'M EATING.
BOY? LEON IS IN MY ROOMS. TAKE HIM OUT FOR ME, WILL YOU? HE PINES.
THERE IS NO SENSE IN THE BOTH OF US SHRIVELING LIKE THIS.
YES, SIR-- VERITY.

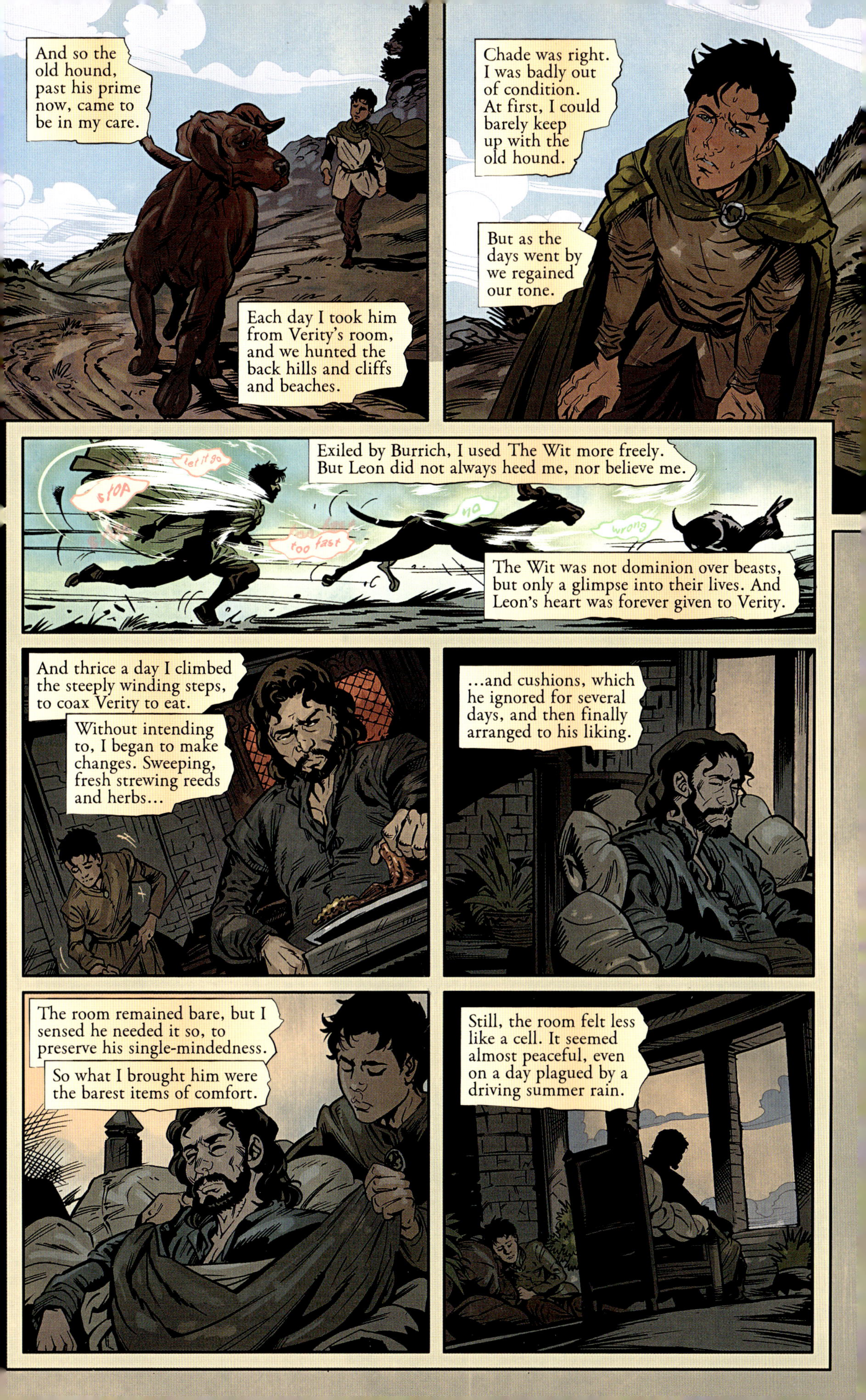
And so the old hound, past his prime now, came to be in my care.
Each day I took him from Verity's room, and we hunted the back hills and cliffs and beaches.
Chade was right. I was badly out of condition. At first, I could barely keep up with the old hound.
But as the days went by we regained our tone.
Exiled by Burrich, I used The Wit more freely. But Leon did not always heed me, nor believe me.
let it go
stop
too fast
no
wrong
The Wit was not dominion over beasts, but only a glimpse into their lives. And Leon's heart was forever given to Verity.
And thrice a day I climbed the steeply winding steps, to coax Verity to eat.
Without intending to, I began to make changes. Sweeping, fresh strewing reeds and herbs...
...and cushions, which he ignored for several days, and then finally arranged to his liking.
The room remained bare, but I sensed he needed it so, to preserve his single-mindedness.
So what I brought him were the barest items of comfort.
Still, the room felt less like a cell. It seemed almost peaceful, even on a day plagued by a driving summer rain.

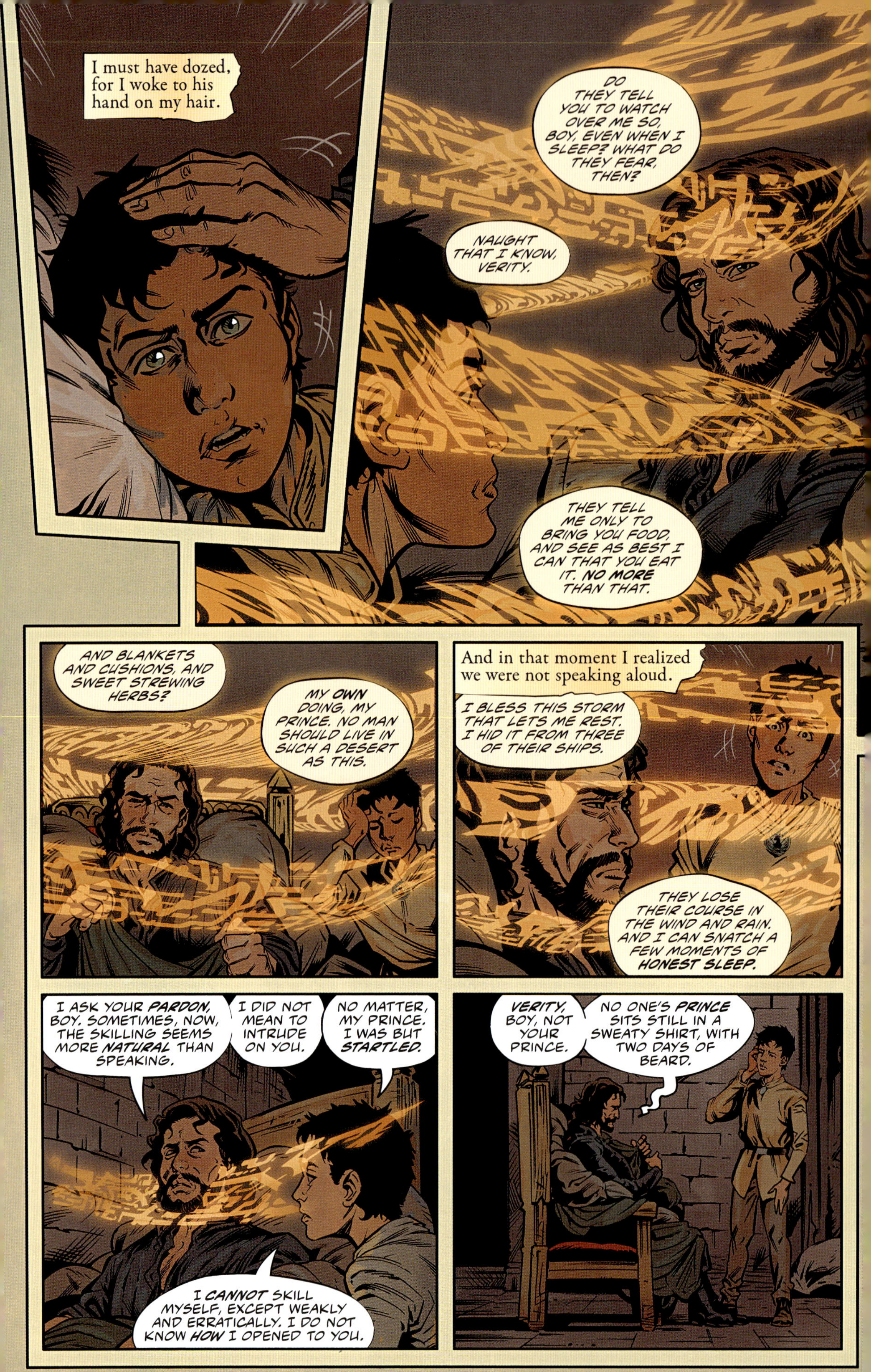
I must have dozed, for I woke to his hand on my hair.
DO THEY TELL YOU TO WATCH OVER ME SO, BOY, EVEN WHEN I SLEEP? WHAT DO THEY FEAR, THEN?
NAUGHT THAT I KNOW, VERITY.
THEY TELL ME ONLY TO BRING YOU FOOD, AND SEE AS BEST I CAN THAT YOU EAT IT. NO MORE THAN THAT.
AND BLANKETS AND CUSHIONS, AND SWEET STREWING HERBS?
MY OWN DOING, MY PRINCE. NO MAN SHOULD LIVE IN SUCH A DESERT AS THIS.
And in that moment I realized we were not speaking aloud.
I BLESS THIS STORM THAT LETS ME REST. I HID IT FROM THREE OF THEIR SHIPS.
THEY LOSE THEIR COURSE IN THE WIND AND RAIN, AND I CAN SNATCH A FEW MOMENTS OF HONEST SLEEP.
I ASK YOUR PARDON, BOY. SOMETIMES, NOW, THE SKILLING SEEMS MORE NATURAL THAN SPEAKING.
I DID NOT MEAN TO INTRUDE ON YOU.
NO MATTER, MY PRINCE. I WAS BUT STARTLED.
I CANNOT SKILL MYSELF, EXCEPT WEAKLY AND ERRATICALLY. I DO NOT KNOW HOW I OPENED TO YOU.
VERITY, BOY, NOT YOUR PRINCE.
NO ONE'S PRINCE SITS STILL IN A SWEATY SHIRT, WITH TWO DAYS OF BEARD.

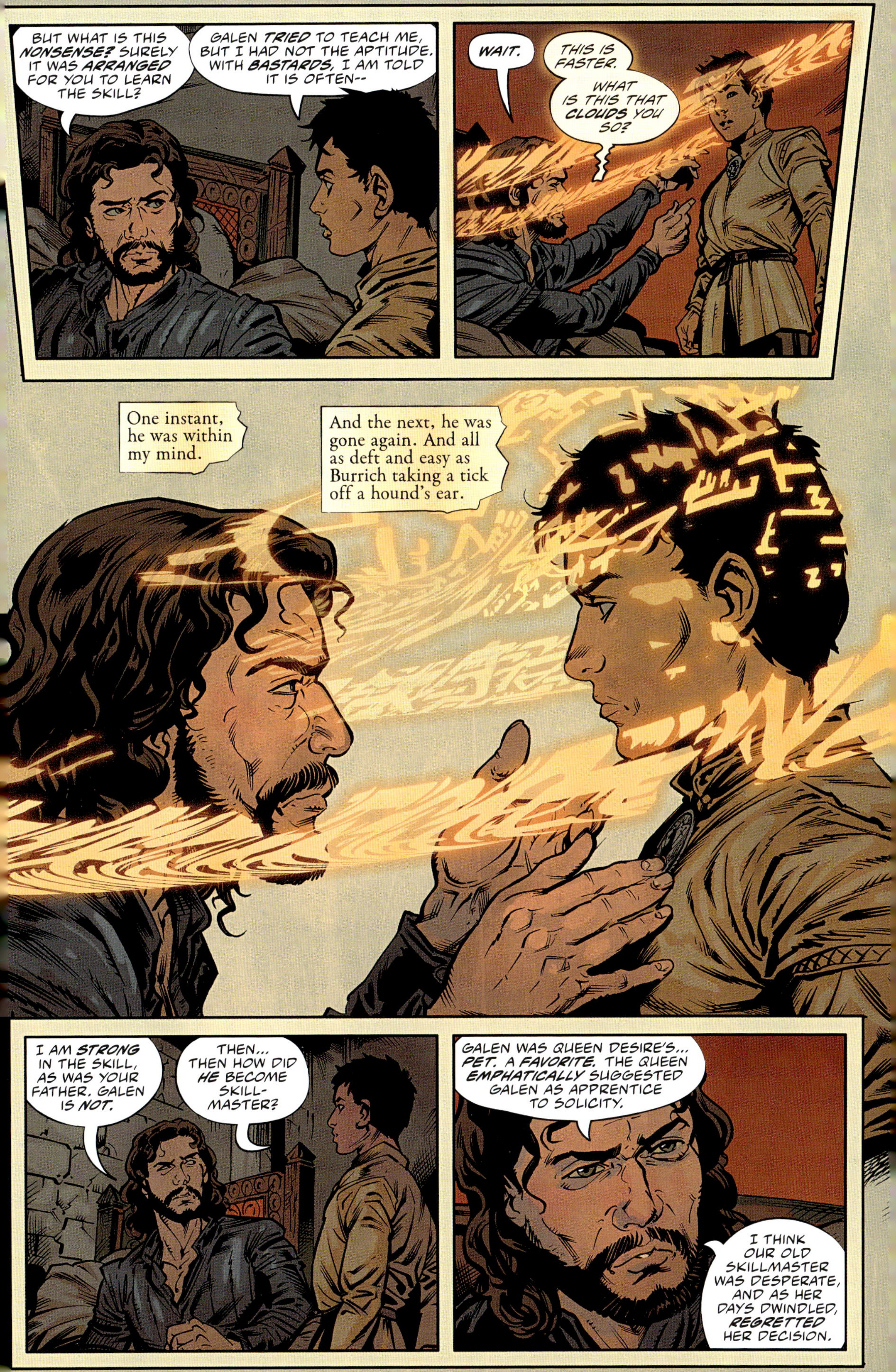

BUT WHAT IS THIS NONSENSE? SURELY IT WAS ARRANGED FOR YOU TO LEARN THE SKILL?
GALEN TRIED TO TEACH ME, BUT I HAD NOT THE APTITUDE. WITH BASTARDS, I AM TOLD IT IS OFTEN--
WAIT.
THIS IS FASTER.
WHAT IS THIS THAT CLOUDS YOU SO?
One instant, he was within my mind.
And the next, he was gone again. And all as deft and easy as Burrich taking a tick off a hound's ear.
I AM STRONG IN THE SKILL, AS WAS YOUR FATHER. GALEN IS NOT.
THEN... THEN HOW DID HE BECOME SKILL-MASTER?
GALEN WAS QUEEN DESIRE'S... PET. A FAVORITE. THE QUEEN EMPHATICALLY SUGGESTED GALEN AS APPRENTICE TO SOLICITY.
I THINK OUR OLD SKILLMASTER WAS DESPERATE, AND AS HER DAYS DWINDLED, REGRETTED HER DECISION.

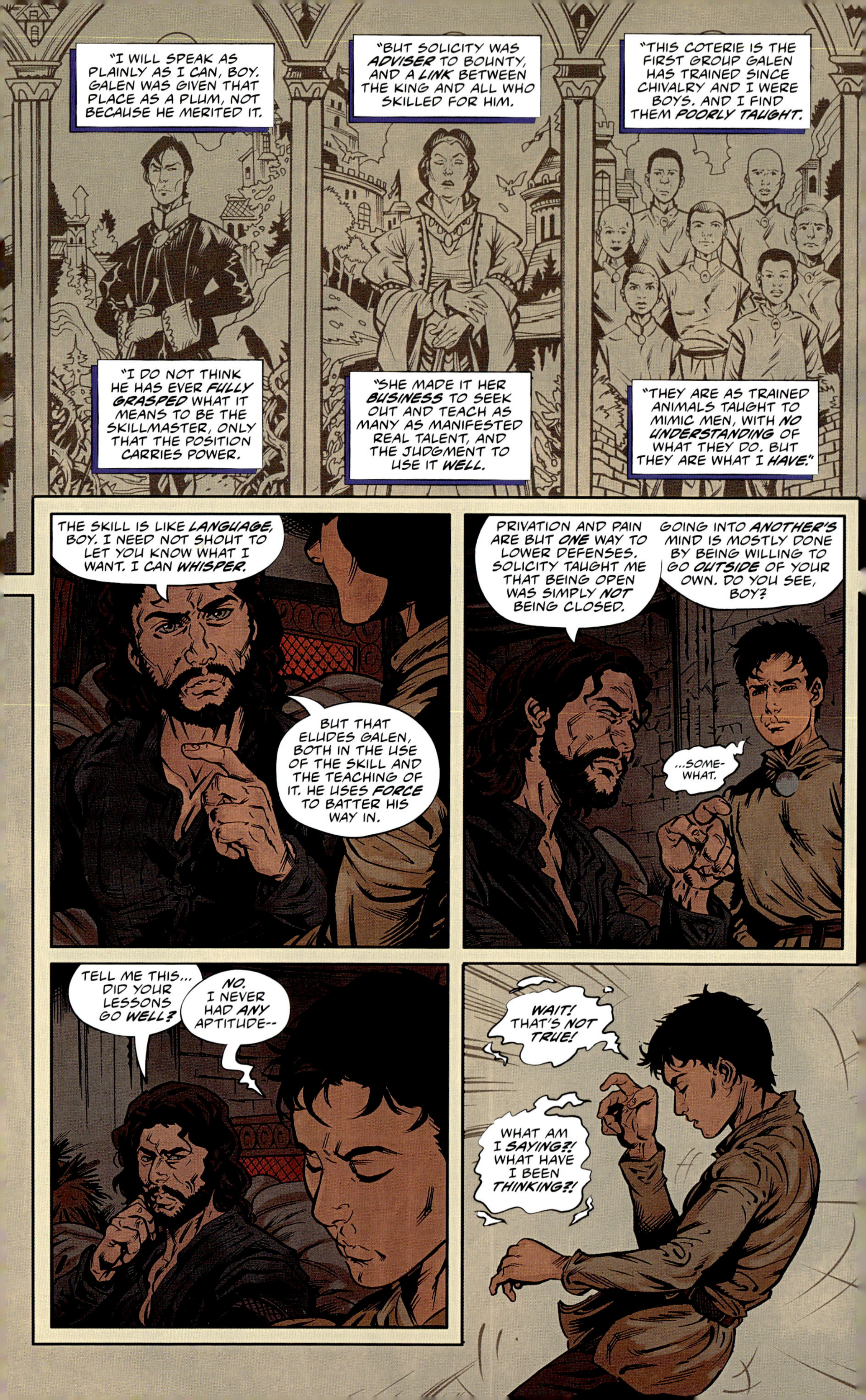
"I WILL SPEAK AS PLAINLY AS I CAN, BOY. GALEN WAS GIVEN THAT PLACE AS A PLUM, NOT BECAUSE HE MERITED IT.
"I DO NOT THINK HE HAS EVER FULLY GRASPED WHAT IT MEANS TO BE THE SKILLMASTER, ONLY THAT THE POSITION CARRIES POWER.
"BUT SOLICITY WAS ADVISER TO BOUNTY, AND A LINK BETWEEN THE KING AND ALL WHO SKILLED FOR HIM.
"SHE MADE IT HER BUSINESS TO SEEK OUT AND TEACH AS MANY AS MANIFESTED REAL TALENT, AND THE JUDGMENT TO USE IT WELL.
"THIS COTERIE IS THE FIRST GROUP GALEN HAS TRAINED SINCE CHIVALRY AND I WERE BOYS. AND I FIND THEM POORLY TAUGHT.
"THEY ARE AS TRAINED ANIMALS TAUGHT TO MIMIC MEN, WITH NO UNDERSTANDING OF WHAT THEY DO. BUT THEY ARE WHAT I HAVE."
THE SKILL IS LIKE LANGUAGE, BOY. I NEED NOT SHOUT TO LET YOU KNOW WHAT I WANT. I CAN WHISPER.
BUT THAT ELUDES GALEN, BOTH IN THE USE OF THE SKILL AND THE TEACHING OF IT. HE USES FORCE TO BATTER HIS WAY IN.
PRIVATION AND PAIN ARE BUT ONE WAY TO LOWER DEFENSES. SOLICITY TAUGHT ME THAT BEING OPEN WAS SIMPLY NOT BEING CLOSED.
GOING INTO ANOTHER'S MIND IS MOSTLY DONE BY BEING WILLING TO GO OUTSIDE OF YOUR OWN. DO YOU SEE, BOY?
...SOME-WHAT.
TELL ME THIS... DID YOUR LESSONS GO WELL?
NO. I NEVER HAD ANY APTITUDE--
WAIT! THAT'S NOT TRUE!
WHAT AM I SAYING?! WHAT HAVE I BEEN THINKING?!

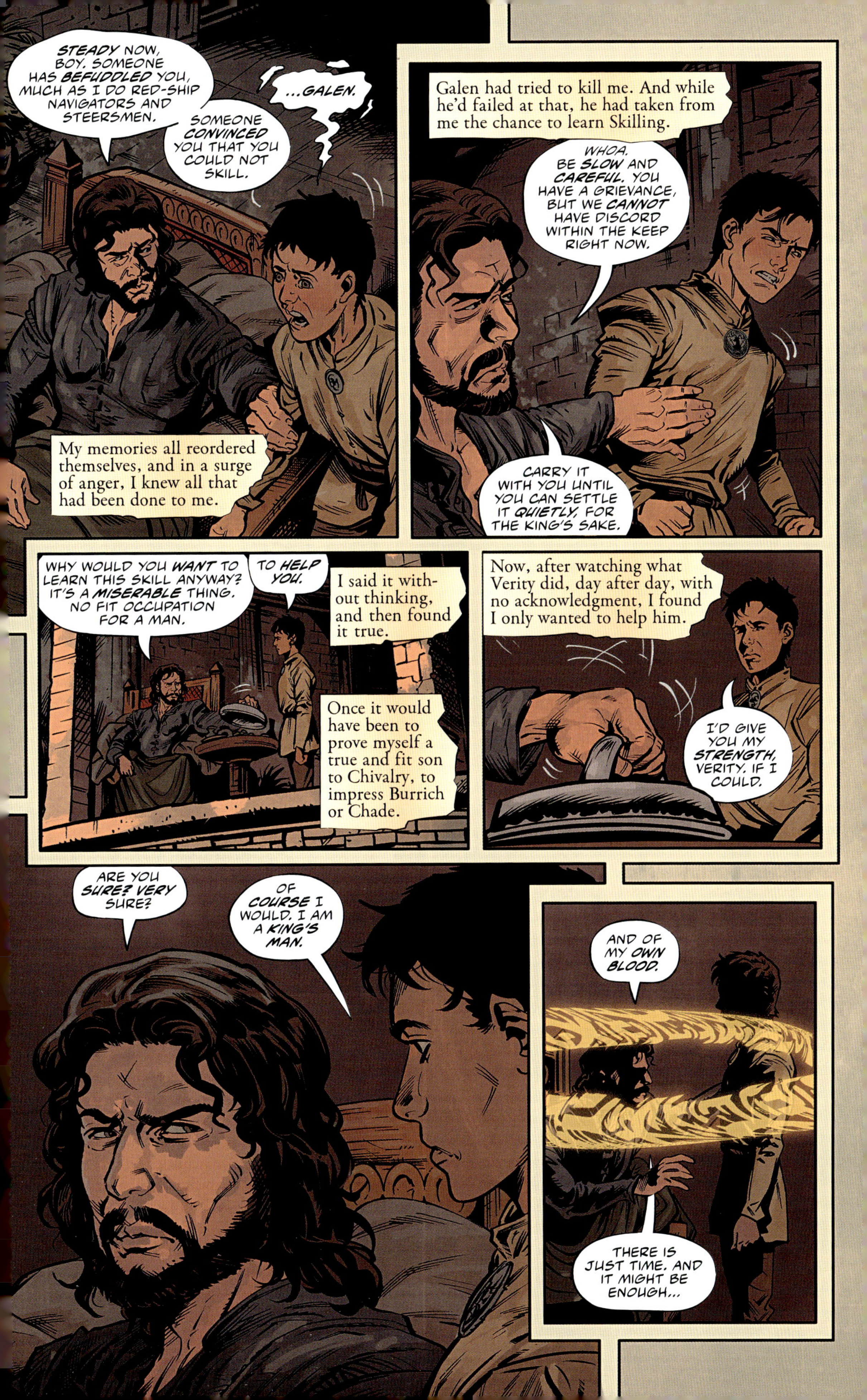
STEADY NOW, BOY. SOMEONE HAS BEFUDDLED YOU, MUCH AS I DO RED-SHIP NAVIGATORS AND STEERSMEN.
SOMEONE CONVINCED YOU THAT YOU COULD NOT SKILL.
...GALEN.
My memories all reordered themselves, and in a surge of anger, I knew all that had been done to me.
Galen had tried to kill me. And while he'd failed at that, he had taken from me the chance to learn Skilling.
WHOA. BE SLOW AND CAREFUL. YOU HAVE A GRIEVANCE, BUT WE CANNOT HAVE DISCORD WITHIN THE KEEP RIGHT NOW.
CARRY IT WITH YOU UNTIL YOU CAN SETTLE IT QUIETLY, FOR THE KING'S SAKE.
WHY WOULD YOU WANT TO LEARN THIS SKILL ANYWAY? IT'S A MISERABLE THING. NO FIT OCCUPATION FOR A MAN.
TO HELP YOU.
I said it without thinking, and then found it true.
Once it would have been to prove myself a true and fit son to Chivalry, to impress Burrich or Chade.
Now, after watching what Verity did, day after day, with no acknowledgment, I found I only wanted to help him.
I'D GIVE YOU MY STRENGTH, VERITY, IF I COULD.
ARE YOU SURE? VERY SURE?
OF COURSE I WOULD. I AM A KING'S MAN.
AND OF MY OWN BLOOD.
THERE IS JUST TIME. AND IT MIGHT BE ENOUGH...

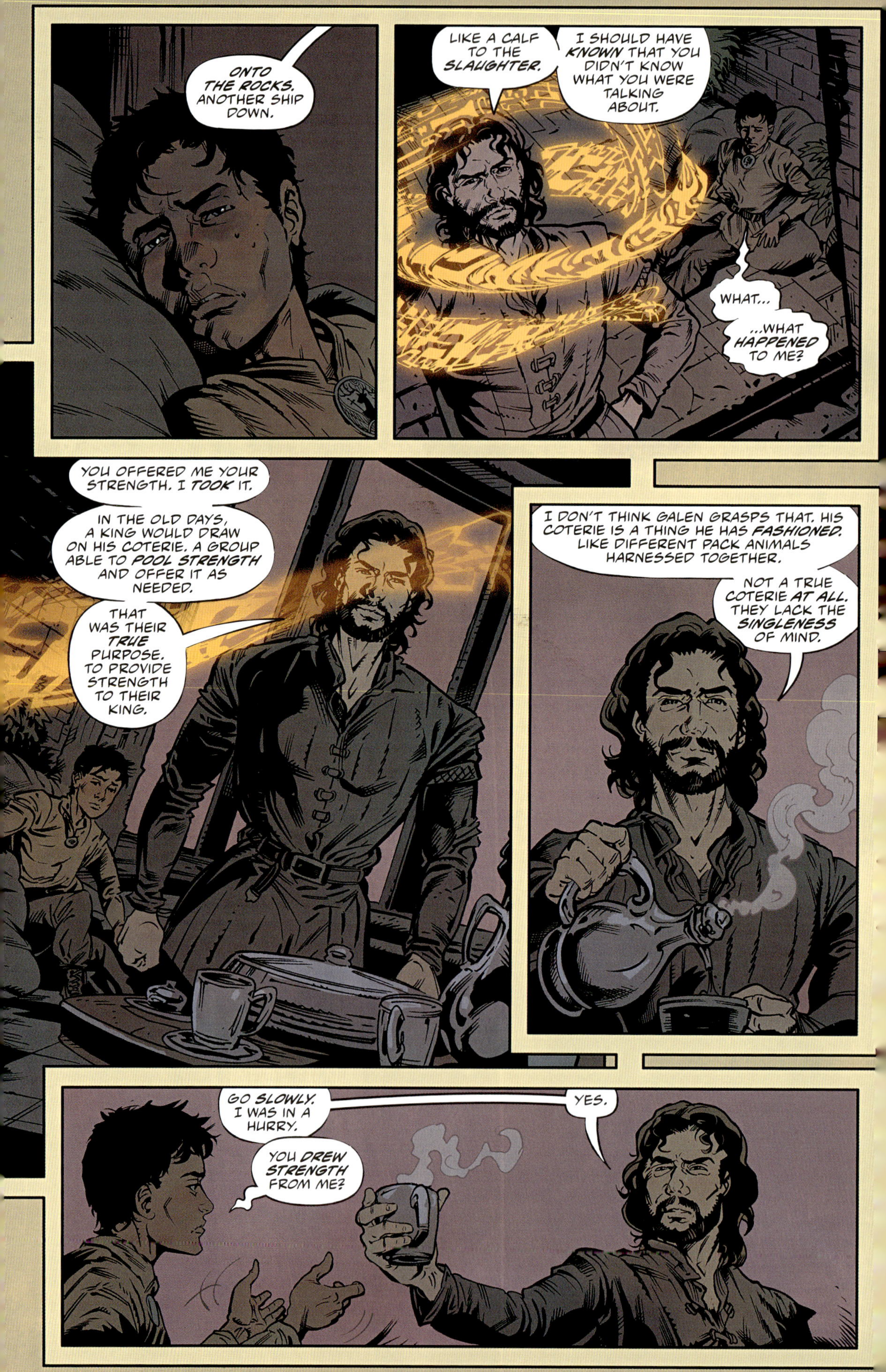
ONTO THE ROCKS. ANOTHER SHIP DOWN.
LIKE A CALF TO THE SLAUGHTER.
I SHOULD HAVE KNOWN THAT YOU DIDN'T KNOW WHAT YOU WERE TALKING ABOUT.
WHAT...
...WHAT HAPPENED TO ME?
YOU OFFERED ME YOUR STRENGTH. I TOOK IT.
IN THE OLD DAYS, A KING WOULD DRAW ON HIS COTERIE. A GROUP ABLE TO POOL STRENGTH AND OFFER IT AS NEEDED.
THAT WAS THEIR TRUE PURPOSE. TO PROVIDE STRENGTH TO THEIR KING.
I DON'T THINK GALEN GRASPS THAT. HIS COTERIE IS A THING HE HAS FASHIONED. LIKE DIFFERENT PACK ANIMALS HARNESSED TOGETHER.
NOT A TRUE COTERIE AT ALL. THEY LACK THE SINGLENESS OF MIND.
GO SLOWLY. I WAS IN A HURRY.
YOU DREW STRENGTH FROM ME?
YES.

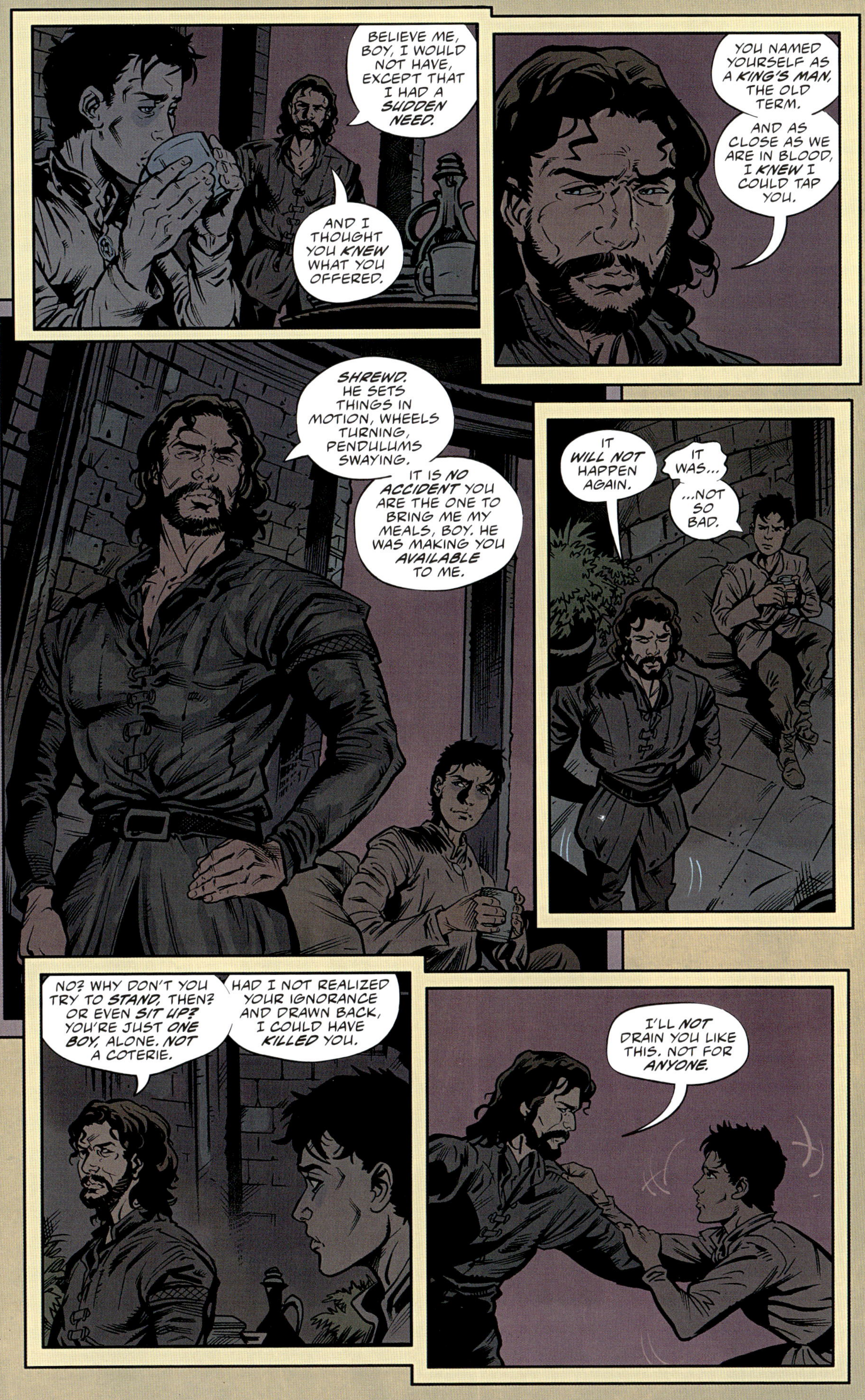
BELIEVE ME, BOY, I WOULD NOT HAVE, EXCEPT THAT I HAD A SUDDEN NEED.
AND I THOUGHT YOU KNEW WHAT YOU OFFERED.
YOU NAMED YOURSELF AS A KING'S MAN, THE OLD TERM.
AND AS CLOSE AS WE ARE IN BLOOD, I KNEW I COULD TAP YOU.
SHREWD. HE SETS THINGS IN MOTION, WHEELS TURNING, PENDULUMS SWAYING.
IT IS NO ACCIDENT YOU ARE THE ONE TO BRING ME MY MEALS, BOY. HE WAS MAKING YOU AVAILABLE TO ME.
IT WILL NOT HAPPEN AGAIN.
IT WAS...
...NOT SO BAD.
NO? WHY DON'T YOU TRY TO STAND, THEN? OR EVEN SIT UP? YOU'RE JUST ONE BOY, ALONE. NOT A COTERIE.
HAD I NOT REALIZED YOUR IGNORANCE AND DRAWN BACK, I COULD HAVE KILLED YOU.
I'LL NOT DRAIN YOU LIKE THIS. NOT FOR ANYONE.

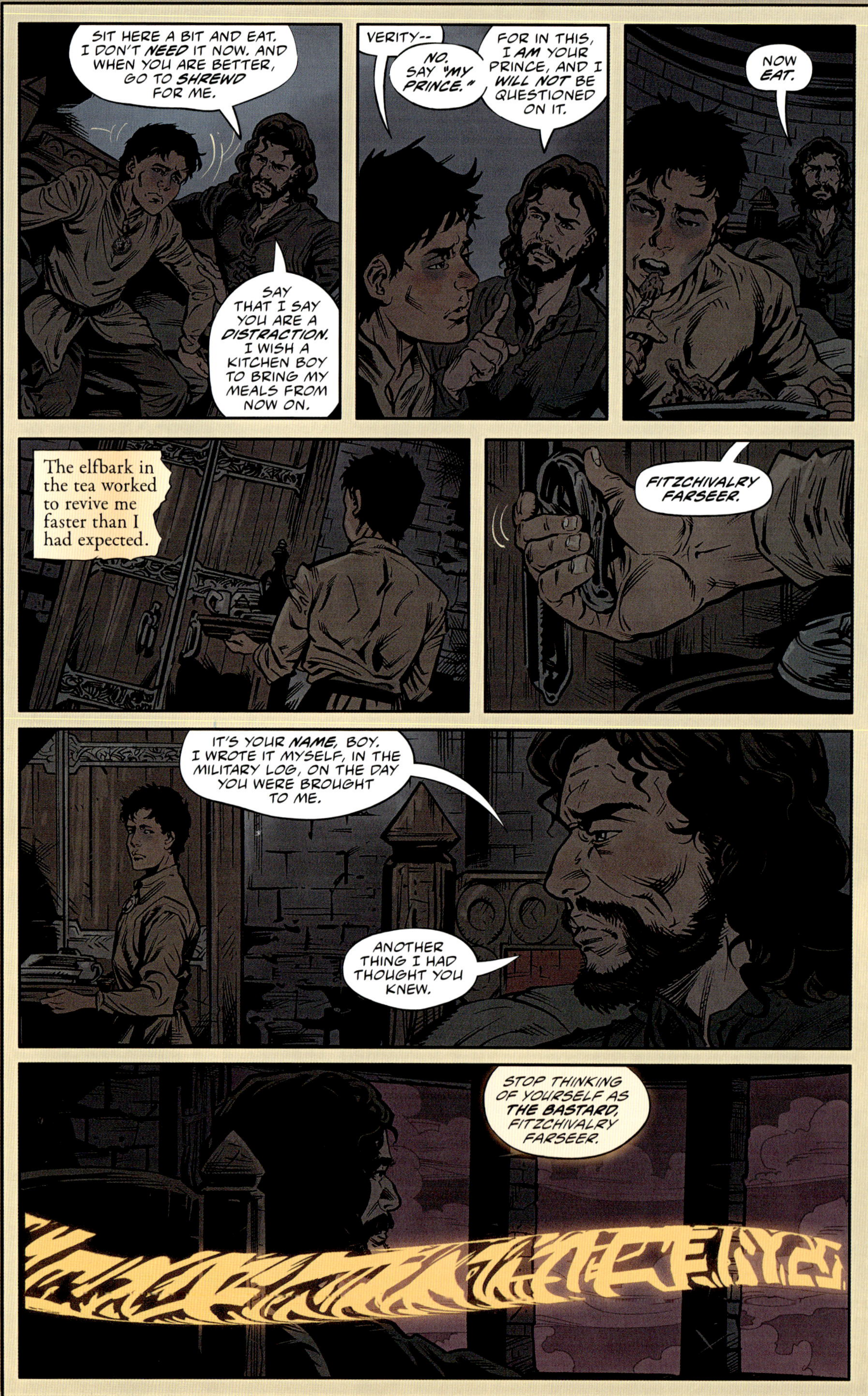
SIT HERE A BIT AND EAT. I DON'T NEED IT NOW. AND WHEN YOU ARE BETTER, GO TO SHREWD FOR ME.
SAY THAT I SAY YOU ARE A DISTRACTION. I WISH A KITCHEN BOY TO BRING MY MEALS FROM NOW ON.
VERITY--
NO. SAY "MY PRINCE."
FOR IN THIS, I AM YOUR PRINCE, AND I WILL NOT BE QUESTIONED ON IT.
NOW EAT.
The elfbark in the tea worked to revive me faster than I had expected.
FITZCHIVALRY FARSEER.
IT'S YOUR NAME, BOY. I WROTE IT MYSELF, IN THE MILITARY LOG, ON THE DAY YOU WERE BROUGHT TO ME.
ANOTHER THING I HAD THOUGHT YOU KNEW.
STOP THINKING OF YOURSELF AS THE BASTARD, FITZCHIVALRY FARSEER.

Chapter Three

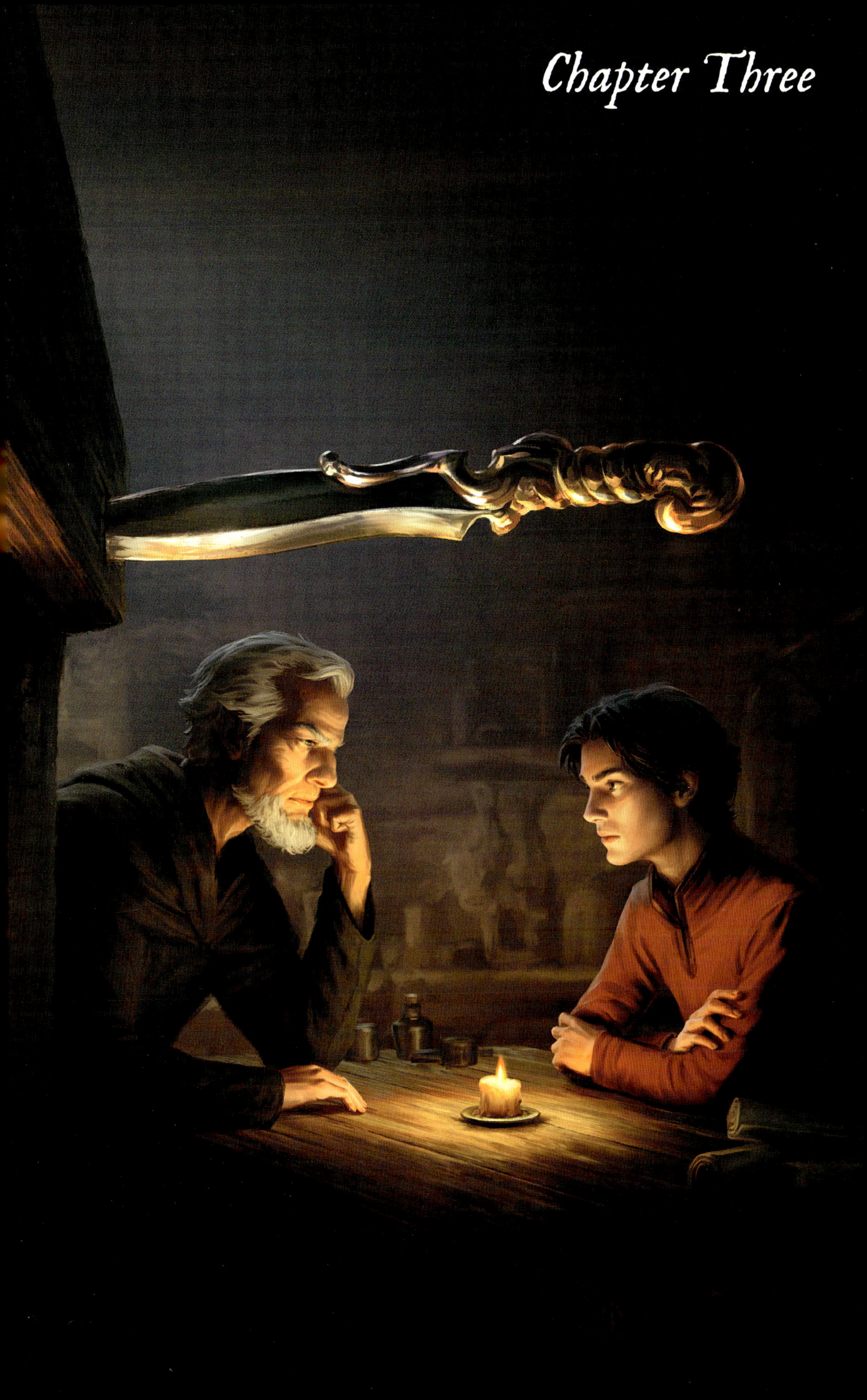

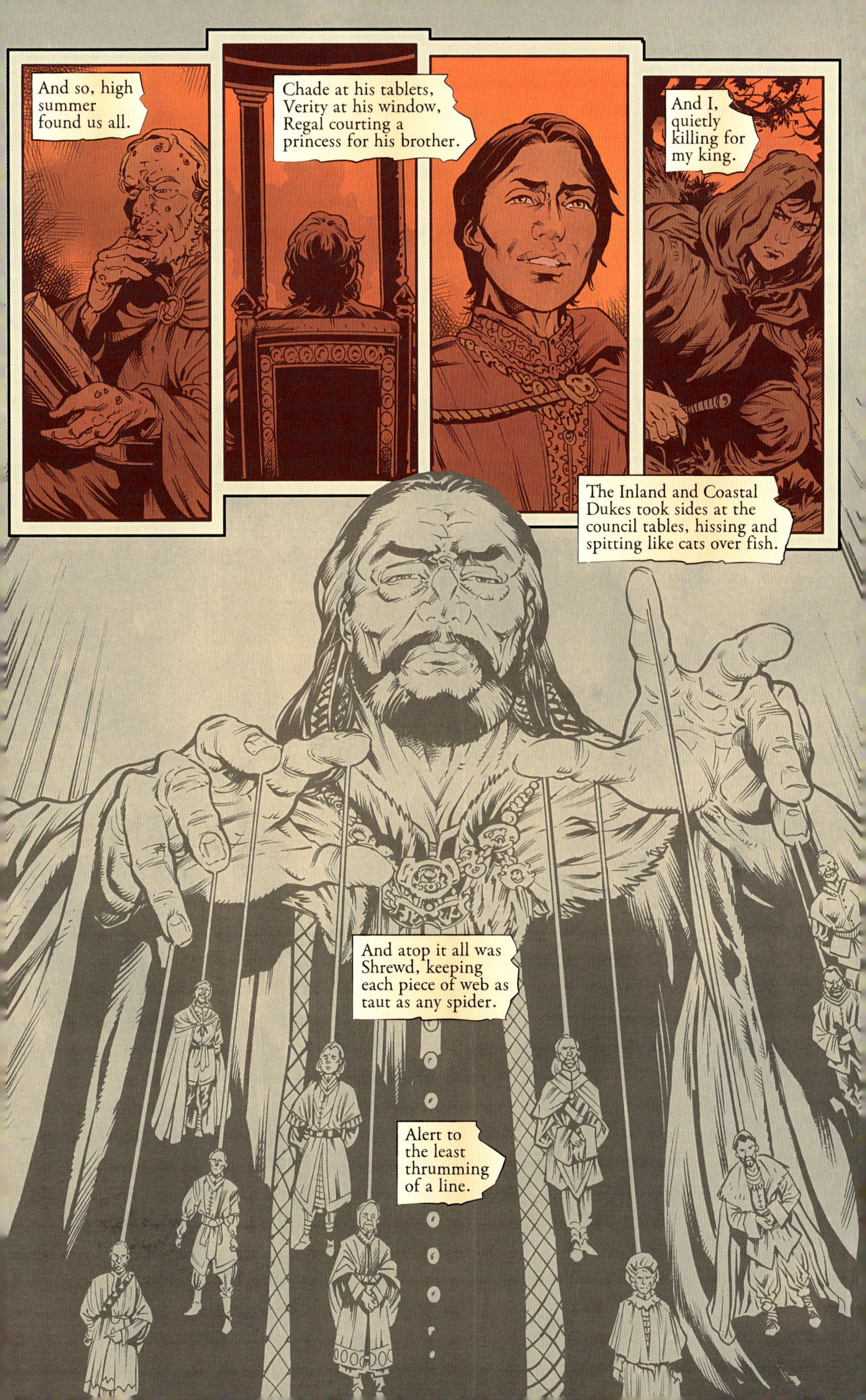
And so, high summer found us all.
Chade at his tablets, Verity at his window, Regal courting a princess for his brother.
And I, quietly killing for my king.
The Inland and Coastal Dukes took sides at the council tables, hissing and spitting like cats over fish.
And atop it all was Shrewd, keeping each piece of web as taut as any spider.
Alert to the least thrumming of a line.

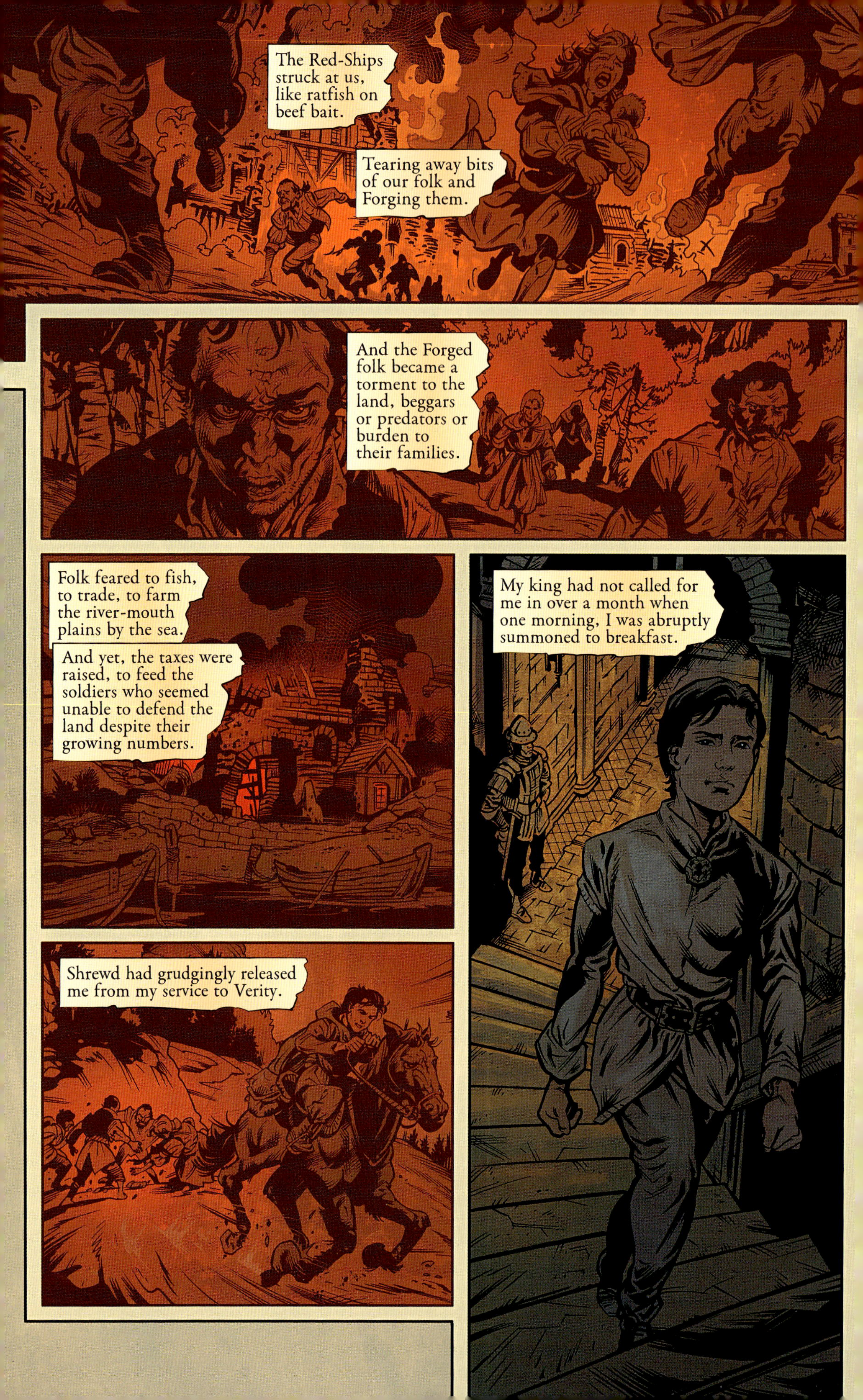

The Red-Ships struck at us, like ratfish on beef bait.
Tearing away bits of our folk and Forging them.
And the Forged folk became a torment to the land, beggars or predators or burden to their families.
Folk feared to fish, to trade, to farm the river-mouth plains by the sea.
And yet, the taxes were raised, to feed the soldiers who seemed unable to defend the land despite their growing numbers.
Shrewd had grudgingly released me from my service to Verity.
My king had not called for me in over a month when one morning, I was abruptly summoned to breakfast.

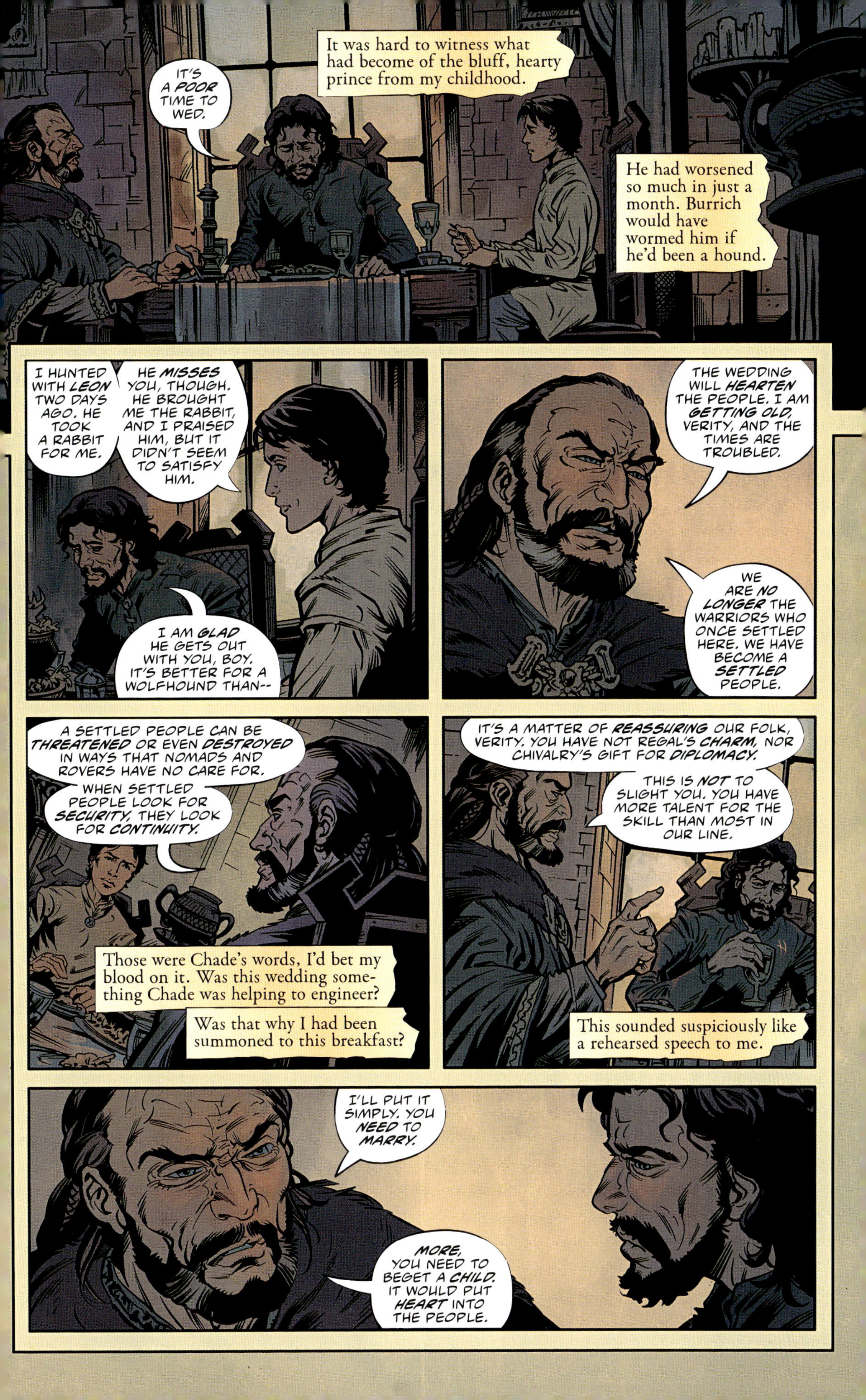
It was hard to witness what had become of the bluff, hearty prince from my childhood.
IT'S A POOR TIME TO WED.
He had worsened so much in just a month. Burrich would have wormed him if he'd been a hound.
I HUNTED WITH LEON TWO DAYS AGO. HE TOOK A RABBIT FOR ME.
HE MISSES YOU, THOUGH. HE BROUGHT ME THE RABBIT, AND I PRAISED HIM, BUT IT DIDN'T SEEM TO SATISFY HIM.
I AM GLAD HE GETS OUT WITH YOU, BOY. IT'S BETTER FOR A WOLFHOUND THAN--
THE WEDDING WILL HEARTEN THE PEOPLE. I AM GETTING OLD, VERITY, AND THE TIMES ARE TROUBLED.
WE ARE NO LONGER THE WARRIORS WHO ONCE SETTLED HERE. WE HAVE BECOME A SETTLED PEOPLE.
A SETTLED PEOPLE CAN BE THREATENED OR EVEN DESTROYED IN WAYS THAT NOMADS AND ROVERS HAVE NO CARE FOR.
WHEN SETTLED PEOPLE LOOK FOR SECURITY, THEY LOOK FOR CONTINUITY.
Those were Chade's words, I'd bet my blood on it. Was this wedding something Chade was helping to engineer?
Was that why I had been summoned to this breakfast?
IT'S A MATTER OF REASSURING OUR FOLK, VERITY. YOU HAVE NOT REGAL'S CHARM, NOR CHIVALRY'S GIFT FOR DIPLOMACY.
THIS IS NOT TO SLIGHT YOU. YOU HAVE MORE TALENT FOR THE SKILL THAN MOST IN OUR LINE.
This sounded suspiciously like a rehearsed speech to me.
I'LL PUT IT SIMPLY. YOU NEED TO MARRY.
MORE, YOU NEED TO BEGET A CHILD. IT WOULD PUT HEART INTO THE PEOPLE.

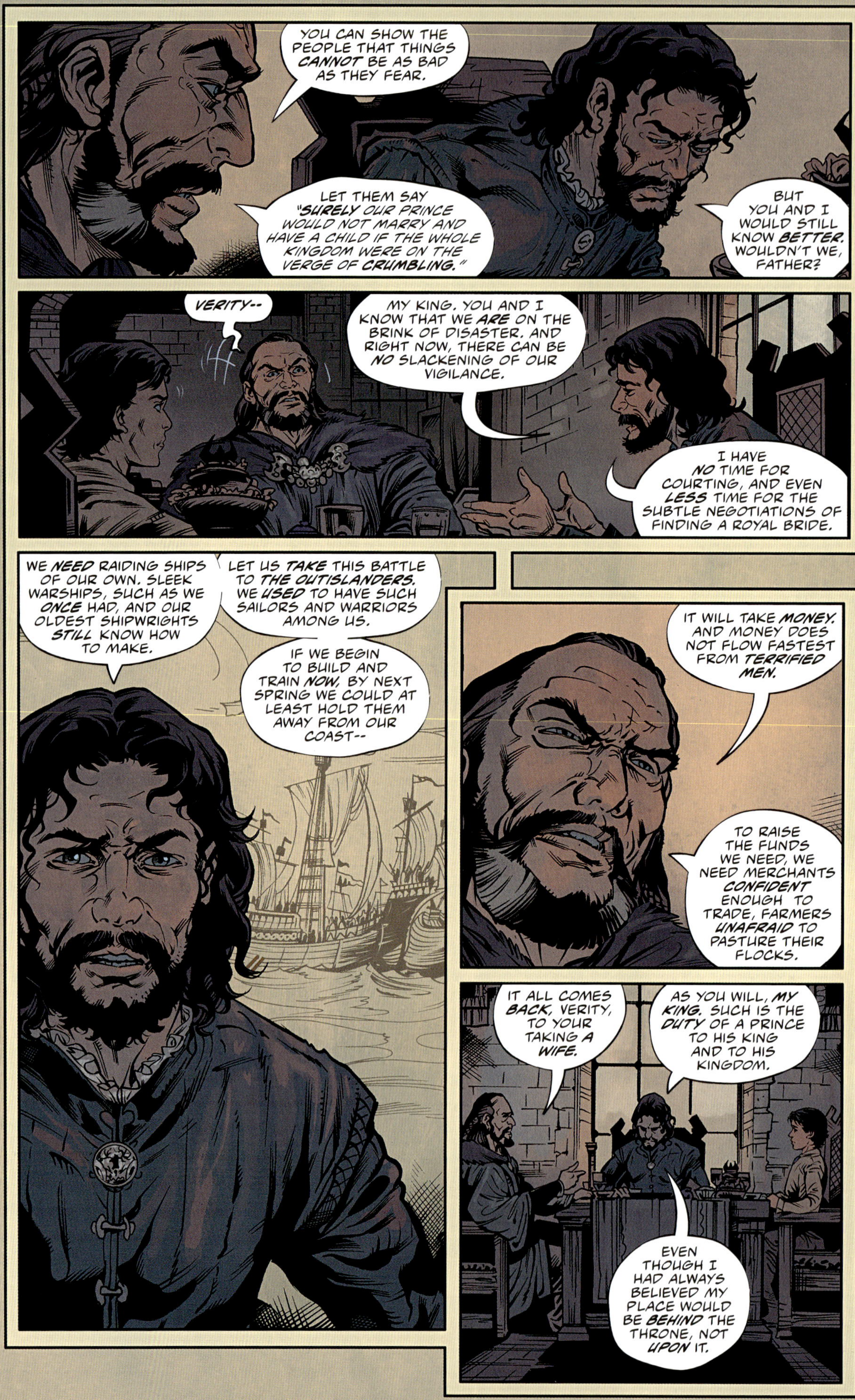
YOU CAN SHOW THE PEOPLE THAT THINGS CANNOT BE AS BAD AS THEY FEAR.
LET THEM SAY "SURELY OUR PRINCE WOULD NOT MARRY AND HAVE A CHILD IF THE WHOLE KINGDOM WERE ON THE VERGE OF CRUMBLING."
BUT YOU AND I WOULD STILL KNOW BETTER. WOULDN'T WE, FATHER?
VERITY--
MY KING. YOU AND I KNOW THAT WE ARE ON THE BRINK OF DISASTER. AND RIGHT NOW, THERE CAN BE NO SLACKENING OF OUR VIGILANCE.
I HAVE NO TIME FOR COURTING, AND EVEN LESS TIME FOR THE SUBTLE NEGOTIATIONS OF FINDING A ROYAL BRIDE.
WE NEED RAIDING SHIPS OF OUR OWN. SLEEK WARSHIPS, SUCH AS WE ONCE HAD, AND OUR OLDEST SHIPWRIGHTS STILL KNOW HOW TO MAKE.
LET US TAKE THIS BATTLE TO THE OUTISLANDERS. WE USED TO HAVE SUCH SAILORS AND WARRIORS AMONG US.
IF WE BEGIN TO BUILD AND TRAIN NOW, BY NEXT SPRING WE COULD AT LEAST HOLD THEM AWAY FROM OUR COAST--
IT WILL TAKE MONEY. AND MONEY DOES NOT FLOW FASTEST FROM TERRIFIED MEN.
TO RAISE THE FUNDS WE NEED, WE NEED MERCHANTS CONFIDENT ENOUGH TO TRADE, FARMERS UNAFRAID TO PASTURE THEIR FLOCKS.
IT ALL COMES BACK, VERITY, TO YOUR TAKING A WIFE.
AS YOU WILL, MY KING. SUCH IS THE DUTY OF A PRINCE TO HIS KING AND TO HIS KINGDOM.
EVEN THOUGH I HAD ALWAYS BELIEVED MY PLACE WOULD BE BEHIND THE THRONE, NOT UPON IT.

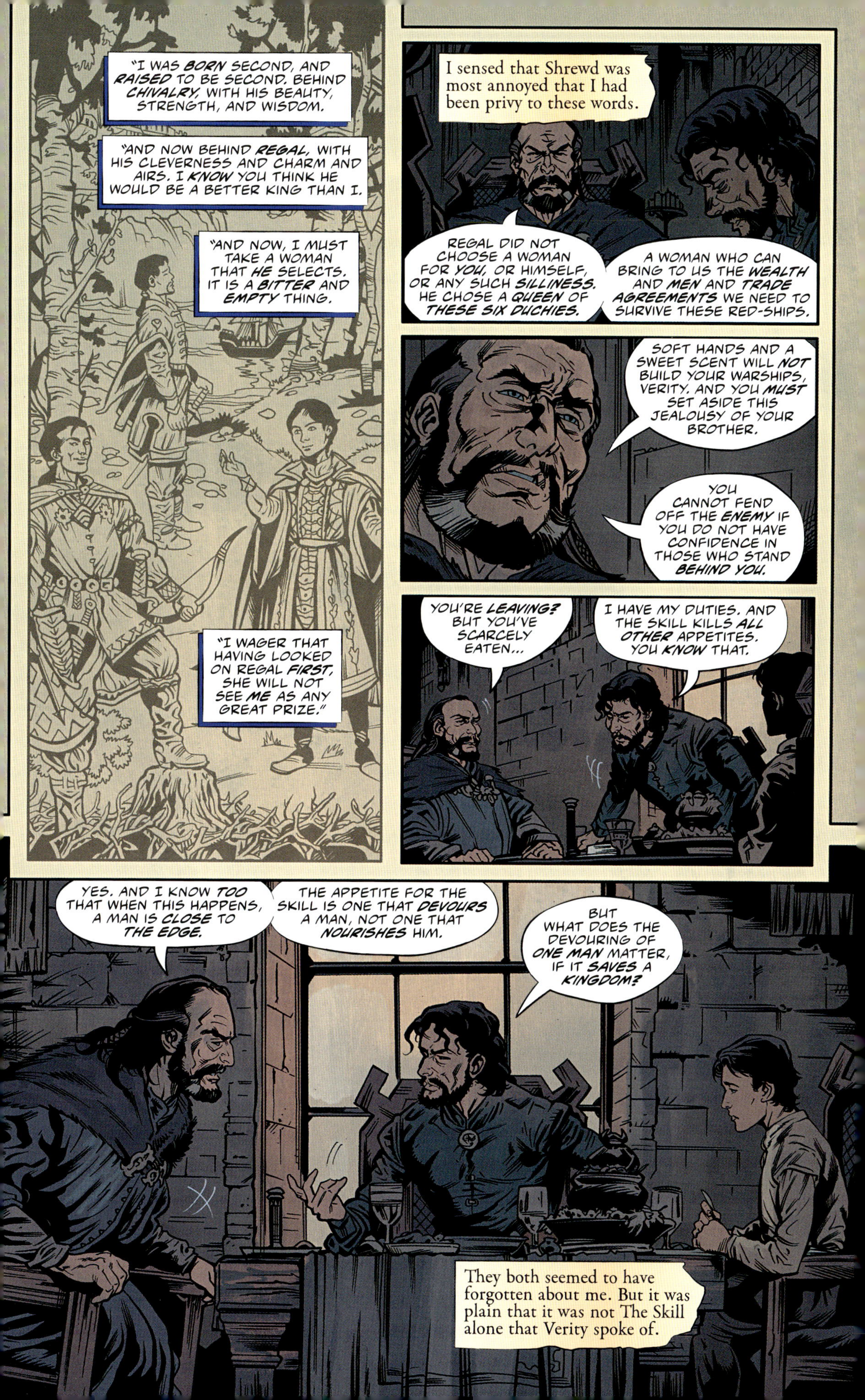
"I WAS BORN SECOND, AND RAISED TO BE SECOND. BEHIND CHIVALRY, WITH HIS BEAUTY, STRENGTH, AND WISDOM.
"AND NOW BEHIND REGAL, WITH HIS CLEVERNESS AND CHARM AND AIRS. I KNOW YOU THINK HE WOULD BE A BETTER KING THAN I.
"AND NOW, I MUST TAKE A WOMAN THAT HE SELECTS. IT IS A BITTER AND EMPTY THING.
"I WAGER THAT HAVING LOOKED ON REGAL FIRST, SHE WILL NOT SEE ME AS ANY GREAT PRIZE."
I sensed that Shrewd was most annoyed that I had been privy to these words.
REGAL DID NOT CHOOSE A WOMAN FOR YOU, OR HIMSELF, OR ANY SUCH SILLINESS. HE CHOSE A QUEEN OF THESE SIX DUCHIES.
A WOMAN WHO CAN BRING TO US THE WEALTH AND MEN AND TRADE AGREEMENTS WE NEED TO SURVIVE THESE RED-SHIPS.
SOFT HANDS AND A SWEET SCENT WILL NOT BUILD YOUR WARSHIPS, VERITY. AND YOU MUST SET ASIDE THIS JEALOUSY OF YOUR BROTHER.
YOU CANNOT FEND OFF THE ENEMY IF YOU DO NOT HAVE CONFIDENCE IN THOSE WHO STAND BEHIND YOU.
YOU'RE LEAVING? BUT YOU'VE SCARCELY EATEN...
I HAVE MY DUTIES. AND THE SKILL KILLS ALL OTHER APPETITES. YOU KNOW THAT.
YES. AND I KNOW TOO THAT WHEN THIS HAPPENS, A MAN IS CLOSE TO THE EDGE.
THE APPETITE FOR THE SKILL IS ONE THAT DEVOURS A MAN, NOT ONE THAT NOURISHES HIM.
BUT WHAT DOES THE DEVOURING OF ONE MAN MATTER, IF IT SAVES A KINGDOM?
They both seemed to have forgotten about me. But it was plain that it was not The Skill alone that Verity spoke of.

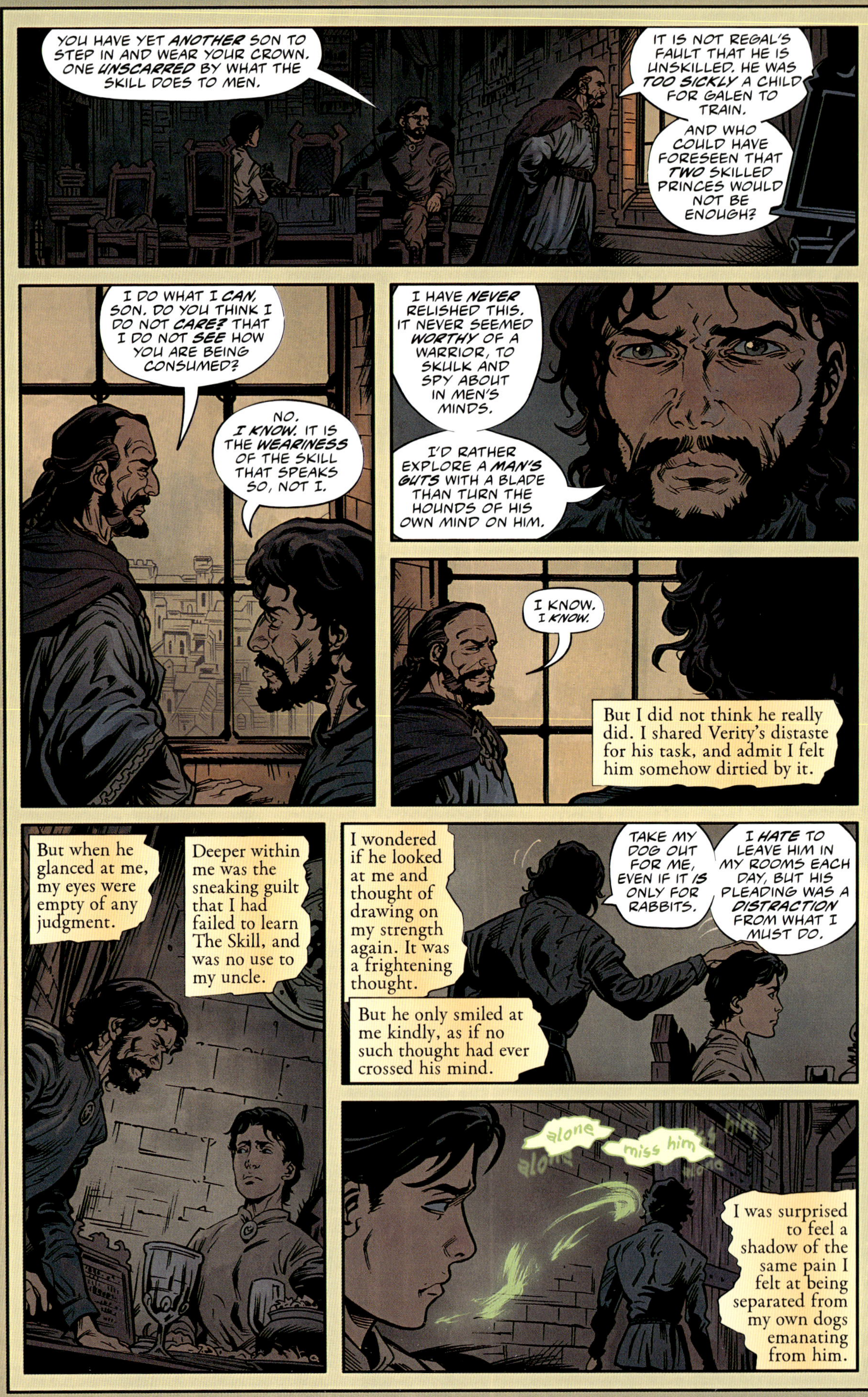

YOU HAVE YET ANOTHER SON TO STEP IN AND WEAR YOUR CROWN. ONE UNSCARRED BY WHAT THE SKILL DOES TO MEN.
IT IS NOT REGAL'S FAULT THAT HE IS UNSKILLED. HE WAS TOO SICKLY A CHILD FOR GALEN TO TRAIN.
AND WHO COULD HAVE FORESEEN THAT TWO SKILLED PRINCES WOULD NOT BE ENOUGH?
I DO WHAT I CAN, SON. DO YOU THINK I DO NOT CARE? THAT I DO NOT SEE HOW YOU ARE BEING CONSUMED?
NO. I KNOW. IT IS THE WEARINESS OF THE SKILL THAT SPEAKS SO, NOT I.
I HAVE NEVER RELISHED THIS. IT NEVER SEEMED WORTHY OF A WARRIOR, TO SKULK AND SPY ABOUT IN MEN'S MINDS.
I'D RATHER EXPLORE A MAN'S GUTS WITH A BLADE THAN TURN THE HOUNDS OF HIS OWN MIND ON HIM.
I KNOW. I KNOW.
But I did not think he really did. I shared Verity's distaste for his task, and admit I felt him somehow dirtied by it.
But when he glanced at me, my eyes were empty of any judgment.
Deeper within me was the sneaking guilt that I had failed to learn The Skill, and was no use to my uncle.
I wondered if he looked at me and thought of drawing on my strength again. It was a frightening thought.
But he only smiled at me kindly, as if no such thought had ever crossed his mind.
TAKE MY DOG OUT FOR ME, EVEN IF IT IS ONLY FOR RABBITS.
I HATE TO LEAVE HIM IN MY ROOMS EACH DAY, BUT HIS PLEADING WAS A DISTRACTION FROM WHAT I MUST DO.
alone
miss him
I was surprised to feel a shadow of the same pain I felt at being separated from my own dogs emanating from him.

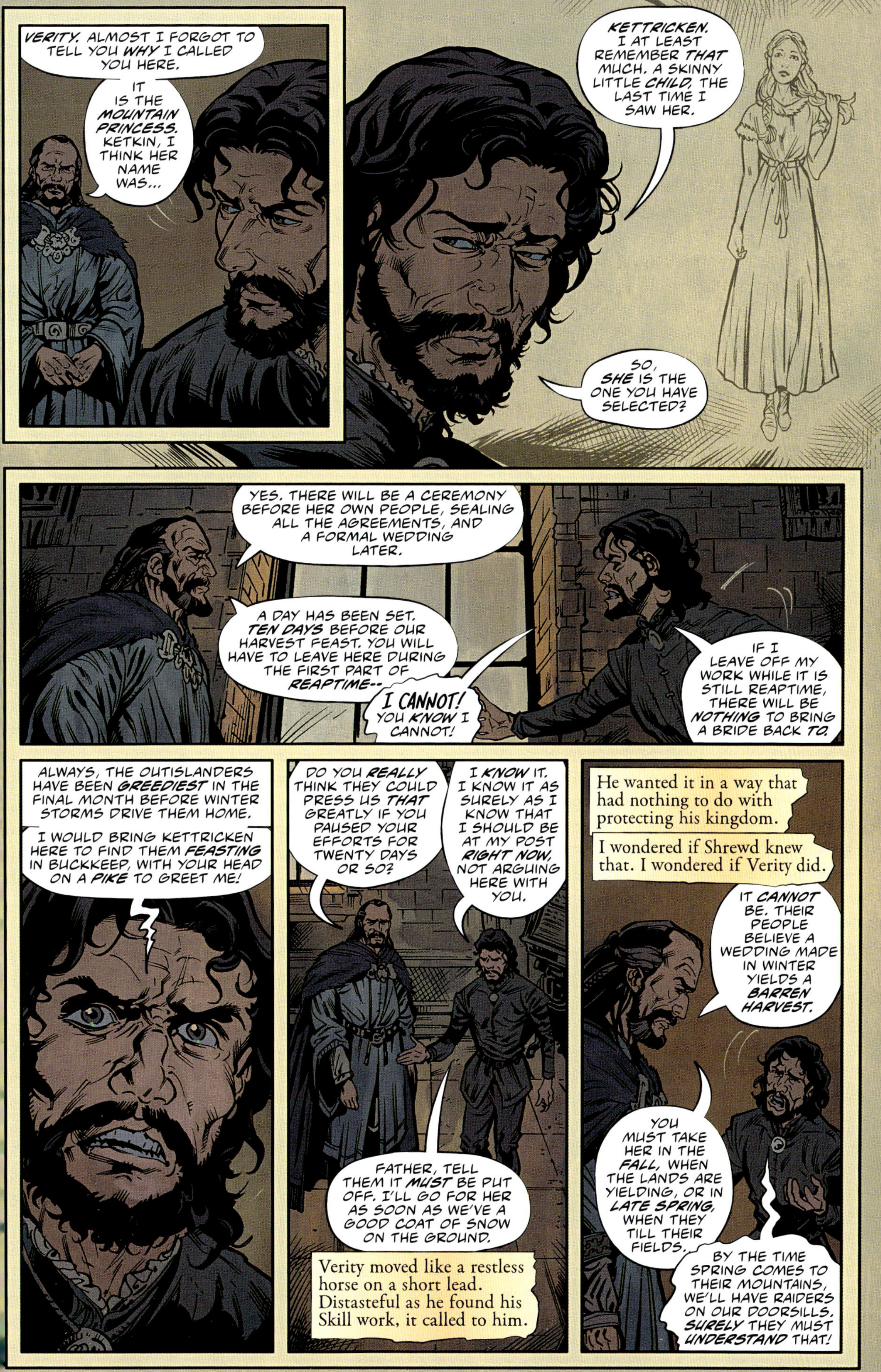
VERITY. ALMOST I FORGOT TO TELL YOU WHY I CALLED YOU HERE.
IT IS THE MOUNTAIN PRINCESS. KETKIN, I THINK HER NAME WAS...
KETTRICKEN. I AT LEAST REMEMBER THAT MUCH. A SKINNY LITTLE CHILD, THE LAST TIME I SAW HER.
SO, SHE IS THE ONE YOU HAVE SELECTED?
YES. THERE WILL BE A CEREMONY BEFORE HER OWN PEOPLE, SEALING ALL THE AGREEMENTS, AND A FORMAL WEDDING LATER.
A DAY HAS BEEN SET. TEN DAYS BEFORE OUR HARVEST FEAST. YOU WILL HAVE TO LEAVE HERE DURING THE FIRST PART OF REAPTIME--
I CANNOT! YOU KNOW I CANNOT!
IF I LEAVE OFF MY WORK WHILE IT IS STILL REAPTIME, THERE WILL BE NOTHING TO BRING A BRIDE BACK TO.
ALWAYS, THE OUTISLANDERS HAVE BEEN GREEDIEST IN THE FINAL MONTH BEFORE WINTER STORMS DRIVE THEM HOME.
I WOULD BRING KETTRICKEN HERE TO FIND THEM FEASTING IN BUCKKEEP, WITH YOUR HEAD ON A PIKE TO GREET ME!
DO YOU REALLY THINK THEY COULD PRESS US THAT GREATLY IF YOU PAUSED YOUR EFFORTS FOR TWENTY DAYS OR SO?
I KNOW IT. I KNOW IT AS SURELY AS I KNOW THAT I SHOULD BE AT MY POST RIGHT NOW, NOT ARGUING HERE WITH YOU.
FATHER, TELL THEM IT MUST BE PUT OFF. I'LL GO FOR HER AS SOON AS WE'VE A GOOD COAT OF SNOW ON THE GROUND.
Verity moved like a restless horse on a short lead. Distasteful as he found his Skill work, it called to him.
He wanted it in a way that had nothing to do with protecting his kingdom.
I wondered if Shrewd knew that. I wondered if Verity did.
IT CANNOT BE. THEIR PEOPLE BELIEVE A WEDDING MADE IN WINTER YIELDS A BARREN HARVEST.
YOU MUST TAKE HER IN THE FALL, WHEN THE LANDS ARE YIELDING, OR IN LATE SPRING, WHEN THEY TILL THEIR FIELDS.
BY THE TIME SPRING COMES TO THEIR MOUNTAINS, WE'LL HAVE RAIDERS ON OUR DOORSILLS. SURELY THEY MUST UNDERSTAND THAT!

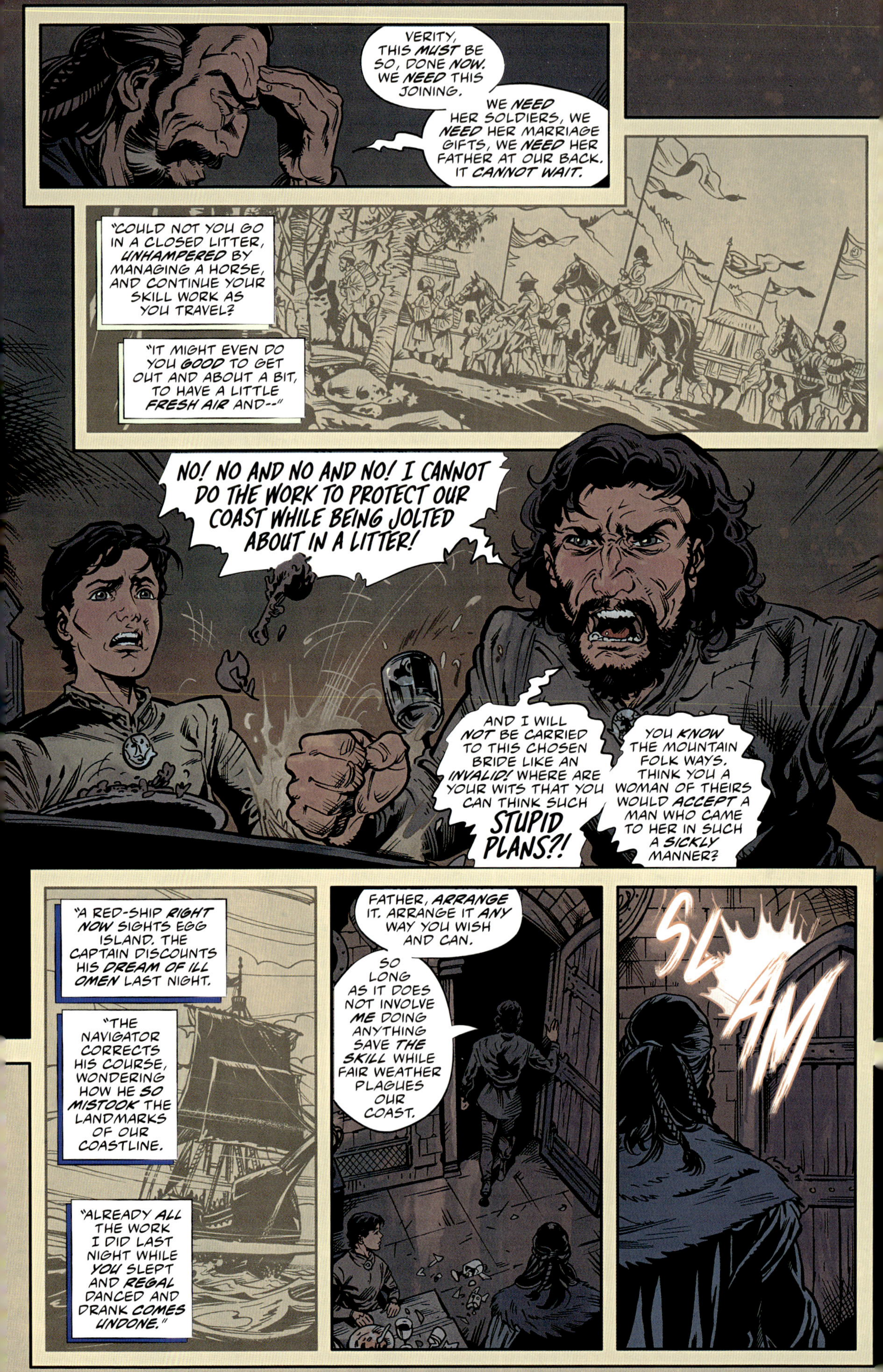

VERITY, THIS MUST BE SO, DONE NOW. WE NEED THIS JOINING.
WE NEED HER SOLDIERS, WE NEED HER MARRIAGE GIFTS, WE NEED HER FATHER AT OUR BACK. IT CANNOT WAIT.
"COULD NOT YOU GO IN A CLOSED LITTER, UNHAMPERED BY MANAGING A HORSE, AND CONTINUE YOUR SKILL WORK AS YOU TRAVEL?
"IT MIGHT EVEN DO YOU GOOD TO GET OUT AND ABOUT A BIT, TO HAVE A LITTLE FRESH AIR AND--"
NO! NO AND NO AND NO! I CANNOT DO THE WORK TO PROTECT OUR COAST WHILE BEING JOLTED ABOUT IN A LITTER!
AND I WILL NOT BE CARRIED TO THIS CHOSEN BRIDE LIKE AN INVALID! WHERE ARE YOUR WITS THAT YOU CAN THINK SUCH STUPID PLANS?!
YOU KNOW THE MOUNTAIN FOLK WAYS. THINK YOU A WOMAN OF THEIRS WOULD ACCEPT A MAN WHO CAME TO HER IN SUCH A SICKLY MANNER?
"A RED-SHIP RIGHT NOW SIGHTS EGG ISLAND. THE CAPTAIN DISCOUNTS HIS DREAM OF ILL OMEN LAST NIGHT.
"THE NAVIGATOR CORRECTS HIS COURSE, WONDERING HOW HE SO MISTOOK THE LANDMARKS OF OUR COASTLINE.
"ALREADY ALL THE WORK I DID LAST NIGHT WHILE YOU SLEPT AND REGAL DANCED AND DRANK COMES UNDONE."
FATHER, ARRANGE IT. ARRANGE IT ANY WAY YOU WISH AND CAN.
SO LONG AS IT DOES NOT INVOLVE ME DOING ANYTHING SAVE THE SKILL WHILE FAIR WEATHER PLAGUES OUR COAST.
SLAM

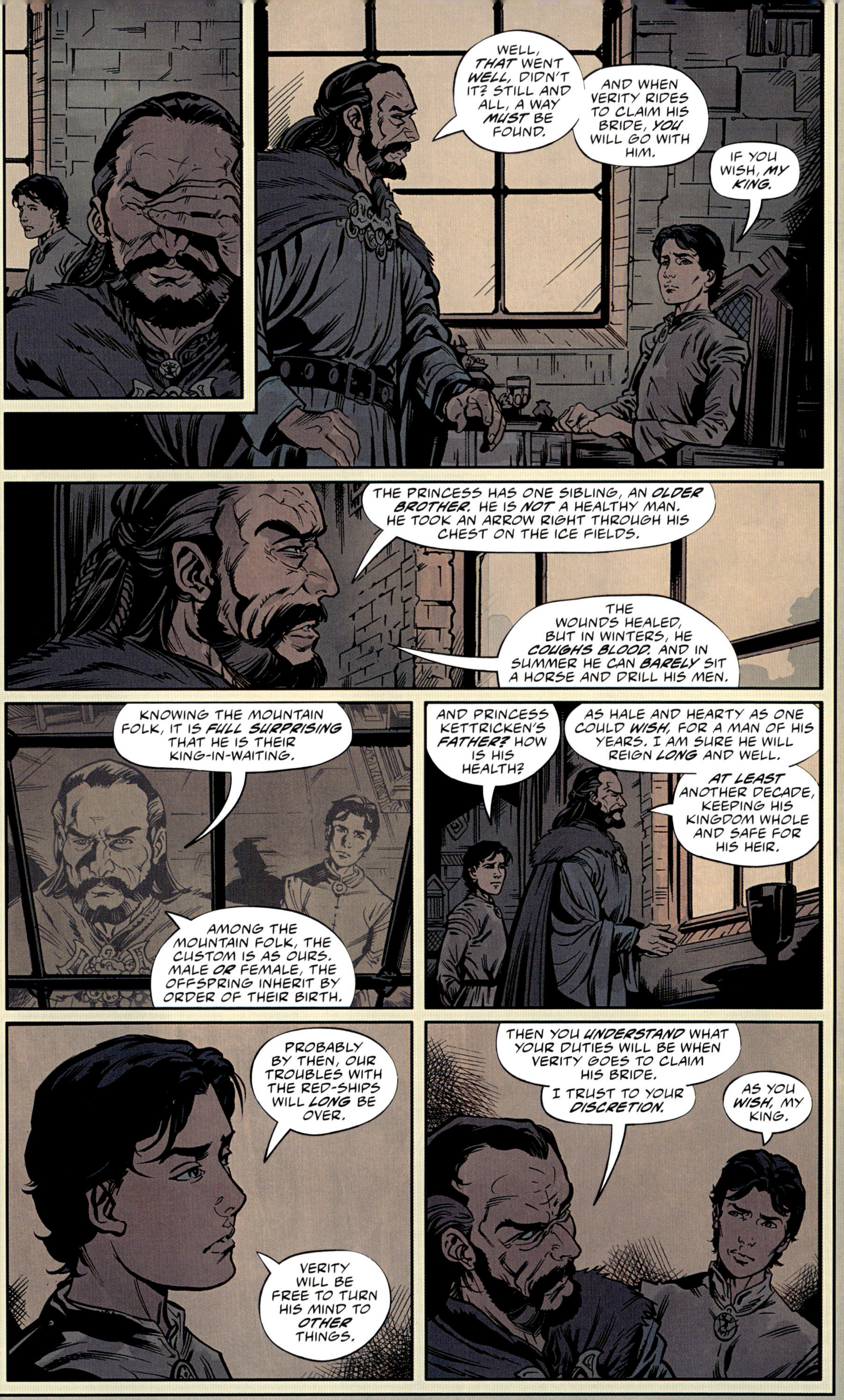
WELL, THAT WENT WELL, DIDN'T IT? STILL AND ALL, A WAY MUST BE FOUND.
AND WHEN VERITY RIDES TO CLAIM HIS BRIDE, YOU WILL GO WITH HIM.
IF YOU WISH, MY KING.
THE PRINCESS HAS ONE SIBLING, AN OLDER BROTHER. HE IS NOT A HEALTHY MAN. HE TOOK AN ARROW RIGHT THROUGH HIS CHEST ON THE ICE FIELDS.
THE WOUNDS HEALED, BUT IN WINTERS, HE COUGHS BLOOD, AND IN SUMMER HE CAN BARELY SIT A HORSE AND DRILL HIS MEN.
KNOWING THE MOUNTAIN FOLK, IT IS FULL SURPRISING THAT HE IS THEIR KING-IN-WAITING.
AMONG THE MOUNTAIN FOLK, THE CUSTOM IS AS OURS. MALE OR FEMALE, THE OFFSPRING INHERIT BY ORDER OF THEIR BIRTH.
AND PRINCESS KETTRICKEN'S FATHER? HOW IS HIS HEALTH?
AS HALE AND HEARTY AS ONE COULD WISH, FOR A MAN OF HIS YEARS. I AM SURE HE WILL REIGN LONG AND WELL.
AT LEAST ANOTHER DECADE, KEEPING HIS KINGDOM WHOLE AND SAFE FOR HIS HEIR.
PROBABLY BY THEN, OUR TROUBLES WITH THE RED-SHIPS WILL LONG BE OVER.
VERITY WILL BE FREE TO TURN HIS MIND TO OTHER THINGS.
THEN YOU UNDERSTAND WHAT YOUR DUTIES WILL BE WHEN VERITY GOES TO CLAIM HIS BRIDE.
I TRUST TO YOUR DISCRETION.
AS YOU WISH, MY KING.

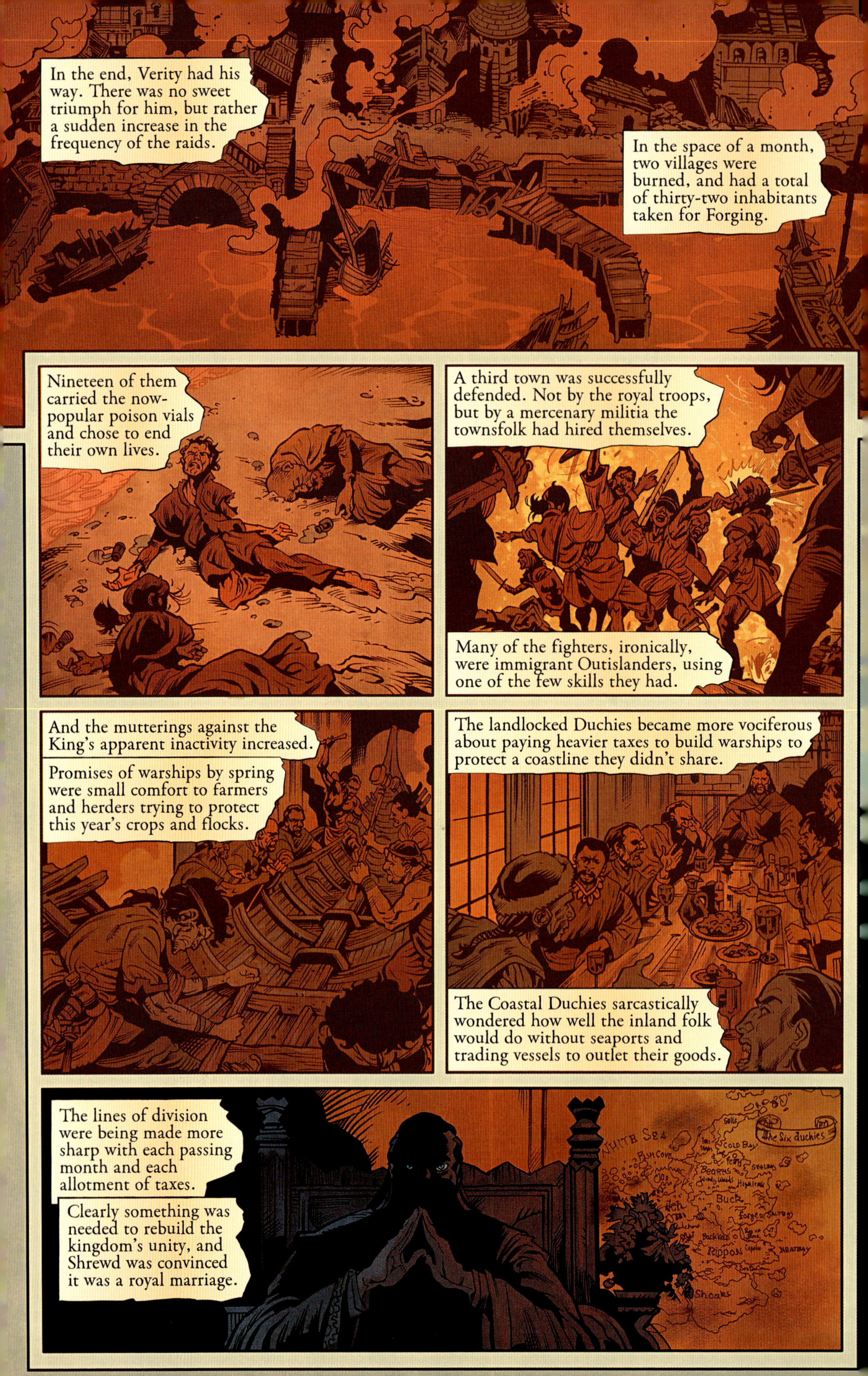
In the end, Verity had his way. There was no sweet triumph for him, but rather a sudden increase in the frequency of the raids.
In the space of a month, two villages were burned, and had a total of thirty-two inhabitants taken for Forging.
Nineteen of them carried the now-popular poison vials and chose to end their own lives.
A third town was successfully defended. Not by the royal troops, but by a mercenary militia the townsfolk had hired themselves.
Many of the fighters, ironically, were immigrant Outislanders, using one of the few skills they had.
And the mutterings against the King's apparent inactivity increased.
Promises of warships by spring were small comfort to farmers and herders trying to protect this year's crops and flocks.
The landlocked Duchies became more vociferous about paying heavier taxes to build warships to protect a coastline they didn't share.
The Coastal Duchies sarcastically wondered how well the inland folk would do without seaports and trading vessels to outlet their goods.
The lines of division were being made more sharp with each passing month and each allotment of taxes.
Clearly something was needed to rebuild the kingdom's unity, and Shrewd was convinced it was a royal marriage.
The Six duchies
COLD BAY
Buck
RIPPON
Shoaks

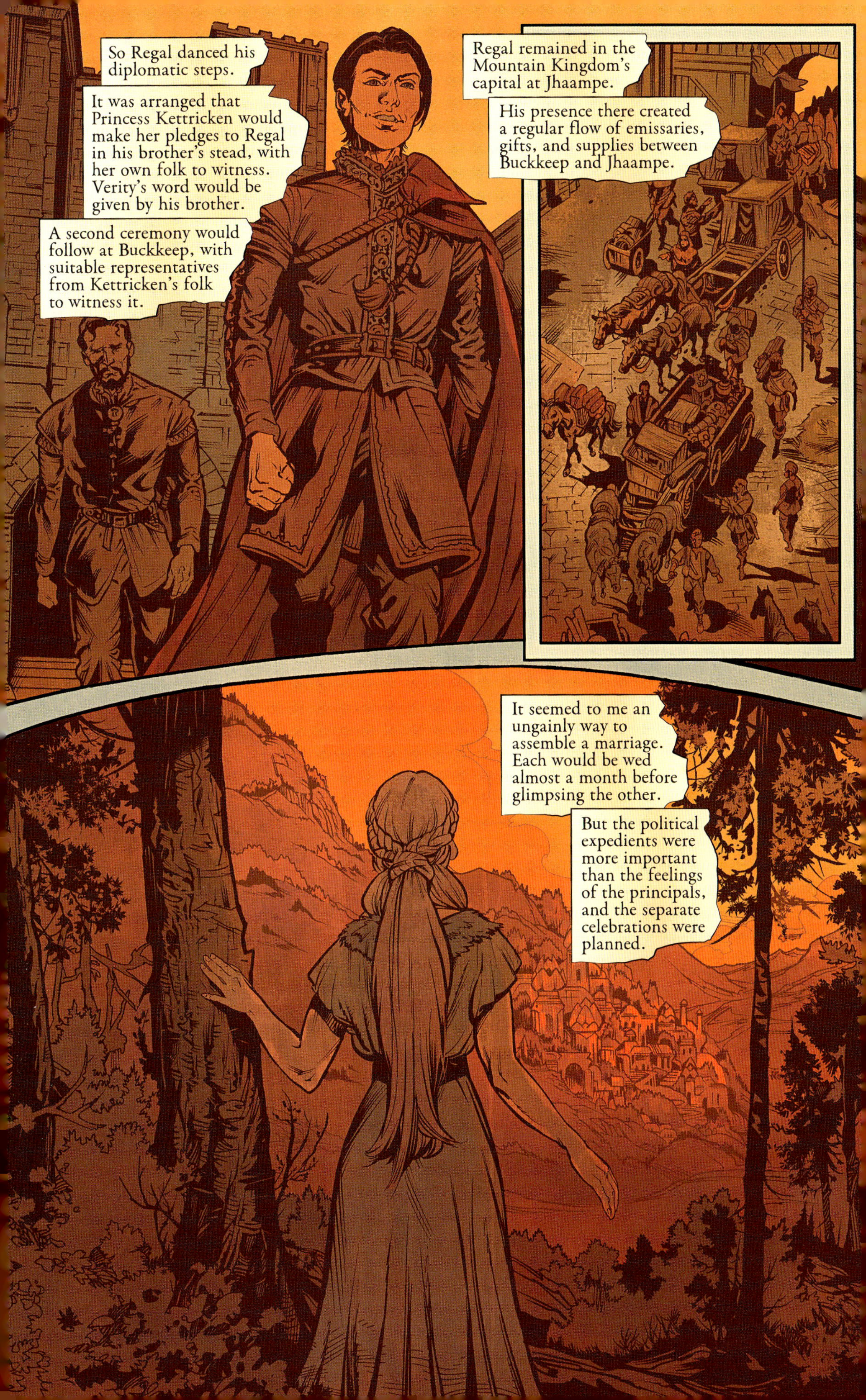
So Regal danced his diplomatic steps.
It was arranged that Princess Kettricken would make her pledges to Regal in his brother's stead, with her own folk to witness. Verity's word would be given by his brother.
A second ceremony would follow at Buckkeep, with suitable representatives from Kettricken's folk to witness it.
Regal remained in the Mountain Kingdom's capital at Jhaampe.
His presence there created a regular flow of emissaries, gifts, and supplies between Buckkeep and Jhaampe.
It seemed to me an ungainly way to assemble a marriage. Each would be wed almost a month before glimpsing the other.
But the political expedients were more important than the feelings of the principals, and the separate celebrations were planned.

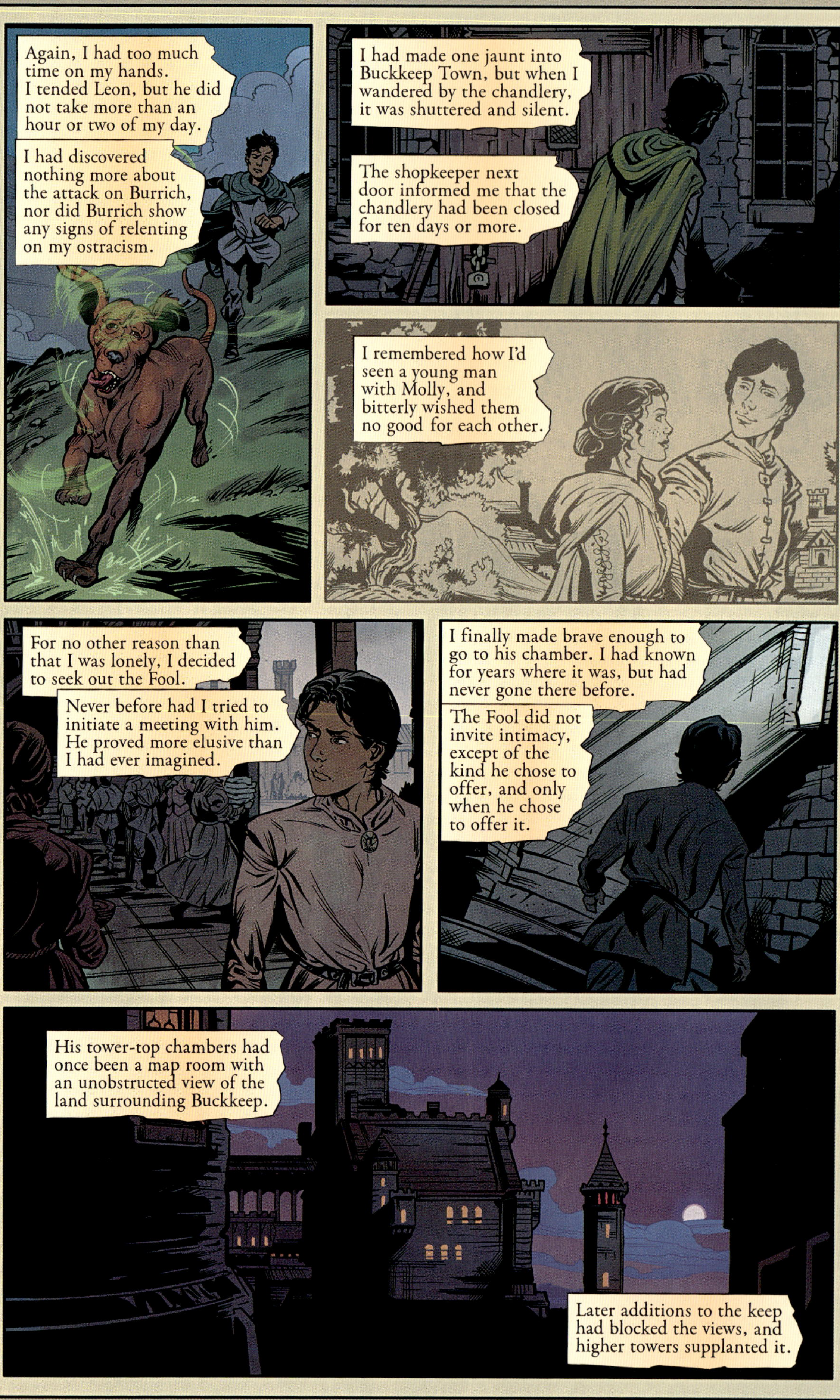
Again, I had too much time on my hands. I tended Leon, but he did not take more than an hour or two of my day.
I had discovered nothing more about the attack on Burrich, nor did Burrich show any signs of relenting on my ostracism.
I had made one jaunt into Buckkeep Town, but when I wandered by the chandlery, it was shuttered and silent.
The shopkeeper next door informed me that the chandlery had been closed for ten days or more.
I remembered how I'd seen a young man with Molly, and bitterly wished them no good for each other.
For no other reason than that I was lonely, I decided to seek out the Fool.
Never before had I tried to initiate a meeting with him. He proved more elusive than I had ever imagined.
I finally made brave enough to go to his chamber. I had known for years where it was, but had never gone there before.
The Fool did not invite intimacy, except of the kind he chose to offer, and only when he chose to offer it.
His tower-top chambers had once been a map room with an unobstructed view of the land surrounding Buckkeep.
Later additions to the keep had blocked the views, and higher towers supplanted it.

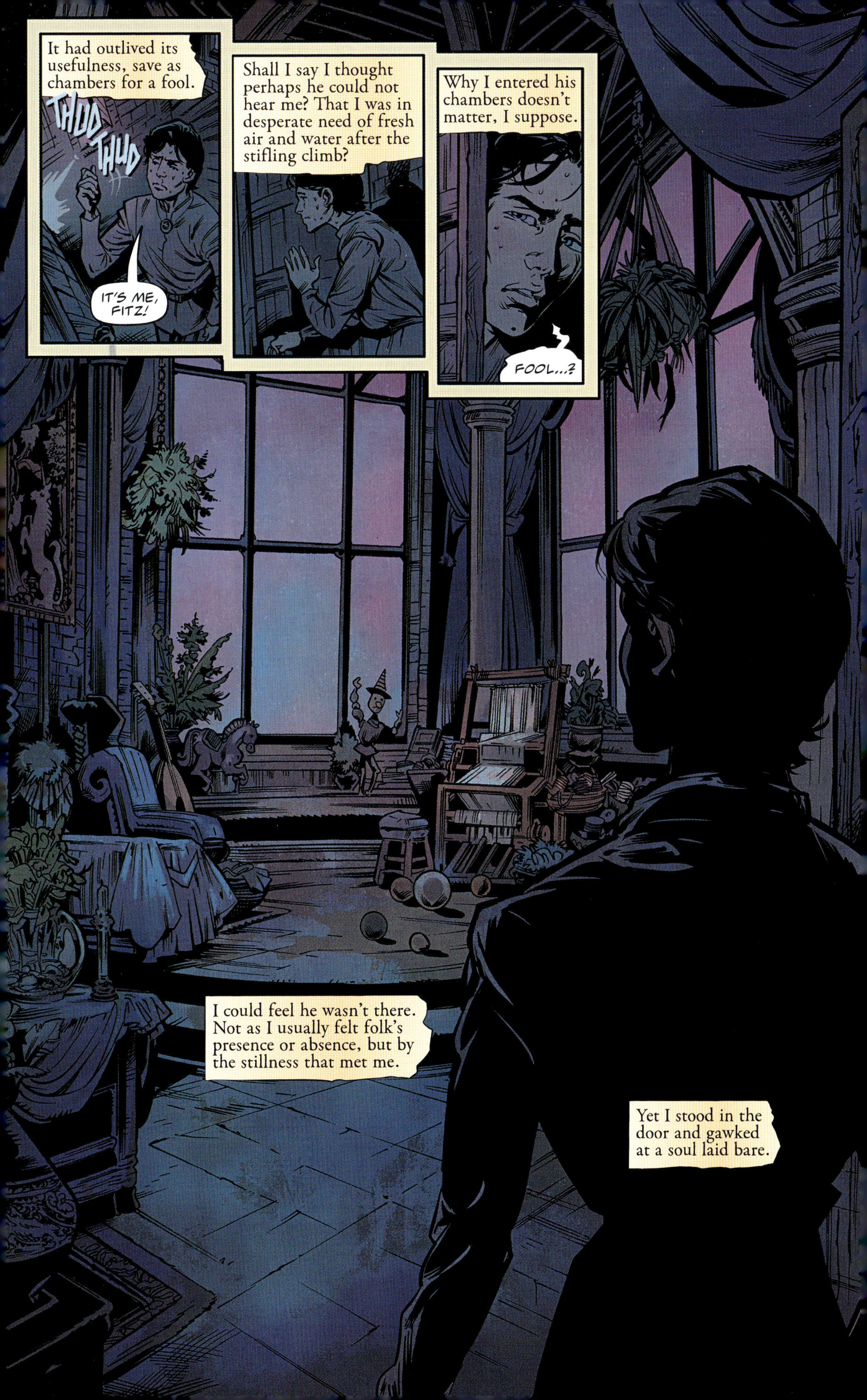
It had outlived its usefulness, save as chambers for a fool.
THUD THUD
IT'S ME, FITZ!
Shall I say I thought perhaps he could not hear me? That I was in desperate need of fresh air and water after the stifling climb?
Why I entered his chambers doesn't matter, I suppose.
FOOL...?
I could feel he wasn't there. Not as I usually felt folk's presence or absence, but by the stillness that met me.
Yet I stood in the door and gawked at a soul laid bare.

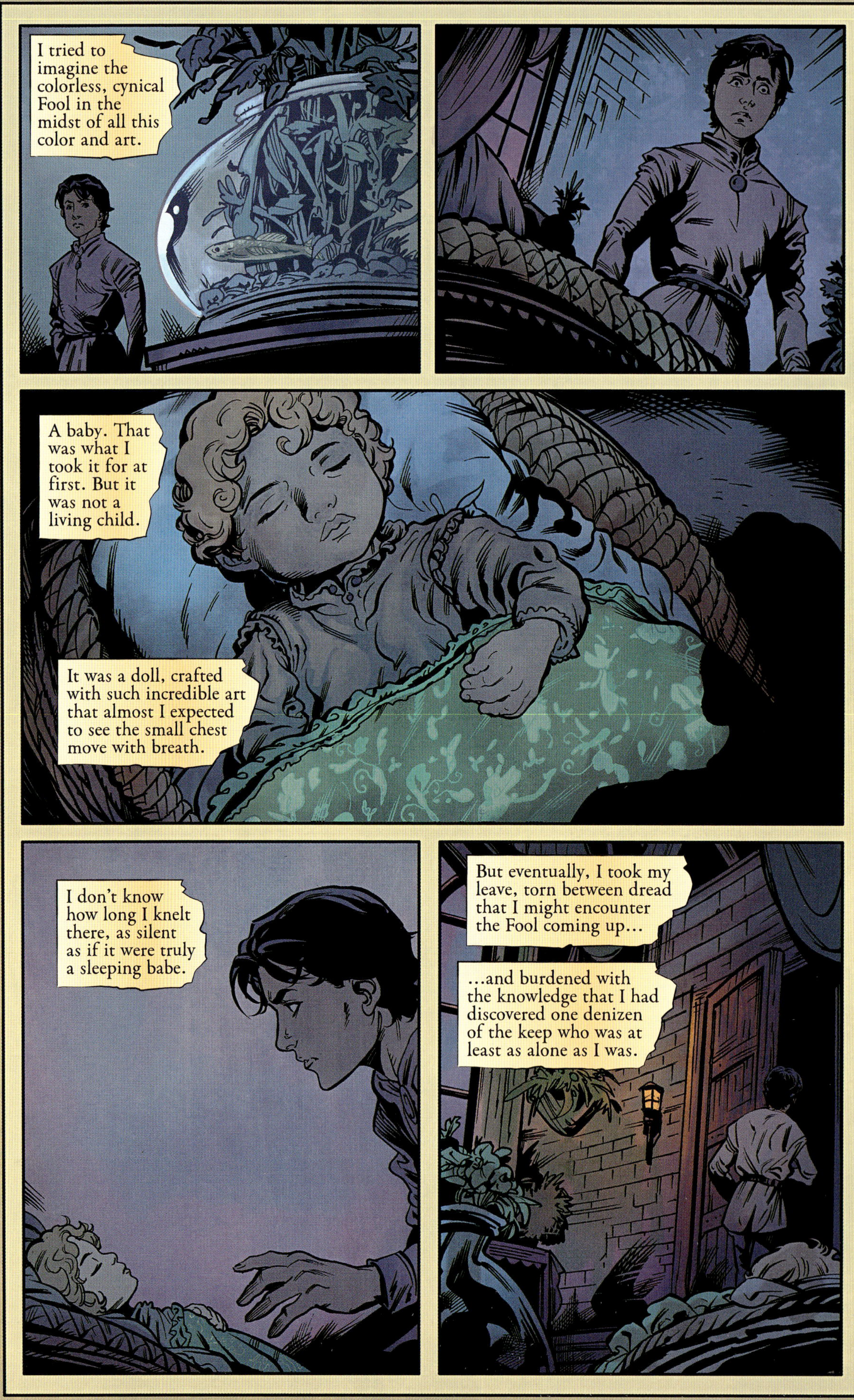
I tried to imagine the colorless, cynical Fool in the midst of all this color and art.
A baby. That was what I took it for at first. But it was not a living child.
It was a doll, crafted with such incredible art that almost I expected to see the small chest move with breath.
I don't know how long I knelt there, as silent as if it were truly a sleeping babe.
But eventually, I took my leave, torn between dread that I might encounter the Fool coming up...
...and burdened with the knowledge that I had discovered one denizen of the keep who was at least as alone as I was.

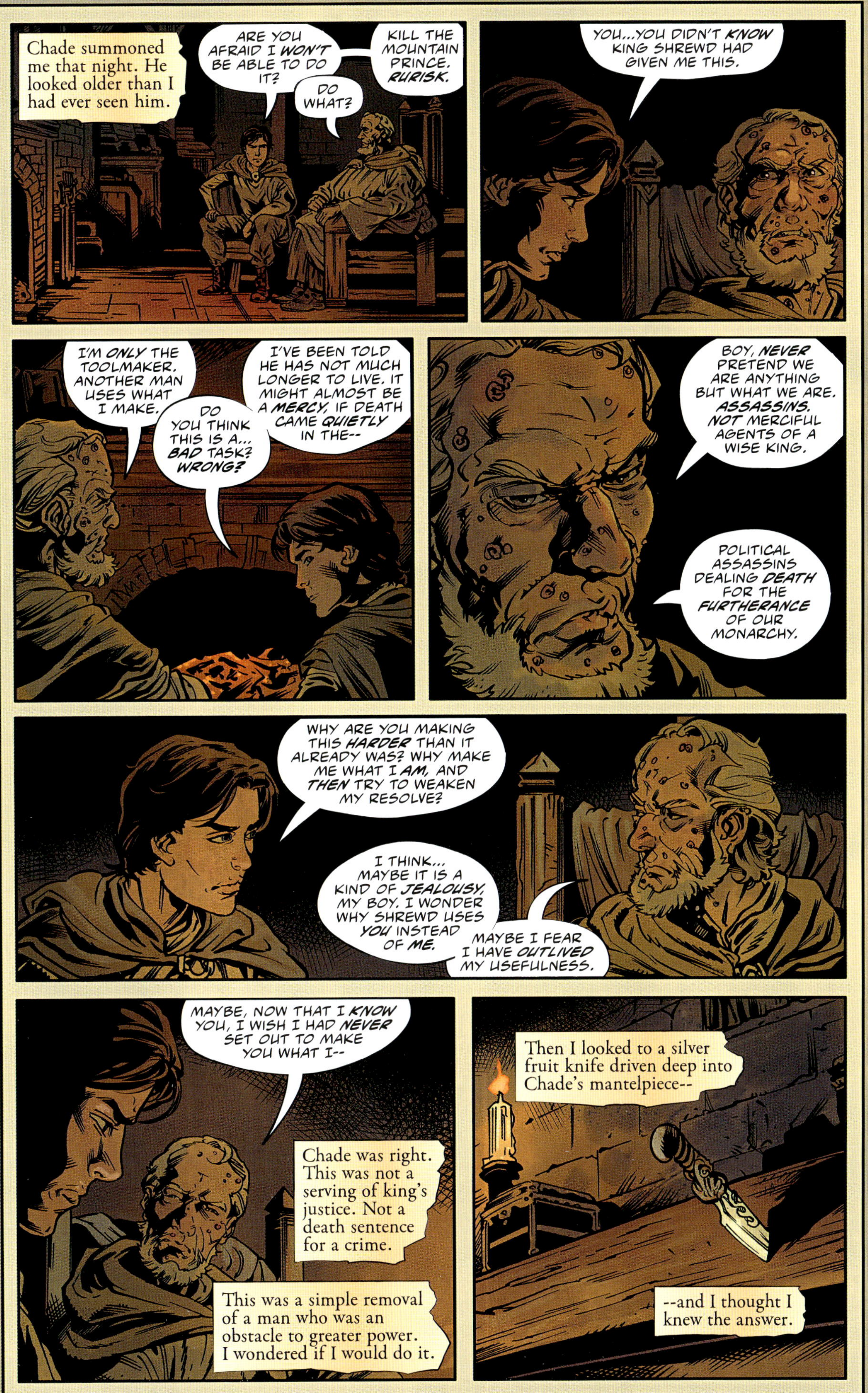

Chade summoned me that night. He looked older than I had ever seen him.
KILL THE MOUNTAIN PRINCE. RURISK.
ARE YOU AFRAID I WON'T BE ABLE TO DO IT?
DO WHAT?
YOU...YOU DIDN'T KNOW KING SHREWD HAD GIVEN ME THIS.
I'M ONLY THE TOOLMAKER. ANOTHER MAN USES WHAT I MAKE.
I'VE BEEN TOLD HE HAS NOT MUCH LONGER TO LIVE. IT MIGHT ALMOST BE A MERCY, IF DEATH CAME QUIETLY IN THE--
DO YOU THINK THIS IS A... BAD TASK? WRONG?
BOY, NEVER PRETEND WE ARE ANYTHING BUT WHAT WE ARE. ASSASSINS. NOT MERCIFUL AGENTS OF A WISE KING.
POLITICAL ASSASSINS DEALING DEATH FOR THE FURTHERANCE OF OUR MONARCHY.
WHY ARE YOU MAKING THIS HARDER THAN IT ALREADY WAS? WHY MAKE ME WHAT I AM, AND THEN TRY TO WEAKEN MY RESOLVE?
I THINK... MAYBE IT IS A KIND OF JEALOUSY, MY BOY. I WONDER WHY SHREWD USES YOU INSTEAD OF ME.
MAYBE I FEAR I HAVE OUTLIVED MY USEFULNESS.
MAYBE, NOW THAT I KNOW YOU, I WISH I HAD NEVER SET OUT TO MAKE YOU WHAT I--
Chade was right. This was not a serving of king's justice. Not a death sentence for a crime.
This was a simple removal of a man who was an obstacle to greater power. I wondered if I would do it.
Then I looked to a silver fruit knife driven deep into Chade's mantelpiece--
--and I thought I knew the answer.

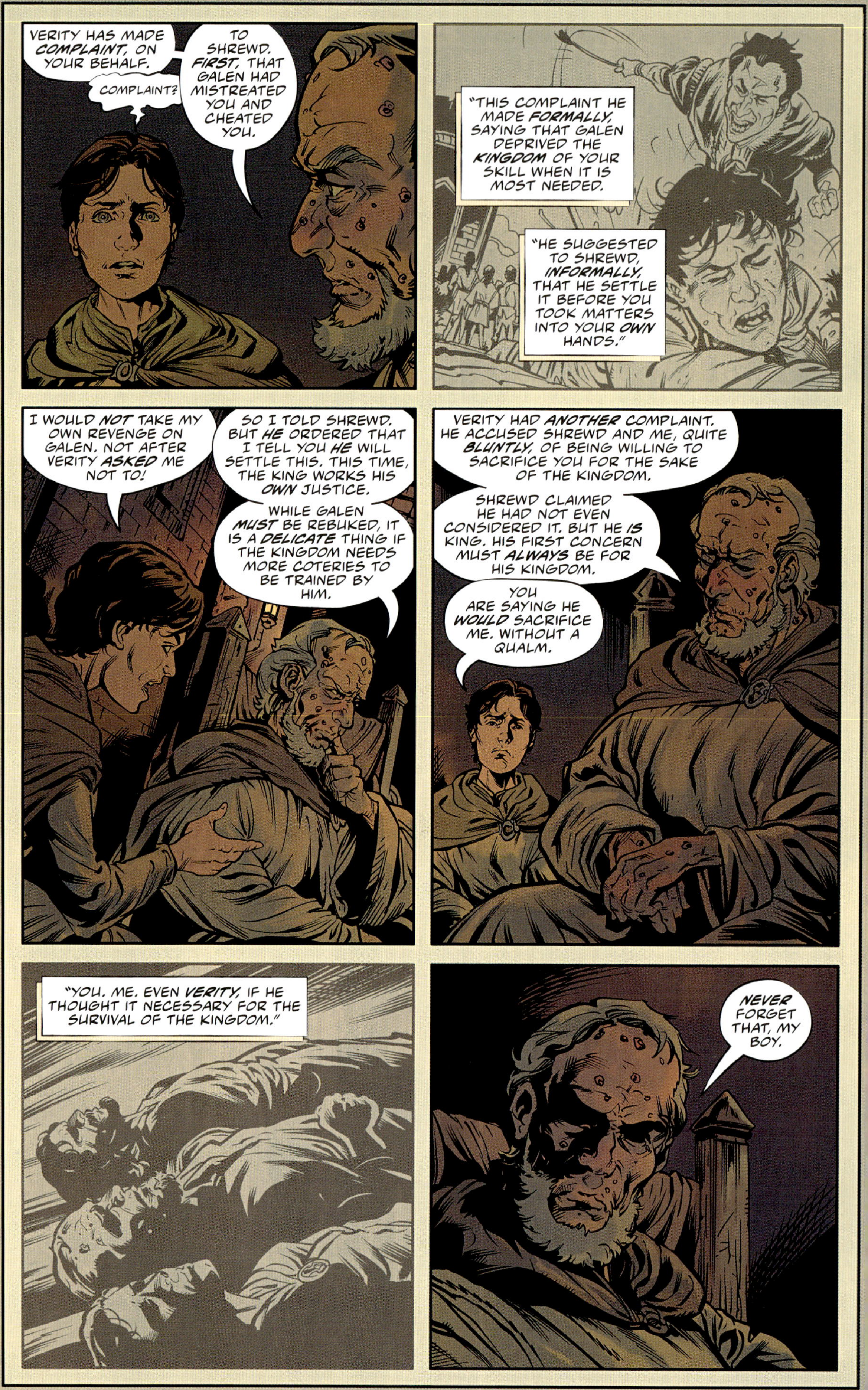
VERITY HAS MADE COMPLAINT, ON YOUR BEHALF.
COMPLAINT?
TO SHREWD. FIRST, THAT GALEN HAD MISTREATED YOU AND CHEATED YOU.
"THIS COMPLAINT HE MADE FORMALLY, SAYING THAT GALEN DEPRIVED THE KINGDOM OF YOUR SKILL WHEN IT IS MOST NEEDED.
"HE SUGGESTED TO SHREWD, INFORMALLY, THAT HE SETTLE IT BEFORE YOU TOOK MATTERS INTO YOUR OWN HANDS."
I WOULD NOT TAKE MY OWN REVENGE ON GALEN. NOT AFTER VERITY ASKED ME NOT TO!
SO I TOLD SHREWD. BUT HE ORDERED THAT I TELL YOU HE WILL SETTLE THIS. THIS TIME, THE KING WORKS HIS OWN JUSTICE.
WHILE GALEN MUST BE REBUKED, IT IS A DELICATE THING IF THE KINGDOM NEEDS MORE COTERIES TO BE TRAINED BY HIM.
VERITY HAD ANOTHER COMPLAINT. HE ACCUSED SHREWD AND ME, QUITE BLUNTLY, OF BEING WILLING TO SACRIFICE YOU FOR THE SAKE OF THE KINGDOM.
SHREWD CLAIMED HE HAD NOT EVEN CONSIDERED IT. BUT HE IS KING. HIS FIRST CONCERN MUST ALWAYS BE FOR HIS KINGDOM.
YOU ARE SAYING HE WOULD SACRIFICE ME. WITHOUT A QUALM.
"YOU. ME. EVEN VERITY, IF HE THOUGHT IT NECESSARY FOR THE SURVIVAL OF THE KINGDOM."
NEVER FORGET THAT, MY BOY.

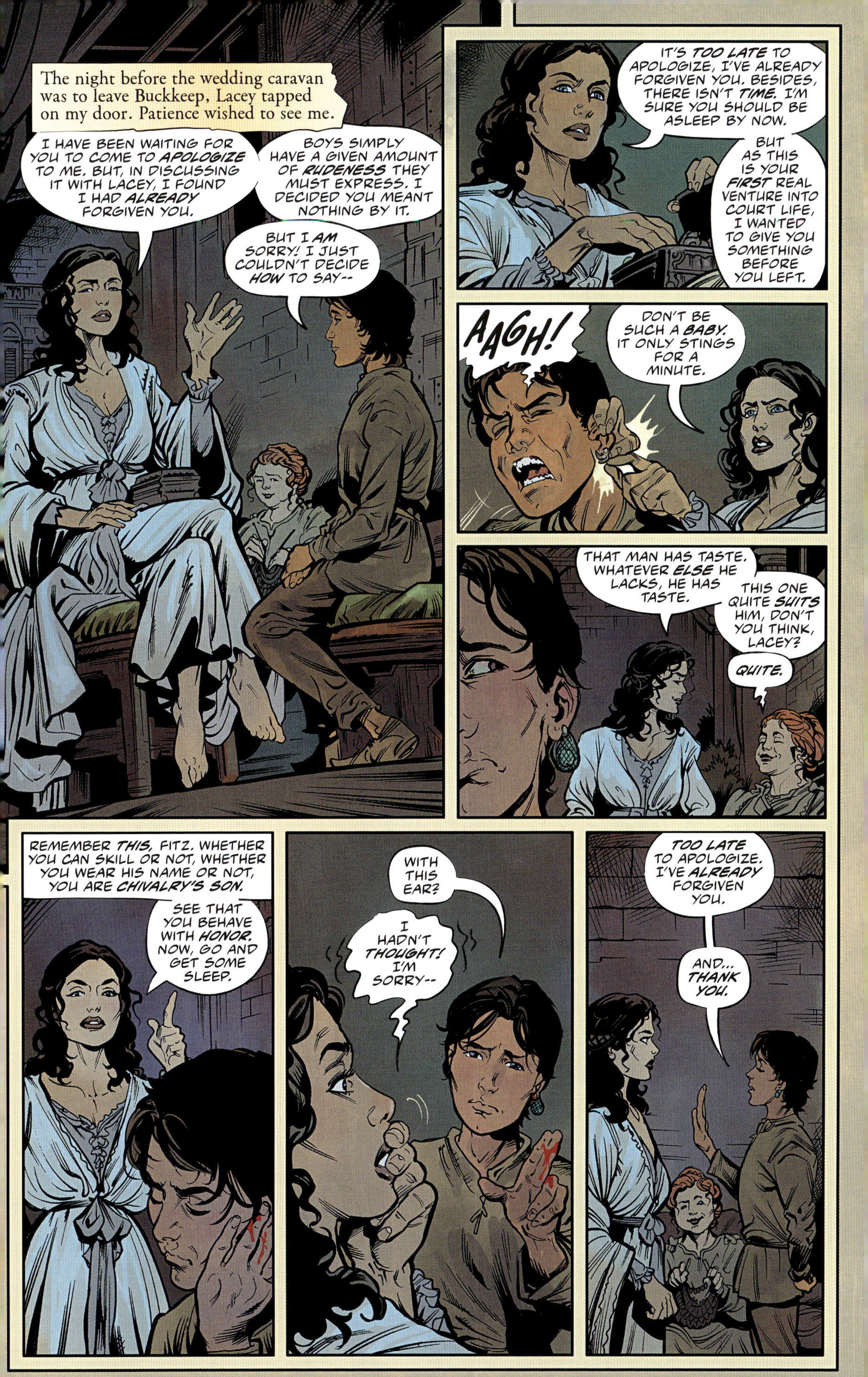
The night before the wedding caravan was to leave Buckkeep, Lacey tapped on my door. Patience wished to see me.
I HAVE BEEN WAITING FOR YOU TO COME TO APOLOGIZE TO ME. BUT, IN DISCUSSING IT WITH LACEY, I FOUND I HAD ALREADY FORGIVEN YOU.
BOYS SIMPLY HAVE A GIVEN AMOUNT OF RUDENESS THEY MUST EXPRESS. I DECIDED YOU MEANT NOTHING BY IT.
BUT I AM SORRY! I JUST COULDN'T DECIDE HOW TO SAY--
IT'S TOO LATE TO APOLOGIZE, I'VE ALREADY FORGIVEN YOU. BESIDES, THERE ISN'T TIME. I'M SURE YOU SHOULD BE ASLEEP BY NOW.
BUT AS THIS IS YOUR FIRST REAL VENTURE INTO COURT LIFE, I WANTED TO GIVE YOU SOMETHING BEFORE YOU LEFT.
AAGH!
DON'T BE SUCH A BABY. IT ONLY STINGS FOR A MINUTE.
THAT MAN HAS TASTE. WHATEVER ELSE HE LACKS, HE HAS TASTE.
THIS ONE QUITE SUITS HIM, DON'T YOU THINK, LACEY?
QUITE.
REMEMBER THIS, FITZ. WHETHER YOU CAN SKILL OR NOT, WHETHER YOU WEAR HIS NAME OR NOT, YOU ARE CHIVALRY'S SON.
SEE THAT YOU BEHAVE WITH HONOR. NOW, GO AND GET SOME SLEEP.
WITH THIS EAR?
I HADN'T THOUGHT! I'M SORRY--
TOO LATE TO APOLOGIZE. I'VE ALREADY FORGIVEN YOU.
AND... THANK YOU.

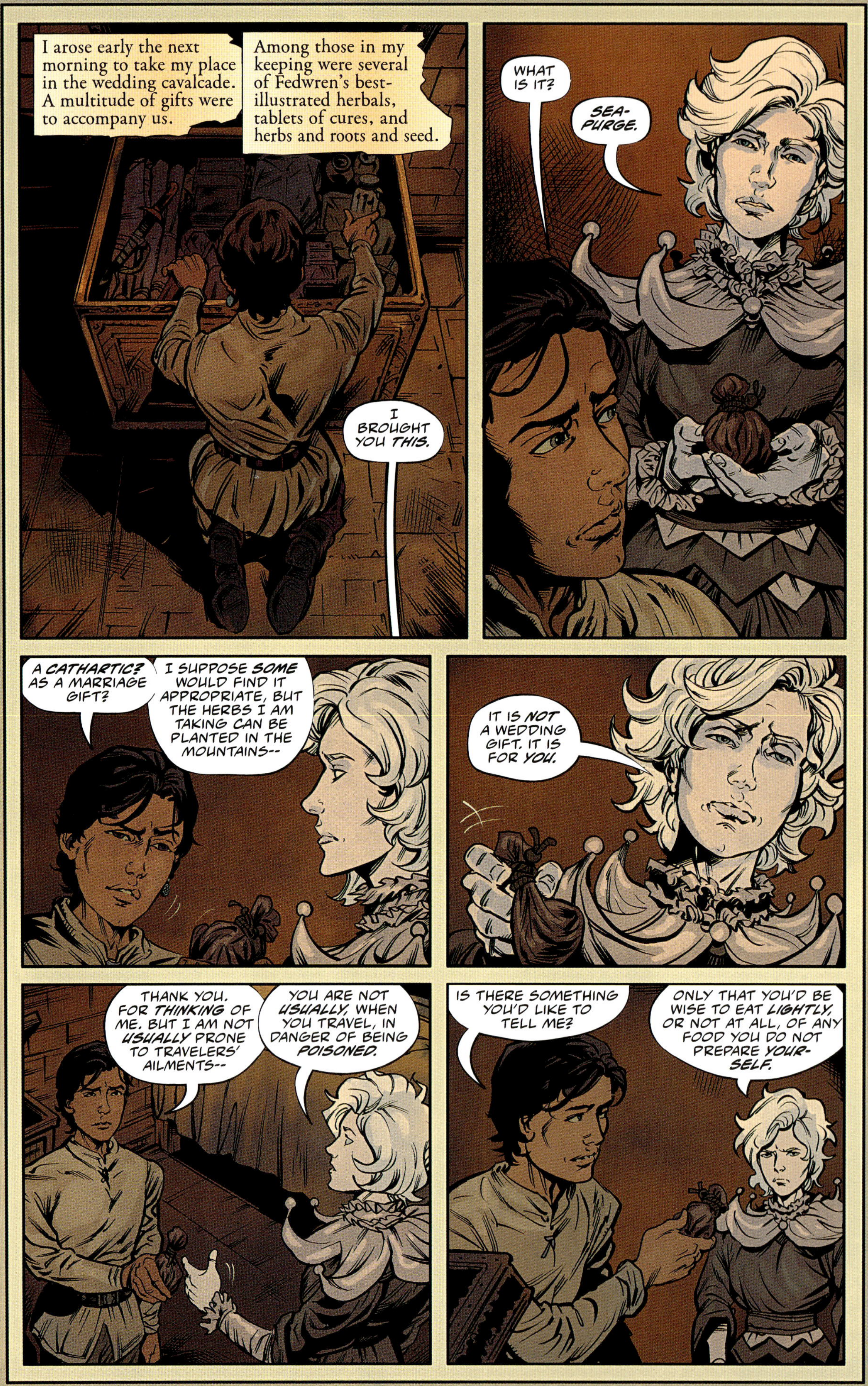
I arose early the next morning to take my place in the wedding cavalcade. A multitude of gifts were to accompany us.
Among those in my keeping were several of Fedwren's best-illustrated herbals, tablets of cures, and herbs and roots and seed.
I BROUGHT YOU *THIS.*
WHAT IS IT?
SEA-PURGE.
A *CATHARTIC?* AS A MARRIAGE GIFT?
I SUPPOSE *SOME* WOULD FIND IT APPROPRIATE, BUT THE HERBS I AM TAKING CAN BE PLANTED IN THE MOUNTAINS--
IT IS *NOT* A WEDDING GIFT. IT IS FOR *YOU.*
THANK YOU. FOR *THINKING* OF ME. BUT I AM NOT *USUALLY* PRONE TO TRAVELERS' AILMENTS--
YOU ARE NOT *USUALLY,* WHEN YOU TRAVEL, IN DANGER OF BEING *POISONED.*
IS THERE SOMETHING YOU'D LIKE TO TELL ME?
ONLY THAT YOU'D BE WISE TO EAT *LIGHTLY,* OR NOT AT ALL, OF ANY FOOD YOU DO NOT PREPARE *YOUR-SELF.*

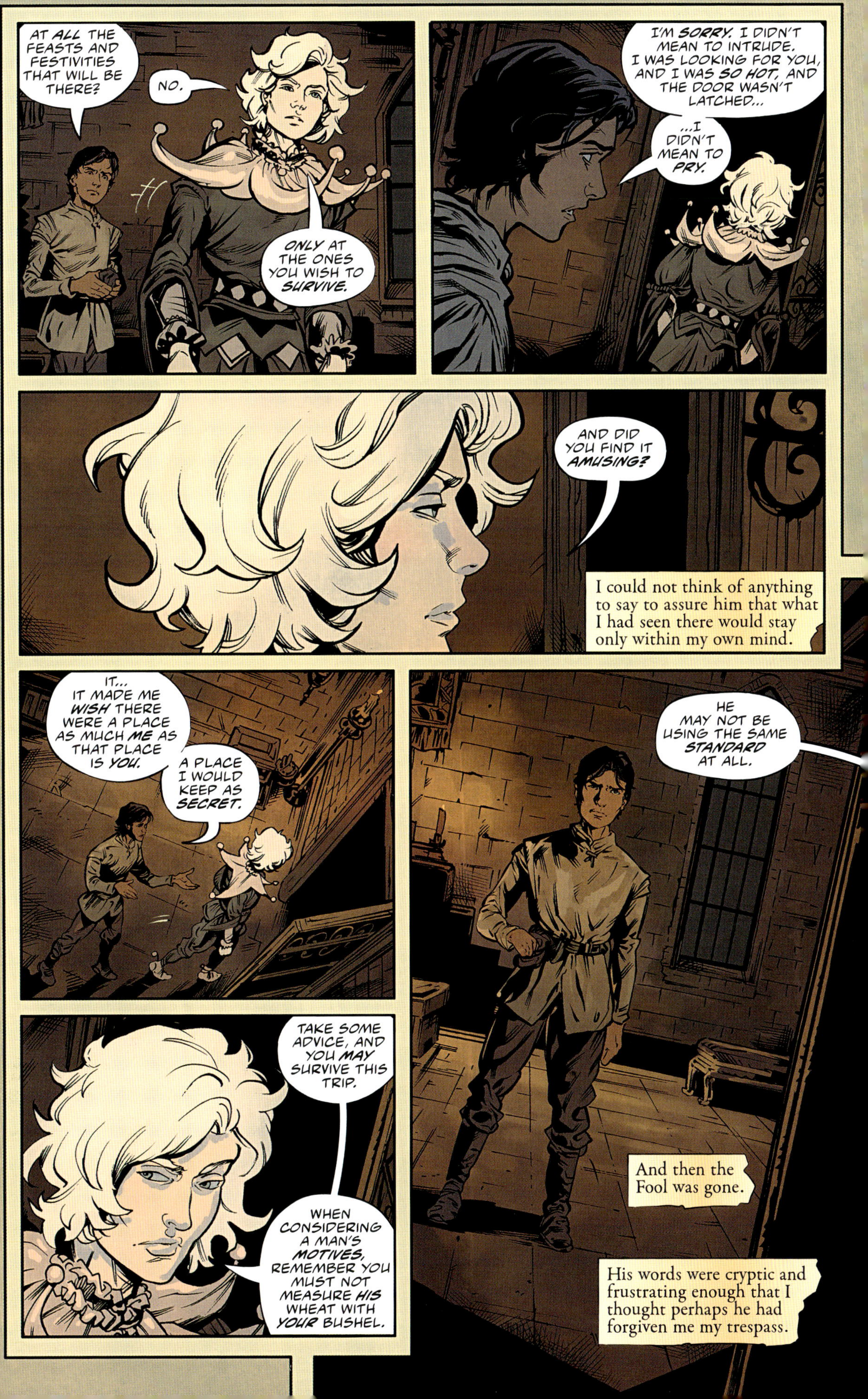

AT ALL THE FEASTS AND FESTIVITIES THAT WILL BE THERE?
NO.
ONLY AT THE ONES YOU WISH TO SURVIVE.
I'M SORRY. I DIDN'T MEAN TO INTRUDE. I WAS LOOKING FOR YOU, AND I WAS SO HOT, AND THE DOOR WASN'T LATCHED...
...I DIDN'T MEAN TO PRY.
AND DID YOU FIND IT AMUSING?
I could not think of anything to say to assure him that what I had seen there would stay only within my own mind.
IT... IT MADE ME WISH THERE WERE A PLACE AS MUCH ME AS THAT PLACE IS YOU.
A PLACE I WOULD KEEP AS SECRET.
TAKE SOME ADVICE, AND YOU MAY SURVIVE THIS TRIP.
WHEN CONSIDERING A MAN'S MOTIVES, REMEMBER YOU MUST NOT MEASURE HIS WHEAT WITH YOUR BUSHEL.
HE MAY NOT BE USING THE SAME STANDARD AT ALL.
And then the Fool was gone.
His words were cryptic and frustrating enough that I thought perhaps he had forgiven me my trespass.

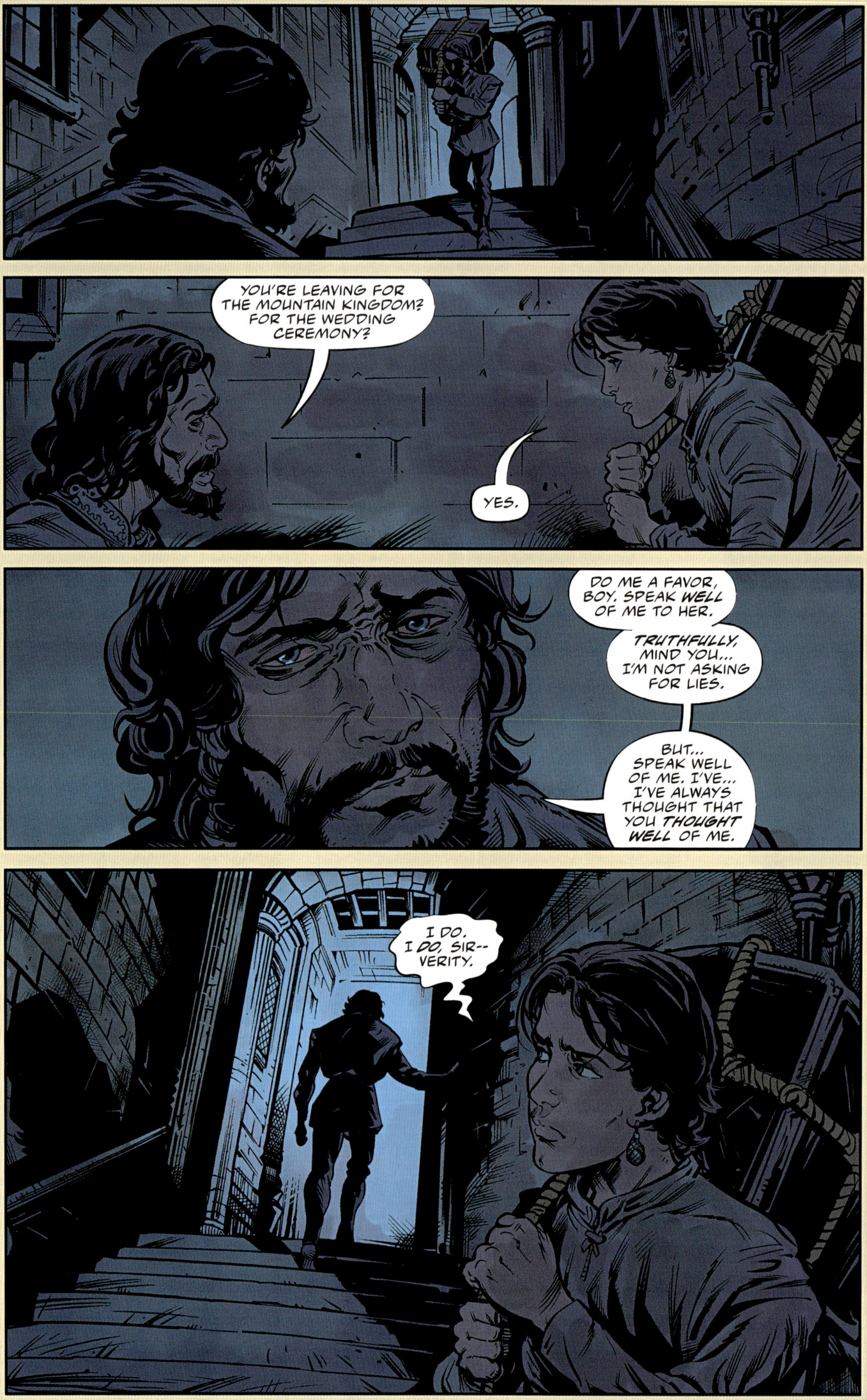
YOU'RE LEAVING FOR THE MOUNTAIN KINGDOM? FOR THE WEDDING CEREMONY?
YES.
DO ME A FAVOR, BOY. SPEAK *WELL* OF ME TO HER.
TRUTHFULLY, MIND YOU... I'M NOT ASKING FOR LIES.
BUT... SPEAK WELL OF ME. I'VE... I'VE ALWAYS THOUGHT THAT YOU *THOUGHT WELL* OF ME.
I DO. I *DO,* SIR-- VERITY.

Chapter Four

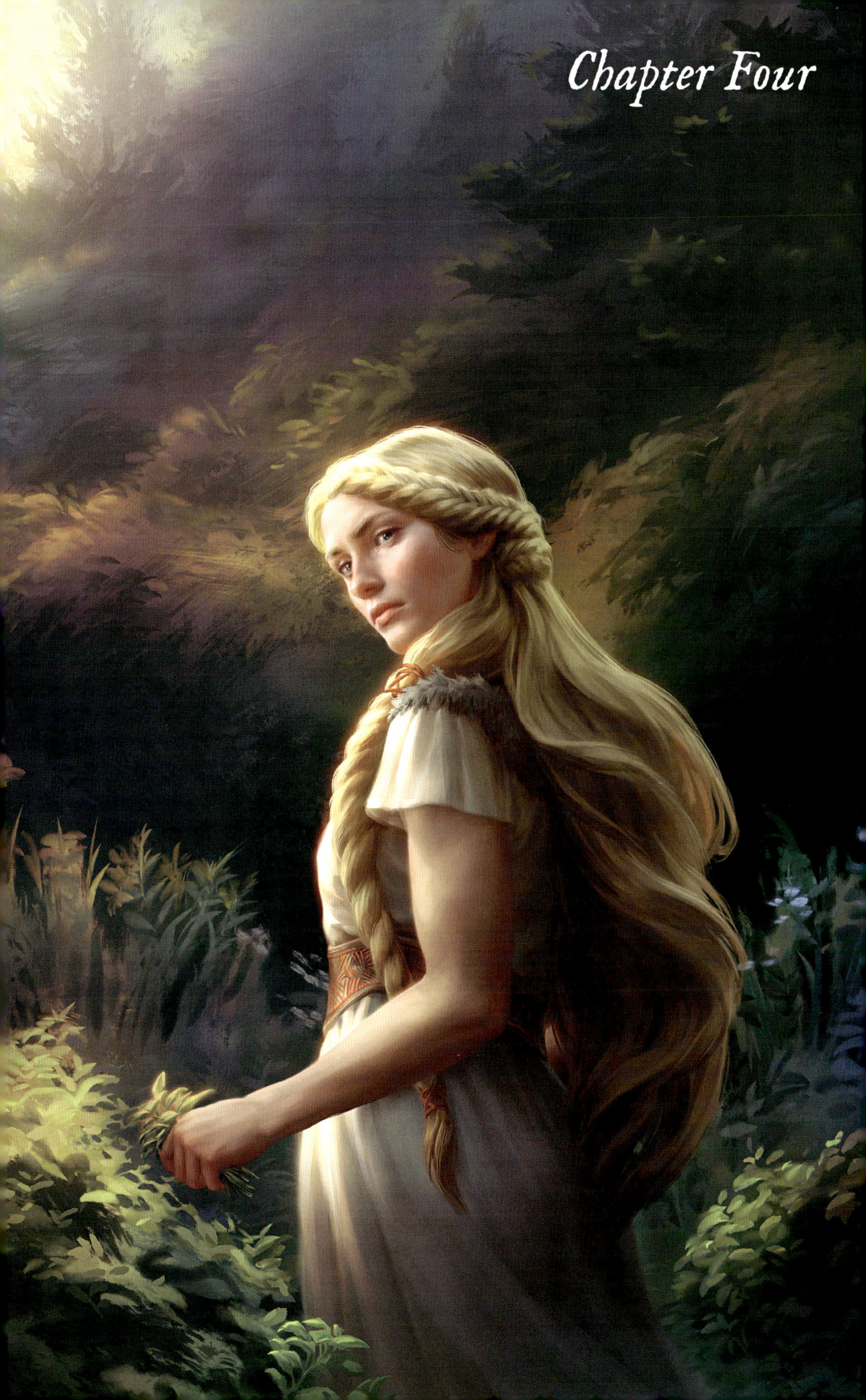

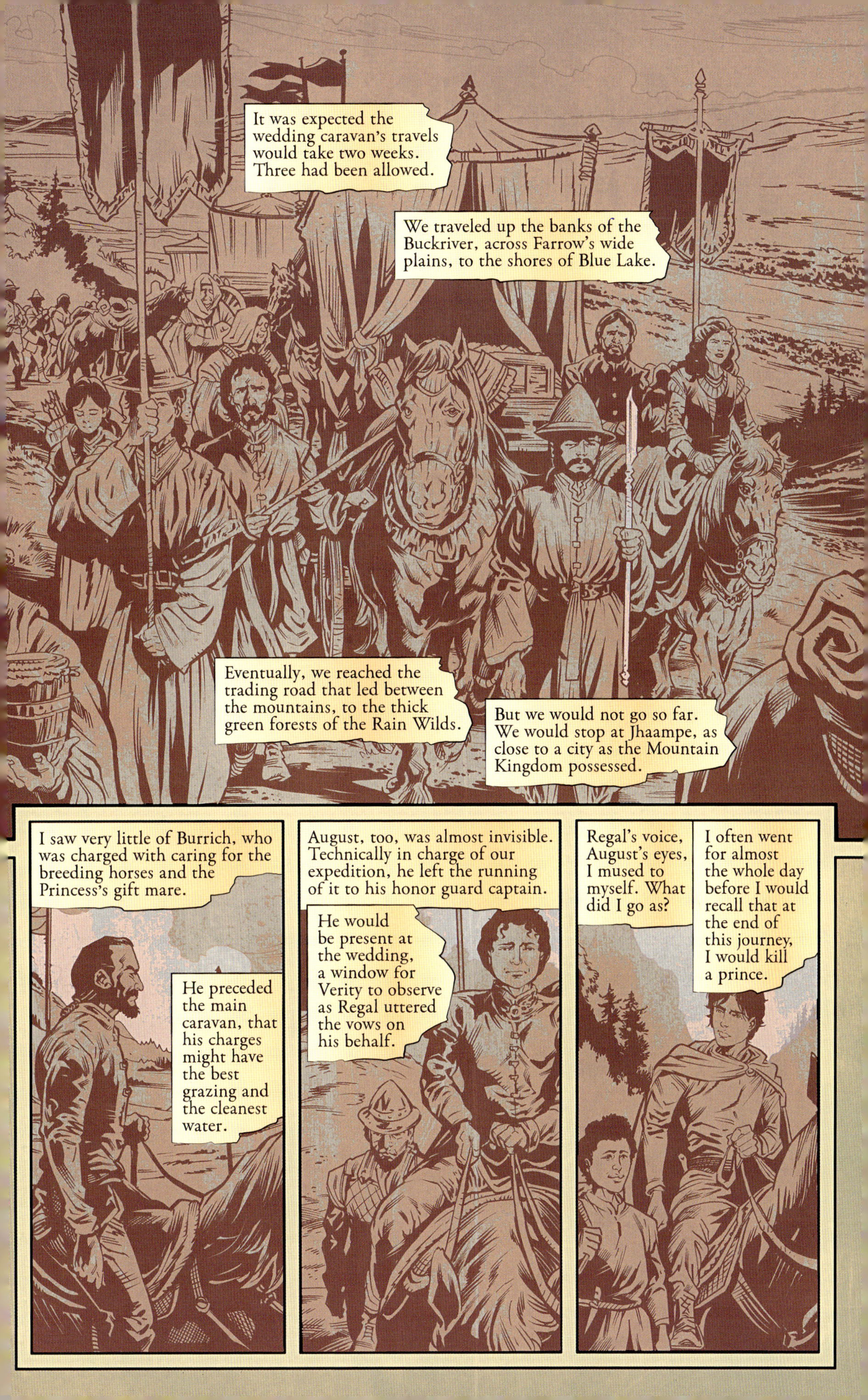

It was expected the wedding caravan's travels would take two weeks. Three had been allowed.
We traveled up the banks of the Buckriver, across Farrow's wide plains, to the shores of Blue Lake.
Eventually, we reached the trading road that led between the mountains, to the thick green forests of the Rain Wilds.
But we would not go so far. We would stop at Jhaampe, as close to a city as the Mountain Kingdom possessed.
I saw very little of Burrich, who was charged with caring for the breeding horses and the Princess's gift mare.
He preceded the main caravan, that his charges might have the best grazing and the cleanest water.
August, too, was almost invisible. Technically in charge of our expedition, he left the running of it to his honor guard captain.
He would be present at the wedding, a window for Verity to observe as Regal uttered the vows on his behalf.
Regal's voice, August's eyes, I mused to myself. What did I go as?
I often went for almost the whole day before I would recall that at the end of this journey, I would kill a prince.

I lay awake many a night, plagued with much anxiety. This assignment must be carried out perfectly.

It would not be an easy death to arrange, without raising even the tiniest suspicion. And the timing was critical.

The Prince must not die while we were at Jhaampe. Or before the Buckkeep ceremonies and the wedding consummation.

It would be seen as an ill omen, and nothing could cast the slightest shadow upon the nuptials.

I wondered why this had been entrusted to me instead of to Chade. Was it a test? Would I be put to death if I failed?

Was Chade too old or too valuable for this challenge? Or could he not be spared from tending Verity's health?

I wondered if I should use a powder that would irritate Rurisk's damaged lungs so he might cough himself to death.

Perhaps I might treat his pillows and bedding with it.

Should I offer him a pain remedy, one that would slowly addict him and lure him into a sleeping death?

If his lungs were chronically bleeding already, a blood-thinning tonic might be enough to send him on his way.

I had one poison, swift and deadly and tasteless as water, if I could arrange for him to encounter it at a safely distant time.

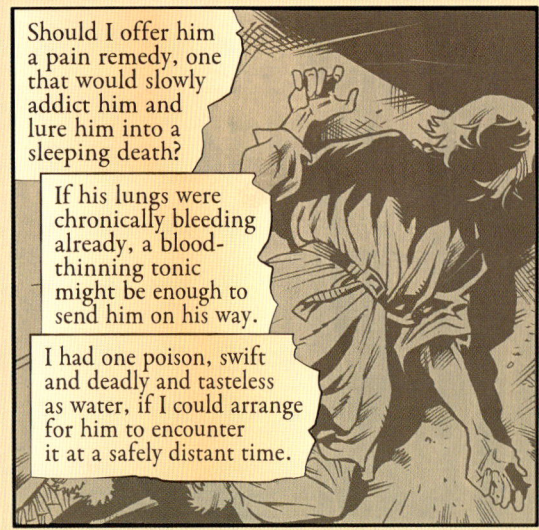

None of these were thoughts conducive to sleep. Yet the fresh air and the exercise of riding could usually counter them.

I often awoke eager for the next day of travel.

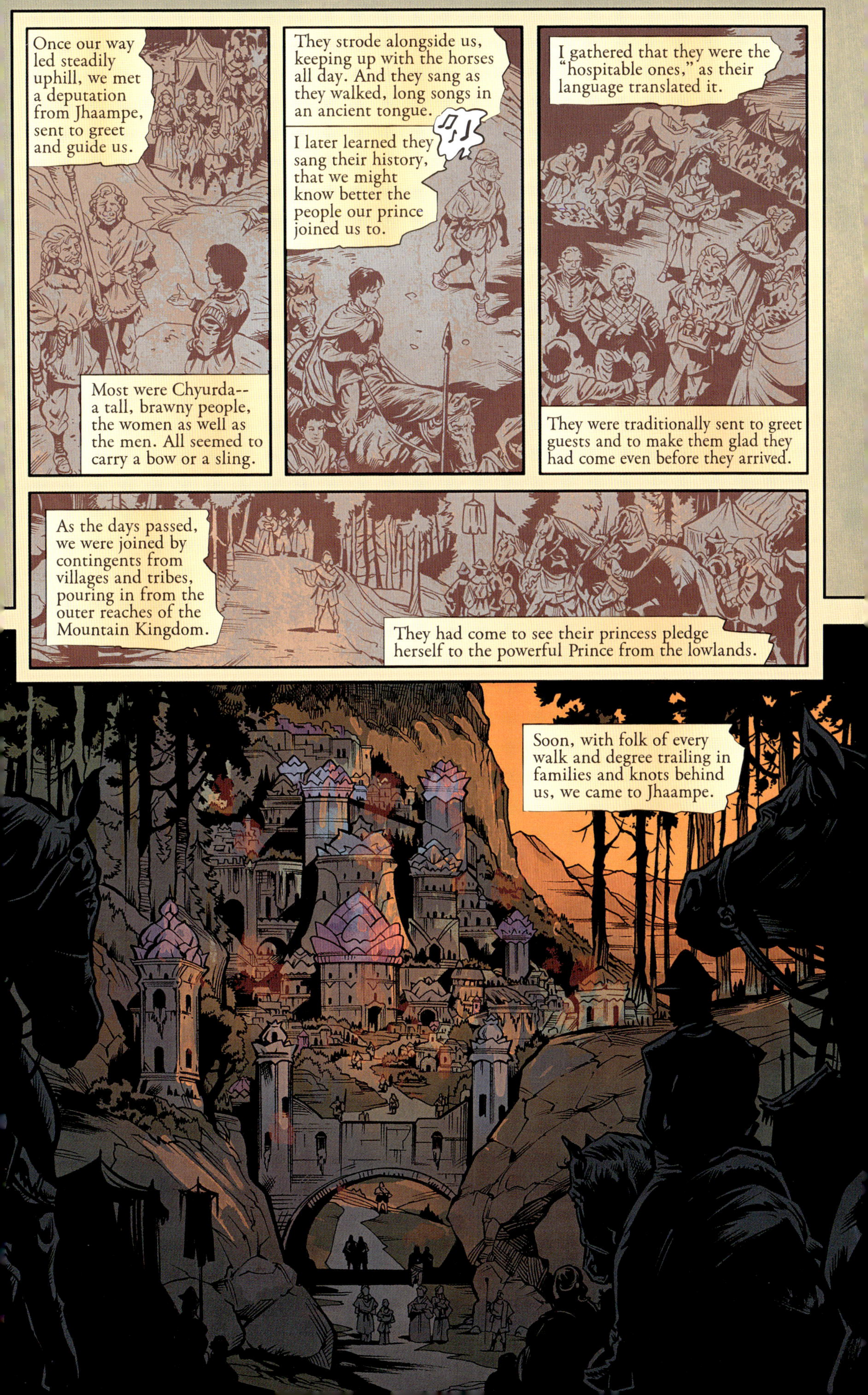
Once our way led steadily uphill, we met a deputation from Jhaampe, sent to greet and guide us.
Most were Chyurda-- a tall, brawny people, the women as well as the men. All seemed to carry a bow or a sling.
They strode alongside us, keeping up with the horses all day. And they sang as they walked, long songs in an ancient tongue.
I later learned they sang their history, that we might know better the people our prince joined us to.
I gathered that they were the "hospitable ones," as their language translated it.
They were traditionally sent to greet guests and to make them glad they had come even before they arrived.
As the days passed, we were joined by contingents from villages and tribes, pouring in from the outer reaches of the Mountain Kingdom.
They had come to see their princess pledge herself to the powerful Prince from the lowlands.
Soon, with folk of every walk and degree trailing in families and knots behind us, we came to Jhaampe.

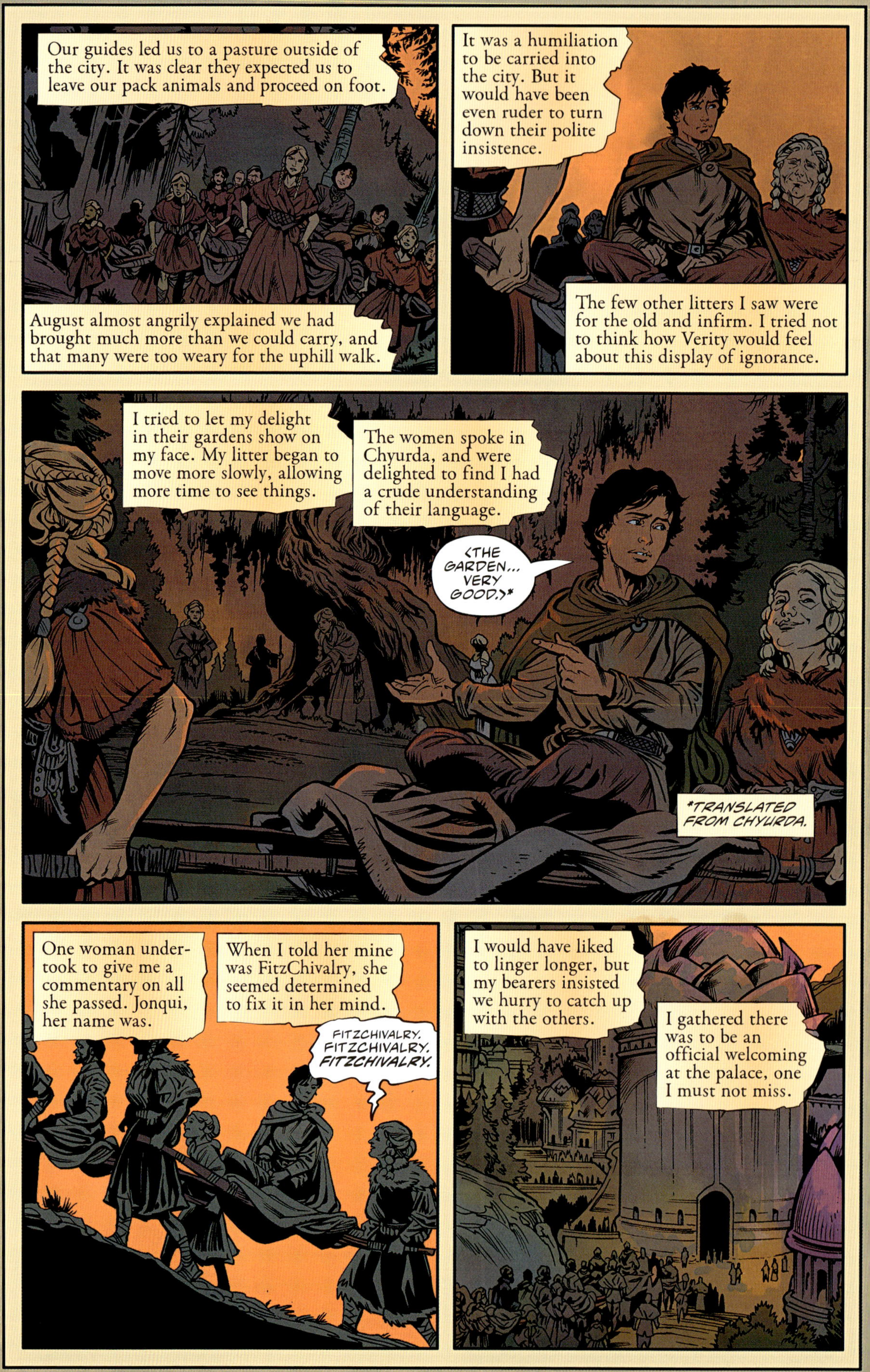
Our guides led us to a pasture outside of the city. It was clear they expected us to leave our pack animals and proceed on foot.
August almost angrily explained we had brought much more than we could carry, and that many were too weary for the uphill walk.
It was a humiliation to be carried into the city. But it would have been even ruder to turn down their polite insistence.
The few other litters I saw were for the old and infirm. I tried not to think how Verity would feel about this display of ignorance.
I tried to let my delight in their gardens show on my face. My litter began to move more slowly, allowing more time to see things.
The women spoke in Chyurda, and were delighted to find I had a crude understanding of their language.
‹THE GARDEN... VERY GOOD.›*
*TRANSLATED FROM CHYURDA.
One woman undertook to give me a commentary on all she passed. Jonqui, her name was.
When I told her mine was FitzChivalry, she seemed determined to fix it in her mind.
FITZCHIVALRY. FITZCHIVALRY. FITZCHIVALRY.
I would have liked to linger longer, but my bearers insisted we hurry to catch up with the others.
I gathered there was to be an official welcoming at the palace, one I must not miss.

<WHAT IS HAPPENING?>

<OUR SACRIFICE-- AH, YOU SAY, KING EYOD, WILL WELCOME YOU. HE WILL SHOW TO YOU HIS DAUGHTER, TO BE YOUR SACRIFICE-- AH, QUEEN.>

<AND HIS SON, WHO WILL RULE FOR HER HERE.>

<AT THE SACRIFICE'S SIDE... THAT IS MY NIECE.>

<AH. SHE... LOOKS HEALTHY. AND STRONG.>

<THE MAN ON THE OTHER SIDE LOOKS SO MUCH LIKE HER... IS HE ALSO A RELATIVE?>

<HE IS MY NEPHEW, YES.>

<AND NOW, WE MUST LISTEN.>

To me, Regal and August, decked in circlets and rings and opulent fabrics, looked more like decorations than princes.

I hoped that our hosts would think their outlandish garb was merely a foreign custom, rather than see them as foppish and vain.

<I PRESENT MY SON, PRINCE RURISK.>

<AND MY DAUGHTER, PRINCESS KETTRICKEN. BETROTHED TO YOUR PRINCE VERITY.>

I realized then that the elderly woman beside me was the King's own sister.

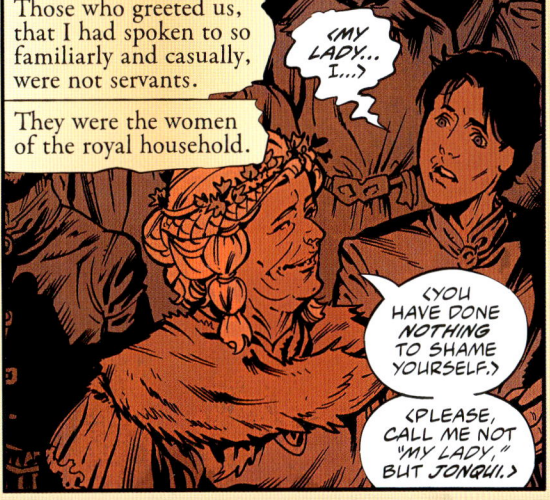

Those who greeted us, that I had spoken to so familiarly and casually, were not servants.

They were the women of the royal household.

<MY LADY... I...>

<YOU HAVE DONE NOTHING TO SHAME YOURSELF.>

<PLEASE, CALL ME NOT "MY LADY," BUT JONQUI.>

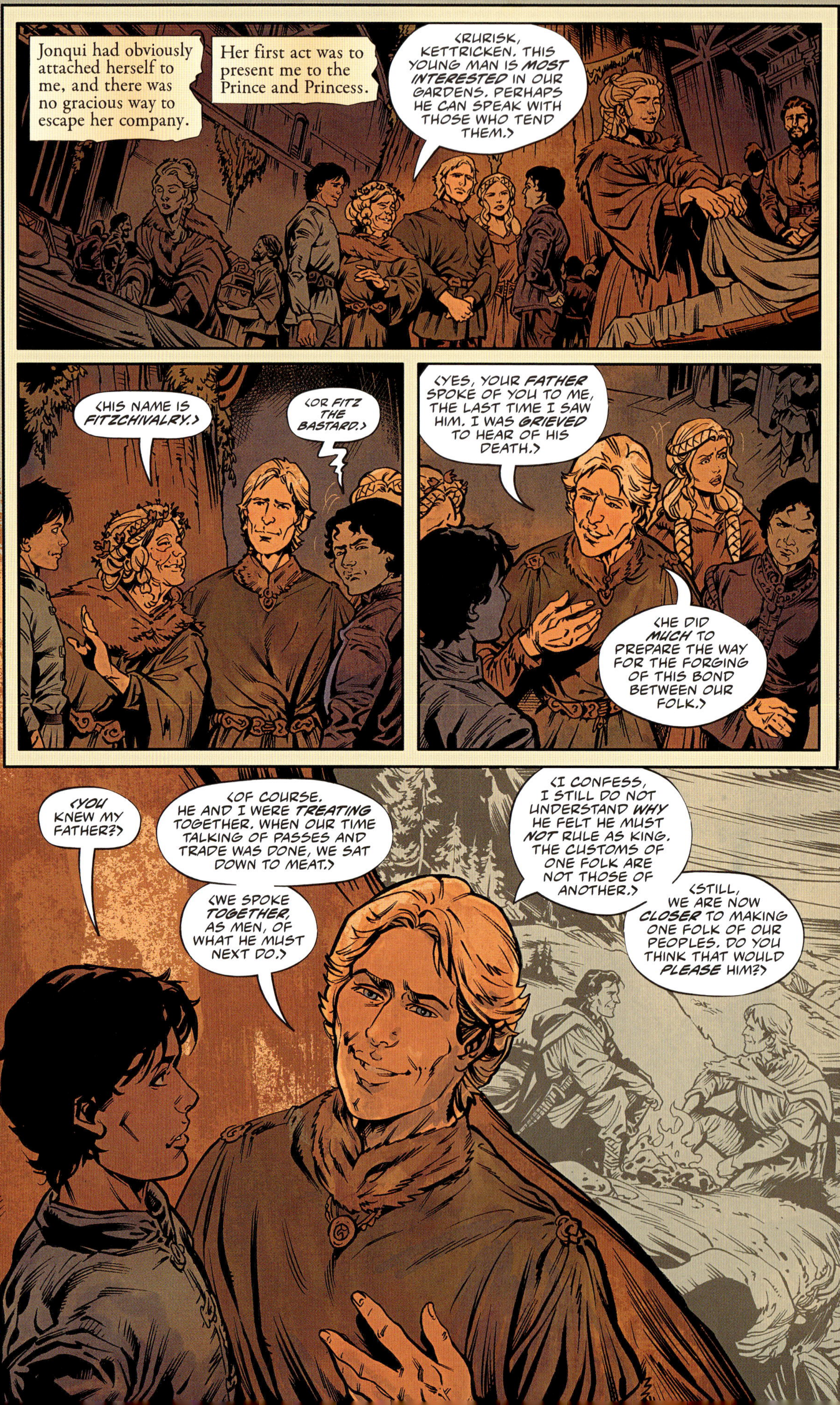

Jonqui had obviously attached herself to me, and there was no gracious way to escape her company.
Her first act was to present me to the Prince and Princess.
<RURISK, KETTRICKEN. THIS YOUNG MAN IS MOST INTERESTED IN OUR GARDENS. PERHAPS HE CAN SPEAK WITH THOSE WHO TEND THEM.>
<HIS NAME IS FITZCHIVALRY.>
<OR FITZ THE BASTARD.>
<YES, YOUR FATHER SPOKE OF YOU TO ME, THE LAST TIME I SAW HIM. I WAS GRIEVED TO HEAR OF HIS DEATH.>
<HE DID MUCH TO PREPARE THE WAY FOR THE FORGING OF THIS BOND BETWEEN OUR FOLK.>
<YOU KNEW MY FATHER?>
<OF COURSE. HE AND I WERE TREATING TOGETHER. WHEN OUR TIME TALKING OF PASSES AND TRADE WAS DONE, WE SAT DOWN TO MEAT.>
<WE SPOKE TOGETHER, AS MEN, OF WHAT HE MUST NEXT DO.>
<I CONFESS, I STILL DO NOT UNDERSTAND WHY HE FELT HE MUST NOT RULE AS KING. THE CUSTOMS OF ONE FOLK ARE NOT THOSE OF ANOTHER.>
<STILL, WE ARE NOW CLOSER TO MAKING ONE FOLK OF OUR PEOPLES. DO YOU THINK THAT WOULD PLEASE HIM?>

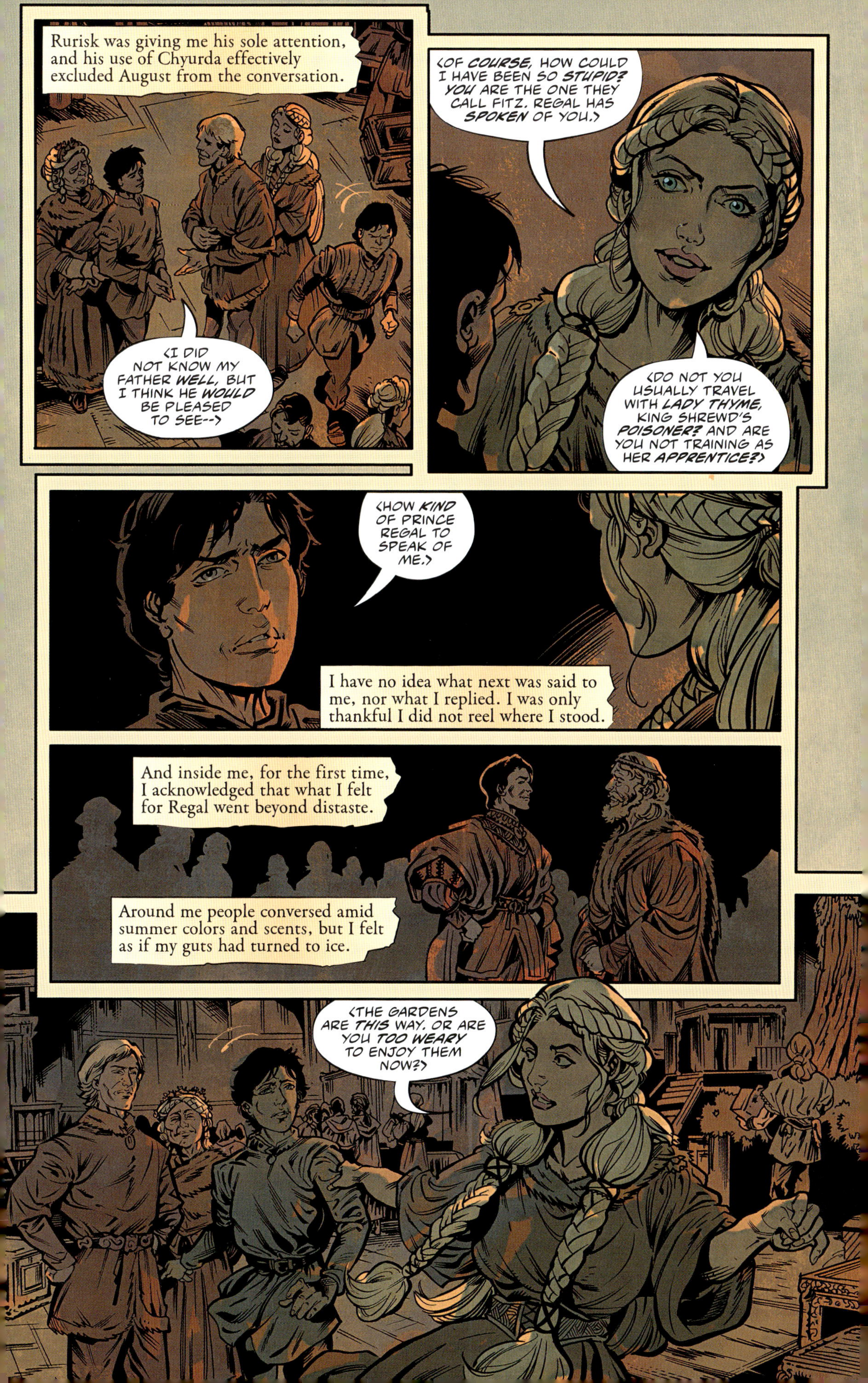
Rurisk was giving me his sole attention, and his use of Chyurda effectively excluded August from the conversation.
<I DID NOT KNOW MY FATHER WELL, BUT I THINK HE WOULD BE PLEASED TO SEE-->
<OF COURSE, HOW COULD I HAVE BEEN SO STUPID? YOU ARE THE ONE THEY CALL FITZ. REGAL HAS SPOKEN OF YOU.>
<DO NOT YOU USUALLY TRAVEL WITH LADY THYME, KING SHREWD'S POISONER? AND ARE YOU NOT TRAINING AS HER APPRENTICE?>
<HOW KIND OF PRINCE REGAL TO SPEAK OF ME.>
I have no idea what next was said to me, nor what I replied. I was only thankful I did not reel where I stood.
And inside me, for the first time, I acknowledged that what I felt for Regal went beyond distaste.
Around me people conversed amid summer colors and scents, but I felt as if my guts had turned to ice.
<THE GARDENS ARE THIS WAY, OR ARE YOU TOO WEARY TO ENJOY THEM NOW?>

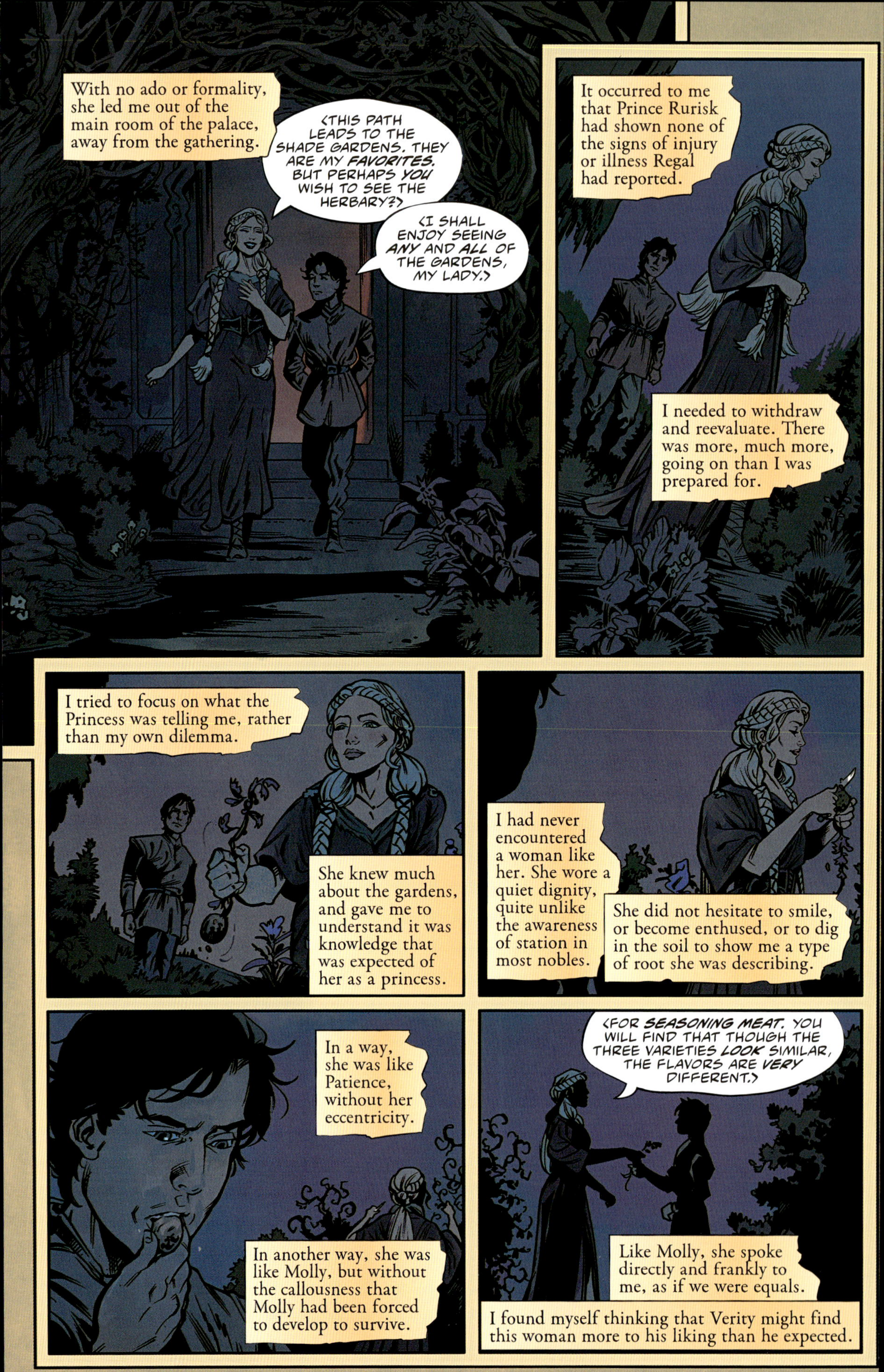

With no ado or formality, she led me out of the main room of the palace, away from the gathering.
<THIS PATH LEADS TO THE SHADE GARDENS. THEY ARE MY FAVORITES. BUT PERHAPS YOU WISH TO SEE THE HERBARY?>
<I SHALL ENJOY SEEING ANY AND ALL OF THE GARDENS, MY LADY.>
It occurred to me that Prince Rurisk had shown none of the signs of injury or illness Regal had reported.
I needed to withdraw and reevaluate. There was more, much more, going on than I was prepared for.
I tried to focus on what the Princess was telling me, rather than my own dilemma.
She knew much about the gardens, and gave me to understand it was knowledge that was expected of her as a princess.
I had never encountered a woman like her. She wore a quiet dignity, quite unlike the awareness of station in most nobles.
She did not hesitate to smile, or become enthused, or to dig in the soil to show me a type of root she was describing.
In a way, she was like Patience, without her eccentricity.
In another way, she was like Molly, but without the callousness that Molly had been forced to develop to survive.
<FOR SEASONING MEAT. YOU WILL FIND THAT THOUGH THE THREE VARIETIES LOOK SIMILAR, THE FLAVORS ARE VERY DIFFERENT.>
Like Molly, she spoke directly and frankly to me, as if we were equals.
I found myself thinking that Verity might find this woman more to his liking than he expected.

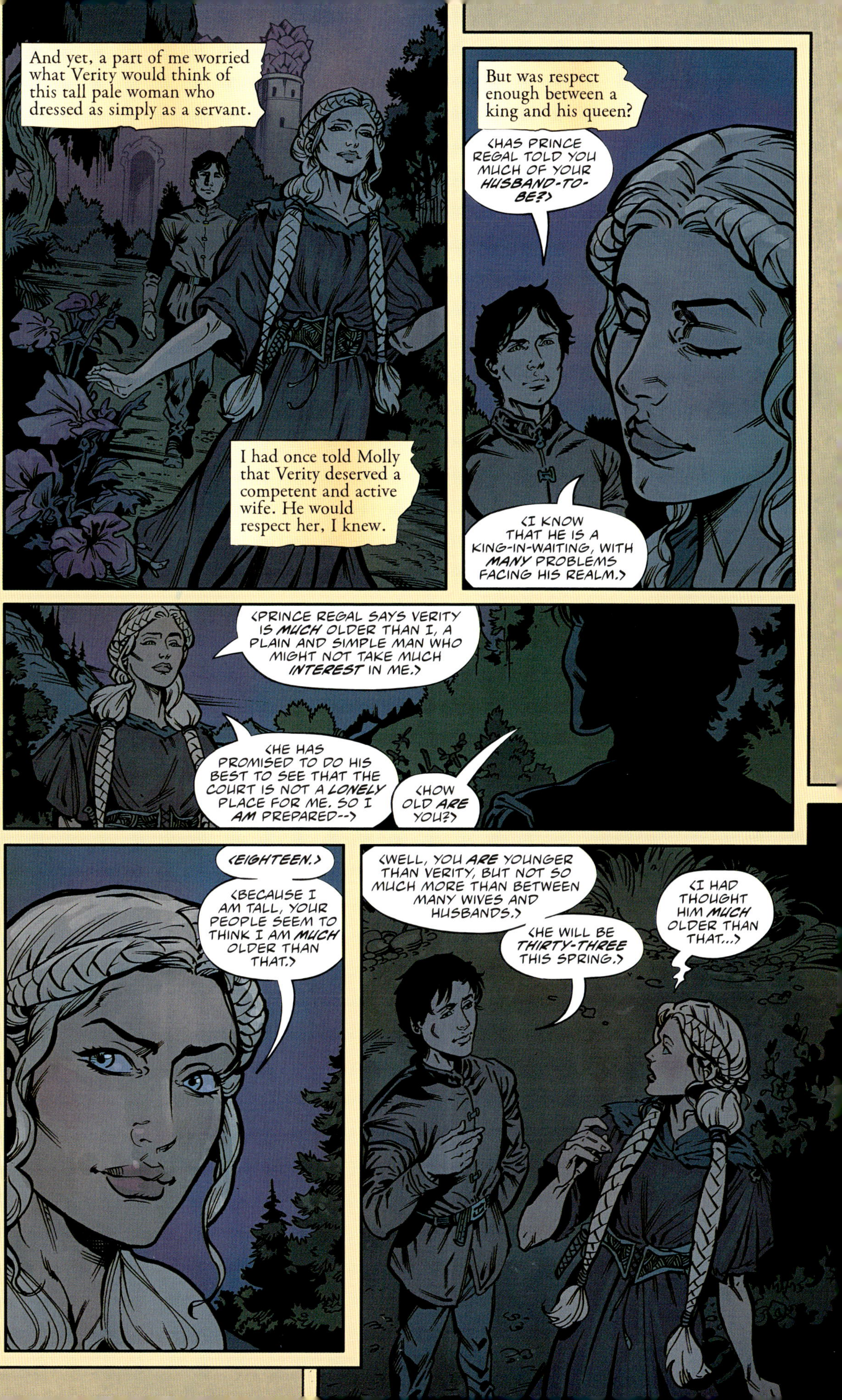
And yet, a part of me worried what Verity would think of this tall pale woman who dressed as simply as a servant.
I had once told Molly that Verity deserved a competent and active wife. He would respect her, I knew.
But was respect enough between a king and his queen?
<HAS PRINCE REGAL TOLD YOU MUCH OF YOUR HUSBAND-TO-BE?>
<I KNOW THAT HE IS A KING-IN-WAITING, WITH MANY PROBLEMS FACING HIS REALM.>
<PRINCE REGAL SAYS VERITY IS MUCH OLDER THAN I, A PLAIN AND SIMPLE MAN WHO MIGHT NOT TAKE MUCH INTEREST IN ME.>
<HE HAS PROMISED TO DO HIS BEST TO SEE THAT THE COURT IS NOT A LONELY PLACE FOR ME. SO I AM PREPARED-->
<HOW OLD ARE YOU?>
<EIGHTEEN.>
<BECAUSE I AM TALL, YOUR PEOPLE SEEM TO THINK I AM MUCH OLDER THAN THAT.>
<WELL, YOU ARE YOUNGER THAN VERITY, BUT NOT SO MUCH MORE THAN BETWEEN MANY WIVES AND HUSBANDS.>
<HE WILL BE THIRTY-THREE THIS SPRING.>
<I HAD THOUGHT HIM MUCH OLDER THAN THAT...>

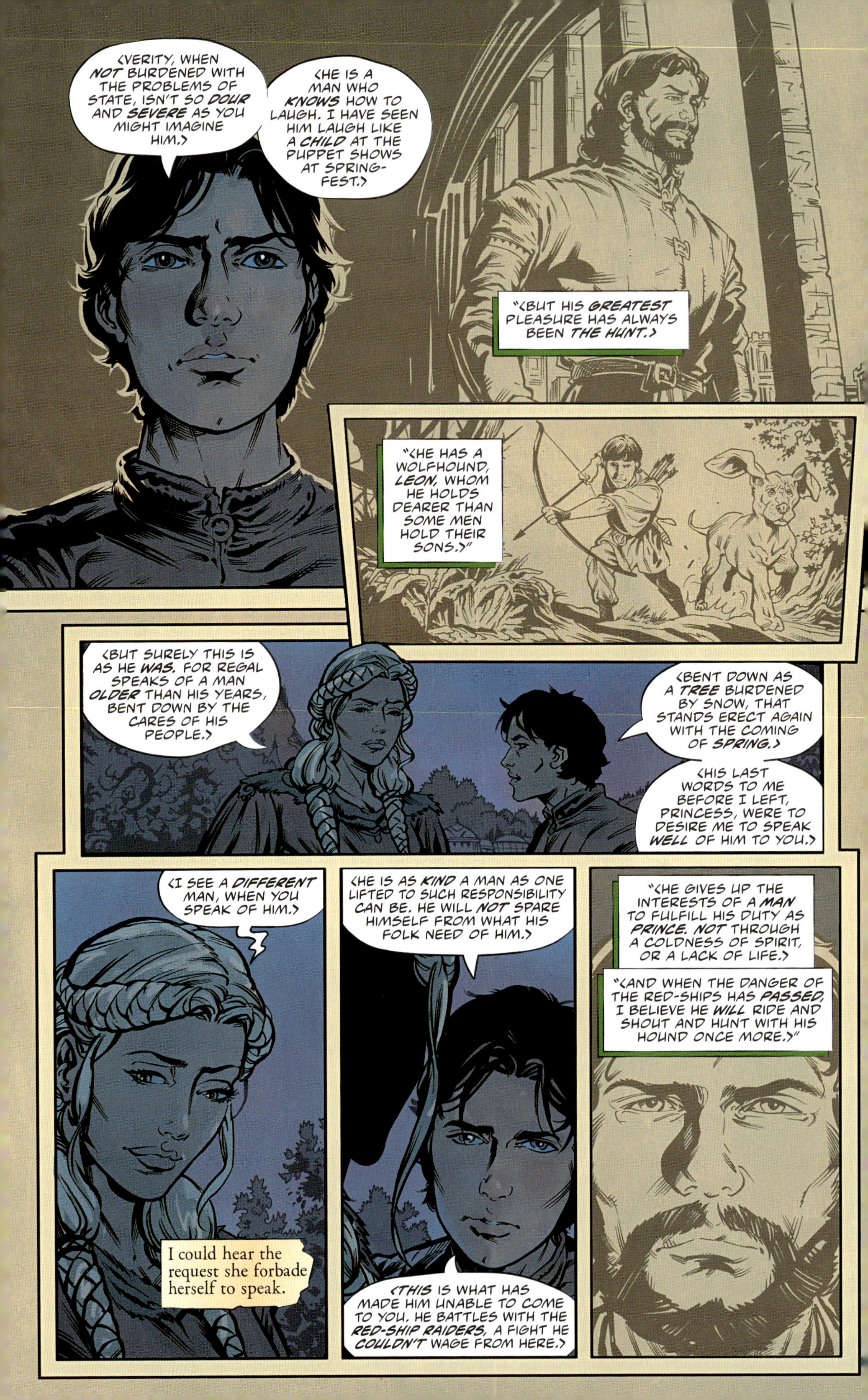
‹VERITY, WHEN NOT BURDENED WITH THE PROBLEMS OF STATE, ISN'T SO DOUR AND SEVERE AS YOU MIGHT IMAGINE HIM.›
‹HE IS A MAN WHO KNOWS HOW TO LAUGH. I HAVE SEEN HIM LAUGH LIKE A CHILD AT THE PUPPET SHOWS AT SPRING-FEST.›
"‹BUT HIS GREATEST PLEASURE HAS ALWAYS BEEN THE HUNT.›
"‹HE HAS A WOLFHOUND, LEON, WHOM HE HOLDS DEARER THAN SOME MEN HOLD THEIR SONS.›"
‹BUT SURELY THIS IS AS HE WAS. FOR REGAL SPEAKS OF A MAN OLDER THAN HIS YEARS, BENT DOWN BY THE CARES OF HIS PEOPLE.›
‹BENT DOWN AS A TREE BURDENED BY SNOW, THAT STANDS ERECT AGAIN WITH THE COMING OF SPRING.›
‹HIS LAST WORDS TO ME BEFORE I LEFT, PRINCESS, WERE TO DESIRE ME TO SPEAK WELL OF HIM TO YOU.›
‹I SEE A DIFFERENT MAN, WHEN YOU SPEAK OF HIM.›
I could hear the request she forbade herself to speak.
‹HE IS AS KIND A MAN AS ONE LIFTED TO SUCH RESPONSIBILITY CAN BE. HE WILL NOT SPARE HIMSELF FROM WHAT HIS FOLK NEED OF HIM.›
‹THIS IS WHAT HAS MADE HIM UNABLE TO COME TO YOU. HE BATTLES WITH THE RED-SHIP RAIDERS, A FIGHT HE COULDN'T WAGE FROM HERE.›
"‹HE GIVES UP THE INTERESTS OF A MAN TO FULFILL HIS DUTY AS PRINCE. NOT THROUGH A COLDNESS OF SPIRIT, OR A LACK OF LIFE.›
"‹AND WHEN THE DANGER OF THE RED-SHIPS HAS PASSED, I BELIEVE HE WILL RIDE AND SHOUT AND HUNT WITH HIS HOUND ONCE MORE.›"

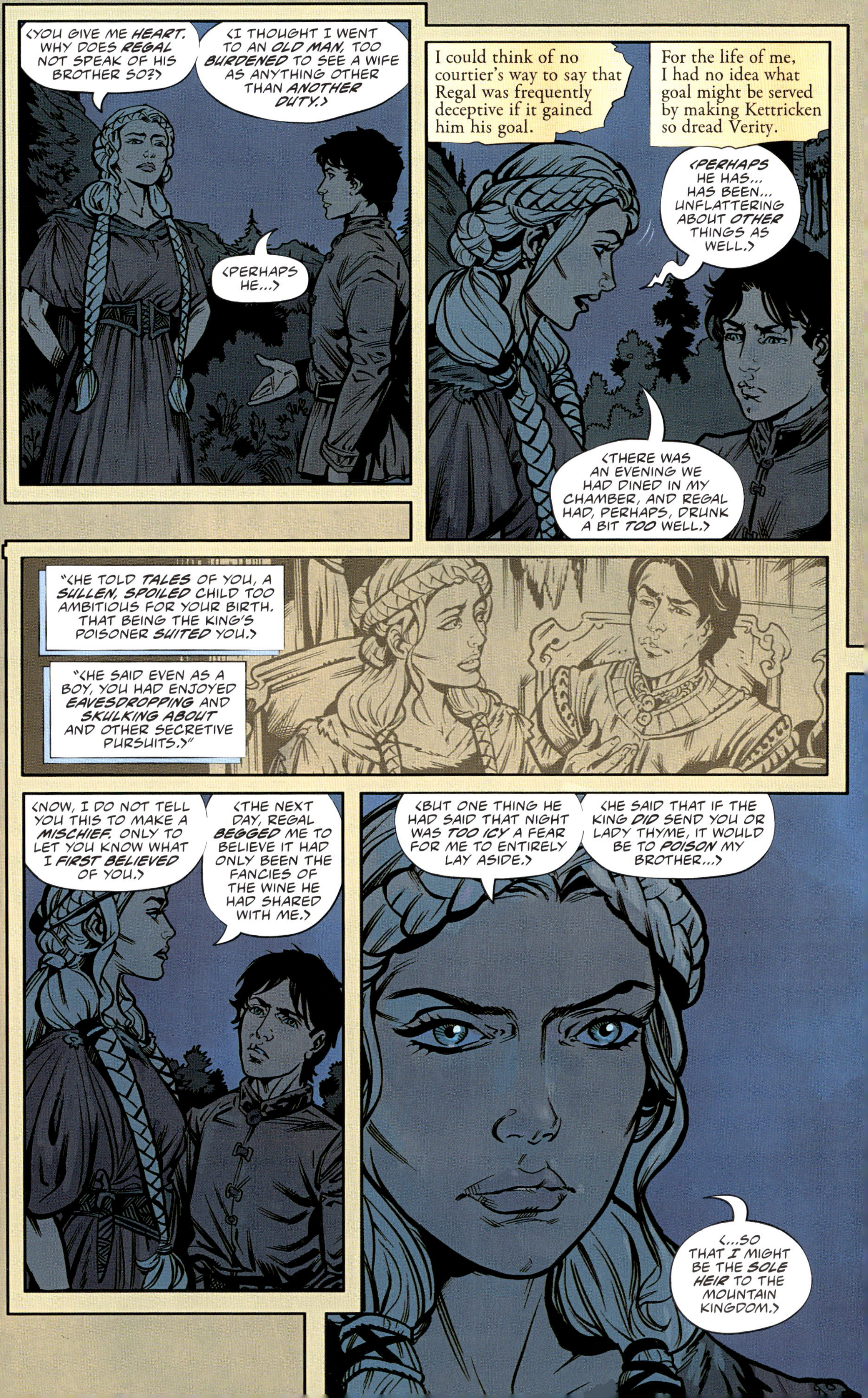
‹YOU GIVE ME HEART. WHY DOES REGAL NOT SPEAK OF HIS BROTHER SO?›
‹I THOUGHT I WENT TO AN OLD MAN, TOO BURDENED TO SEE A WIFE AS ANYTHING OTHER THAN ANOTHER DUTY.›
‹PERHAPS HE...›
I could think of no courtier's way to say that Regal was frequently deceptive if it gained him his goal.
For the life of me, I had no idea what goal might be served by making Kettricken so dread Verity.
‹PERHAPS HE HAS... HAS BEEN... UNFLATTERING ABOUT OTHER THINGS AS WELL.›
‹THERE WAS AN EVENING WE HAD DINED IN MY CHAMBER, AND REGAL HAD, PERHAPS, DRUNK A BIT TOO WELL.›
"‹HE TOLD TALES OF YOU, A SULLEN, SPOILED CHILD TOO AMBITIOUS FOR YOUR BIRTH. THAT BEING THE KING'S POISONER SUITED YOU.›
"‹HE SAID EVEN AS A BOY, YOU HAD ENJOYED EAVESDROPPING AND SKULKING ABOUT AND OTHER SECRETIVE PURSUITS.›"
‹NOW, I DO NOT TELL YOU THIS TO MAKE A MISCHIEF. ONLY TO LET YOU KNOW WHAT I FIRST BELIEVED OF YOU.›
‹THE NEXT DAY, REGAL BEGGED ME TO BELIEVE IT HAD ONLY BEEN THE FANCIES OF THE WINE HE HAD SHARED WITH ME.›
‹BUT ONE THING HE HAD SAID THAT NIGHT WAS TOO ICY A FEAR FOR ME TO ENTIRELY LAY ASIDE.›
‹HE SAID THAT IF THE KING DID SEND YOU OR LADY THYME, IT WOULD BE TO POISON MY BROTHER...›
‹...SO THAT I MIGHT BE THE SOLE HEIR TO THE MOUNTAIN KINGDOM.›

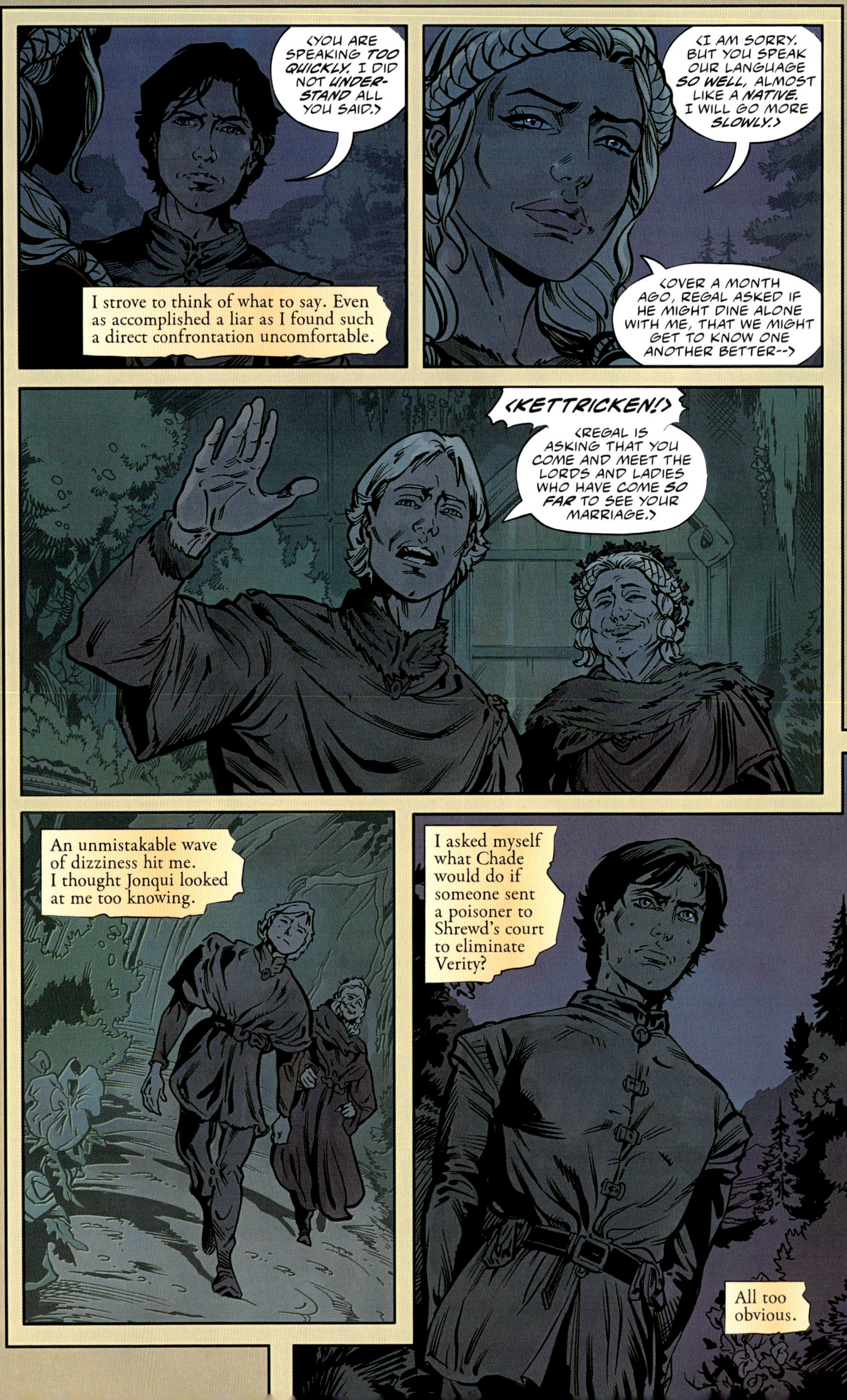

<YOU ARE SPEAKING TOO QUICKLY. I DID NOT UNDERSTAND ALL YOU SAID.>
I strove to think of what to say. Even as accomplished a liar as I found such a direct confrontation uncomfortable.
<I AM SORRY. BUT YOU SPEAK OUR LANGUAGE SO WELL, ALMOST LIKE A NATIVE. I WILL GO MORE SLOWLY.>
<OVER A MONTH AGO, REGAL ASKED IF HE MIGHT DINE ALONE WITH ME, THAT WE MIGHT GET TO KNOW ONE ANOTHER BETTER-->
<KETTRICKEN!>
<REGAL IS ASKING THAT YOU COME AND MEET THE LORDS AND LADIES WHO HAVE COME SO FAR TO SEE YOUR MARRIAGE.>
An unmistakable wave of dizziness hit me. I thought Jonqui looked at me too knowing.
I asked myself what Chade would do if someone sent a poisoner to Shrewd's court to eliminate Verity?
All too obvious.

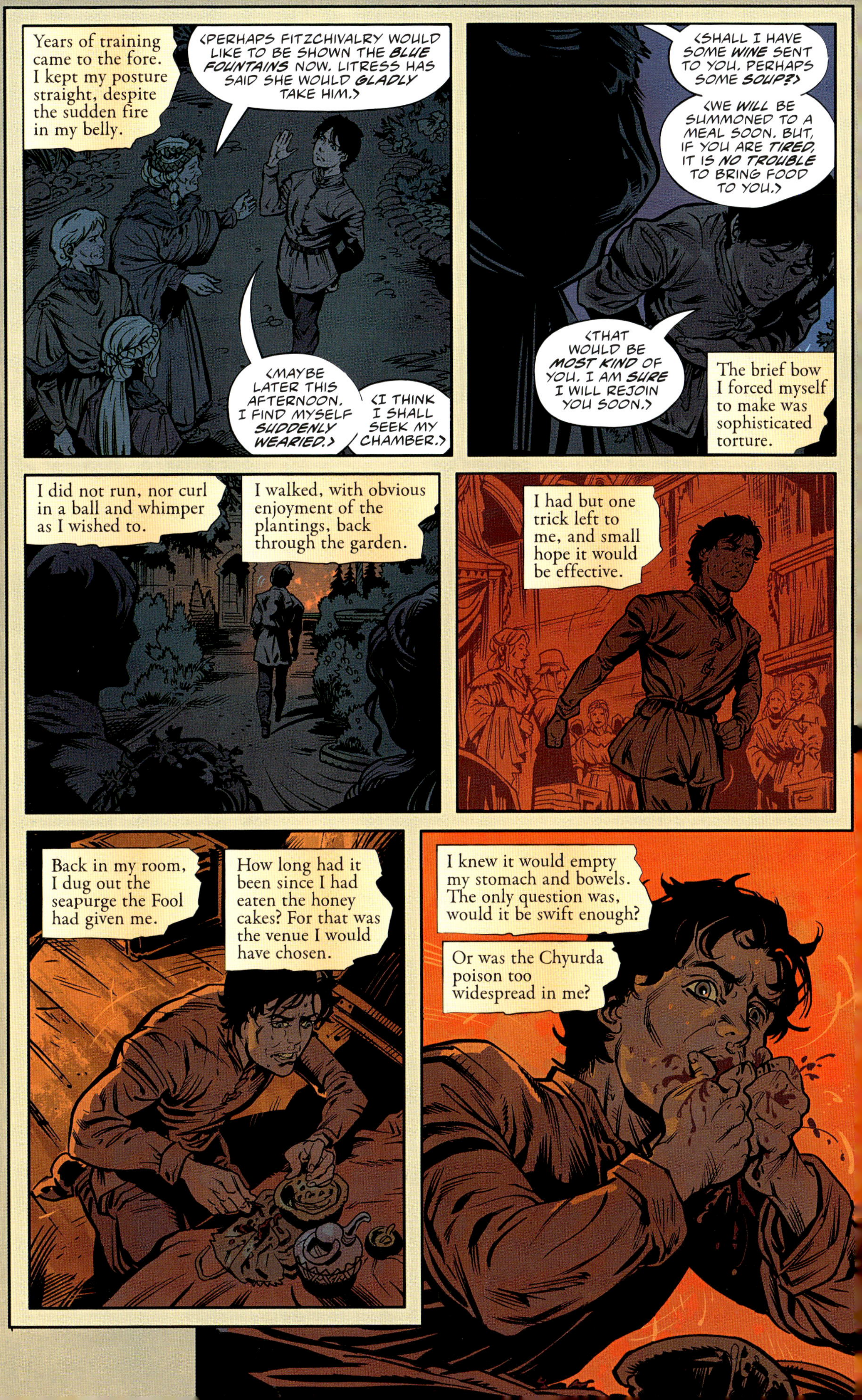

Years of training came to the fore. I kept my posture straight, despite the sudden fire in my belly.
<PERHAPS FITZCHIVALRY WOULD LIKE TO BE SHOWN THE BLUE FOUNTAINS NOW. LITRESS HAS SAID SHE WOULD GLADLY TAKE HIM.>
<MAYBE LATER THIS AFTERNOON. I FIND MYSELF SUDDENLY WEARIED.>
<I THINK I SHALL SEEK MY CHAMBER.>
<SHALL I HAVE SOME WINE SENT TO YOU. PERHAPS SOME SOUP?>
<WE WILL BE SUMMONED TO A MEAL SOON. BUT, IF YOU ARE TIRED, IT IS NO TROUBLE TO BRING FOOD TO YOU.>
<THAT WOULD BE MOST KIND OF YOU. I AM SURE I WILL REJOIN YOU SOON.>
The brief bow I forced myself to make was sophisticated torture.
I did not run, nor curl in a ball and whimper as I wished to.
I walked, with obvious enjoyment of the plantings, back through the garden.
I had but one trick left to me, and small hope it would be effective.
Back in my room, I dug out the seapurge the Fool had given me.
How long had it been since I had eaten the honey cakes? For that was the venue I would have chosen.
I knew it would empty my stomach and bowels. The only question was, would it be swift enough?
Or was the Chyurda poison too widespread in me?

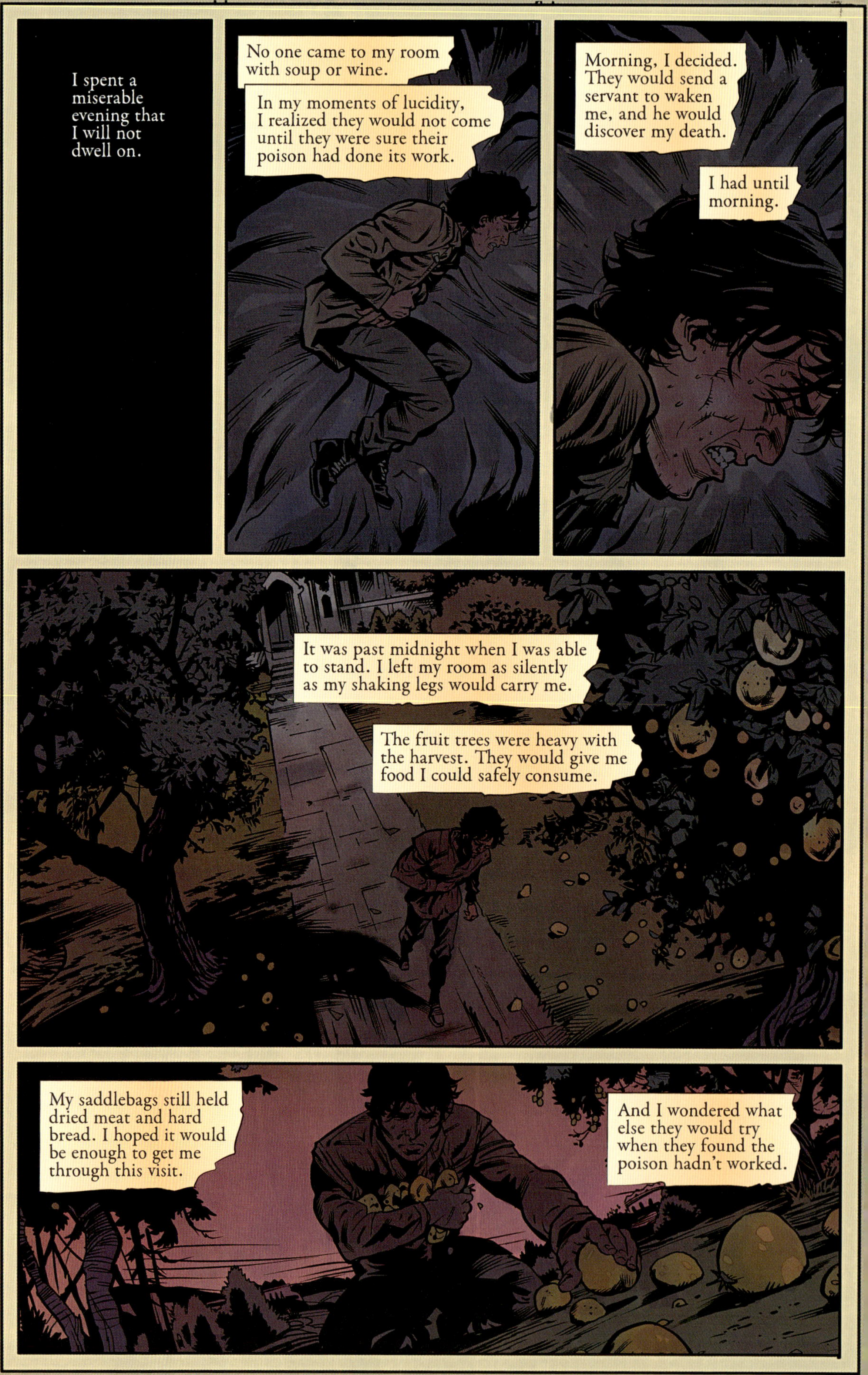
I spent a miserable evening that I will not dwell on.
No one came to my room with soup or wine.
In my moments of lucidity, I realized they would not come until they were sure their poison had done its work.
Morning, I decided. They would send a servant to waken me, and he would discover my death.
I had until morning.
It was past midnight when I was able to stand. I left my room as silently as my shaking legs would carry me.
The fruit trees were heavy with the harvest. They would give me food I could safely consume.
My saddlebags still held dried meat and hard bread. I hoped it would be enough to get me through this visit.
And I wondered what else they would try when they found the poison hadn't worked.

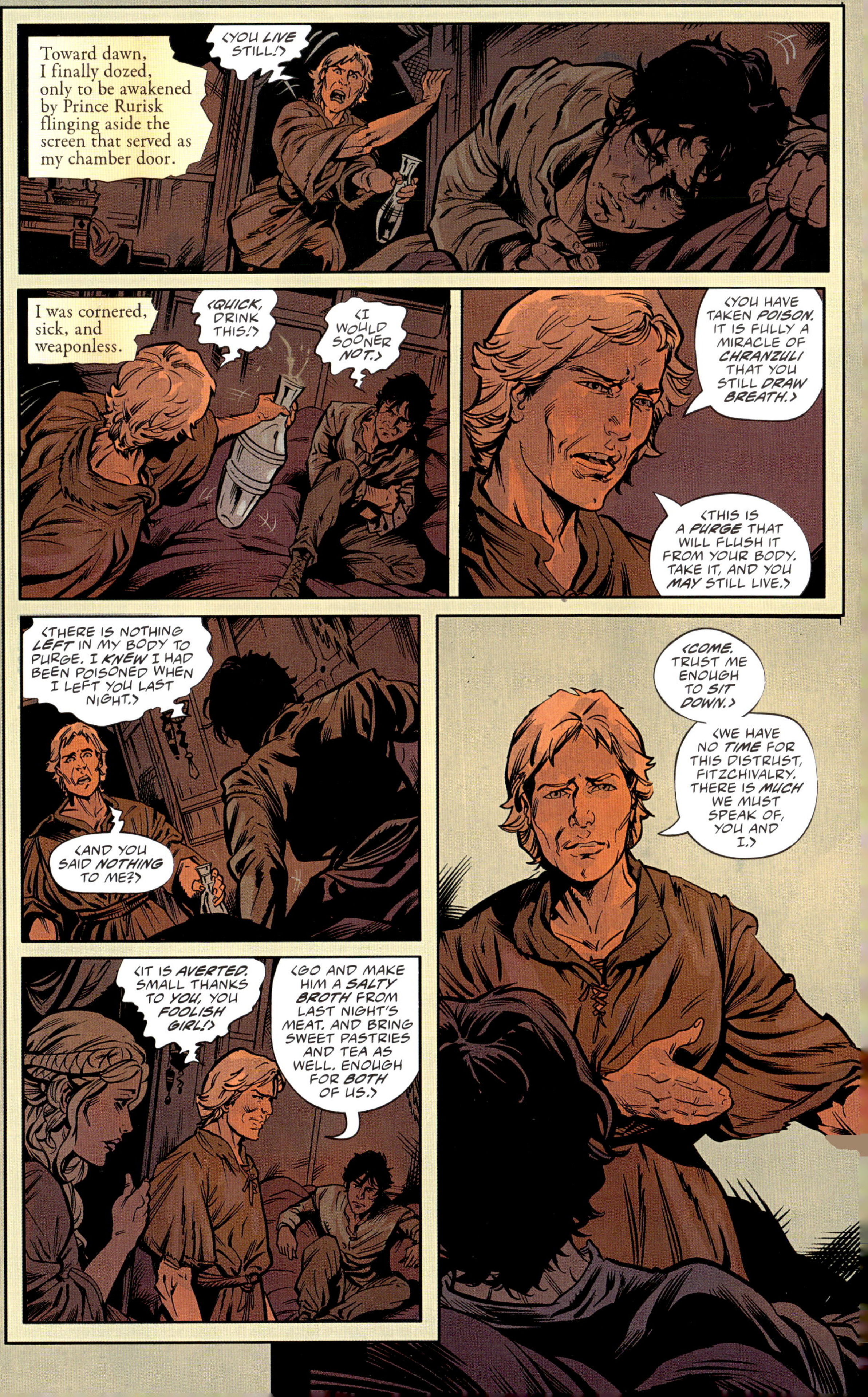

Toward dawn, I finally dozed, only to be awakened by Prince Rurisk flinging aside the screen that served as my chamber door.
‹YOU LIVE STILL!›
I was cornered, sick, and weaponless.
‹QUICK, DRINK THIS!›
‹I WOULD SOONER NOT.›
‹YOU HAVE TAKEN POISON. IT IS FULLY A MIRACLE OF CHRANZULI THAT YOU STILL DRAW BREATH.›
‹THIS IS A PURGE THAT WILL FLUSH IT FROM YOUR BODY. TAKE IT, AND YOU MAY STILL LIVE.›
‹THERE IS NOTHING LEFT IN MY BODY TO PURGE. I KNEW I HAD BEEN POISONED WHEN I LEFT YOU LAST NIGHT.›
‹AND YOU SAID NOTHING TO ME?›
‹COME. TRUST ME ENOUGH TO SIT DOWN.›
‹WE HAVE NO TIME FOR THIS DISTRUST, FITZCHIVALRY. THERE IS MUCH WE MUST SPEAK OF, YOU AND I.›
‹IT IS AVERTED. SMALL THANKS TO YOU, YOU FOOLISH GIRL!›
‹GO AND MAKE HIM A SALTY BROTH FROM LAST NIGHT'S MEAT, AND BRING SWEET PASTRIES AND TEA AS WELL. ENOUGH FOR BOTH OF US.›

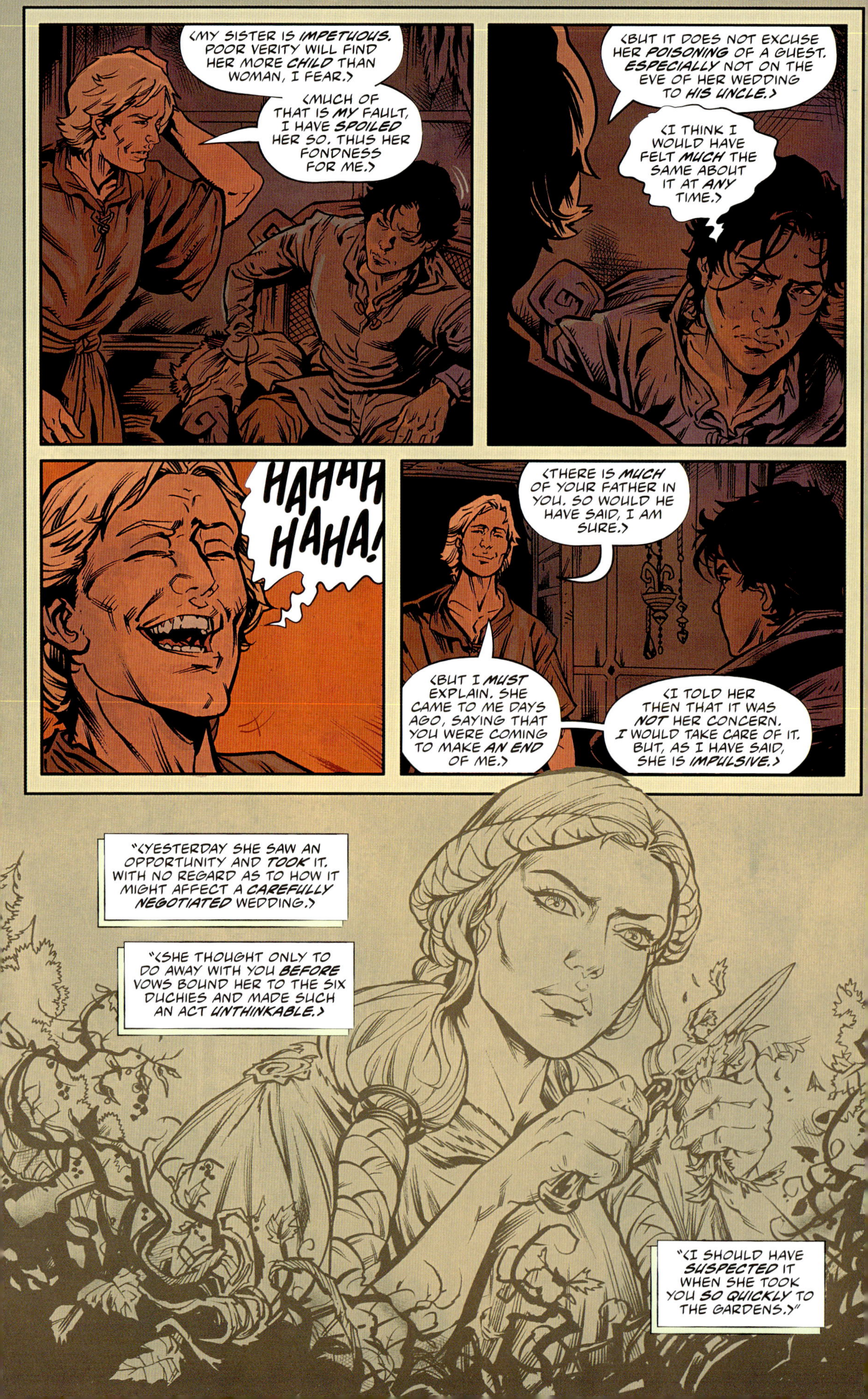
<MY SISTER IS IMPETUOUS. POOR VERITY WILL FIND HER MORE CHILD THAN WOMAN, I FEAR.>
<MUCH OF THAT IS MY FAULT, I HAVE SPOILED HER SO. THUS HER FONDNESS FOR ME.>
<BUT IT DOES NOT EXCUSE HER POISONING OF A GUEST. ESPECIALLY NOT ON THE EVE OF HER WEDDING TO HIS UNCLE.>
<I THINK I WOULD HAVE FELT MUCH THE SAME ABOUT IT AT ANY TIME.>
HAHAH HAHA!
<THERE IS MUCH OF YOUR FATHER IN YOU. SO WOULD HE HAVE SAID, I AM SURE.>
<BUT I MUST EXPLAIN. SHE CAME TO ME DAYS AGO, SAYING THAT YOU WERE COMING TO MAKE AN END OF ME.>
<I TOLD HER THEN THAT IT WAS NOT HER CONCERN. I WOULD TAKE CARE OF IT. BUT, AS I HAVE SAID, SHE IS IMPULSIVE.>
"<YESTERDAY SHE SAW AN OPPORTUNITY AND TOOK IT. WITH NO REGARD AS TO HOW IT MIGHT AFFECT A CAREFULLY NEGOTIATED WEDDING.>
"<SHE THOUGHT ONLY TO DO AWAY WITH YOU BEFORE VOWS BOUND HER TO THE SIX DUCHIES AND MADE SUCH AN ACT UNTHINKABLE.>
"<I SHOULD HAVE SUSPECTED IT WHEN SHE TOOK YOU SO QUICKLY TO THE GARDENS.>"

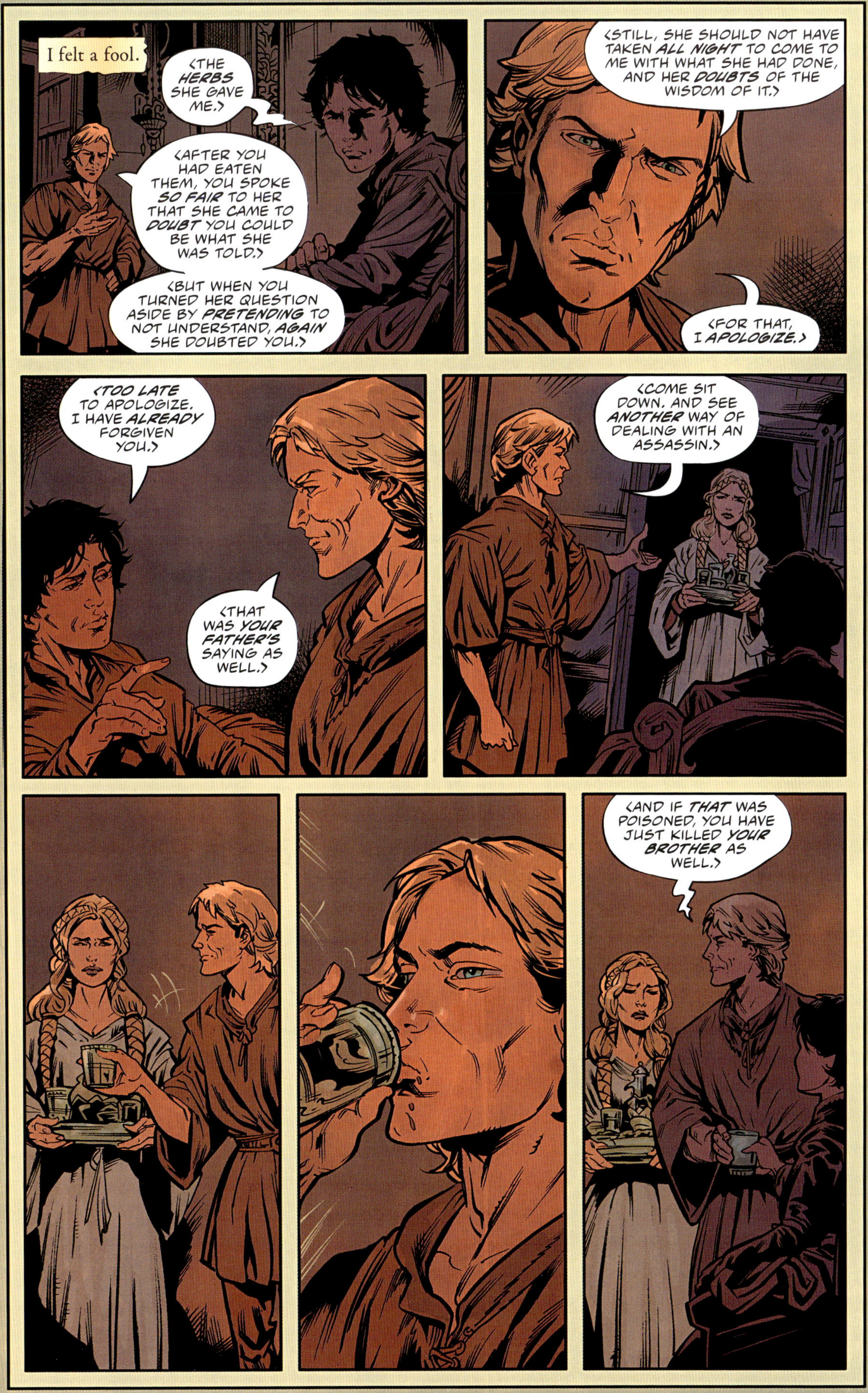
I felt a fool.
<THE HERBS SHE GAVE ME.>
<AFTER YOU HAD EATEN THEM, YOU SPOKE SO FAIR TO HER THAT SHE CAME TO DOUBT YOU COULD BE WHAT SHE WAS TOLD.>
<BUT WHEN YOU TURNED HER QUESTION ASIDE BY PRETENDING TO NOT UNDERSTAND, AGAIN SHE DOUBTED YOU.>
<STILL, SHE SHOULD NOT HAVE TAKEN ALL NIGHT TO COME TO ME WITH WHAT SHE HAD DONE, AND HER DOUBTS OF THE WISDOM OF IT.>
<FOR THAT, I APOLOGIZE.>
<TOO LATE TO APOLOGIZE. I HAVE ALREADY FORGIVEN YOU.>
<THAT WAS YOUR FATHER'S SAYING AS WELL.>
<COME SIT DOWN. AND SEE ANOTHER WAY OF DEALING WITH AN ASSASSIN.>
<AND IF THAT WAS POISONED, YOU HAVE JUST KILLED YOUR BROTHER AS WELL.>

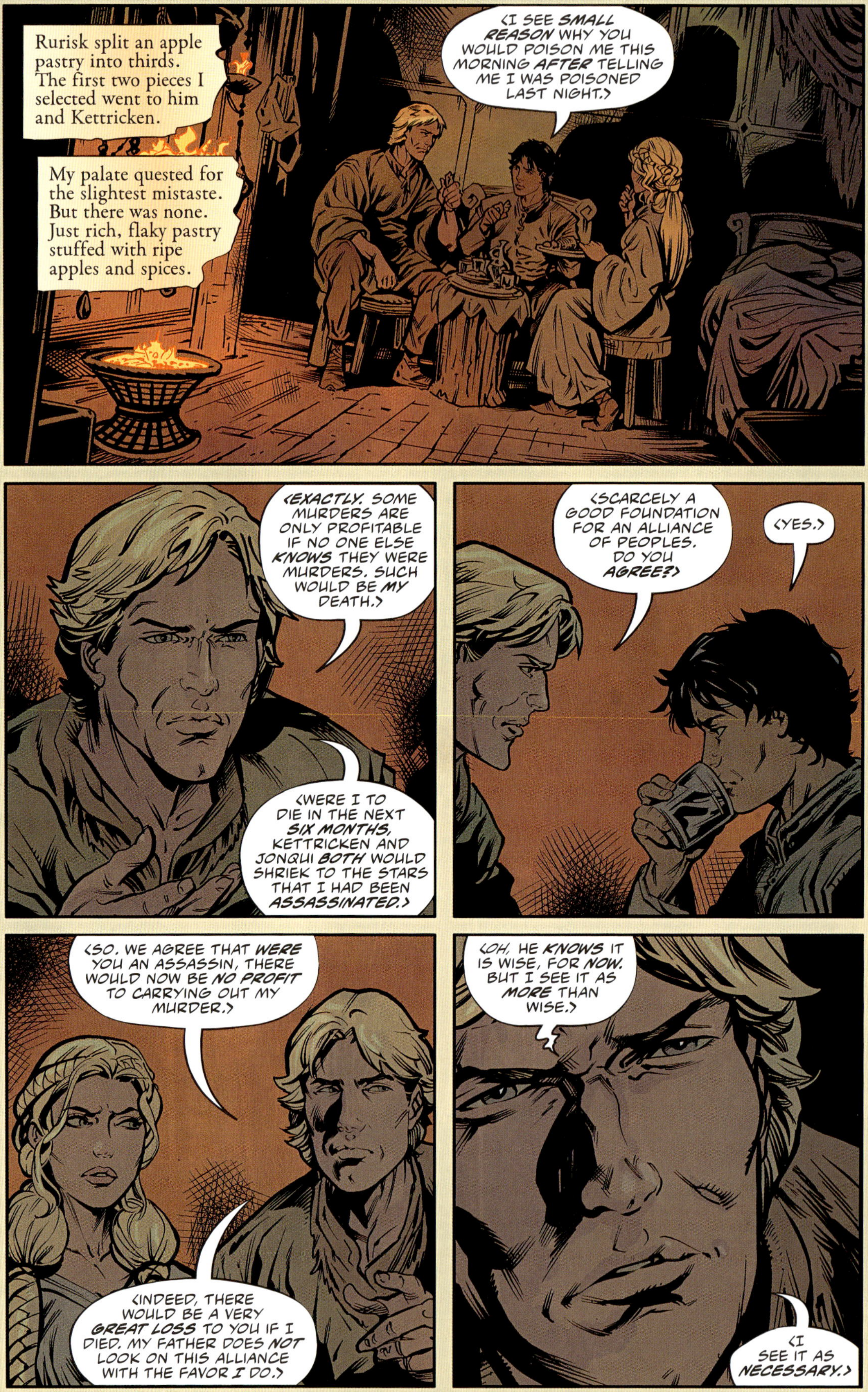

Rurisk split an apple pastry into thirds. The first two pieces I selected went to him and Kettricken.
My palate quested for the slightest mistaste. But there was none. Just rich, flaky pastry stuffed with ripe apples and spices.
‹I SEE SMALL REASON WHY YOU WOULD POISON ME THIS MORNING AFTER TELLING ME I WAS POISONED LAST NIGHT.›
‹EXACTLY. SOME MURDERS ARE ONLY PROFITABLE IF NO ONE ELSE KNOWS THEY WERE MURDERS. SUCH WOULD BE MY DEATH.›
‹WERE I TO DIE IN THE NEXT SIX MONTHS, KETTRICKEN AND JONQUI BOTH WOULD SHRIEK TO THE STARS THAT I HAD BEEN ASSASSINATED.›
‹SCARCELY A GOOD FOUNDATION FOR AN ALLIANCE OF PEOPLES. DO YOU AGREE?›
‹YES.›
‹SO, WE AGREE THAT WERE YOU AN ASSASSIN, THERE WOULD NOW BE NO PROFIT TO CARRYING OUT MY MURDER.›
‹INDEED, THERE WOULD BE A VERY GREAT LOSS TO YOU IF I DIED. MY FATHER DOES NOT LOOK ON THIS ALLIANCE WITH THE FAVOR I DO.›
‹OH, HE KNOWS IT IS WISE, FOR NOW. BUT I SEE IT AS MORE THAN WISE.›
‹I SEE IT AS NECESSARY.›

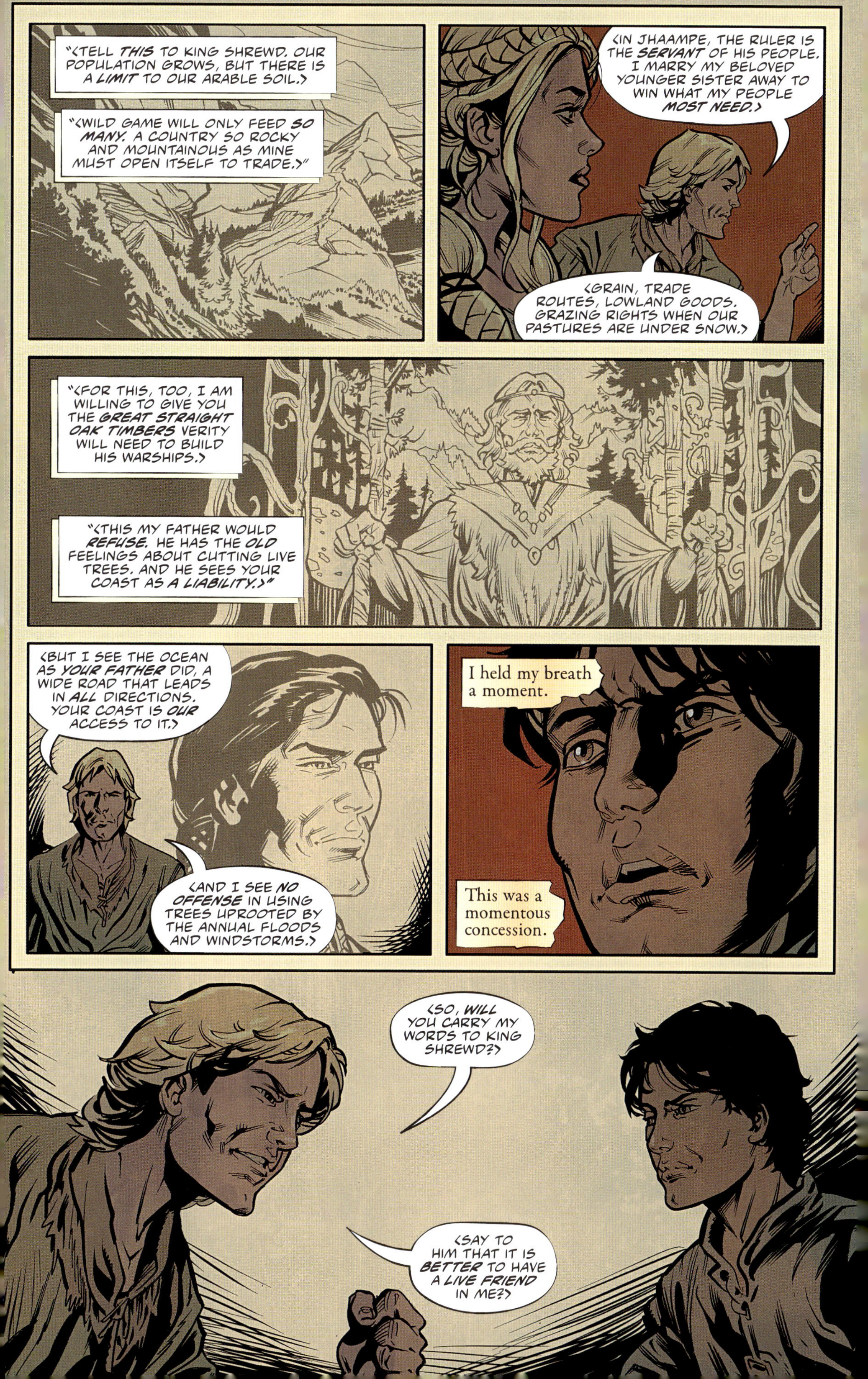
"<TELL THIS TO KING SHREWD. OUR POPULATION GROWS, BUT THERE IS A LIMIT TO OUR ARABLE SOIL.>
"<WILD GAME WILL ONLY FEED SO MANY. A COUNTRY SO ROCKY AND MOUNTAINOUS AS MINE MUST OPEN ITSELF TO TRADE.>"
<IN JHAAMPE, THE RULER IS THE SERVANT OF HIS PEOPLE. I MARRY MY BELOVED YOUNGER SISTER AWAY TO WIN WHAT MY PEOPLE MOST NEED.>
<GRAIN, TRADE ROUTES, LOWLAND GOODS. GRAZING RIGHTS WHEN OUR PASTURES ARE UNDER SNOW.>
"<FOR THIS, TOO, I AM WILLING TO GIVE YOU THE GREAT STRAIGHT OAK TIMBERS VERITY WILL NEED TO BUILD HIS WARSHIPS.>
"<THIS MY FATHER WOULD REFUSE. HE HAS THE OLD FEELINGS ABOUT CUTTING LIVE TREES. AND HE SEES YOUR COAST AS A LIABILITY.>"
<BUT I SEE THE OCEAN AS YOUR FATHER DID, A WIDE ROAD THAT LEADS IN ALL DIRECTIONS. YOUR COAST IS OUR ACCESS TO IT.>
<AND I SEE NO OFFENSE IN USING TREES UPROOTED BY THE ANNUAL FLOODS AND WINDSTORMS.>
I held my breath a moment.
This was a momentous concession.
<SO, WILL YOU CARRY MY WORDS TO KING SHREWD?>
<SAY TO HIM THAT IT IS BETTER TO HAVE A LIVE FRIEND IN ME?>

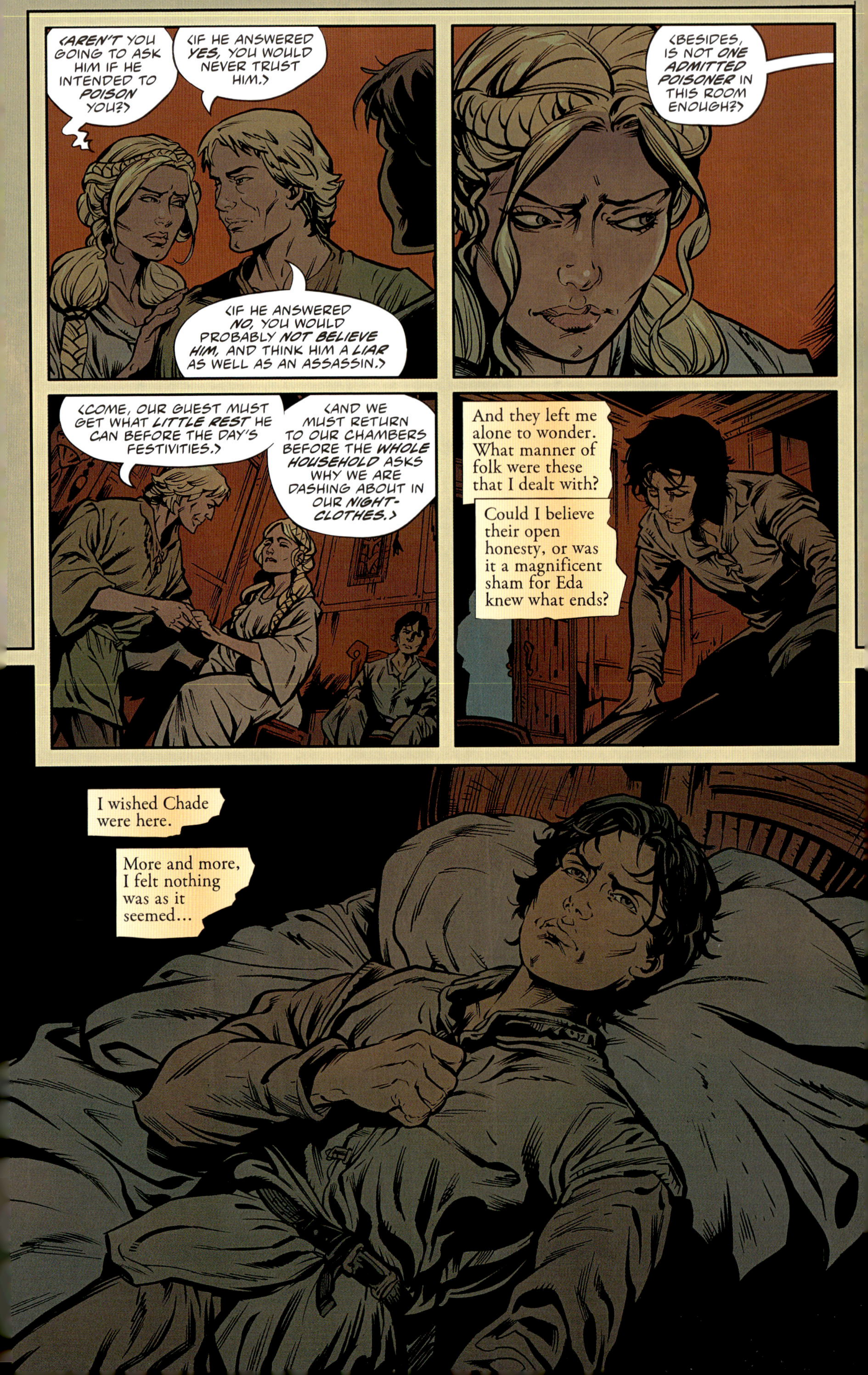

<AREN'T YOU GOING TO ASK HIM IF HE INTENDED TO POISON YOU?>
<IF HE ANSWERED YES, YOU WOULD NEVER TRUST HIM.>
<IF HE ANSWERED NO, YOU WOULD PROBABLY NOT BELIEVE HIM, AND THINK HIM A LIAR AS WELL AS AN ASSASSIN.>
<BESIDES, IS NOT ONE ADMITTED POISONER IN THIS ROOM ENOUGH?>
<COME, OUR GUEST MUST GET WHAT LITTLE REST HE CAN BEFORE THE DAY'S FESTIVITIES.>
<AND WE MUST RETURN TO OUR CHAMBERS BEFORE THE WHOLE HOUSEHOLD ASKS WHY WE ARE DASHING ABOUT IN OUR NIGHT-CLOTHES.>
And they left me alone to wonder. What manner of folk were these that I dealt with?
Could I believe their open honesty, or was it a magnificent sham for Eda knew what ends?
I wished Chade were here.
More and more, I felt nothing was as it seemed...

Chapter Five

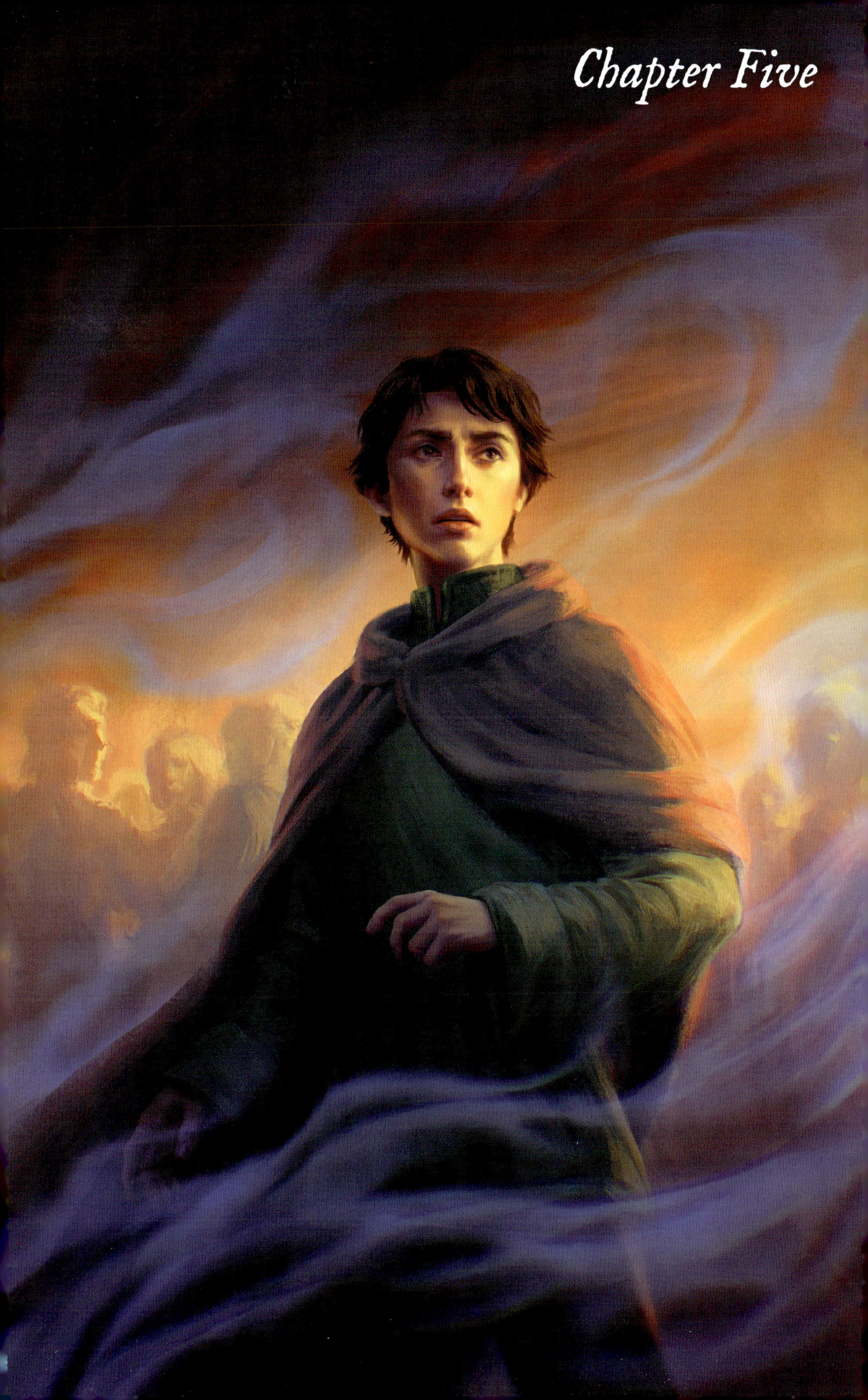

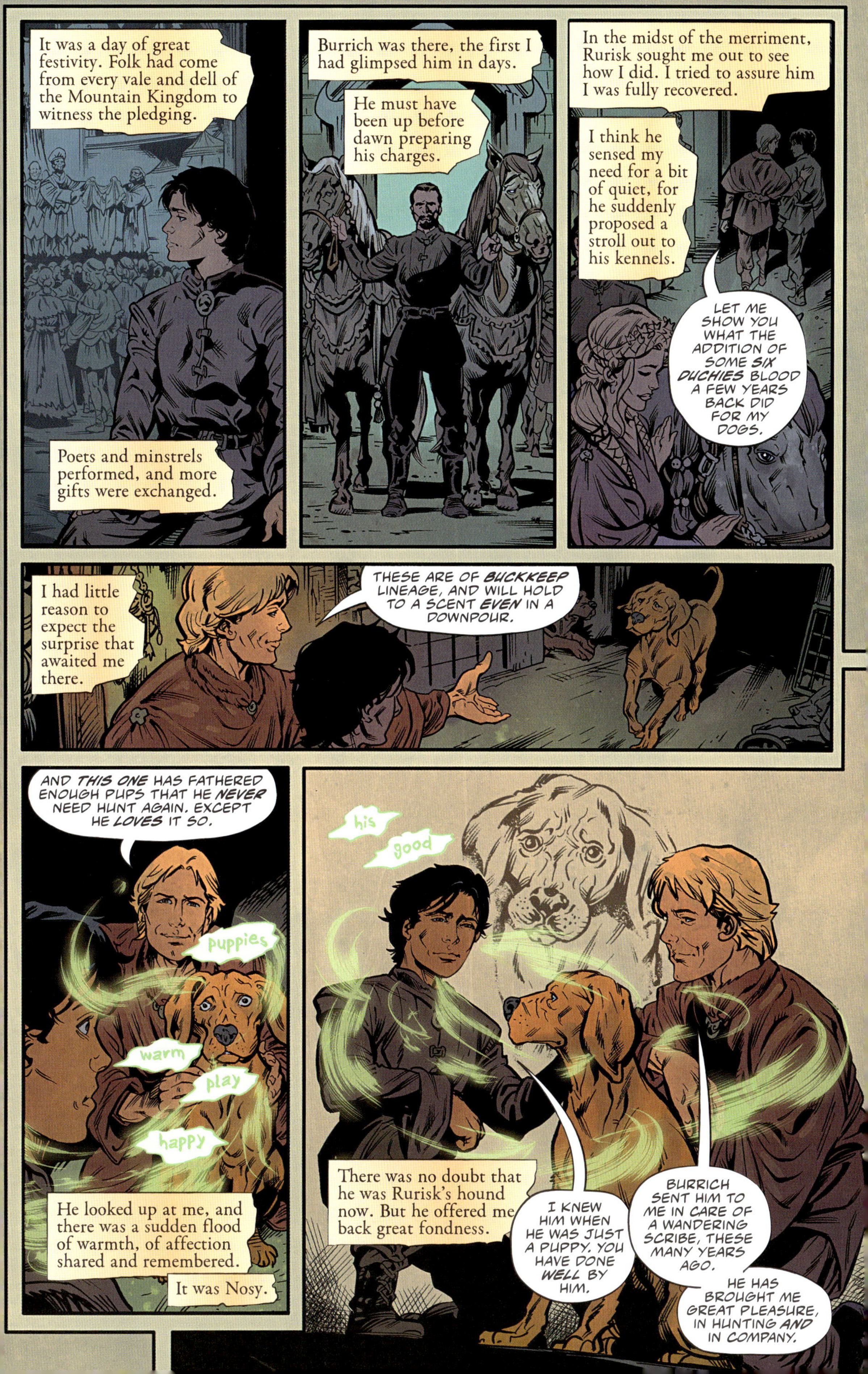

It was a day of great festivity. Folk had come from every vale and dell of the Mountain Kingdom to witness the pledging.
Poets and minstrels performed, and more gifts were exchanged.
Burrich was there, the first I had glimpsed him in days.
He must have been up before dawn preparing his charges.
In the midst of the merriment, Rurisk sought me out to see how I did. I tried to assure him I was fully recovered.
I think he sensed my need for a bit of quiet, for he suddenly proposed a stroll out to his kennels.
LET ME SHOW YOU WHAT THE ADDITION OF SOME SIX DUCHIES BLOOD A FEW YEARS BACK DID FOR MY DOGS.
I had little reason to expect the surprise that awaited me there.
THESE ARE OF BUCKKEEP LINEAGE, AND WILL HOLD TO A SCENT EVEN IN A DOWNPOUR.
AND THIS ONE HAS FATHERED ENOUGH PUPS THAT HE NEVER NEED HUNT AGAIN. EXCEPT HE LOVES IT SO.
puppies
warm
play
happy
He looked up at me, and there was a sudden flood of warmth, of affection shared and remembered.
It was Nosy.
his
good
There was no doubt that he was Rurisk's hound now. But he offered me back great fondness.
I KNEW HIM WHEN HE WAS JUST A PUPPY. YOU HAVE DONE WELL BY HIM.
BURRICH SENT HIM TO ME IN CARE OF A WANDERING SCRIBE, THESE MANY YEARS AGO.
HE HAS BROUGHT ME GREAT PLEASURE, IN HUNTING AND IN COMPANY.

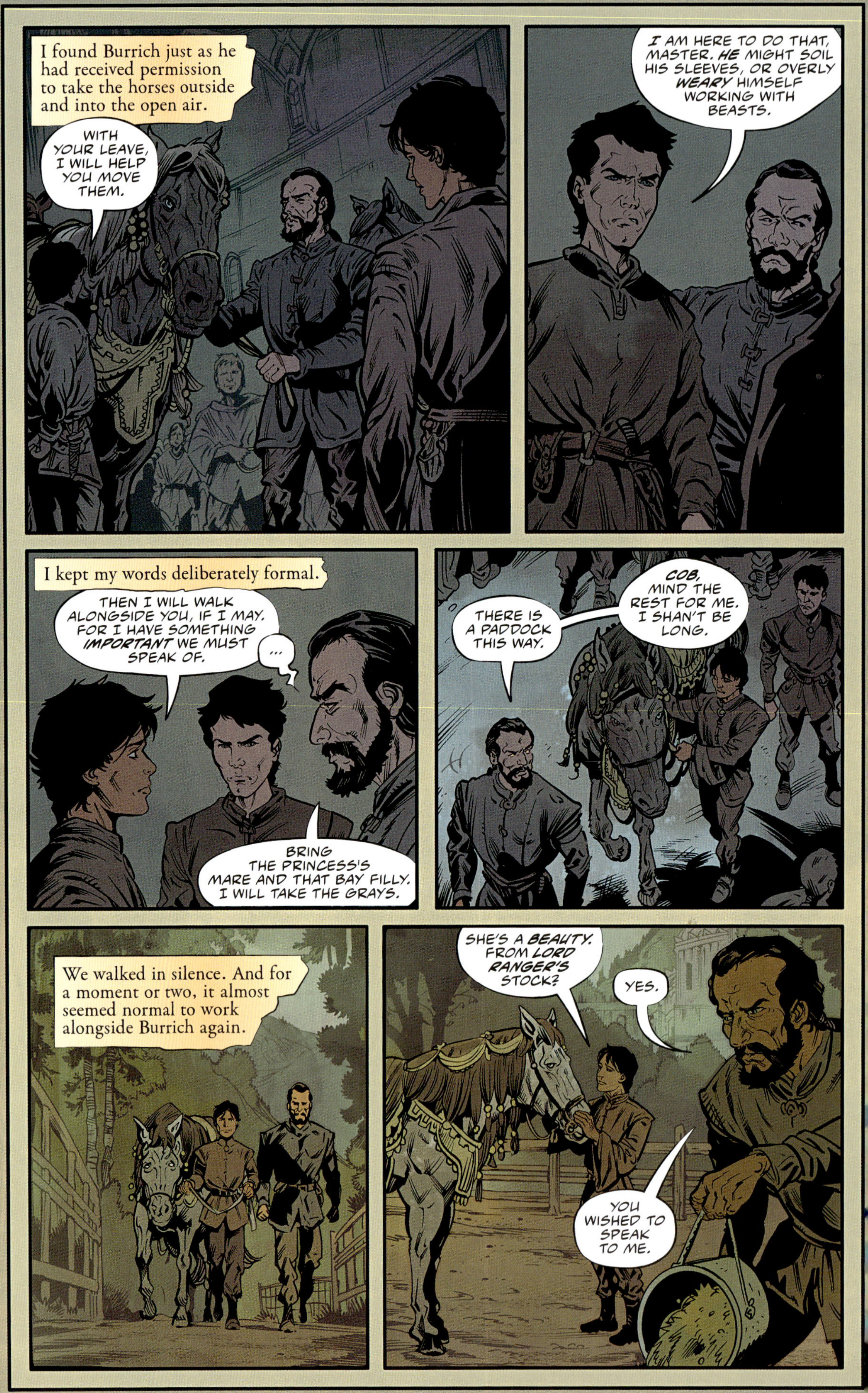

I found Burrich just as he had received permission to take the horses outside and into the open air.
WITH YOUR LEAVE, I WILL HELP YOU MOVE THEM.
I AM HERE TO DO THAT, MASTER. HE MIGHT SOIL HIS SLEEVES, OR OVERLY WEARY HIMSELF WORKING WITH BEASTS.
I kept my words deliberately formal.
THEN I WILL WALK ALONGSIDE YOU, IF I MAY. FOR I HAVE SOMETHING IMPORTANT WE MUST SPEAK OF.
...
BRING THE PRINCESS'S MARE AND THAT BAY FILLY. I WILL TAKE THE GRAYS.
THERE IS A PADDOCK THIS WAY.
COB, MIND THE REST FOR ME. I SHAN'T BE LONG.
We walked in silence. And for a moment or two, it almost seemed normal to work alongside Burrich again.
SHE'S A BEAUTY. FROM LORD RANGER'S STOCK?
YES.
YOU WISHED TO SPEAK TO ME.

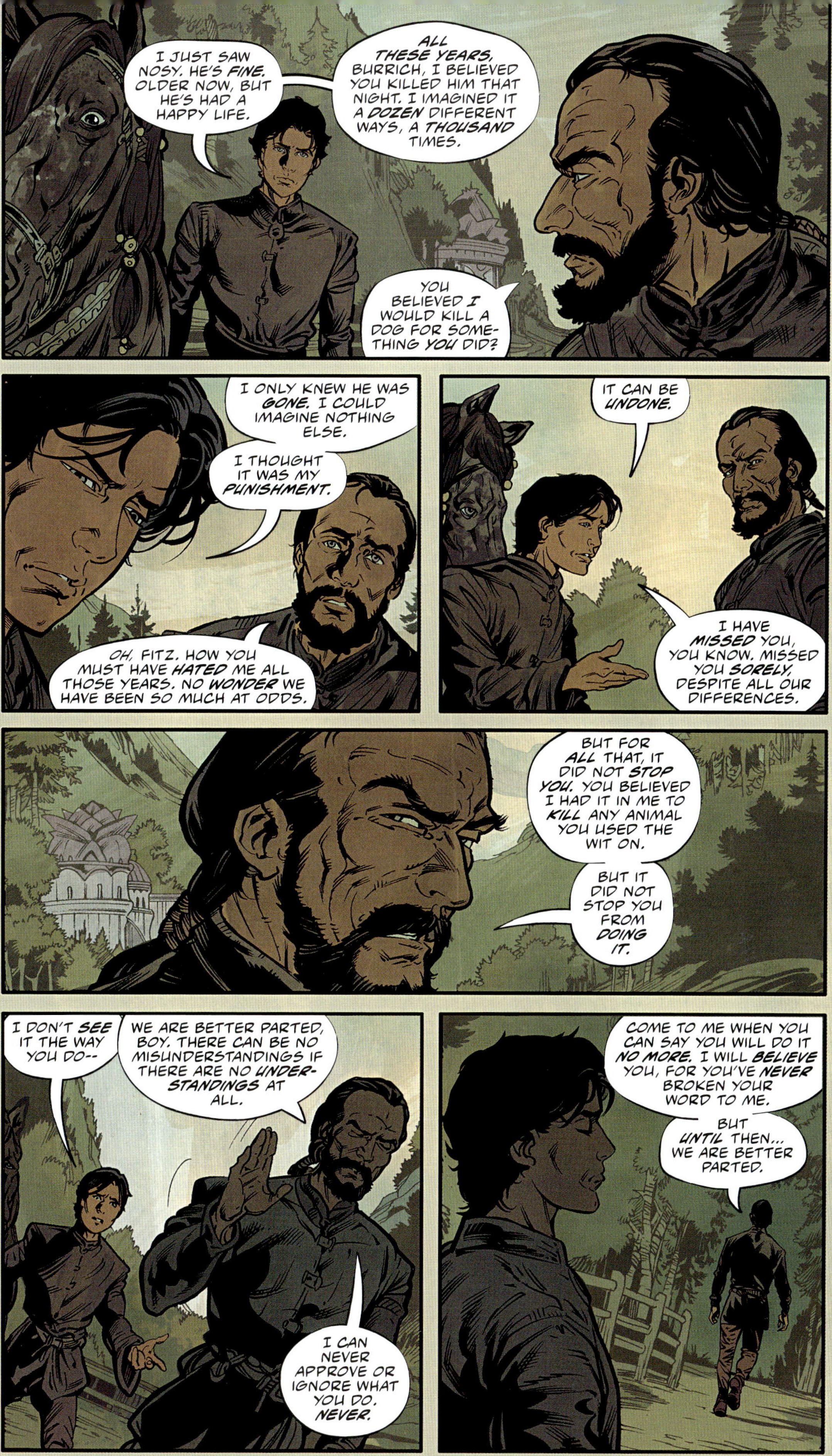

I JUST SAW NOSY. HE'S FINE. OLDER NOW, BUT HE'S HAD A HAPPY LIFE.
ALL THESE YEARS, BURRICH, I BELIEVED YOU KILLED HIM THAT NIGHT. I IMAGINED IT A DOZEN DIFFERENT WAYS, A THOUSAND TIMES.
YOU BELIEVED I WOULD KILL A DOG FOR SOMETHING YOU DID?
I ONLY KNEW HE WAS GONE. I COULD IMAGINE NOTHING ELSE.
I THOUGHT IT WAS MY PUNISHMENT.
OH, FITZ. HOW YOU MUST HAVE HATED ME ALL THOSE YEARS. NO WONDER WE HAVE BEEN SO MUCH AT ODDS.
IT CAN BE UNDONE.
I HAVE MISSED YOU, YOU KNOW. MISSED YOU SORELY, DESPITE ALL OUR DIFFERENCES.
BUT FOR ALL THAT, IT DID NOT STOP YOU. YOU BELIEVED I HAD IT IN ME TO KILL ANY ANIMAL YOU USED THE WIT ON.
BUT IT DID NOT STOP YOU FROM DOING IT.
I DON'T SEE IT THE WAY YOU DO--
WE ARE BETTER PARTED, BOY. THERE CAN BE NO MISUNDERSTANDINGS IF THERE ARE NO UNDERSTANDINGS AT ALL.
I CAN NEVER APPROVE OR IGNORE WHAT YOU DO. NEVER.
COME TO ME WHEN YOU CAN SAY YOU WILL DO IT NO MORE. I WILL BELIEVE YOU, FOR YOU'VE NEVER BROKEN YOUR WORD TO ME.
BUT UNTIL THEN... WE ARE BETTER PARTED.

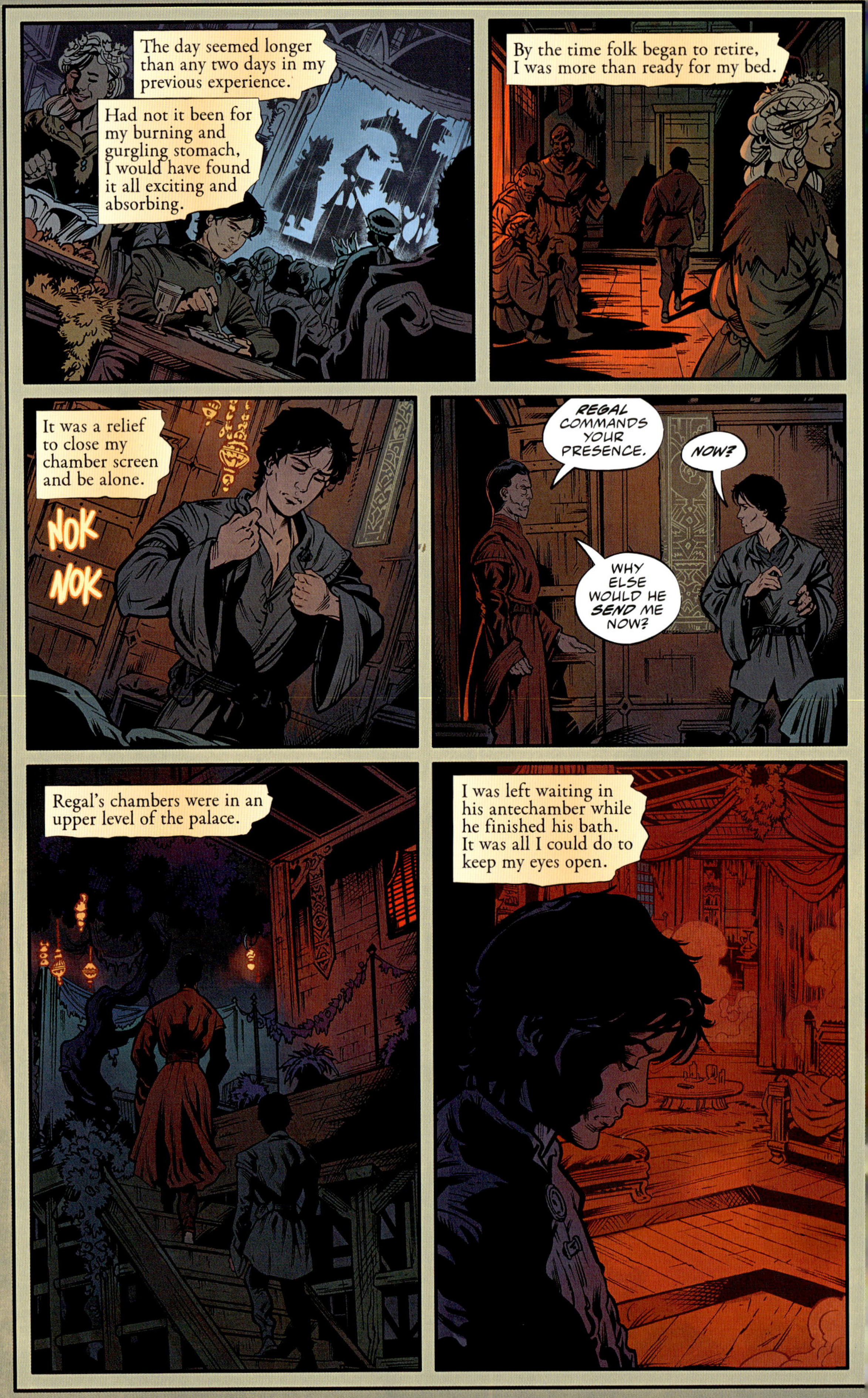
The day seemed longer than any two days in my previous experience.
Had not it been for my burning and gurgling stomach, I would have found it all exciting and absorbing.
By the time folk began to retire, I was more than ready for my bed.
It was a relief to close my chamber screen and be alone.
NOK NOK
REGAL COMMANDS YOUR PRESENCE.
NOW?
WHY ELSE WOULD HE SEND ME NOW?
Regal's chambers were in an upper level of the palace.
I was left waiting in his antechamber while he finished his bath. It was all I could do to keep my eyes open.

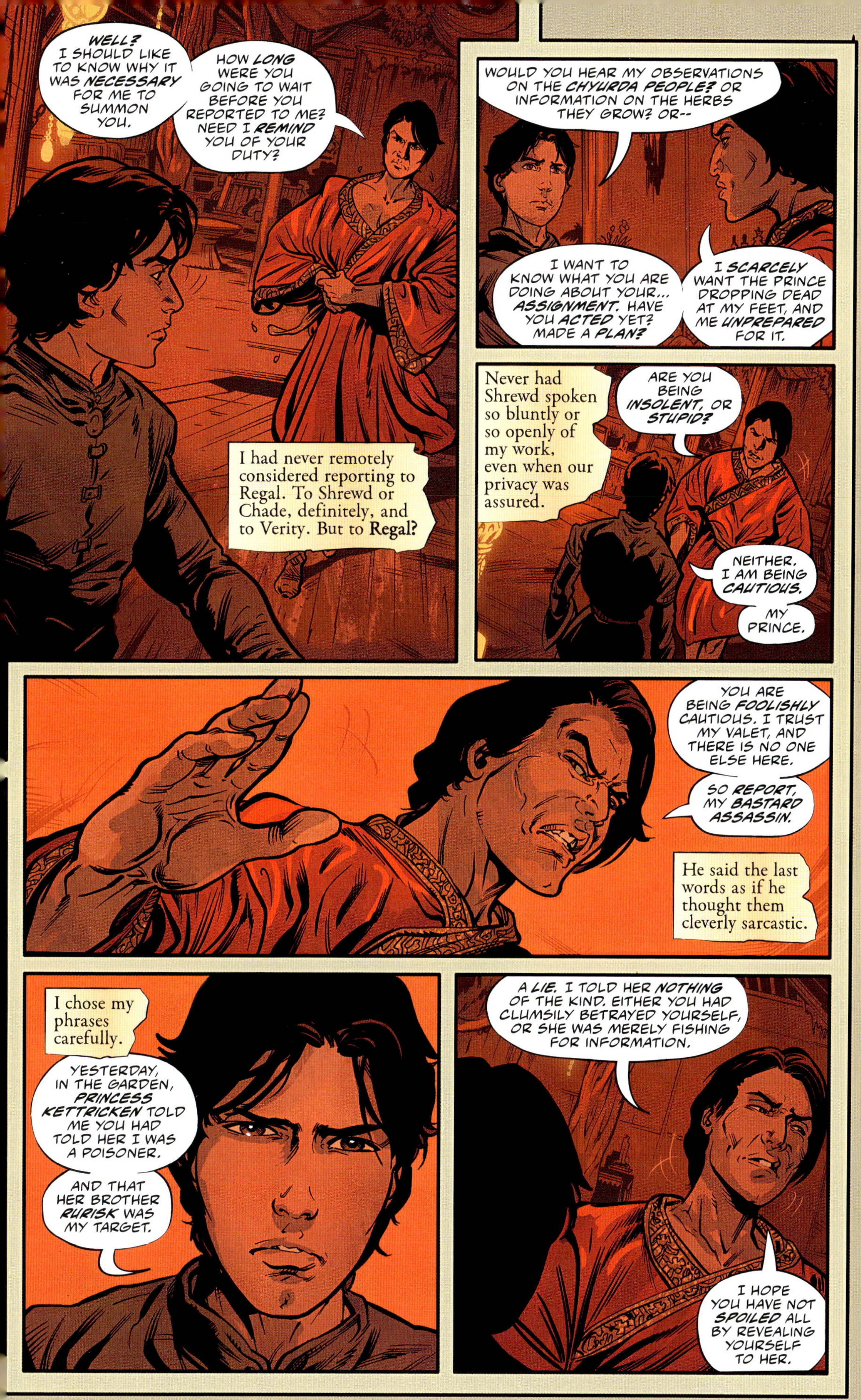
WELL? I SHOULD LIKE TO KNOW WHY IT WAS NECESSARY FOR ME TO SUMMON YOU.
HOW LONG WERE YOU GOING TO WAIT BEFORE YOU REPORTED TO ME? NEED I REMIND YOU OF YOUR DUTY?
I had never remotely considered reporting to Regal. To Shrewd or Chade, definitely, and to Verity. But to Regal?
WOULD YOU HEAR MY OBSERVATIONS ON THE CHYURDA PEOPLE? OR INFORMATION ON THE HERBS THEY GROW? OR--
I WANT TO KNOW WHAT YOU ARE DOING ABOUT YOUR... ASSIGNMENT. HAVE YOU ACTED YET? MADE A PLAN?
I SCARCELY WANT THE PRINCE DROPPING DEAD AT MY FEET, AND ME UNPREPARED FOR IT.
Never had Shrewd spoken so bluntly or so openly of my work, even when our privacy was assured.
ARE YOU BEING INSOLENT, OR STUPID?
NEITHER. I AM BEING CAUTIOUS.
MY PRINCE.
YOU ARE BEING FOOLISHLY CAUTIOUS. I TRUST MY VALET, AND THERE IS NO ONE ELSE HERE.
SO REPORT, MY BASTARD ASSASSIN.
He said the last words as if he thought them cleverly sarcastic.
I chose my phrases carefully.
YESTERDAY, IN THE GARDEN, PRINCESS KETTRICKEN TOLD ME YOU HAD TOLD HER I WAS A POISONER.
AND THAT HER BROTHER RURISK WAS MY TARGET.
A LIE. I TOLD HER NOTHING OF THE KIND. EITHER YOU HAD CLUMSILY BETRAYED YOURSELF, OR SHE WAS MERELY FISHING FOR INFORMATION.
I HOPE YOU HAVE NOT SPOILED ALL BY REVEALING YOURSELF TO HER.

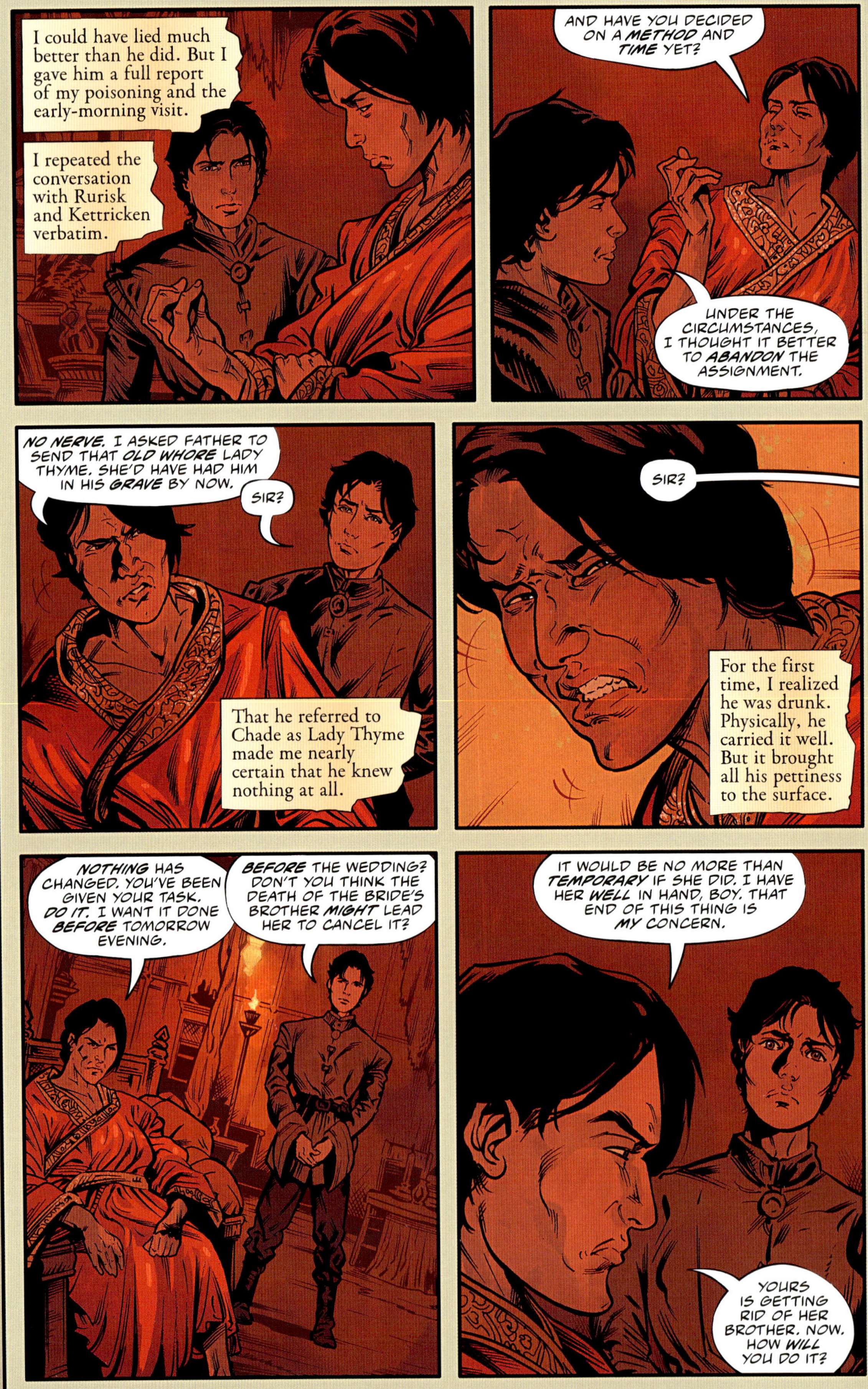
I could have lied much better than he did. But I gave him a full report of my poisoning and the early-morning visit.
I repeated the conversation with Rurisk and Kettricken verbatim.
AND HAVE YOU DECIDED ON A METHOD AND TIME YET?
UNDER THE CIRCUMSTANCES, I THOUGHT IT BETTER TO ABANDON THE ASSIGNMENT.
NO NERVE. I ASKED FATHER TO SEND THAT OLD WHORE LADY THYME. SHE'D HAVE HAD HIM IN HIS GRAVE BY NOW.
SIR?
That he referred to Chade as Lady Thyme made me nearly certain that he knew nothing at all.
SIR?
For the first time, I realized he was drunk. Physically, he carried it well. But it brought all his pettiness to the surface.
NOTHING HAS CHANGED. YOU'VE BEEN GIVEN YOUR TASK. DO IT. I WANT IT DONE BEFORE TOMORROW EVENING.
BEFORE THE WEDDING? DON'T YOU THINK THE DEATH OF THE BRIDE'S BROTHER MIGHT LEAD HER TO CANCEL IT?
IT WOULD BE NO MORE THAN TEMPORARY IF SHE DID. I HAVE HER WELL IN HAND, BOY. THAT END OF THIS THING IS MY CONCERN.
YOURS IS GETTING RID OF HER BROTHER. NOW. HOW WILL YOU DO IT?

I'VE NO IDEA. THESE THINGS CANNOT BE DONE RECKLESSLY OR SLOPPILY.
That seemed a better answer than saying I had no intention. I would return to Buckkeep and report to Shrewd and Chade.
If they said I had chosen wrongly, then they might do with me as they wished.
But I remembered Regal's own voice, from so long ago, quoting Shrewd.
DON'T DO WHAT YOU CAN'T UNDO, UNTIL YOU'VE CONSIDERED WHAT YOU CAN'T DO ONCE YOU'VE DONE IT.
I NEED TO STUDY THE MAN AND HIS HABITS, EXPLORE HIS CHAMBERS, LEARN THE HABITS OF HIS SERVANTS--
I ALREADY KNOW ALL OF THESE THINGS. EASIEST, THEN, FOR ME TO PLAN IT FOR YOU.
COME TO ME TOMORROW NIGHT, AND I WILL GIVE YOU YOUR ORDERS.
MIND THIS WELL, BASTARD. DO NOT ACT BEFORE YOU HAVE INFORMED ME. I WOULD FIND ANY SURPRISE UNPLEASANT. YOU WOULD FIND IT DEADLY.
YOU ARE DISMISSED. REPORT HERE TOMORROW NIGHT, AT THE SAME TIME. DO NOT MAKE ME SEND SEVRENS TO FETCH YOU.
MY FATHER WILL REGRET NOT SENDING BITCH THYME TO DO THIS LITTLE DEED.
I caught a whiff of wine, and a subtle smoke. I wondered if he was learning his mother's habits.
I returned to my chambers, intending to ponder carefully all my options and formulate a plan.

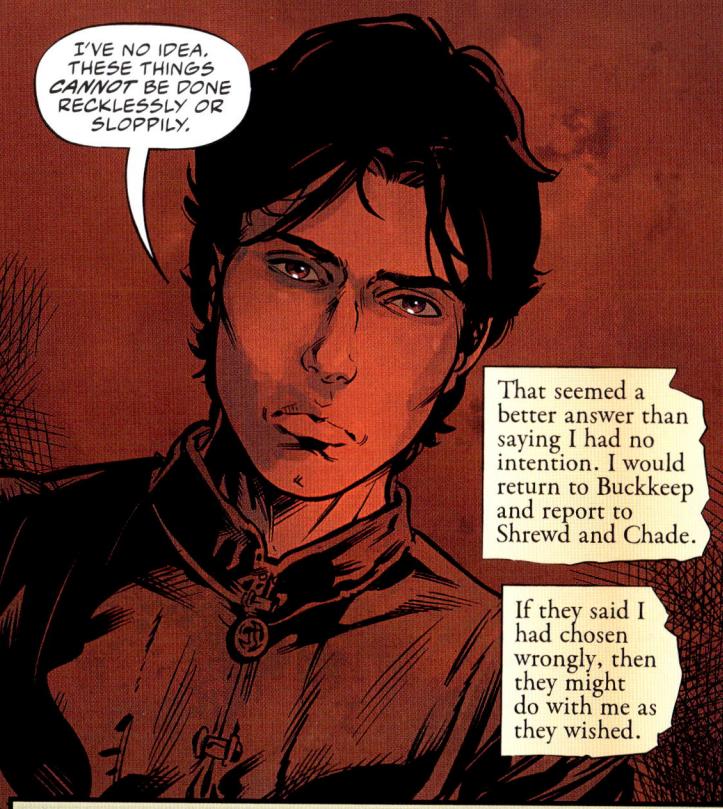

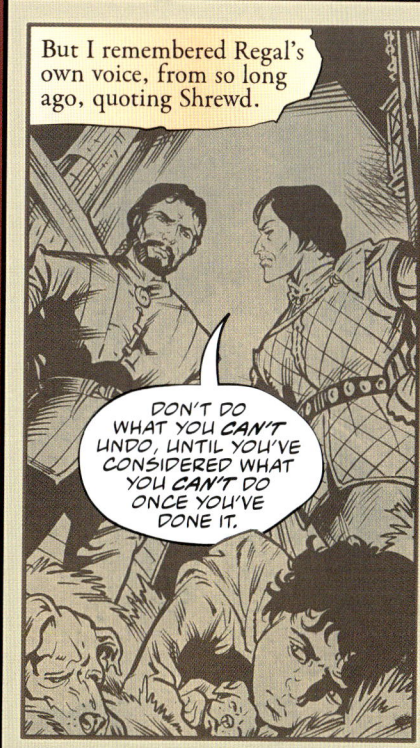

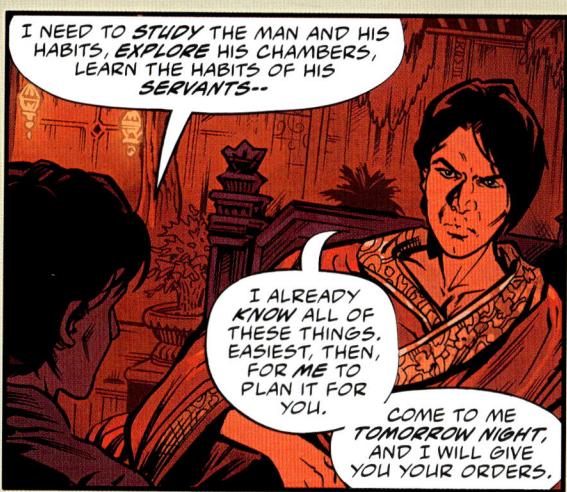

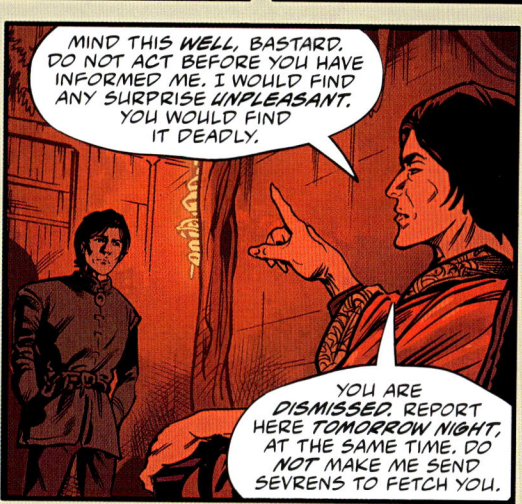

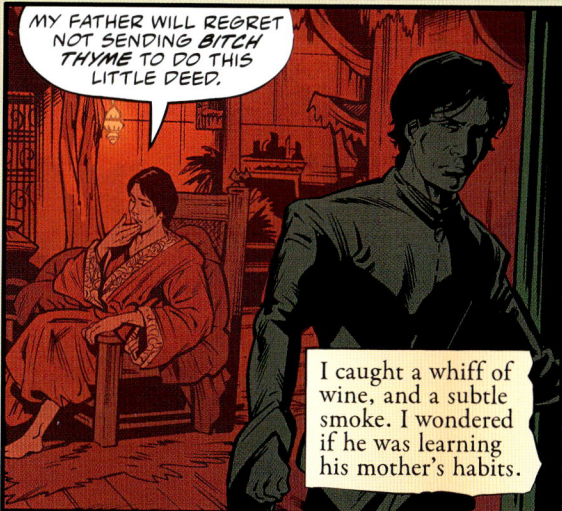

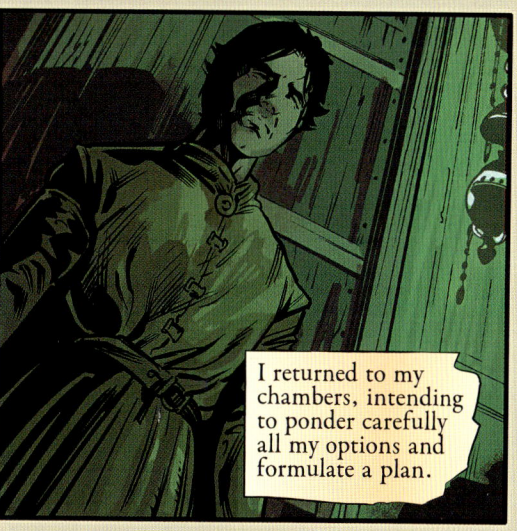

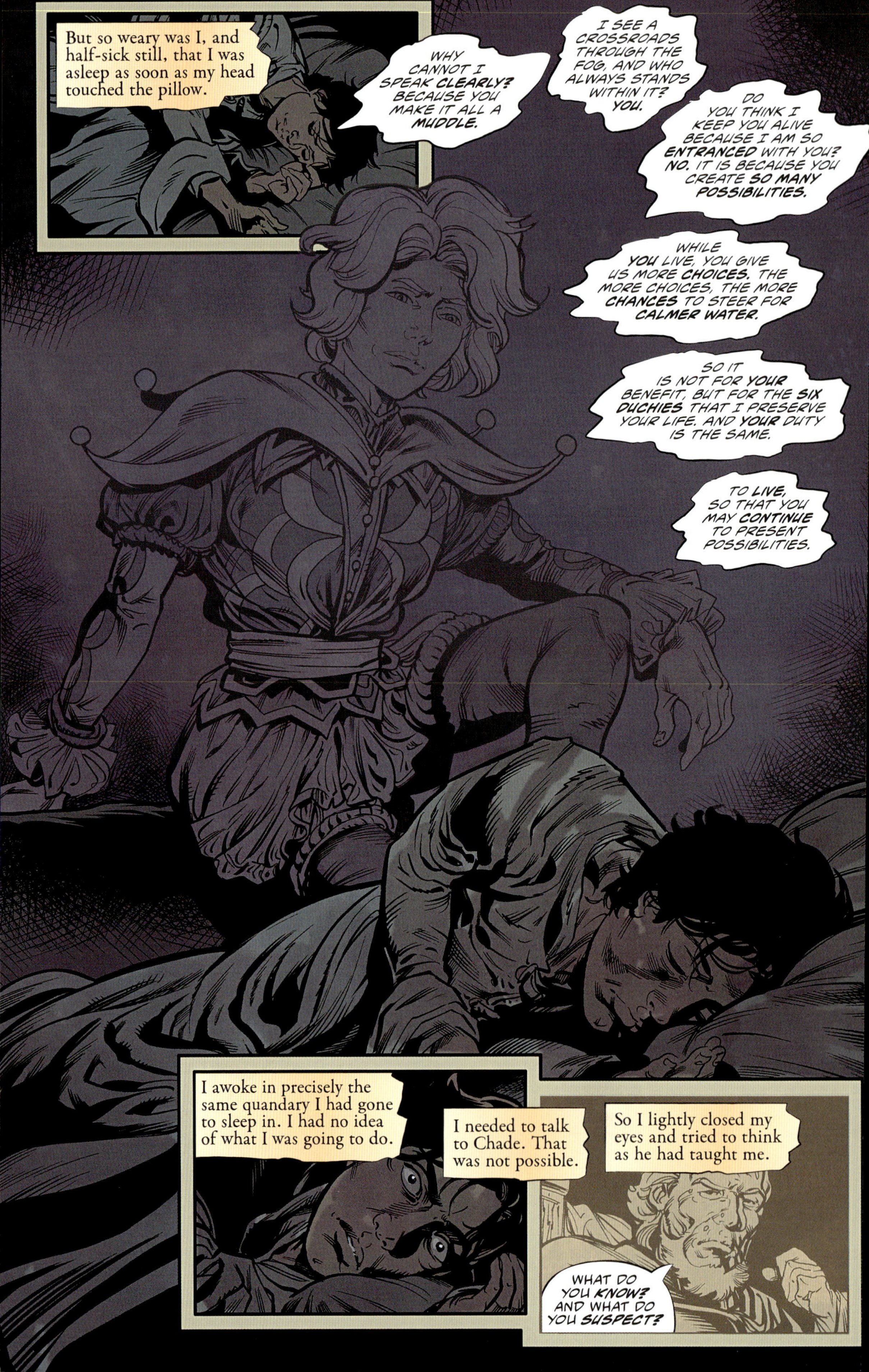
But so weary was I, and half-sick still, that I was asleep as soon as my head touched the pillow.
WHY CANNOT I SPEAK CLEARLY? BECAUSE YOU MAKE IT ALL A MUDDLE.
I SEE A CROSSROADS THROUGH THE FOG, AND WHO ALWAYS STANDS WITHIN IT? YOU.
DO YOU THINK I KEEP YOU ALIVE BECAUSE I AM SO ENTRANCED WITH YOU? NO. IT IS BECAUSE YOU CREATE SO MANY POSSIBILITIES.
WHILE YOU LIVE, YOU GIVE US MORE CHOICES. THE MORE CHOICES, THE MORE CHANCES TO STEER FOR CALMER WATER.
SO IT IS NOT FOR YOUR BENEFIT, BUT FOR THE SIX DUCHIES THAT I PRESERVE YOUR LIFE. AND YOUR DUTY IS THE SAME.
TO LIVE, SO THAT YOU MAY CONTINUE TO PRESENT POSSIBILITIES.
I awoke in precisely the same quandary I had gone to sleep in. I had no idea of what I was going to do.
I needed to talk to Chade. That was not possible.
So I lightly closed my eyes and tried to think as he had taught me.
WHAT DO YOU KNOW? AND WHAT DO YOU SUSPECT?

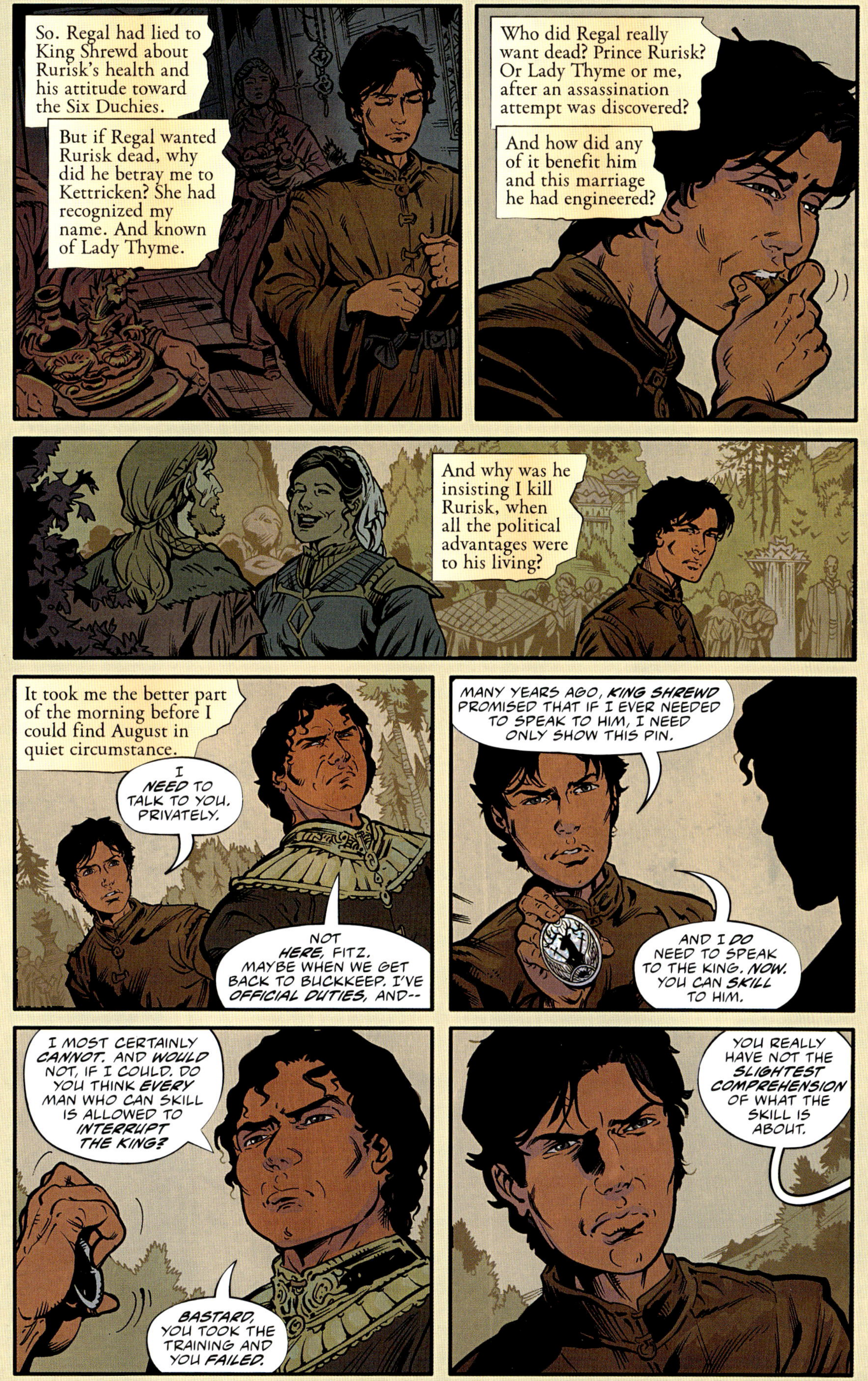
So. Regal had lied to King Shrewd about Rurisk's health and his attitude toward the Six Duchies.
But if Regal wanted Rurisk dead, why did he betray me to Kettricken? She had recognized my name. And known of Lady Thyme.
Who did Regal really want dead? Prince Rurisk? Or Lady Thyme or me, after an assassination attempt was discovered?
And how did any of it benefit him and this marriage he had engineered?
And why was he insisting I kill Rurisk, when all the political advantages were to his living?
It took me the better part of the morning before I could find August in quiet circumstance.
I NEED TO TALK TO YOU, PRIVATELY.
NOT HERE, FITZ. MAYBE WHEN WE GET BACK TO BUCKKEEP. I'VE OFFICIAL DUTIES, AND--
MANY YEARS AGO, KING SHREWD PROMISED THAT IF I EVER NEEDED TO SPEAK TO HIM, I NEED ONLY SHOW THIS PIN.
AND I DO NEED TO SPEAK TO THE KING. NOW. YOU CAN SKILL TO HIM.
I MOST CERTAINLY CANNOT. AND WOULD NOT, IF I COULD. DO YOU THINK EVERY MAN WHO CAN SKILL IS ALLOWED TO INTERRUPT THE KING?
BASTARD, YOU TOOK THE TRAINING AND YOU FAILED.
YOU REALLY HAVE NOT THE SLIGHTEST COMPREHENSION OF WHAT THE SKILL IS ABOUT.

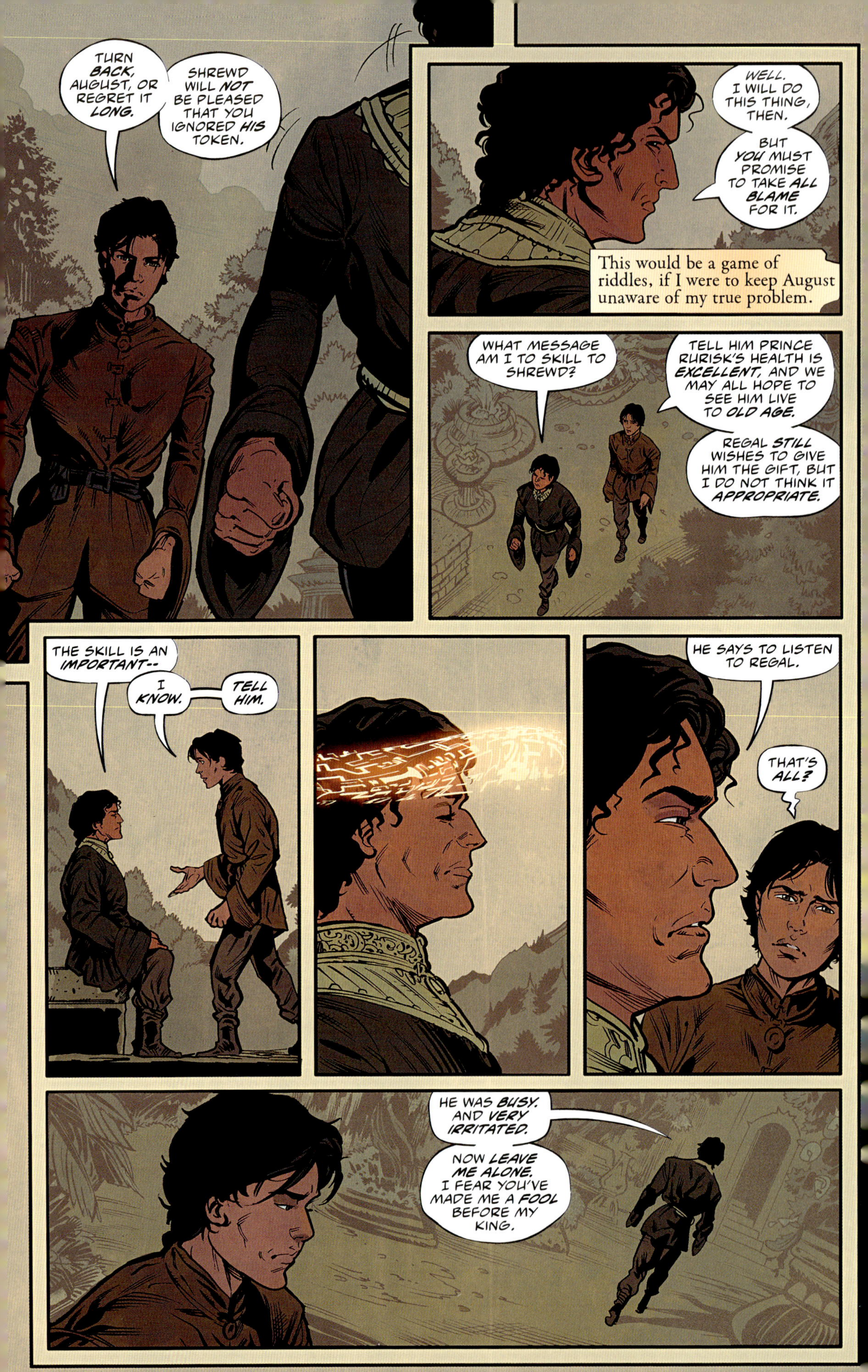

TURN BACK, AUGUST, OR REGRET IT LONG.
SHREWD WILL NOT BE PLEASED THAT YOU IGNORED HIS TOKEN.
WELL. I WILL DO THIS THING, THEN.
BUT YOU MUST PROMISE TO TAKE ALL BLAME FOR IT.
This would be a game of riddles, if I were to keep August unaware of my true problem.
WHAT MESSAGE AM I TO SKILL TO SHREWD?
TELL HIM PRINCE RURISK'S HEALTH IS EXCELLENT, AND WE MAY ALL HOPE TO SEE HIM LIVE TO OLD AGE.
REGAL STILL WISHES TO GIVE HIM THE GIFT, BUT I DO NOT THINK IT APPROPRIATE.
THE SKILL IS AN IMPORTANT--
I KNOW.
TELL HIM.
HE SAYS TO LISTEN TO REGAL.
THAT'S ALL?
HE WAS BUSY. AND VERY IRRITATED.
NOW LEAVE ME ALONE. I FEAR YOU'VE MADE ME A FOOL BEFORE MY KING.

That day, at noon, Kettricken formally announced that she was binding herself to the people of the Six Duchies.

From this moment hence, she was their Sacrifice, in all things, for any reason that they commanded it of her.

Tomorrow would be her day to pledge herself to Verity as a woman to a man.

Regal and August would stand beside her in Verity's stead, August Skilling so that Verity might see his bride make her vows.

The day dragged for me.

I did my best to be interested and pleasant when Jonqui took me to visit the Blue Fountains.

We returned to the palace for more feasting, and that evening's displays of arts by the mountain people.

Blue smoke was very much in evidence. I understood that it was a holiday indulgence. But I was unused to it.

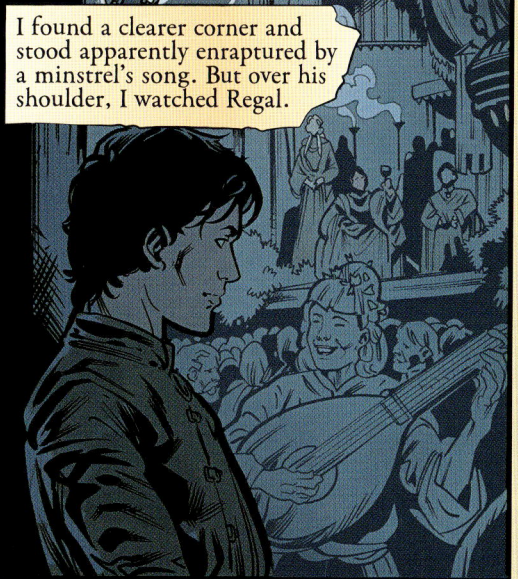

I found a clearer corner and stood apparently enraptured by a minstrel's song. But over his shoulder, I watched Regal.

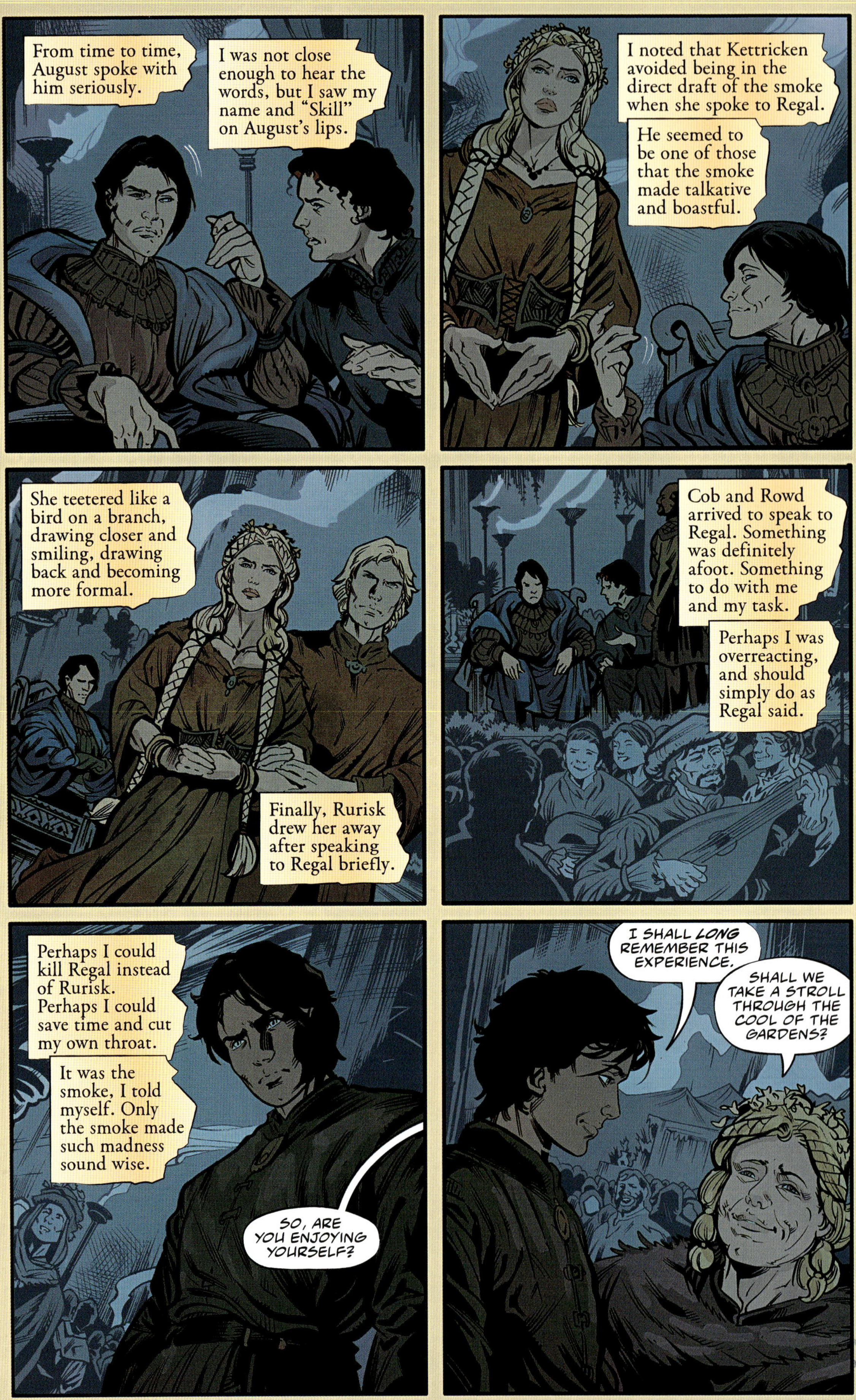
From time to time, August spoke with him seriously.
I was not close enough to hear the words, but I saw my name and "Skill" on August's lips.
I noted that Kettricken avoided being in the direct draft of the smoke when she spoke to Regal.
He seemed to be one of those that the smoke made talkative and boastful.
She teetered like a bird on a branch, drawing closer and smiling, drawing back and becoming more formal.
Finally, Rurisk drew her away after speaking to Regal briefly.
Cob and Rowd arrived to speak to Regal. Something was definitely afoot. Something to do with me and my task.
Perhaps I was overreacting, and should simply do as Regal said.
Perhaps I could kill Regal instead of Rurisk. Perhaps I could save time and cut my own throat.
It was the smoke, I told myself. Only the smoke made such madness sound wise.
SO, ARE YOU ENJOYING YOURSELF?
I SHALL LONG REMEMBER THIS EXPERIENCE.
SHALL WE TAKE A STROLL THROUGH THE COOL OF THE GARDENS?

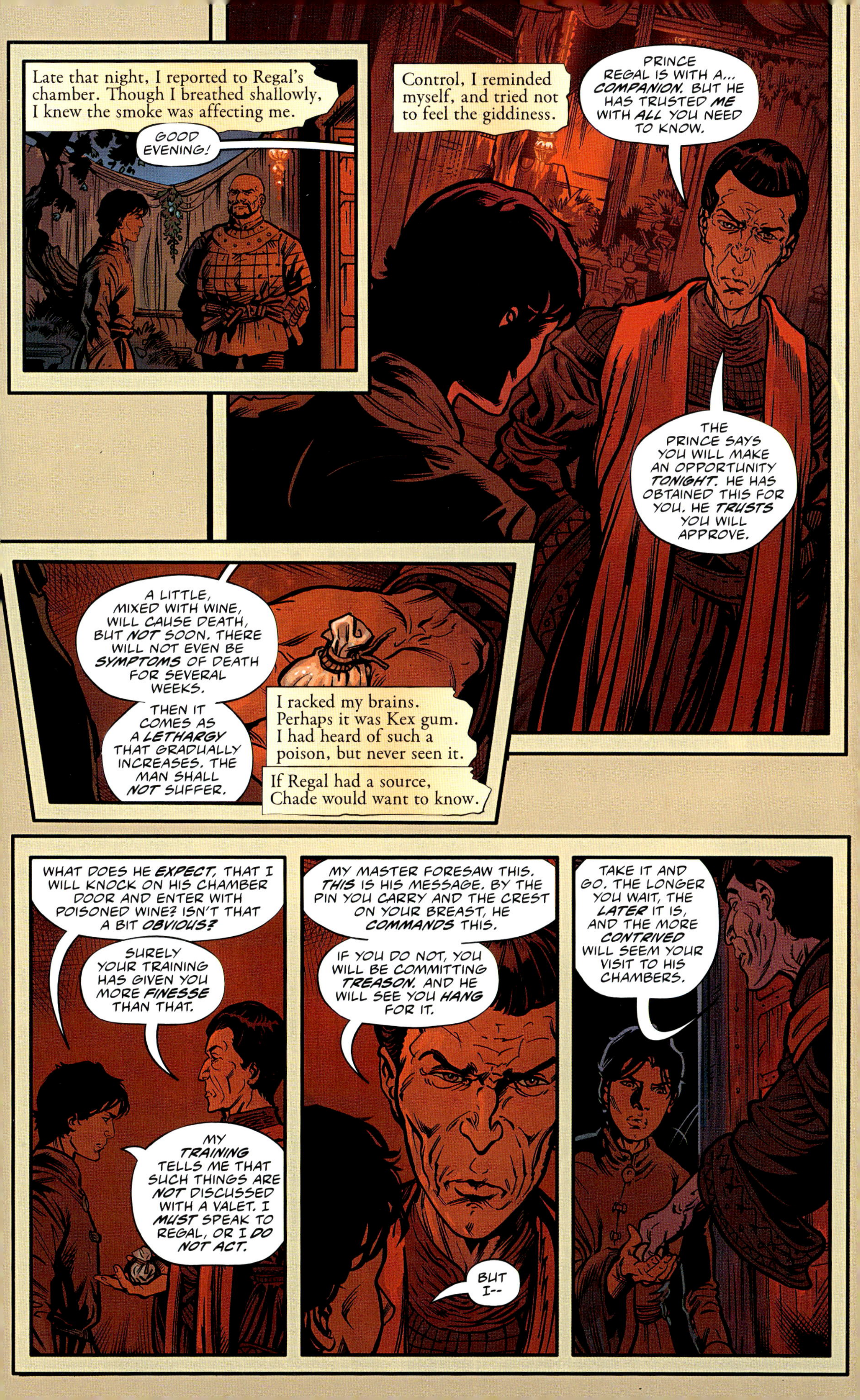

Late that night, I reported to Regal's chamber. Though I breathed shallowly, I knew the smoke was affecting me.
GOOD EVENING!
Control, I reminded myself, and tried not to feel the giddiness.
PRINCE REGAL IS WITH A... COMPANION. BUT HE HAS TRUSTED ME WITH ALL YOU NEED TO KNOW.
THE PRINCE SAYS YOU WILL MAKE AN OPPORTUNITY TONIGHT. HE HAS OBTAINED THIS FOR YOU. HE TRUSTS YOU WILL APPROVE.
A LITTLE, MIXED WITH WINE, WILL CAUSE DEATH, BUT NOT SOON. THERE WILL NOT EVEN BE SYMPTOMS OF DEATH FOR SEVERAL WEEKS.
THEN IT COMES AS A LETHARGY THAT GRADUALLY INCREASES. THE MAN SHALL NOT SUFFER.
I racked my brains. Perhaps it was Kex gum. I had heard of such a poison, but never seen it.
If Regal had a source, Chade would want to know.
WHAT DOES HE EXPECT, THAT I WILL KNOCK ON HIS CHAMBER DOOR AND ENTER WITH POISONED WINE? ISN'T THAT A BIT OBVIOUS?
SURELY YOUR TRAINING HAS GIVEN YOU MORE FINESSE THAN THAT.
MY TRAINING TELLS ME THAT SUCH THINGS ARE NOT DISCUSSED WITH A VALET. I MUST SPEAK TO REGAL, OR I DO NOT ACT.
MY MASTER FORESAW THIS. THIS IS HIS MESSAGE. BY THE PIN YOU CARRY AND THE CREST ON YOUR BREAST, HE COMMANDS THIS.
IF YOU DO NOT, YOU WILL BE COMMITTING TREASON. AND HE WILL SEE YOU HANG FOR IT.
BUT I--
TAKE IT AND GO. THE LONGER YOU WAIT, THE LATER IT IS, AND THE MORE CONTRIVED WILL SEEM YOUR VISIT TO HIS CHAMBERS.

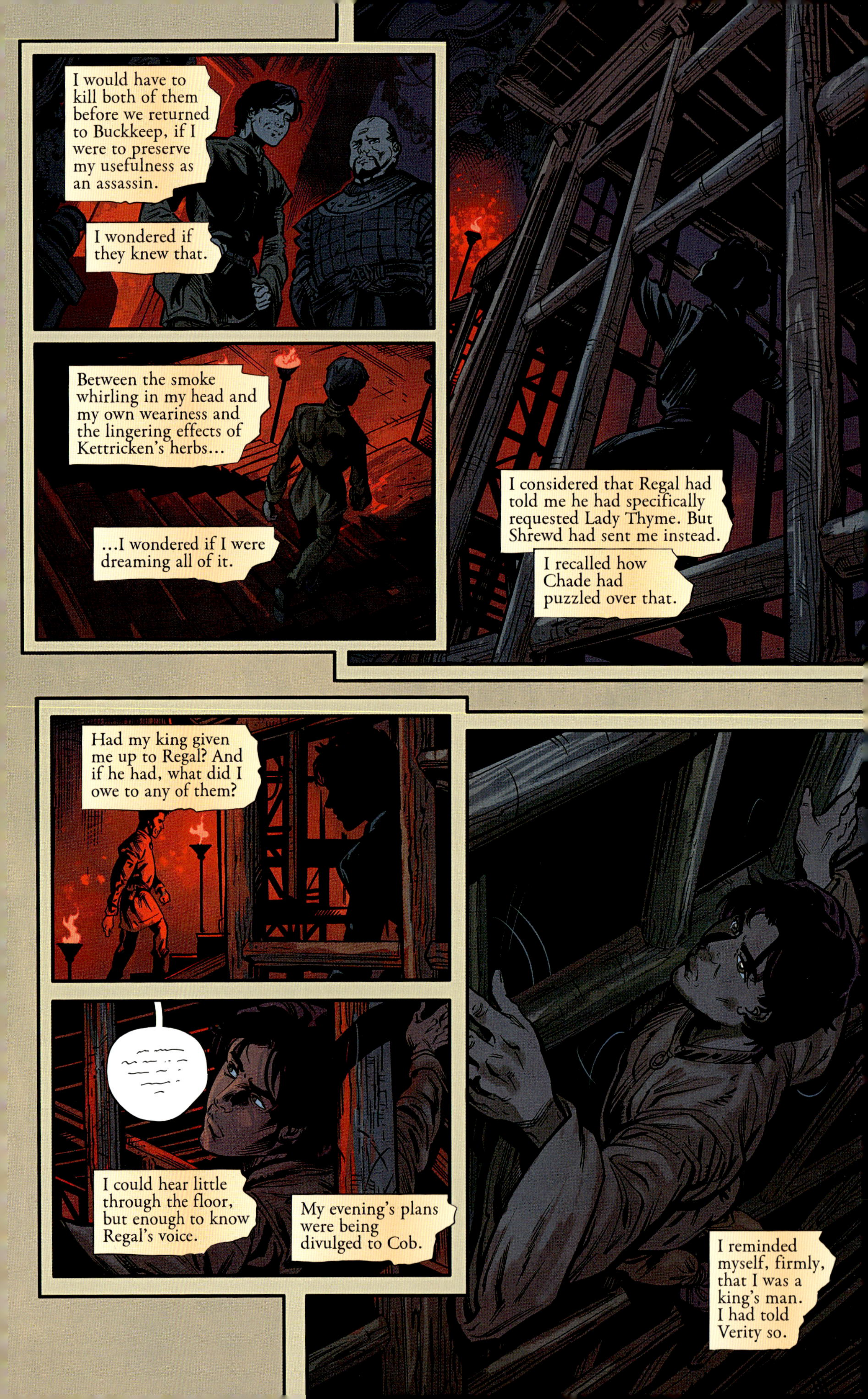
I would have to kill both of them before we returned to Buckkeep, if I were to preserve my usefulness as an assassin.
I wondered if they knew that.
Between the smoke whirling in my head and my own weariness and the lingering effects of Kettricken's herbs...
...I wondered if I were dreaming all of it.
I considered that Regal had told me he had specifically requested Lady Thyme. But Shrewd had sent me instead.
I recalled how Chade had puzzled over that.
Had my king given me up to Regal? And if he had, what did I owe to any of them?
I could hear little through the floor, but enough to know Regal's voice.
My evening's plans were being divulged to Cob.
I reminded myself, firmly, that I was a king's man. I had told Verity so.

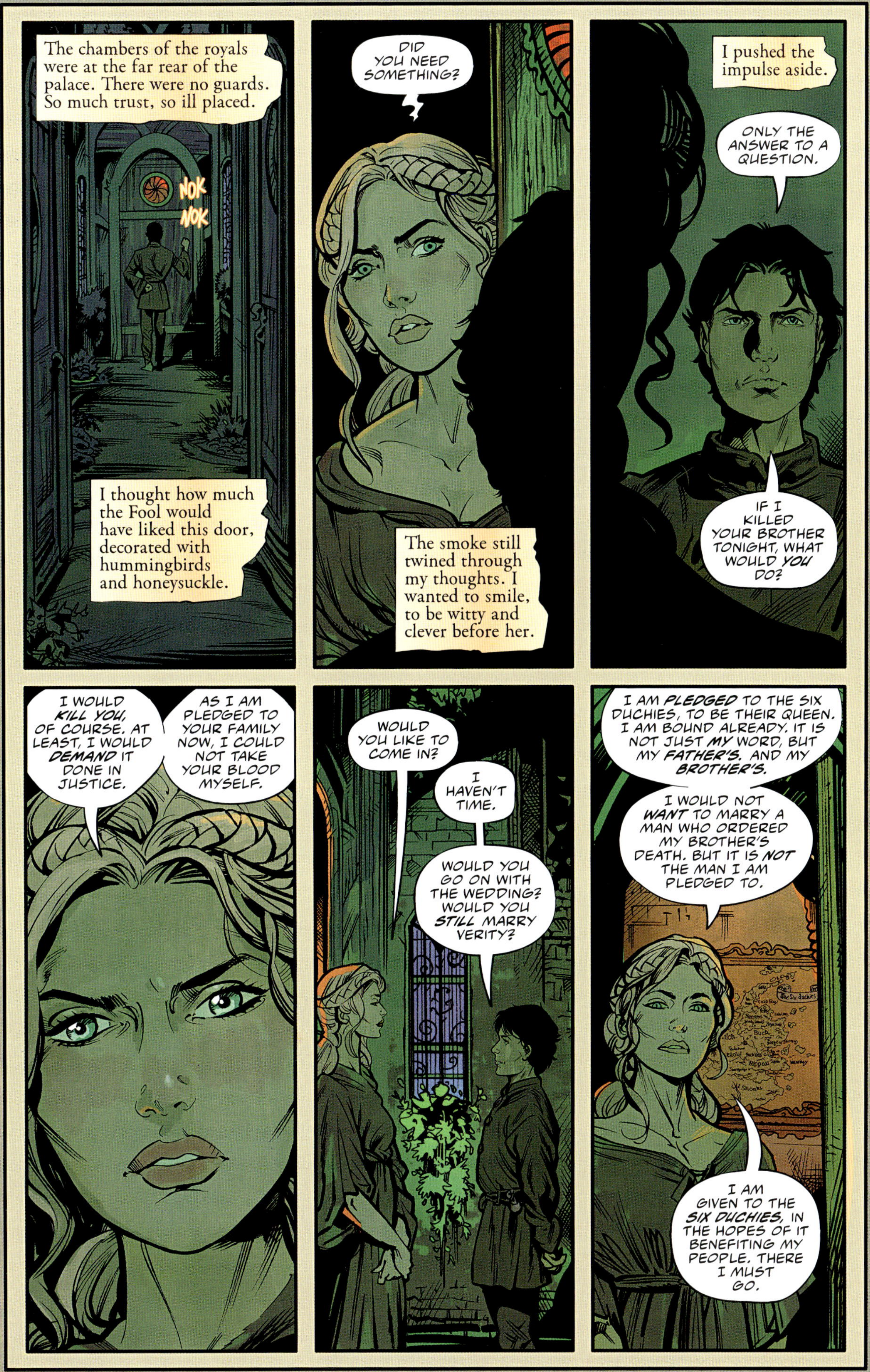
The chambers of the royals were at the far rear of the palace. There were no guards. So much trust, so ill placed.
NOK NOK
I thought how much the Fool would have liked this door, decorated with hummingbirds and honeysuckle.
DID YOU NEED SOMETHING?
The smoke still twined through my thoughts. I wanted to smile, to be witty and clever before her.
I pushed the impulse aside.
ONLY THE ANSWER TO A QUESTION.
IF I KILLED YOUR BROTHER TONIGHT, WHAT WOULD *YOU* DO?
I WOULD *KILL YOU,* OF COURSE. AT LEAST, I WOULD *DEMAND* IT DONE IN JUSTICE.
AS I AM PLEDGED TO YOUR FAMILY NOW, I COULD NOT TAKE YOUR BLOOD MYSELF.
WOULD YOU LIKE TO COME IN?
I HAVEN'T TIME.
WOULD YOU GO ON WITH THE WEDDING? WOULD YOU *STILL* MARRY VERITY?
I AM *PLEDGED* TO THE SIX DUCHIES, TO BE THEIR QUEEN. I AM BOUND ALREADY. IT IS NOT JUST *MY* WORD, BUT MY *FATHER'S*. AND MY *BROTHER'S*.
I WOULD NOT *WANT* TO MARRY A MAN WHO ORDERED MY BROTHER'S DEATH. BUT IT IS *NOT* THE MAN I AM PLEDGED TO.
I AM GIVEN TO THE *SIX DUCHIES*, IN THE HOPES OF IT BENEFITING MY PEOPLE. THERE I MUST GO.

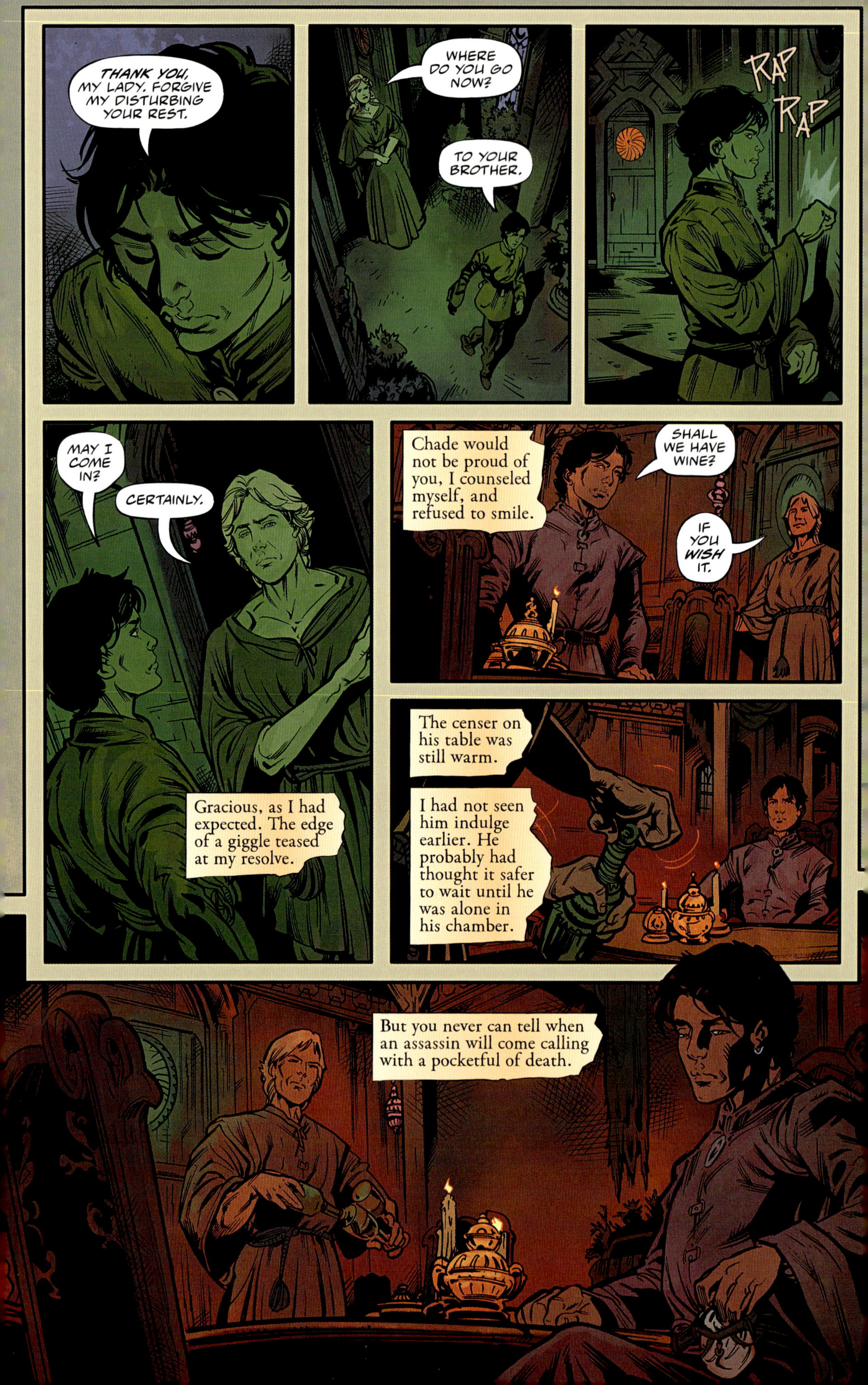
THANK YOU, MY LADY. FORGIVE MY DISTURBING YOUR REST.
WHERE DO YOU GO NOW?
TO YOUR BROTHER.
RAP
RAP
MAY I COME IN?
CERTAINLY.
Gracious, as I had expected. The edge of a giggle teased at my resolve.
Chade would not be proud of you, I counseled myself, and refused to smile.
SHALL WE HAVE WINE?
IF YOU WISH IT.
The censer on his table was still warm.
I had not seen him indulge earlier. He probably had thought it safer to wait until he was alone in his chamber.
But you never can tell when an assassin will come calling with a pocketful of death.

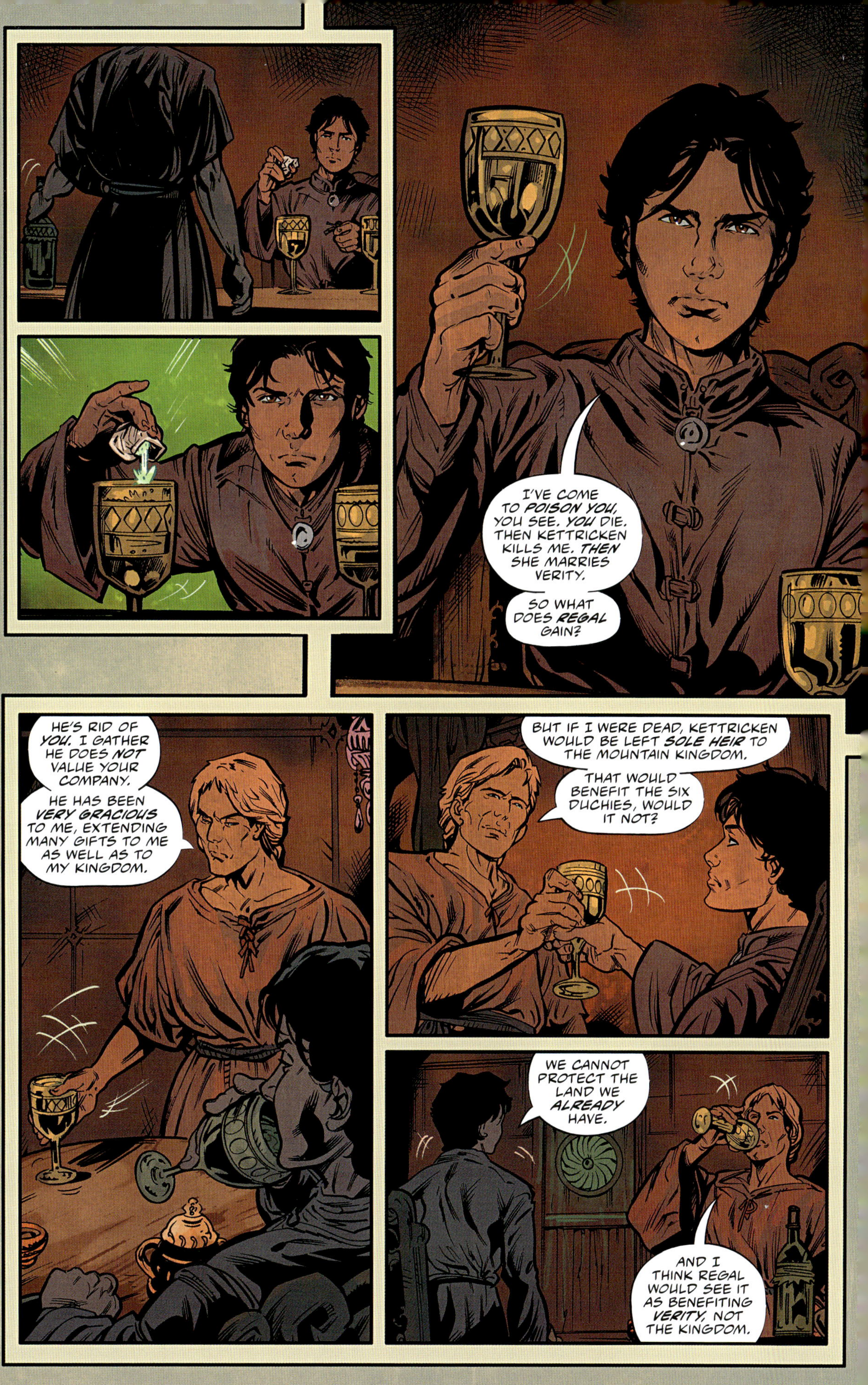
I'VE COME TO POISON YOU, YOU SEE. YOU DIE. THEN KETTRICKEN KILLS ME. THEN SHE MARRIES VERITY.
SO WHAT DOES REGAL GAIN?
HE'S RID OF YOU. I GATHER HE DOES NOT VALUE YOUR COMPANY.
HE HAS BEEN VERY GRACIOUS TO ME, EXTENDING MANY GIFTS TO ME AS WELL AS TO MY KINGDOM.
BUT IF I WERE DEAD, KETTRICKEN WOULD BE LEFT SOLE HEIR TO THE MOUNTAIN KINGDOM.
THAT WOULD BENEFIT THE SIX DUCHIES, WOULD IT NOT?
WE CANNOT PROTECT THE LAND WE ALREADY HAVE.
AND I THINK REGAL WOULD SEE IT AS BENEFITING VERITY, NOT THE KINGDOM.

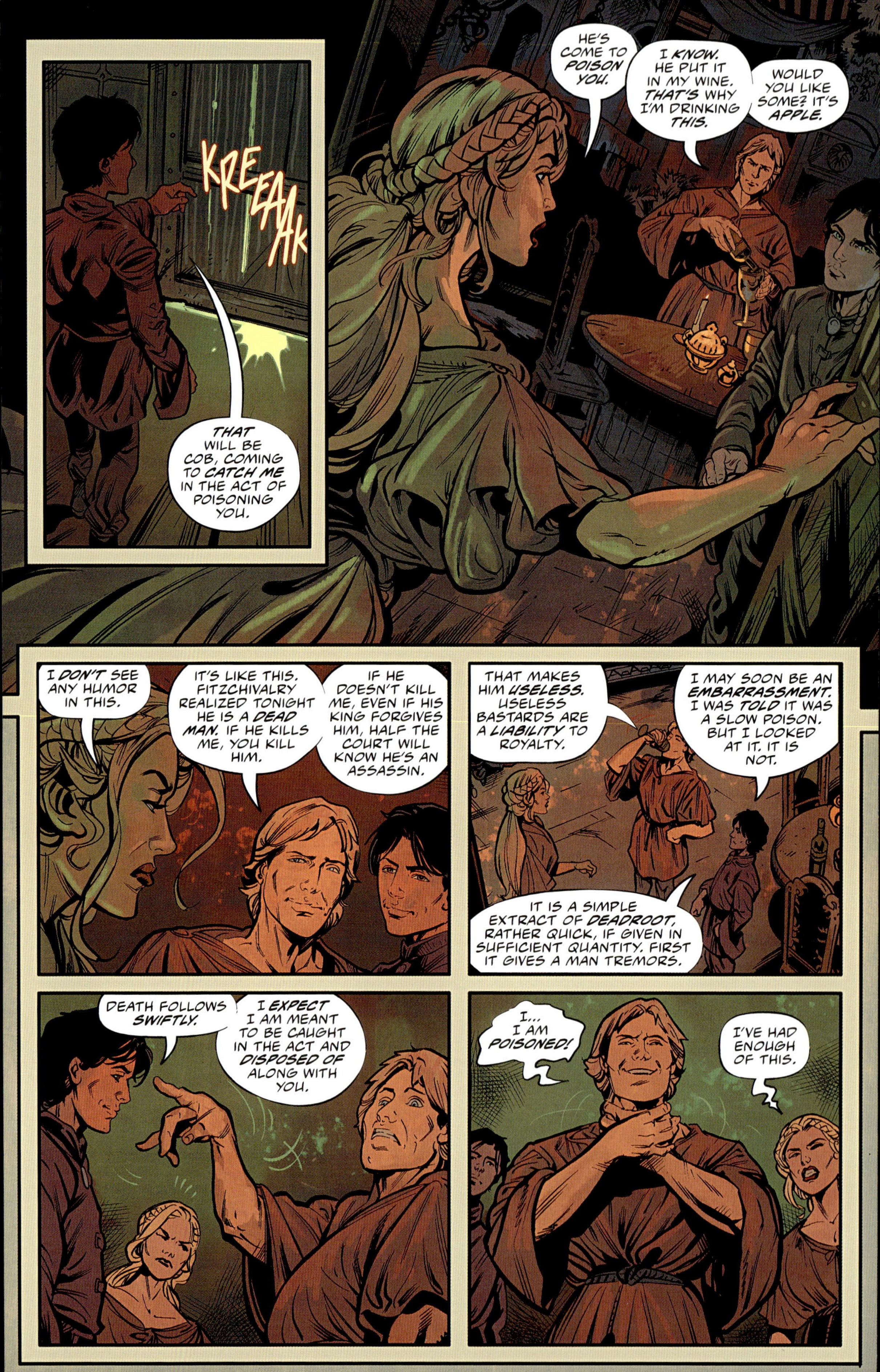
KREEAAK
THAT WILL BE COB, COMING TO CATCH ME IN THE ACT OF POISONING YOU.
HE'S COME TO POISON YOU.
I KNOW. HE PUT IT IN MY WINE. THAT'S WHY I'M DRINKING THIS.
WOULD YOU LIKE SOME? IT'S APPLE.
I DON'T SEE ANY HUMOR IN THIS.
IT'S LIKE THIS. FITZCHIVALRY REALIZED TONIGHT HE IS A DEAD MAN. IF HE KILLS ME, YOU KILL HIM.
IF HE DOESN'T KILL ME, EVEN IF HIS KING FORGIVES HIM, HALF THE COURT WILL KNOW HE'S AN ASSASSIN.
THAT MAKES HIM USELESS. USELESS BASTARDS ARE A LIABILITY TO ROYALTY.
I MAY SOON BE AN EMBARRASSMENT. I WAS TOLD IT WAS A SLOW POISON. BUT I LOOKED AT IT. IT IS NOT.
IT IS A SIMPLE EXTRACT OF DEADROOT, RATHER QUICK, IF GIVEN IN SUFFICIENT QUANTITY. FIRST IT GIVES A MAN TREMORS.
DEATH FOLLOWS SWIFTLY.
I EXPECT I AM MEANT TO BE CAUGHT IN THE ACT AND DISPOSED OF ALONG WITH YOU.
I... I AM POISONED!
I'VE HAD ENOUGH OF THIS.

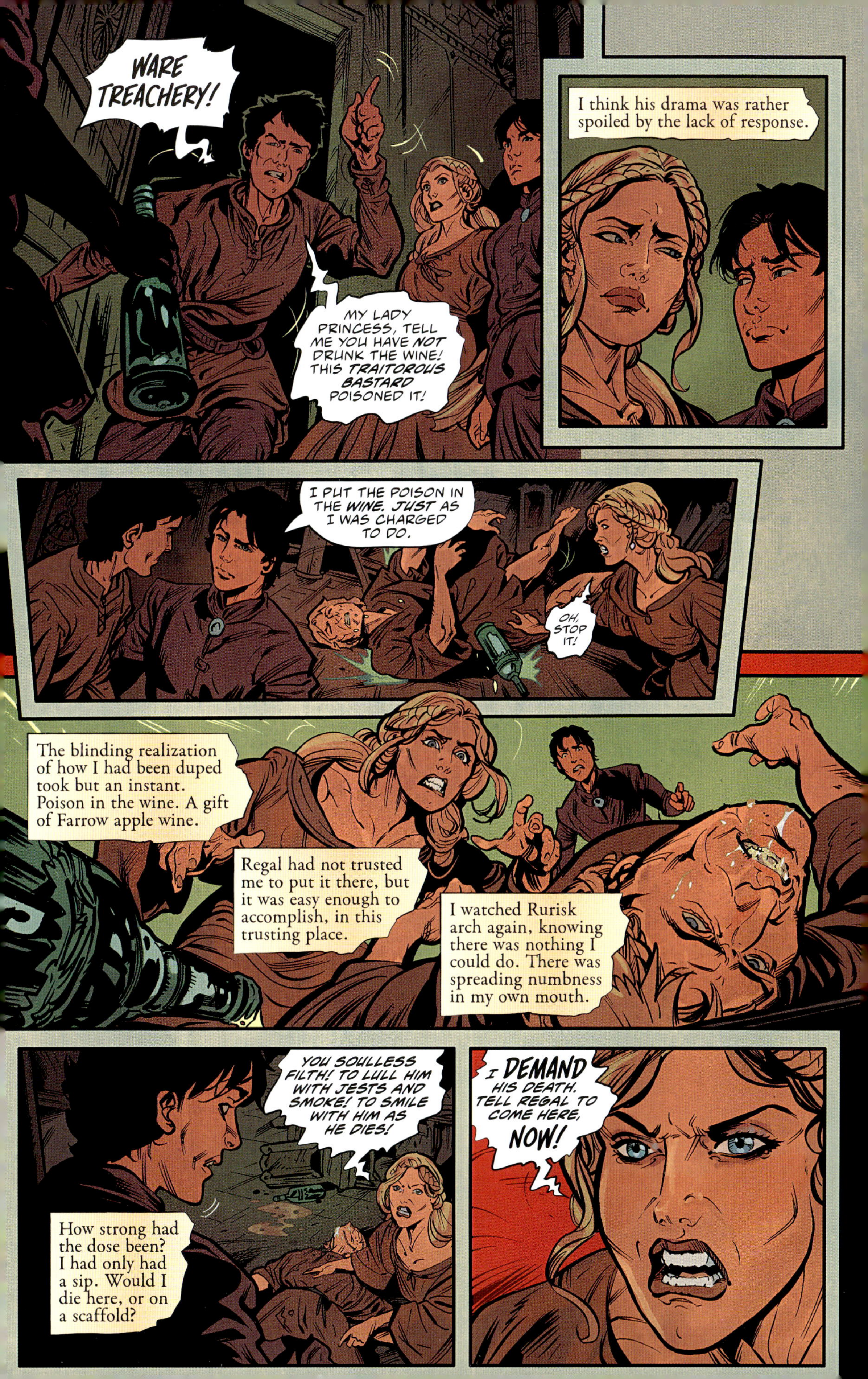

WARE TREACHERY!
MY LADY PRINCESS, TELL ME YOU HAVE NOT DRUNK THE WINE! THIS TRAITOROUS BASTARD POISONED IT!
I think his drama was rather spoiled by the lack of response.
I PUT THE POISON IN THE WINE, JUST AS I WAS CHARGED TO DO.
OH, STOP IT!
The blinding realization of how I had been duped took but an instant. Poison in the wine. A gift of Farrow apple wine.
Regal had not trusted me to put it there, but it was easy enough to accomplish, in this trusting place.
I watched Rurisk arch again, knowing there was nothing I could do. There was spreading numbness in my own mouth.
YOU SOULLESS FILTH! TO LULL HIM WITH JESTS AND SMOKE! TO SMILE WITH HIM AS HE DIES!
How strong had the dose been? I had only had a sip. Would I die here, or on a scaffold?
I DEMAND HIS DEATH. TELL REGAL TO COME HERE, NOW!

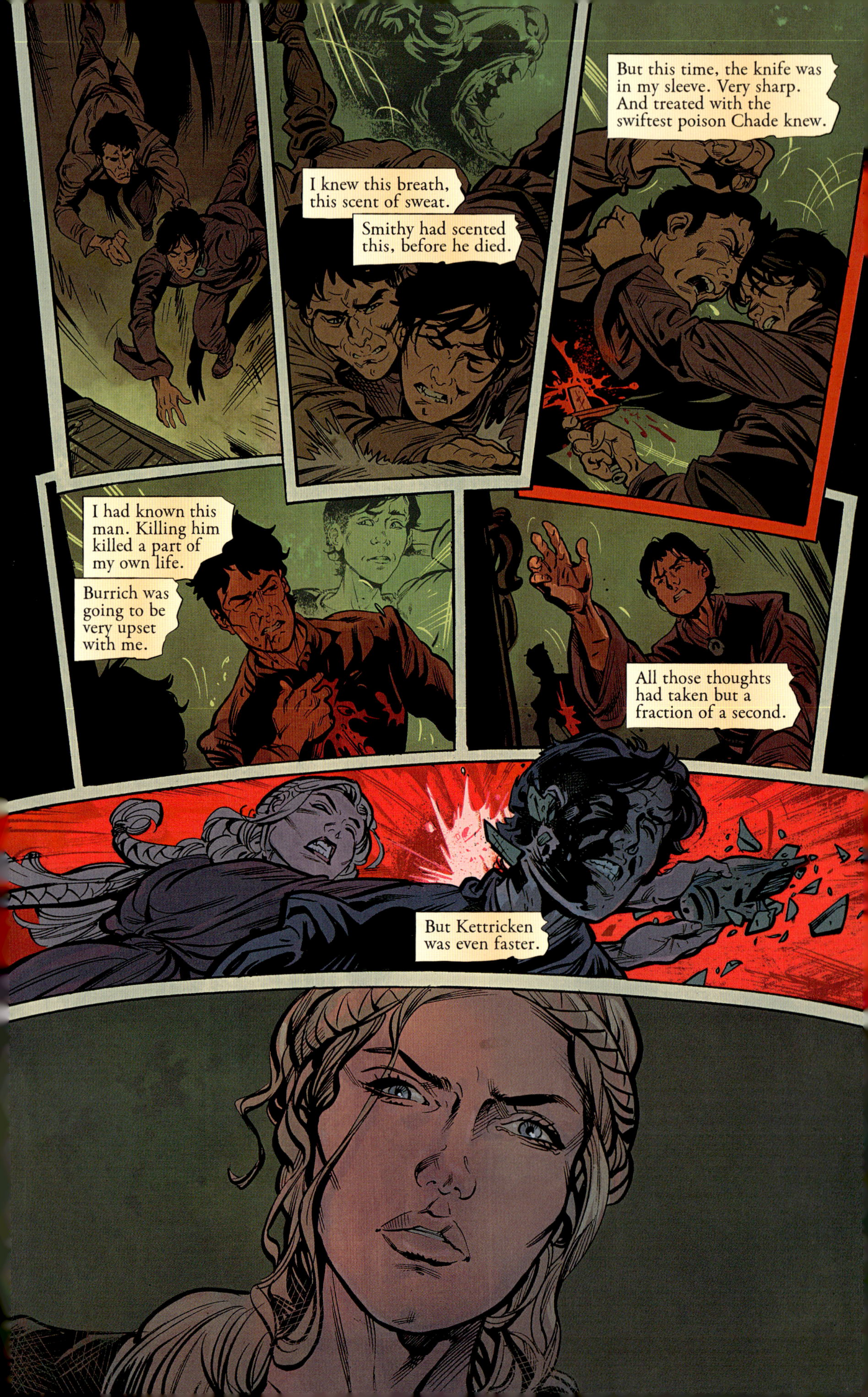

I knew this breath, this scent of sweat.
Smithy had scented this, before he died.
But this time, the knife was in my sleeve. Very sharp. And treated with the swiftest poison Chade knew.
I had known this man. Killing him killed a part of my own life.
Burrich was going to be very upset with me.
All those thoughts had taken but a fraction of a second.
But Kettricken was even faster.

Chapter Six

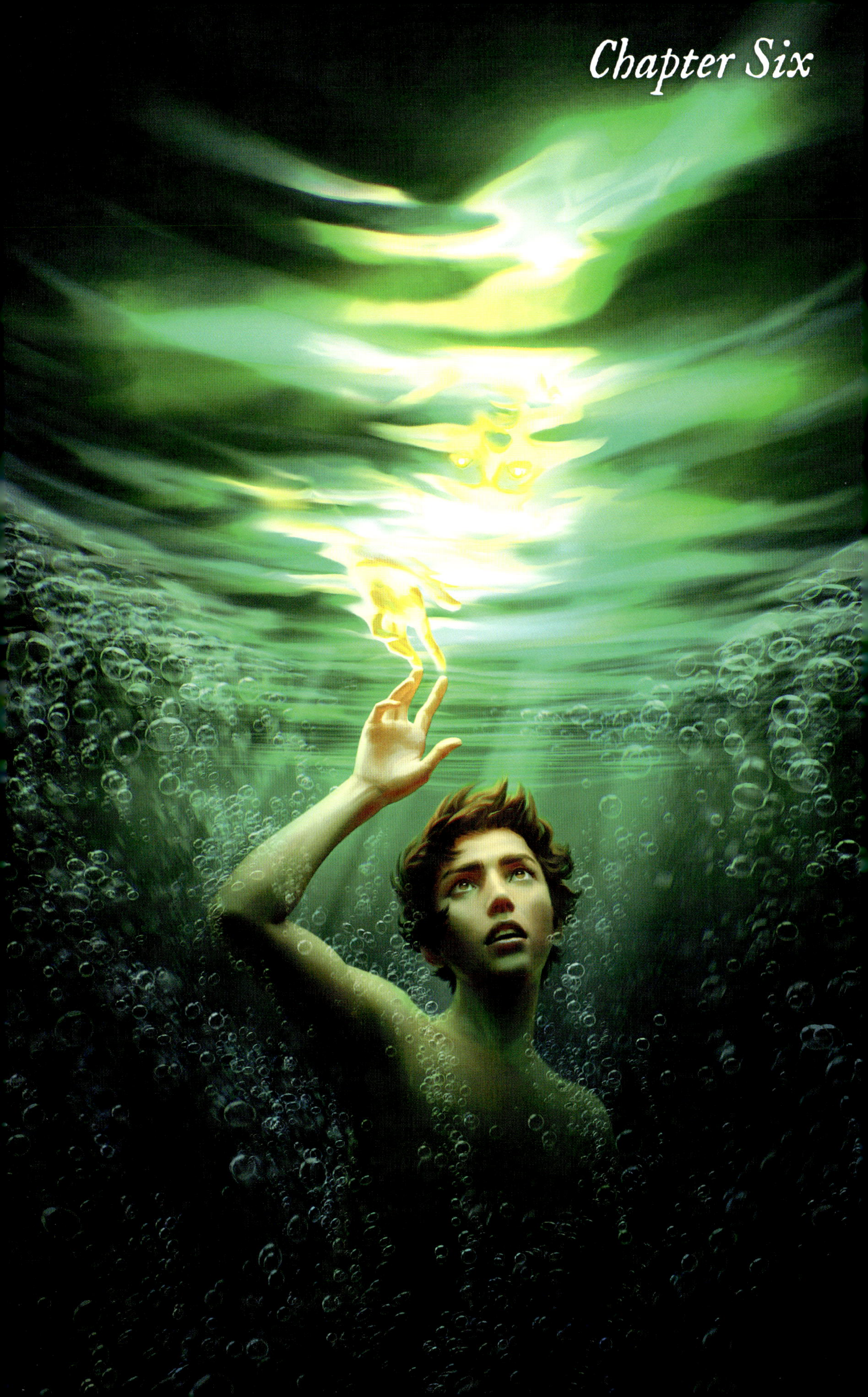

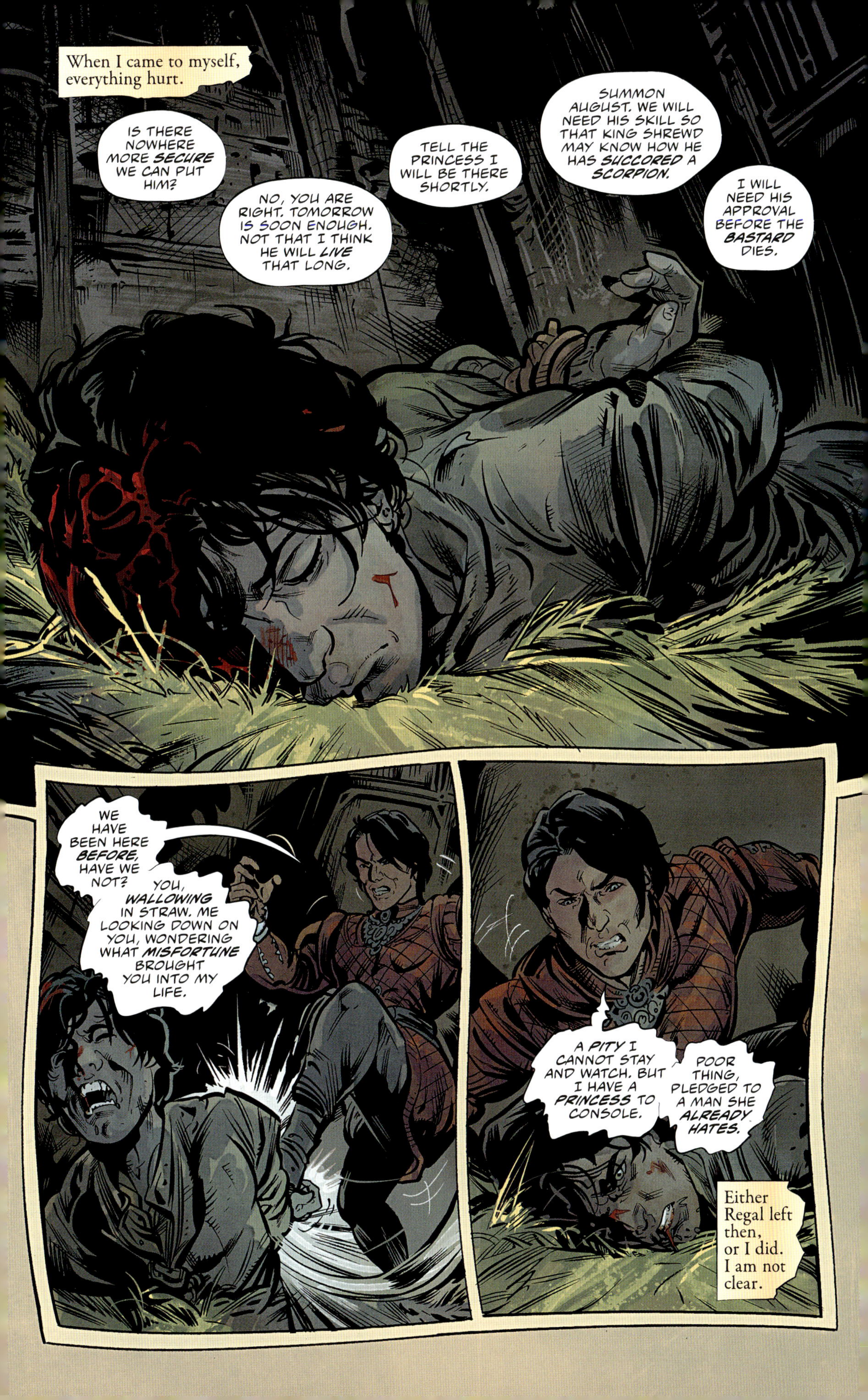
When I came to myself, everything hurt.
IS THERE NOWHERE MORE SECURE WE CAN PUT HIM?
NO, YOU ARE RIGHT. TOMORROW IS SOON ENOUGH. NOT THAT I THINK HE WILL LIVE THAT LONG.
TELL THE PRINCESS I WILL BE THERE SHORTLY.
SUMMON AUGUST. WE WILL NEED HIS SKILL SO THAT KING SHREWD MAY KNOW HOW HE HAS SUCCORED A SCORPION.
I WILL NEED HIS APPROVAL BEFORE THE BASTARD DIES.
WE HAVE BEEN HERE BEFORE, HAVE WE NOT?
YOU, WALLOWING IN STRAW. ME LOOKING DOWN ON YOU, WONDERING WHAT MISFORTUNE BROUGHT YOU INTO MY LIFE.
A PITY I CANNOT STAY AND WATCH. BUT I HAVE A PRINCESS TO CONSOLE.
POOR THING, PLEDGED TO A MAN SHE ALREADY HATES.
Either Regal left then, or I did. I am not clear.

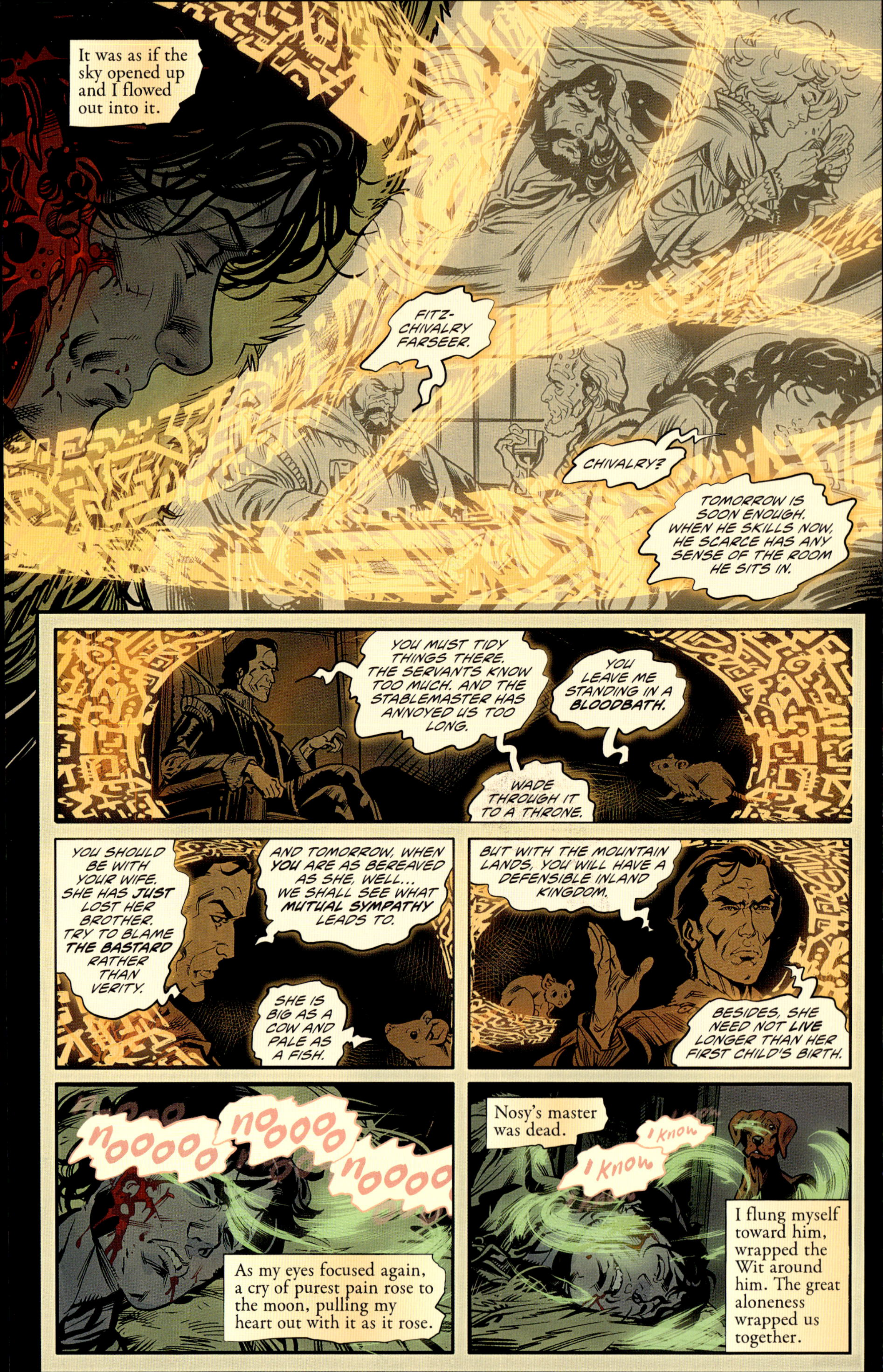

It was as if the sky opened up and I flowed out into it.
FITZ-CHIVALRY FARSEER.
CHIVALRY?
TOMORROW IS SOON ENOUGH. WHEN HE SKILLS NOW, HE SCARCE HAS ANY SENSE OF THE ROOM HE SITS IN.
YOU MUST TIDY THINGS THERE. THE SERVANTS KNOW TOO MUCH. AND THE STABLEMASTER HAS ANNOYED US TOO LONG.
YOU LEAVE ME STANDING IN A BLOODBATH.
WADE THROUGH IT TO A THRONE.
YOU SHOULD BE WITH YOUR WIFE. SHE HAS JUST LOST HER BROTHER. TRY TO BLAME THE BASTARD RATHER THAN VERITY.
AND TOMORROW, WHEN YOU ARE AS BEREAVED AS SHE, WELL... WE SHALL SEE WHAT MUTUAL SYMPATHY LEADS TO.
SHE IS BIG AS A COW AND PALE AS A FISH.
BUT WITH THE MOUNTAIN LANDS, YOU WILL HAVE A DEFENSIBLE INLAND KINGDOM.
BESIDES, SHE NEED NOT LIVE LONGER THAN HER FIRST CHILD'S BIRTH.
nooooo noooo nooooo
As my eyes focused again, a cry of purest pain rose to the moon, pulling my heart out with it as it rose.
Nosy's master was dead.
I know
I know
I flung myself toward him, wrapped the Wit around him. The great aloneness wrapped us together.

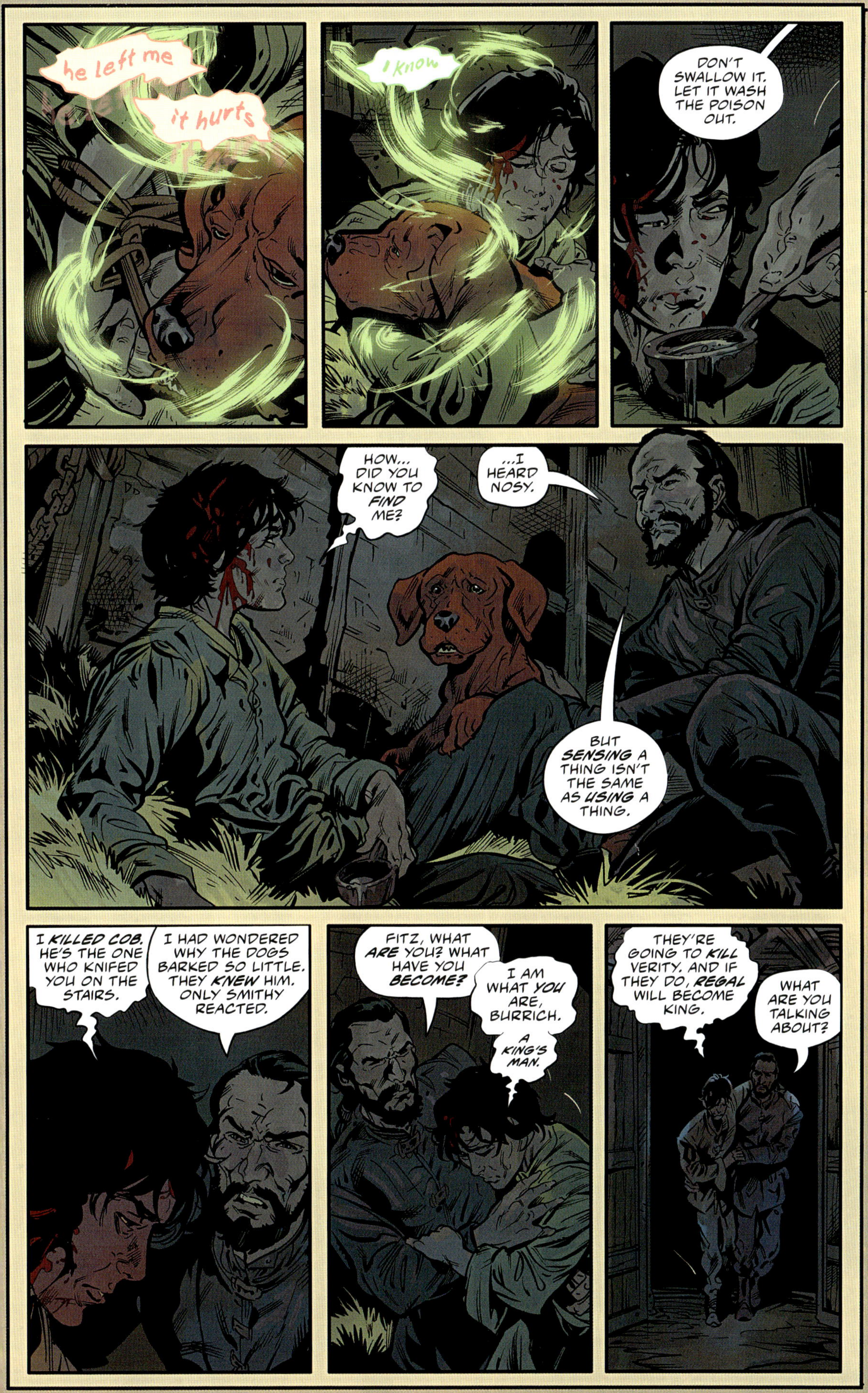
he left me
it hurts
I know
DON'T SWALLOW IT. LET IT WASH THE POISON OUT.
HOW... DID YOU KNOW TO FIND ME?
...I HEARD NOSY.
BUT SENSING A THING ISN'T THE SAME AS USING A THING.
I KILLED COB. HE'S THE ONE WHO KNIFED YOU ON THE STAIRS.
I HAD WONDERED WHY THE DOGS BARKED SO LITTLE. THEY KNEW HIM. ONLY SMITHY REACTED.
FITZ, WHAT ARE YOU? WHAT HAVE YOU BECOME?
I AM WHAT YOU ARE, BURRICH.
A KING'S MAN.
THEY'RE GOING TO KILL VERITY. AND IF THEY DO, REGAL WILL BECOME KING.
WHAT ARE YOU TALKING ABOUT?

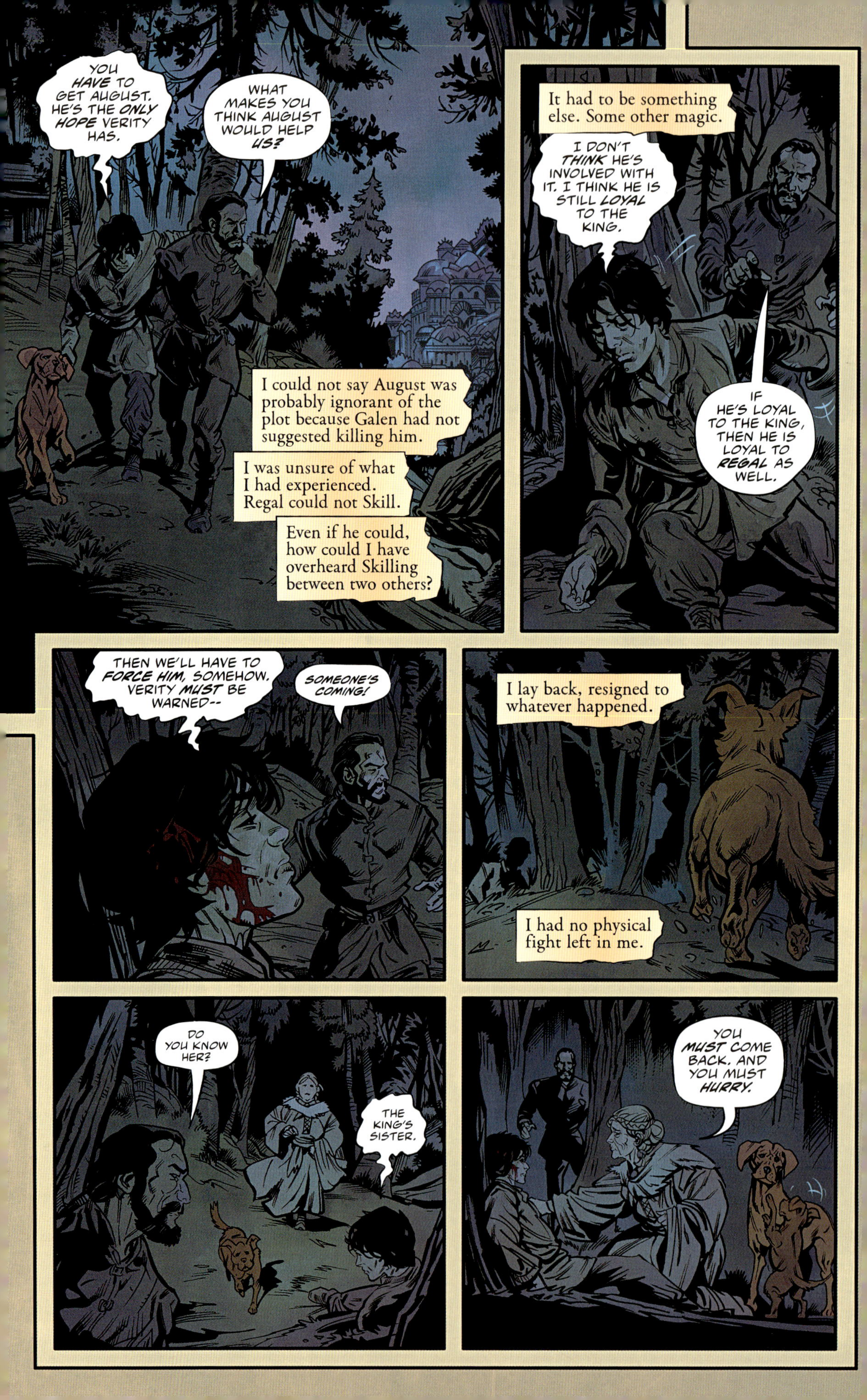

YOU HAVE TO GET AUGUST. HE'S THE ONLY HOPE VERITY HAS.
WHAT MAKES YOU THINK AUGUST WOULD HELP US?
I could not say August was probably ignorant of the plot because Galen had not suggested killing him.
I was unsure of what I had experienced. Regal could not Skill.
Even if he could, how could I have overheard Skilling between two others?
It had to be something else. Some other magic.
I DON'T THINK HE'S INVOLVED WITH IT. I THINK HE IS STILL LOYAL TO THE KING.
IF HE'S LOYAL TO THE KING, THEN HE IS LOYAL TO REGAL AS WELL.
THEN WE'LL HAVE TO FORCE HIM, SOMEHOW. VERITY MUST BE WARNED--
SOMEONE'S COMING!
I lay back, resigned to whatever happened.
I had no physical fight left in me.
DO YOU KNOW HER?
THE KING'S SISTER.
YOU MUST COME BACK. AND YOU MUST HURRY.

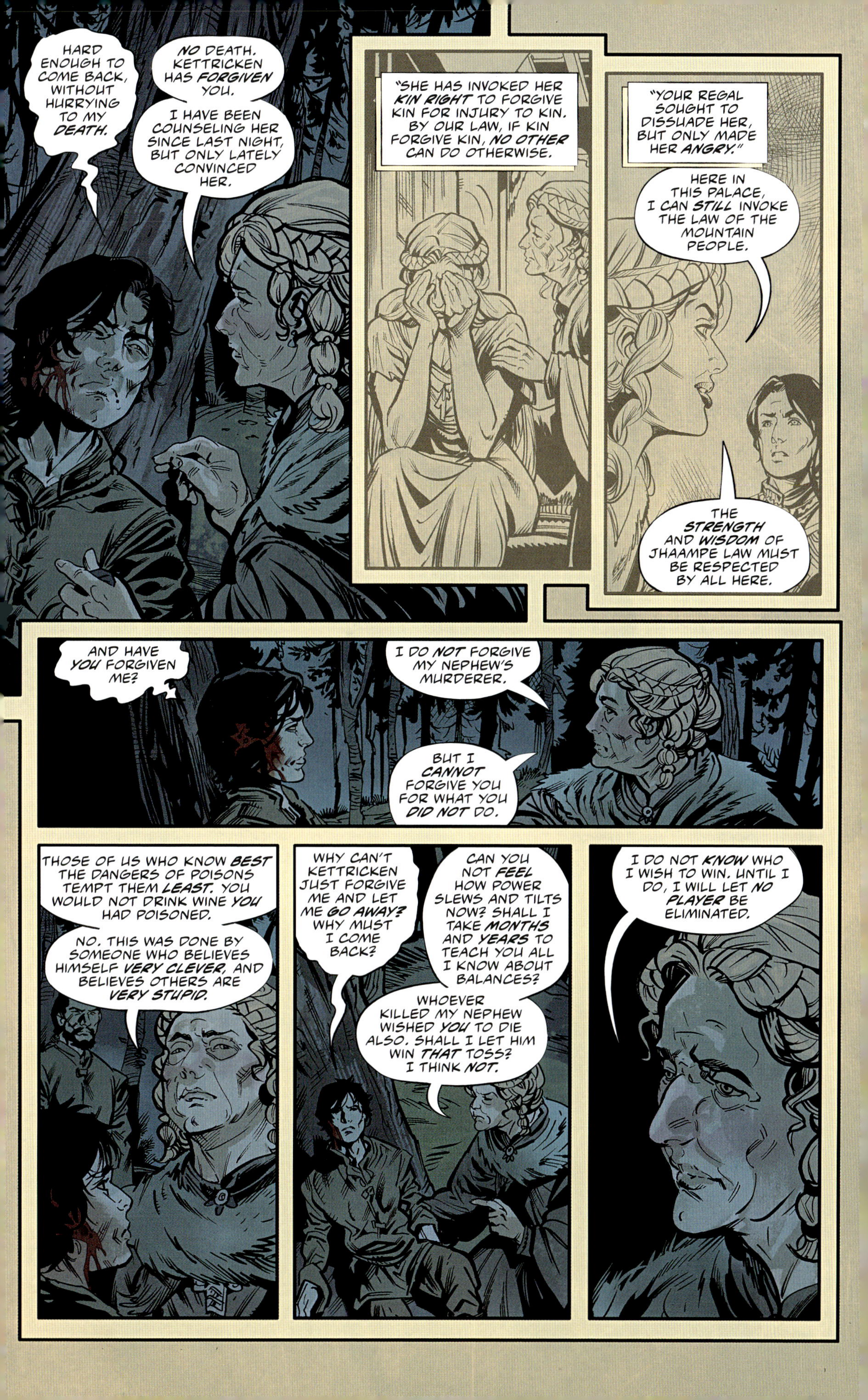
HARD ENOUGH TO COME BACK, WITHOUT HURRYING TO MY DEATH.
NO DEATH. KETTRICKEN HAS FORGIVEN YOU.
I HAVE BEEN COUNSELING HER SINCE LAST NIGHT, BUT ONLY LATELY CONVINCED HER.
"SHE HAS INVOKED HER KIN RIGHT TO FORGIVE KIN FOR INJURY TO KIN. BY OUR LAW, IF KIN FORGIVE KIN, NO OTHER CAN DO OTHERWISE.
"YOUR REGAL SOUGHT TO DISSUADE HER, BUT ONLY MADE HER ANGRY."
HERE IN THIS PALACE, I CAN STILL INVOKE THE LAW OF THE MOUNTAIN PEOPLE.
THE STRENGTH AND WISDOM OF JHAAMPE LAW MUST BE RESPECTED BY ALL HERE.
AND HAVE YOU FORGIVEN ME?
I DO NOT FORGIVE MY NEPHEW'S MURDERER.
BUT I CANNOT FORGIVE YOU FOR WHAT YOU DID NOT DO.
THOSE OF US WHO KNOW BEST THE DANGERS OF POISONS TEMPT THEM LEAST. YOU WOULD NOT DRINK WINE YOU HAD POISONED.
NO. THIS WAS DONE BY SOMEONE WHO BELIEVES HIMSELF VERY CLEVER, AND BELIEVES OTHERS ARE VERY STUPID.
WHY CAN'T KETTRICKEN JUST FORGIVE ME AND LET ME GO AWAY? WHY MUST I COME BACK?
CAN YOU NOT FEEL HOW POWER SLEWS AND TILTS NOW? SHALL I TAKE MONTHS AND YEARS TO TEACH YOU ALL I KNOW ABOUT BALANCES?
WHOEVER KILLED MY NEPHEW WISHED YOU TO DIE ALSO. SHALL I LET HIM WIN THAT TOSS? I THINK NOT.
I DO NOT KNOW WHO I WISH TO WIN. UNTIL I DO, I WILL LET NO PLAYER BE ELIMINATED.

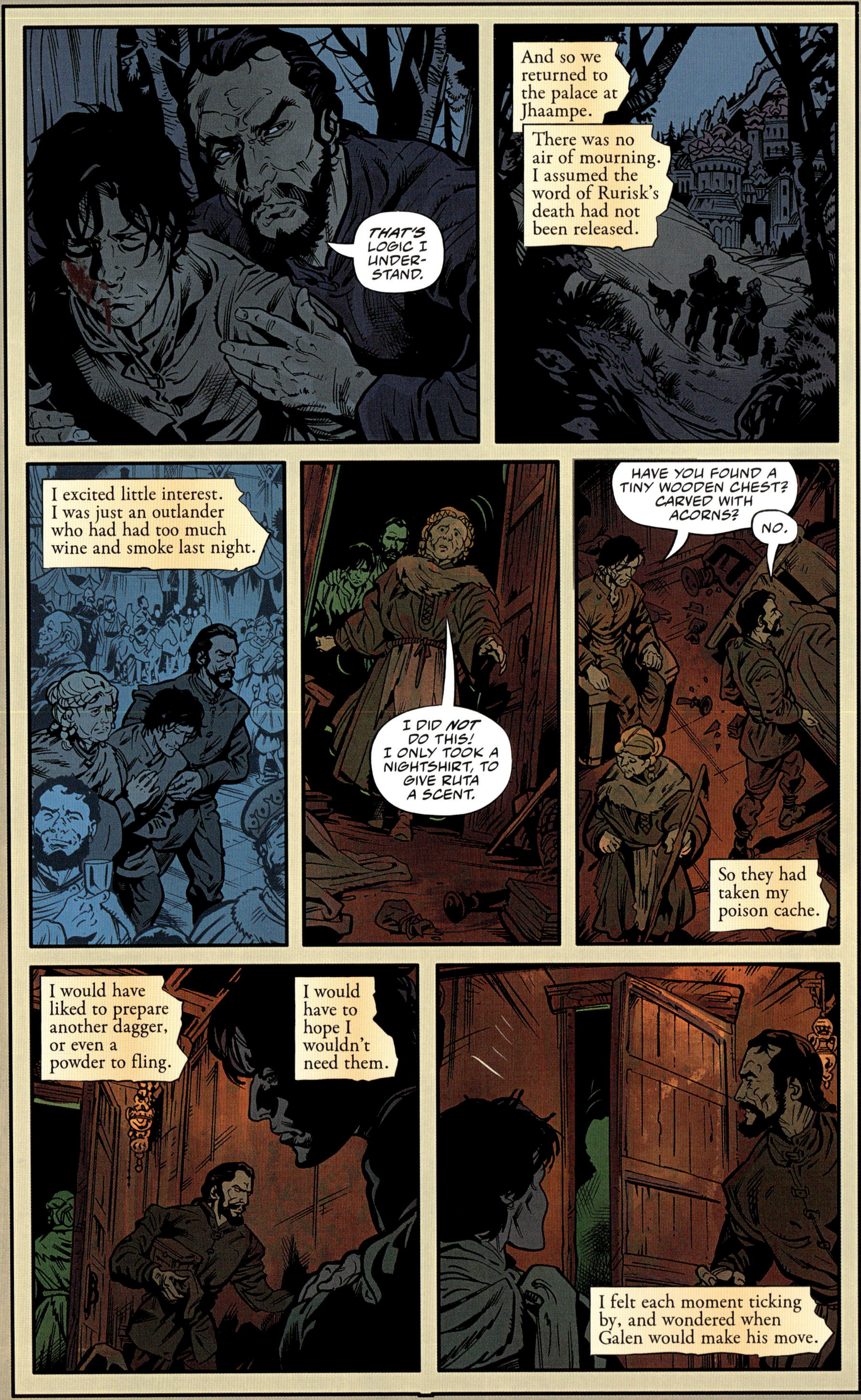
THAT'S LOGIC I UNDER-STAND.
And so we returned to the palace at Jhaampe.
There was no air of mourning. I assumed the word of Rurisk's death had not been released.
I excited little interest. I was just an outlander who had had too much wine and smoke last night.
I DID NOT DO THIS! I ONLY TOOK A NIGHTSHIRT, TO GIVE RUTA A SCENT.
HAVE YOU FOUND A TINY WOODEN CHEST? CARVED WITH ACORNS?
NO.
So they had taken my poison cache.
I would have liked to prepare another dagger, or even a powder to fling.
I would have to hope I wouldn't need them.
I felt each moment ticking by, and wondered when Galen would make his move.

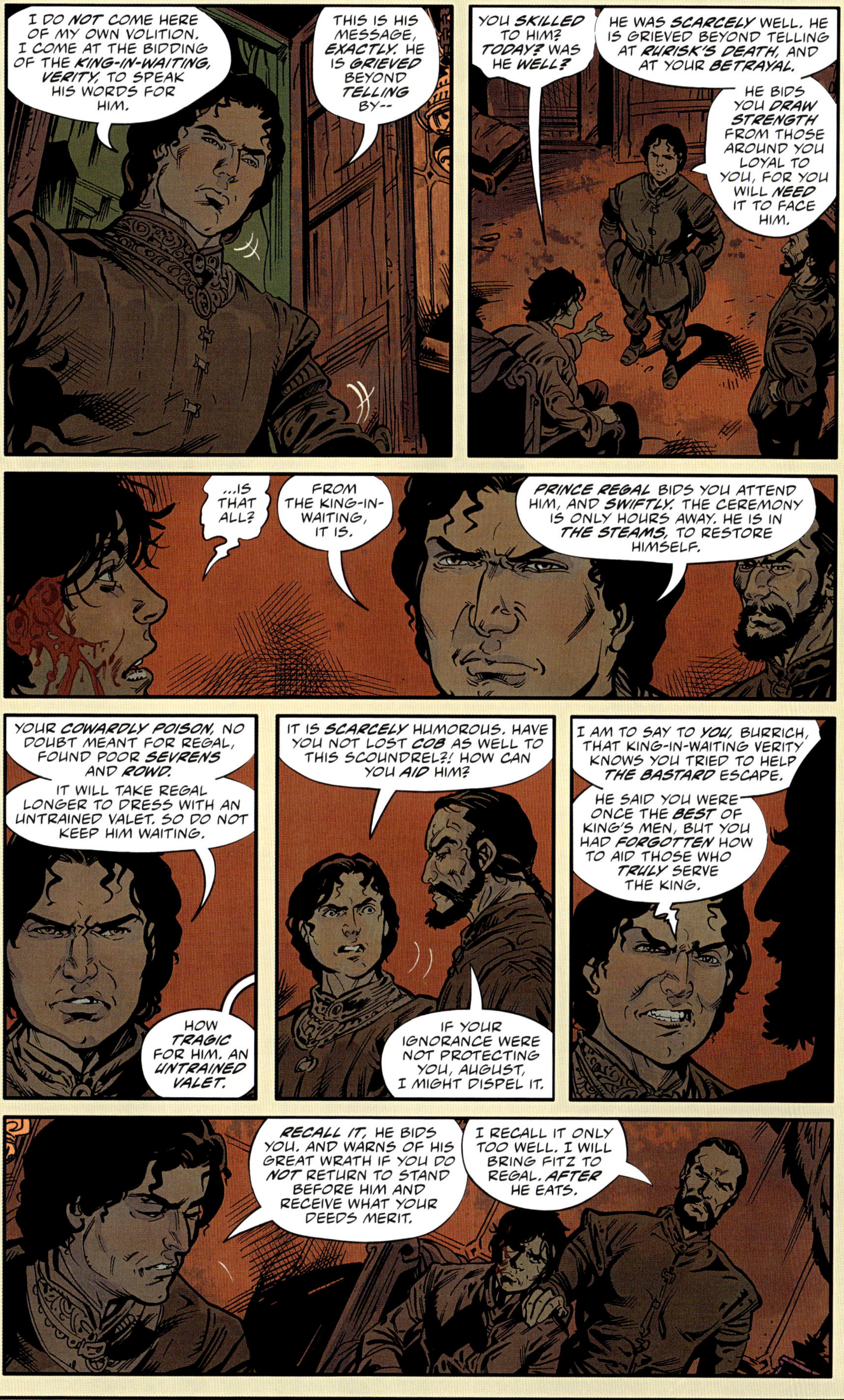
I DO NOT COME HERE OF MY OWN VOLITION. I COME AT THE BIDDING OF THE KING-IN-WAITING, VERITY, TO SPEAK HIS WORDS FOR HIM.
THIS IS HIS MESSAGE, EXACTLY. HE IS GRIEVED BEYOND TELLING BY--
YOU SKILLED TO HIM? TODAY? WAS HE WELL?
HE WAS SCARCELY WELL. HE IS GRIEVED BEYOND TELLING AT RURISK'S DEATH, AND AT YOUR BETRAYAL.
HE BIDS YOU DRAW STRENGTH FROM THOSE AROUND YOU LOYAL TO YOU, FOR YOU WILL NEED IT TO FACE HIM.
...IS THAT ALL?
FROM THE KING-IN-WAITING, IT IS.
PRINCE REGAL BIDS YOU ATTEND HIM, AND SWIFTLY. THE CEREMONY IS ONLY HOURS AWAY. HE IS IN THE STEAMS, TO RESTORE HIMSELF.
YOUR COWARDLY POISON, NO DOUBT MEANT FOR REGAL, FOUND POOR SEVRENS AND ROWD.
IT WILL TAKE REGAL LONGER TO DRESS WITH AN UNTRAINED VALET. SO DO NOT KEEP HIM WAITING.
HOW TRAGIC FOR HIM. AN UNTRAINED VALET.
IT IS SCARCELY HUMOROUS. HAVE YOU NOT LOST COB AS WELL TO THIS SCOUNDREL?! HOW CAN YOU AID HIM?
IF YOUR IGNORANCE WERE NOT PROTECTING YOU, AUGUST, I MIGHT DISPEL IT.
I AM TO SAY TO YOU, BURRICH, THAT KING-IN-WAITING VERITY KNOWS YOU TRIED TO HELP THE BASTARD ESCAPE.
HE SAID YOU WERE ONCE THE BEST OF KING'S MEN, BUT YOU HAD FORGOTTEN HOW TO AID THOSE WHO TRULY SERVE THE KING.
RECALL IT, HE BIDS YOU. AND WARNS OF HIS GREAT WRATH IF YOU DO NOT RETURN TO STAND BEFORE HIM AND RECEIVE WHAT YOUR DEEDS MERIT.
I RECALL IT ONLY TOO WELL. I WILL BRING FITZ TO REGAL. AFTER HE EATS.

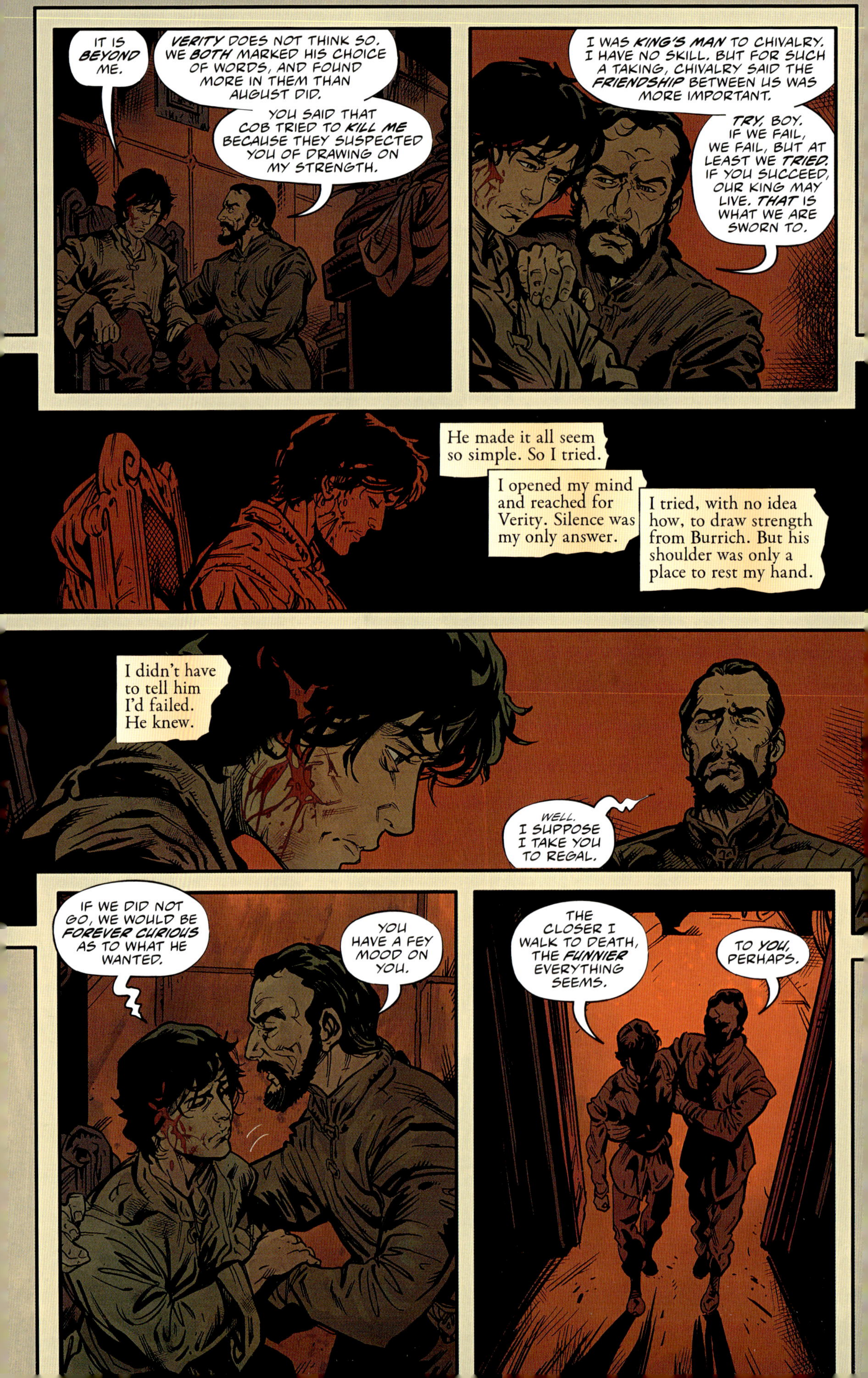
IT IS BEYOND ME.
VERITY DOES NOT THINK SO. WE BOTH MARKED HIS CHOICE OF WORDS, AND FOUND MORE IN THEM THAN AUGUST DID.
YOU SAID THAT COB TRIED TO KILL ME BECAUSE THEY SUSPECTED YOU OF DRAWING ON MY STRENGTH.
I WAS KING'S MAN TO CHIVALRY. I HAVE NO SKILL. BUT FOR SUCH A TAKING, CHIVALRY SAID THE FRIENDSHIP BETWEEN US WAS MORE IMPORTANT.
TRY, BOY. IF WE FAIL, WE FAIL, BUT AT LEAST WE TRIED. IF YOU SUCCEED, OUR KING MAY LIVE. THAT IS WHAT WE ARE SWORN TO.
He made it all seem so simple. So I tried.
I opened my mind and reached for Verity. Silence was my only answer.
I tried, with no idea how, to draw strength from Burrich. But his shoulder was only a place to rest my hand.
I didn't have to tell him I'd failed. He knew.
WELL. I SUPPOSE I TAKE YOU TO REGAL.
IF WE DID NOT GO, WE WOULD BE FOREVER CURIOUS AS TO WHAT HE WANTED.
YOU HAVE A FEY MOOD ON YOU.
THE CLOSER I WALK TO DEATH, THE FUNNIER EVERYTHING SEEMS.
TO YOU, PERHAPS.

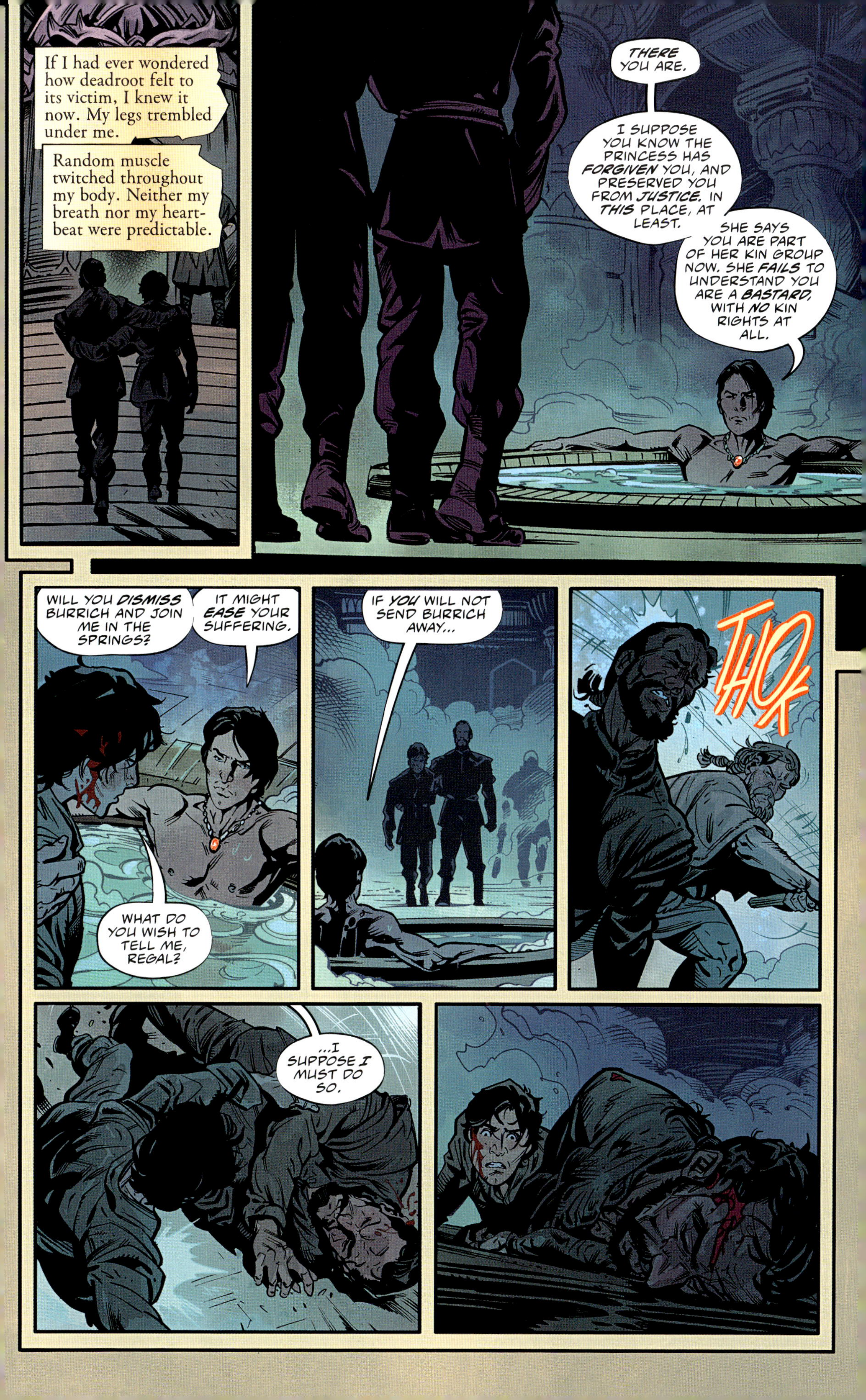

If I had ever wondered how deadroot felt to its victim, I knew it now. My legs trembled under me.
Random muscle twitched throughout my body. Neither my breath nor my heart-beat were predictable.
THERE YOU ARE.
I SUPPOSE YOU KNOW THE PRINCESS HAS FORGIVEN YOU, AND PRESERVED YOU FROM JUSTICE. IN THIS PLACE, AT LEAST.
SHE SAYS YOU ARE PART OF HER KIN GROUP NOW. SHE FAILS TO UNDERSTAND YOU ARE A BASTARD, WITH NO KIN RIGHTS AT ALL.
WILL YOU DISMISS BURRICH AND JOIN ME IN THE SPRINGS?
IT MIGHT EASE YOUR SUFFERING.
WHAT DO YOU WISH TO TELL ME, REGAL?
IF YOU WILL NOT SEND BURRICH AWAY...
THOK
...I SUPPOSE I MUST DO SO.

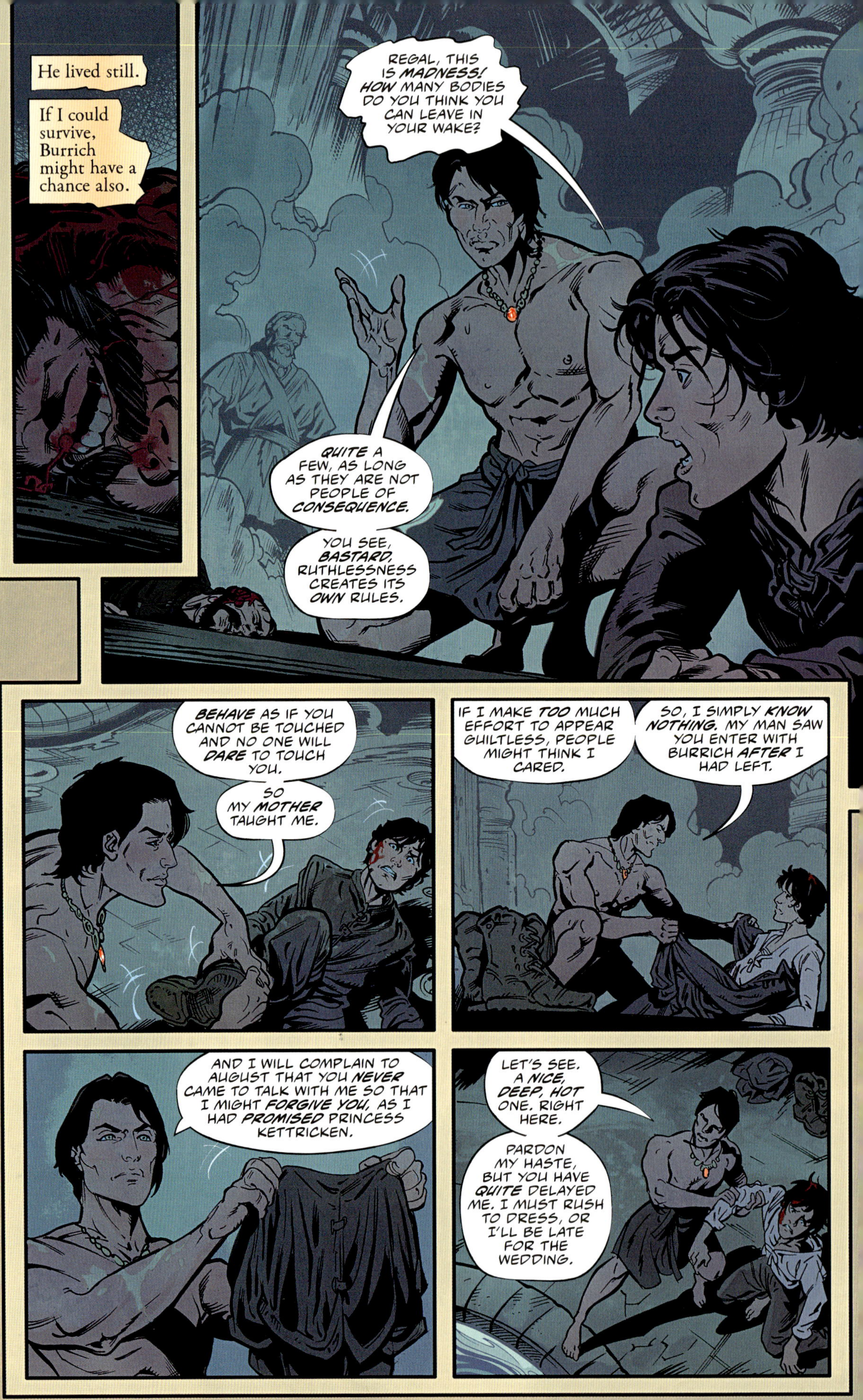
He lived still.
If I could survive, Burrich might have a chance also.
REGAL, THIS IS MADNESS! HOW MANY BODIES DO YOU THINK YOU CAN LEAVE IN YOUR WAKE?
QUITE A FEW, AS LONG AS THEY ARE NOT PEOPLE OF CONSEQUENCE.
YOU SEE, BASTARD, RUTHLESSNESS CREATES ITS OWN RULES.
BEHAVE AS IF YOU CANNOT BE TOUCHED AND NO ONE WILL DARE TO TOUCH YOU.
SO MY MOTHER TAUGHT ME.
IF I MAKE TOO MUCH EFFORT TO APPEAR GUILTLESS, PEOPLE MIGHT THINK I CARED.
SO, I SIMPLY KNOW NOTHING. MY MAN SAW YOU ENTER WITH BURRICH AFTER I HAD LEFT.
AND I WILL COMPLAIN TO AUGUST THAT YOU NEVER CAME TO TALK WITH ME SO THAT I MIGHT FORGIVE YOU, AS I HAD PROMISED PRINCESS KETTRICKEN.
LET'S SEE. A NICE, DEEP, HOT ONE. RIGHT HERE.
PARDON MY HASTE, BUT YOU HAVE QUITE DELAYED ME. I MUST RUSH TO DRESS, OR I'LL BE LATE FOR THE WEDDING.

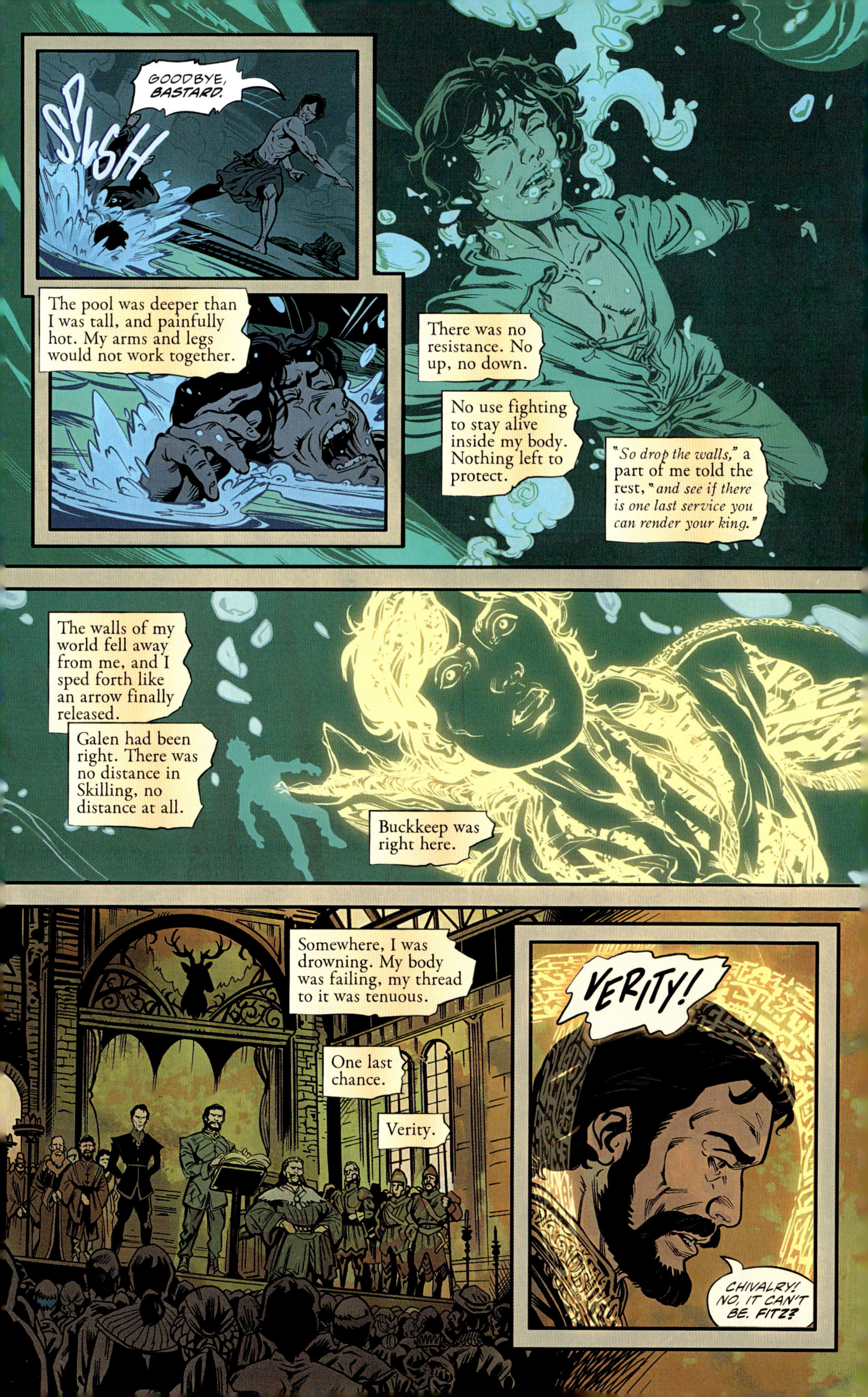
GOODBYE, BASTARD.
SPLSH
The pool was deeper than I was tall, and painfully hot. My arms and legs would not work together.
There was no resistance. No up, no down.
No use fighting to stay alive inside my body. Nothing left to protect.
"So drop the walls," a part of me told the rest, "and see if there is one last service you can render your king."
The walls of my world fell away from me, and I sped forth like an arrow finally released.
Galen had been right. There was no distance in Skilling, no distance at all.
Buckkeep was right here.
Somewhere, I was drowning. My body was failing, my thread to it was tenuous.
One last chance.
Verity.
VERITY!
CHIVALRY! NO, IT CAN'T BE. FITZ?

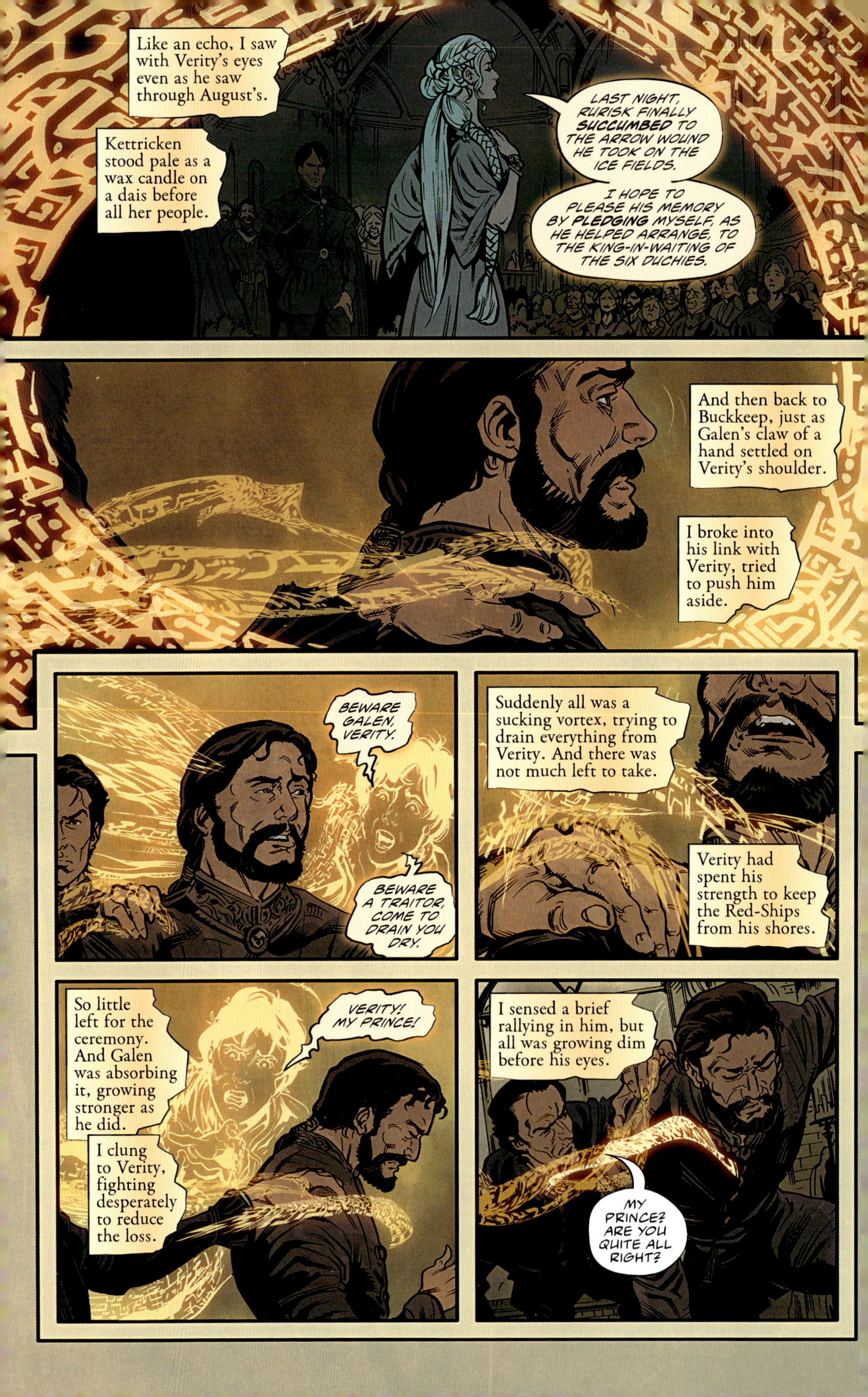
Like an echo, I saw with Verity's eyes even as he saw through August's.
Kettricken stood pale as a wax candle on a dais before all her people.
LAST NIGHT, RURISK FINALLY SUCCUMBED TO THE ARROW WOUND HE TOOK ON THE ICE FIELDS.
I HOPE TO PLEASE HIS MEMORY BY PLEDGING MYSELF, AS HE HELPED ARRANGE, TO THE KING-IN-WAITING OF THE SIX DUCHIES.
And then back to Buckkeep, just as Galen's claw of a hand settled on Verity's shoulder.
I broke into his link with Verity, tried to push him aside.
BEWARE GALEN, VERITY.
BEWARE A TRAITOR, COME TO DRAIN YOU DRY.
Suddenly all was a sucking vortex, trying to drain everything from Verity. And there was not much left to take.
Verity had spent his strength to keep the Red-Ships from his shores.
So little left for the ceremony. And Galen was absorbing it, growing stronger as he did.
VERITY! MY PRINCE!
I clung to Verity, fighting desperately to reduce the loss.
I sensed a brief rallying in him, but all was growing dim before his eyes.
MY PRINCE? ARE YOU QUITE ALL RIGHT?

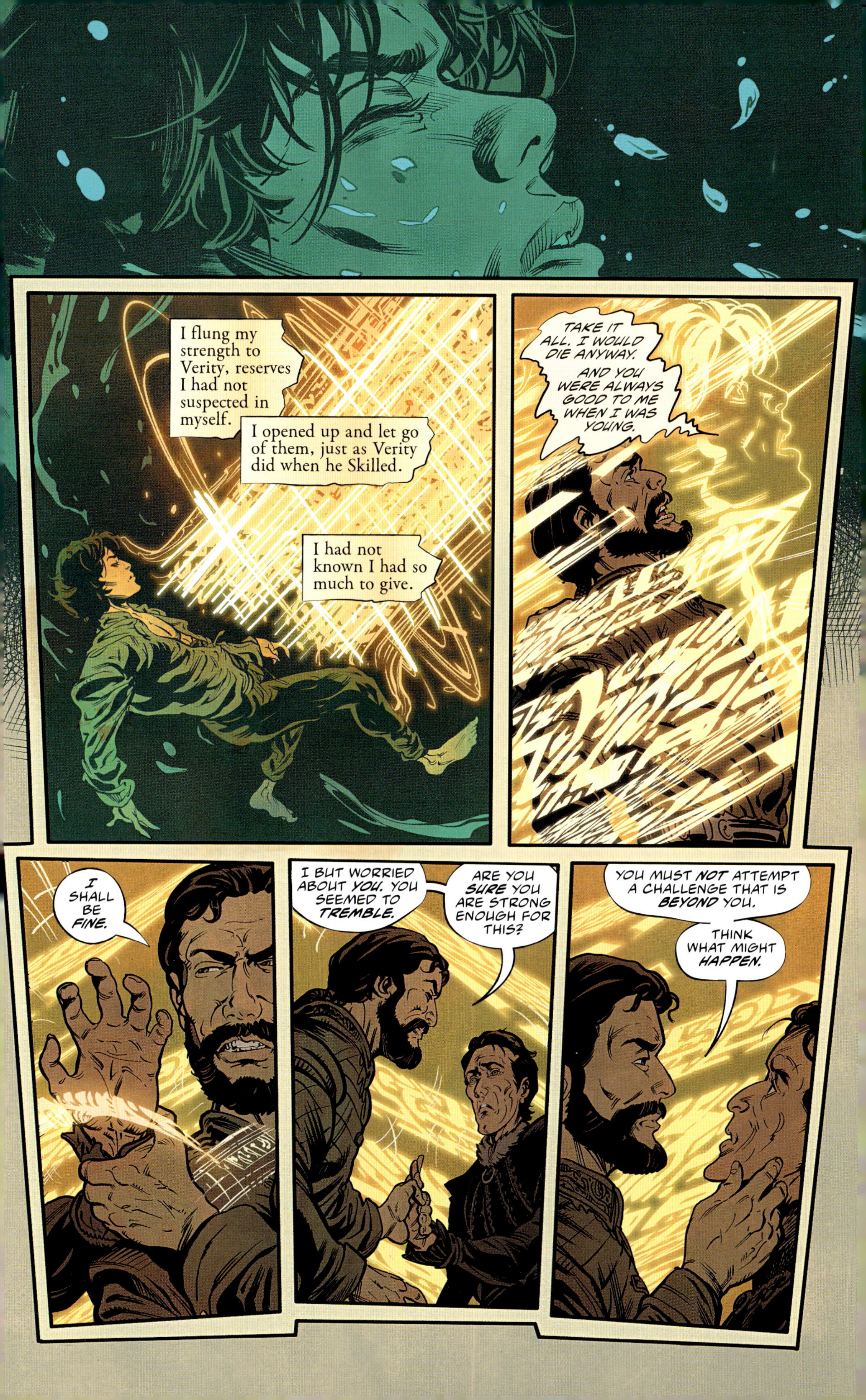
I flung my strength to Verity, reserves I had not suspected in myself.
I opened up and let go of them, just as Verity did when he Skilled.
I had not known I had so much to give.
TAKE IT ALL. I WOULD DIE ANYWAY.
AND YOU WERE ALWAYS GOOD TO ME WHEN I WAS YOUNG.
I SHALL BE *FINE.*
I BUT WORRIED ABOUT *YOU.* YOU SEEMED TO *TREMBLE.*
ARE YOU *SURE* YOU ARE STRONG ENOUGH FOR THIS?
YOU MUST *NOT* ATTEMPT A CHALLENGE THAT IS *BEYOND* YOU.
THINK WHAT MIGHT *HAPPEN.*

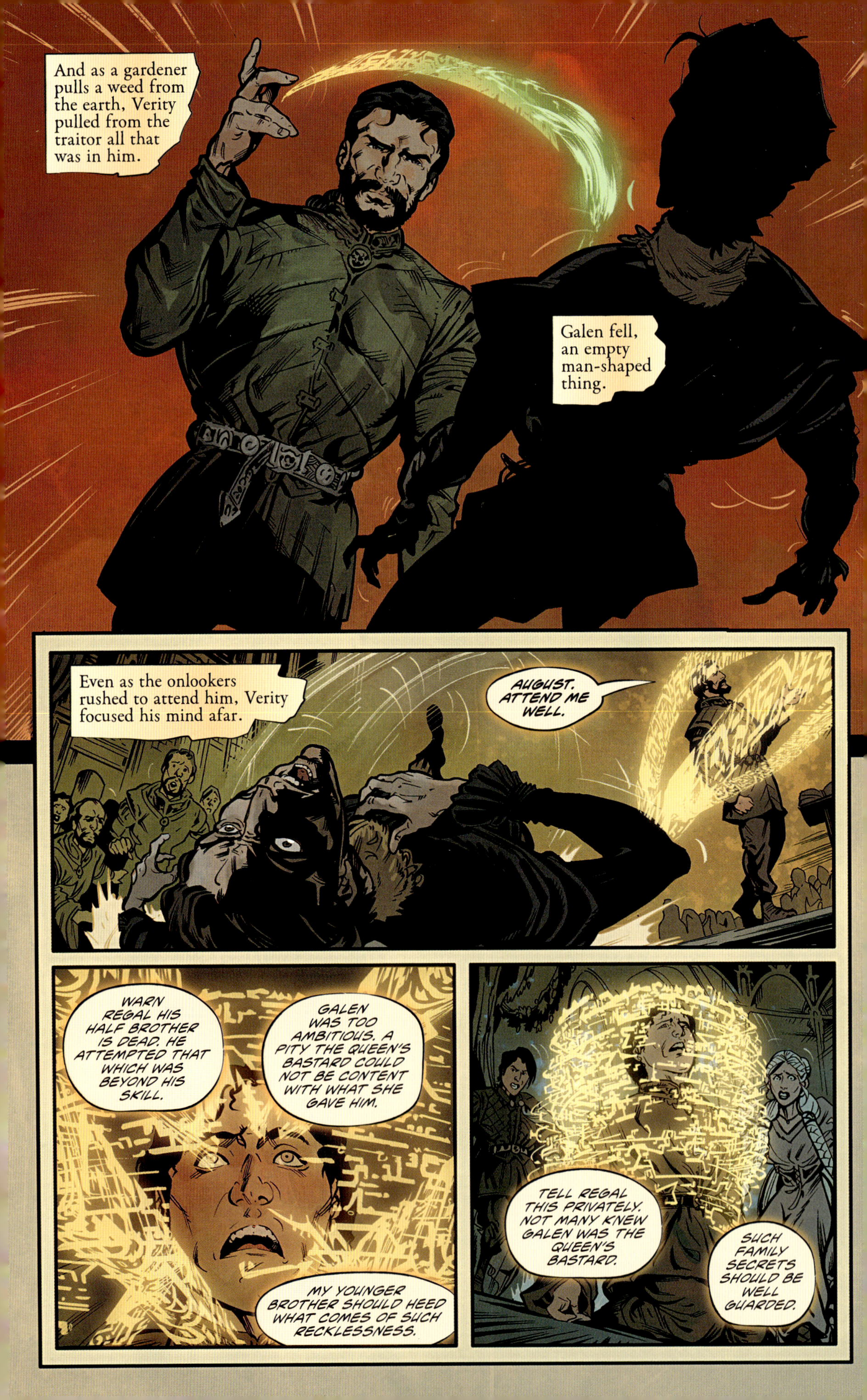
And as a gardener pulls a weed from the earth, Verity pulled from the traitor all that was in him.
Galen fell, an empty man-shaped thing.
Even as the onlookers rushed to attend him, Verity focused his mind afar.
AUGUST. ATTEND ME WELL.
WARN REGAL HIS HALF BROTHER IS DEAD. HE ATTEMPTED THAT WHICH WAS BEYOND HIS SKILL.
GALEN WAS TOO AMBITIOUS. A PITY THE QUEEN'S BASTARD COULD NOT BE CONTENT WITH WHAT SHE GAVE HIM.
MY YOUNGER BROTHER SHOULD HEED WHAT COMES OF SUCH RECKLESSNESS.
TELL REGAL THIS PRIVATELY. NOT MANY KNEW GALEN WAS THE QUEEN'S BASTARD.
SUCH FAMILY SECRETS SHOULD BE WELL GUARDED.

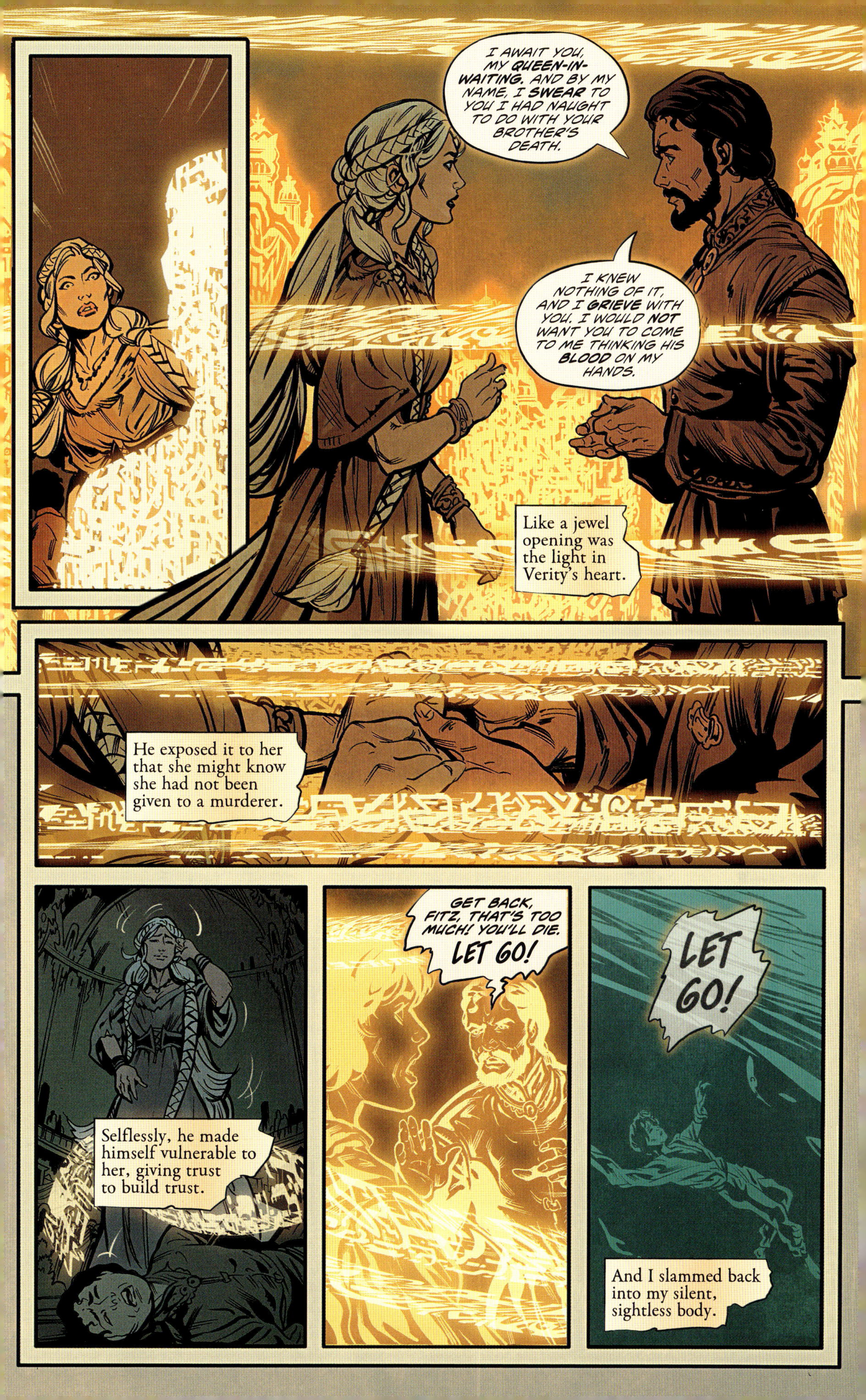
I AWAIT YOU, MY QUEEN-IN-WAITING. AND BY MY NAME, I SWEAR TO YOU I HAD NAUGHT TO DO WITH YOUR BROTHER'S DEATH.
I KNEW NOTHING OF IT, AND I GRIEVE WITH YOU. I WOULD NOT WANT YOU TO COME TO ME THINKING HIS BLOOD ON MY HANDS.
Like a jewel opening was the light in Verity's heart.
He exposed it to her that she might know she had not been given to a murderer.
Selflessly, he made himself vulnerable to her, giving trust to build trust.
GET BACK, FITZ, THAT'S TOO MUCH! YOU'LL DIE. LET GO!
LET GO!
And I slammed back into my silent, sightless body.

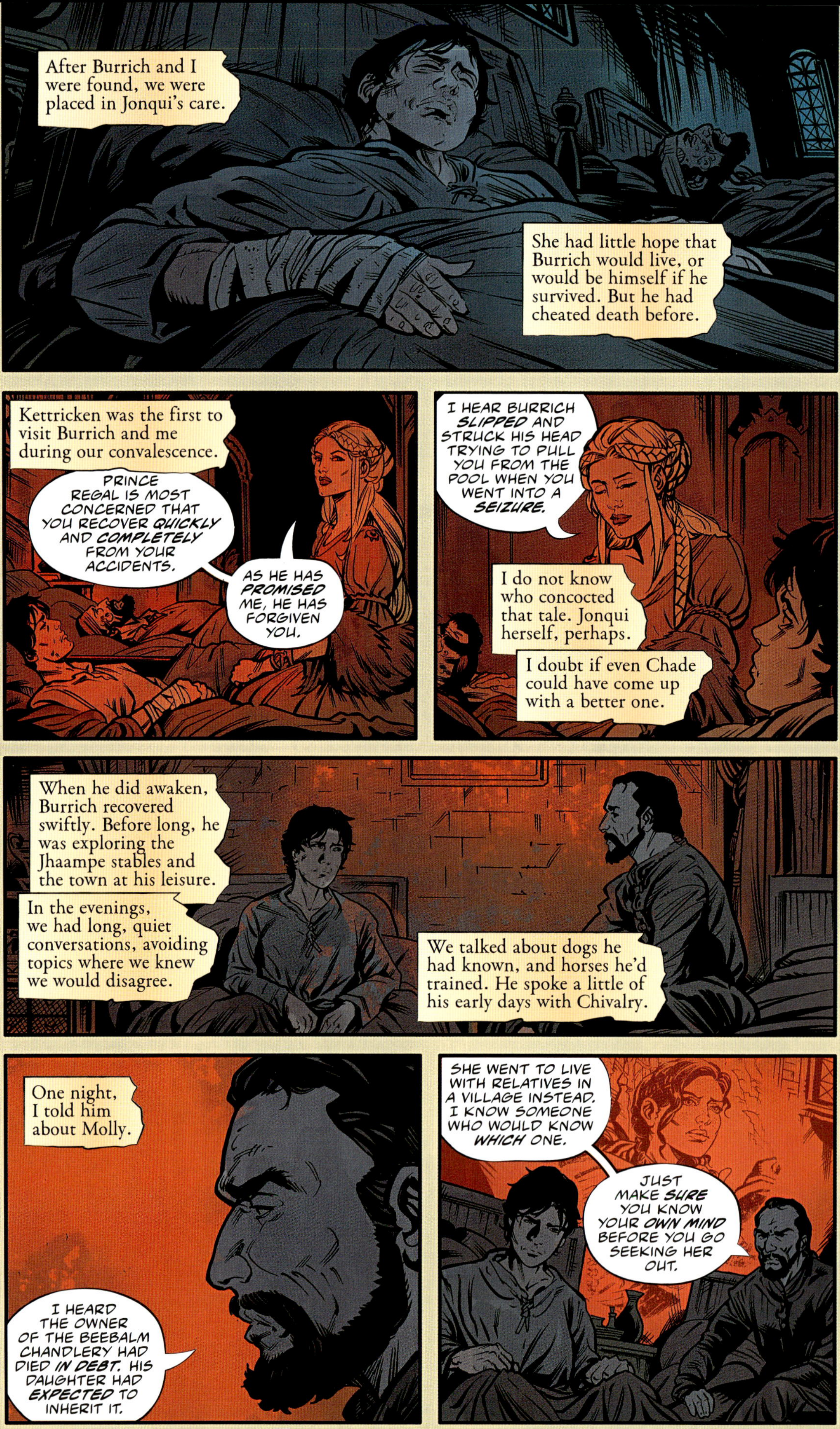
After Burrich and I were found, we were placed in Jonqui's care.
She had little hope that Burrich would live, or would be himself if he survived. But he had cheated death before.
Kettricken was the first to visit Burrich and me during our convalescence.
PRINCE REGAL IS MOST CONCERNED THAT YOU RECOVER *QUICKLY* AND *COMPLETELY* FROM YOUR ACCIDENTS.
AS HE HAS *PROMISED* ME, HE HAS FORGIVEN YOU.
I HEAR BURRICH *SLIPPED* AND STRUCK HIS HEAD TRYING TO PULL YOU FROM THE POOL WHEN YOU WENT INTO A *SEIZURE.*
I do not know who concocted that tale. Jonqui herself, perhaps.
I doubt if even Chade could have come up with a better one.
When he did awaken, Burrich recovered swiftly. Before long, he was exploring the Jhaampe stables and the town at his leisure.
In the evenings, we had long, quiet conversations, avoiding topics where we knew we would disagree.
We talked about dogs he had known, and horses he'd trained. He spoke a little of his early days with Chivalry.
One night, I told him about Molly.
I HEARD THE OWNER OF THE BEEBALM CHANDLERY HAD DIED *IN DEBT.* HIS DAUGHTER HAD *EXPECTED* TO INHERIT IT.
SHE WENT TO LIVE WITH RELATIVES IN A VILLAGE INSTEAD. I KNOW SOMEONE WHO WOULD KNOW *WHICH* ONE.
JUST MAKE *SURE* YOU KNOW YOUR *OWN MIND* BEFORE YOU GO SEEKING HER OUT.

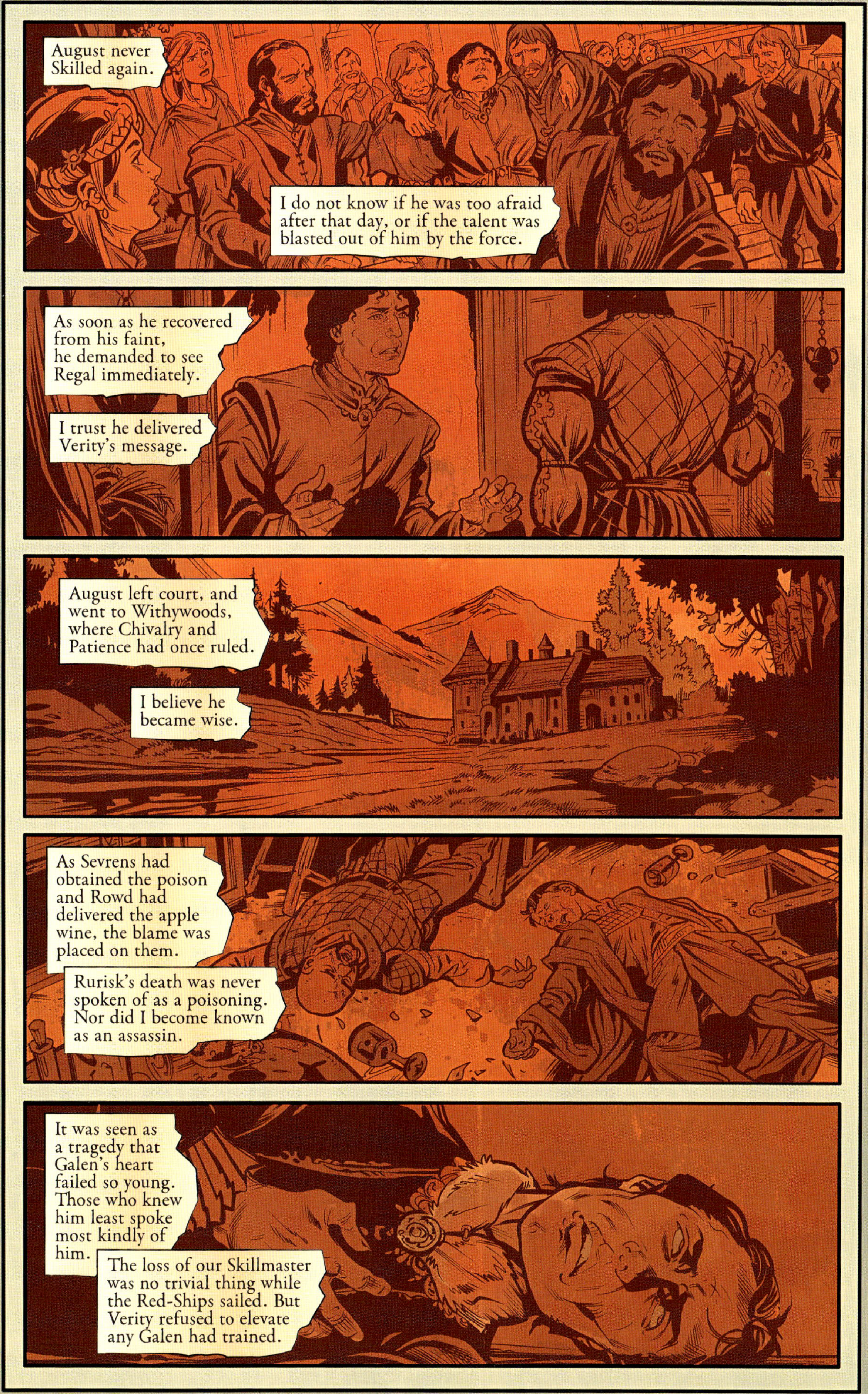

August never Skilled again.
I do not know if he was too afraid after that day, or if the talent was blasted out of him by the force.
As soon as he recovered from his faint, he demanded to see Regal immediately.
I trust he delivered Verity's message.
August left court, and went to Withywoods, where Chivalry and Patience had once ruled.
I believe he became wise.
As Sevrens had obtained the poison and Rowd had delivered the apple wine, the blame was placed on them.
Rurisk's death was never spoken of as a poisoning. Nor did I become known as an assassin.
It was seen as a tragedy that Galen's heart failed so young. Those who knew him least spoke most kindly of him.
The loss of our Skillmaster was no trivial thing while the Red-Ships sailed. But Verity refused to elevate any Galen had trained.

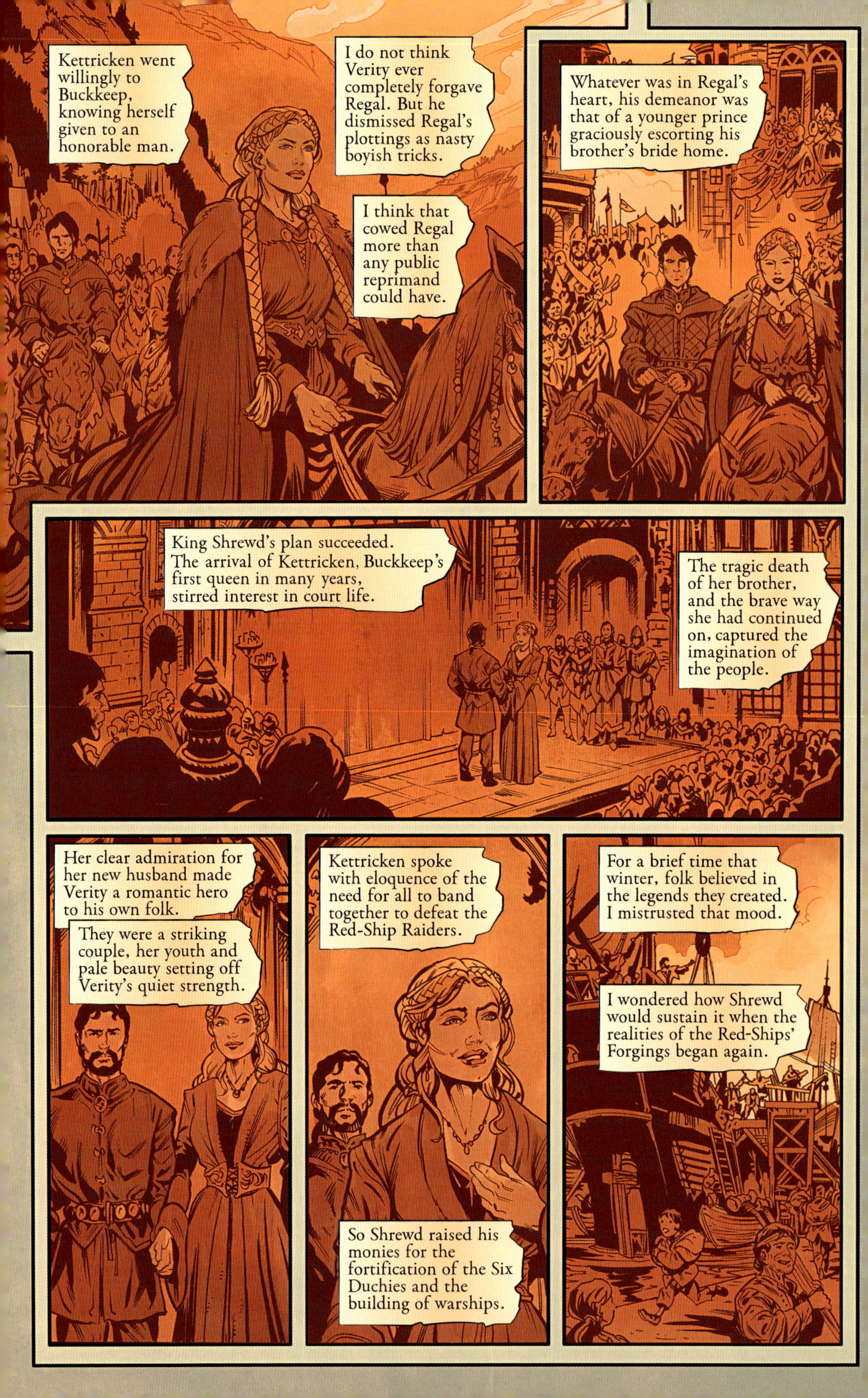
Kettricken went willingly to Buckkeep, knowing herself given to an honorable man.
I do not think Verity ever completely forgave Regal. But he dismissed Regal's plottings as nasty boyish tricks.
I think that cowed Regal more than any public reprimand could have.
Whatever was in Regal's heart, his demeanor was that of a younger prince graciously escorting his brother's bride home.
King Shrewd's plan succeeded. The arrival of Kettricken, Buckkeep's first queen in many years, stirred interest in court life.
The tragic death of her brother, and the brave way she had continued on, captured the imagination of the people.
Her clear admiration for her new husband made Verity a romantic hero to his own folk.
They were a striking couple, her youth and pale beauty setting off Verity's quiet strength.
Kettricken spoke with eloquence of the need for all to band together to defeat the Red-Ship Raiders.
So Shrewd raised his monies for the fortification of the Six Duchies and the building of warships.
For a brief time that winter, folk believed in the legends they created. I mistrusted that mood.
I wondered how Shrewd would sustain it when the realities of the Red-Ships' Forgings began again.

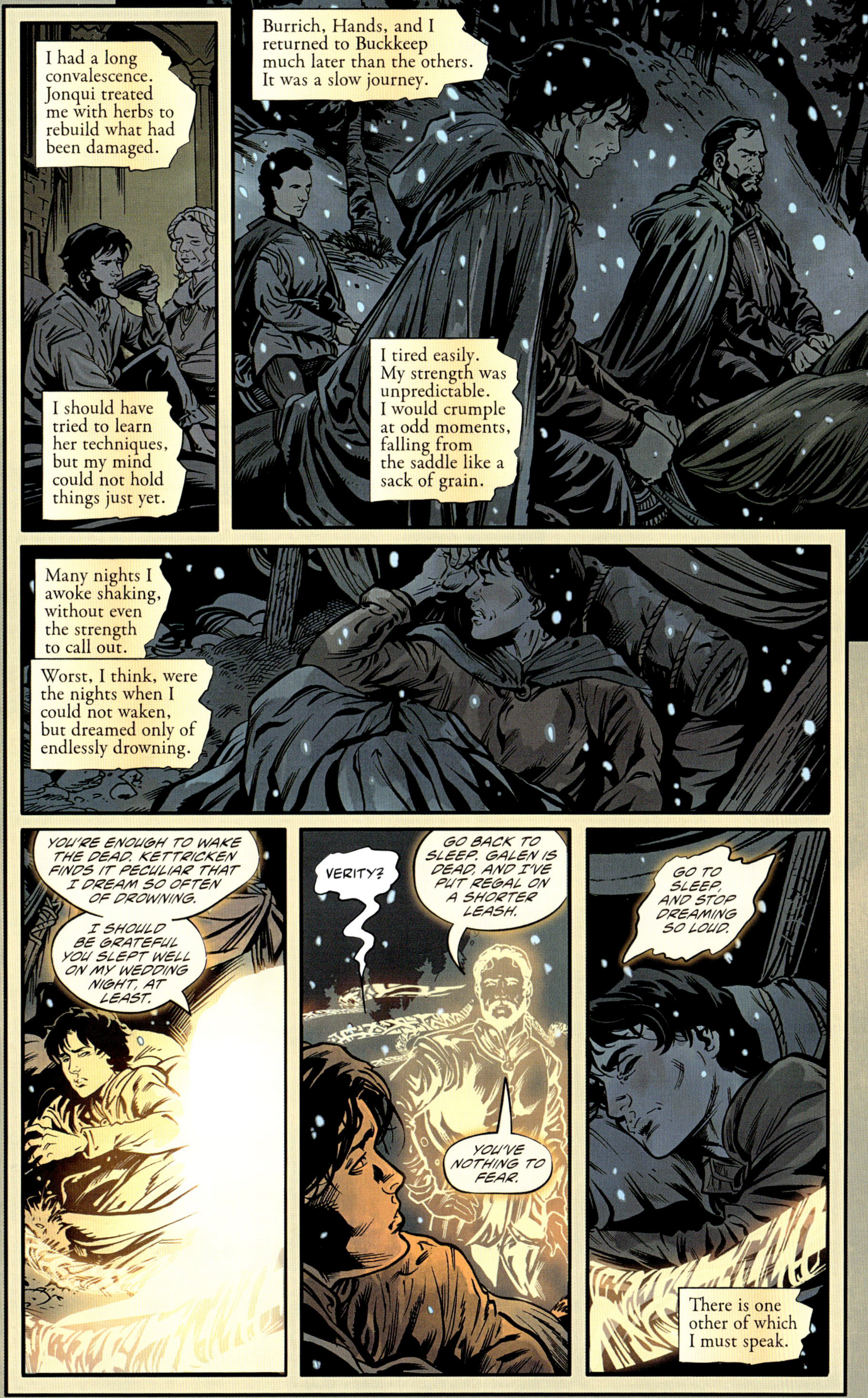
I had a long convalescence. Jonqui treated me with herbs to rebuild what had been damaged.
I should have tried to learn her techniques, but my mind could not hold things just yet.
Burrich, Hands, and I returned to Buckkeep much later than the others. It was a slow journey.
I tired easily. My strength was unpredictable. I would crumple at odd moments, falling from the saddle like a sack of grain.
Many nights I awoke shaking, without even the strength to call out.
Worst, I think, were the nights when I could not waken, but dreamed only of endlessly drowning.
YOU'RE ENOUGH TO WAKE THE DEAD. KETTRICKEN FINDS IT PECULIAR THAT I DREAM SO OFTEN OF DROWNING.
I SHOULD BE GRATEFUL YOU SLEPT WELL ON MY WEDDING NIGHT, AT LEAST.
VERITY?
GO BACK TO SLEEP. GALEN IS DEAD, AND I'VE PUT REGAL ON A SHORTER LEASH.
YOU'VE NOTHING TO FEAR.
GO TO SLEEP, AND STOP DREAMING SO LOUD.
There is one other of which I must speak.

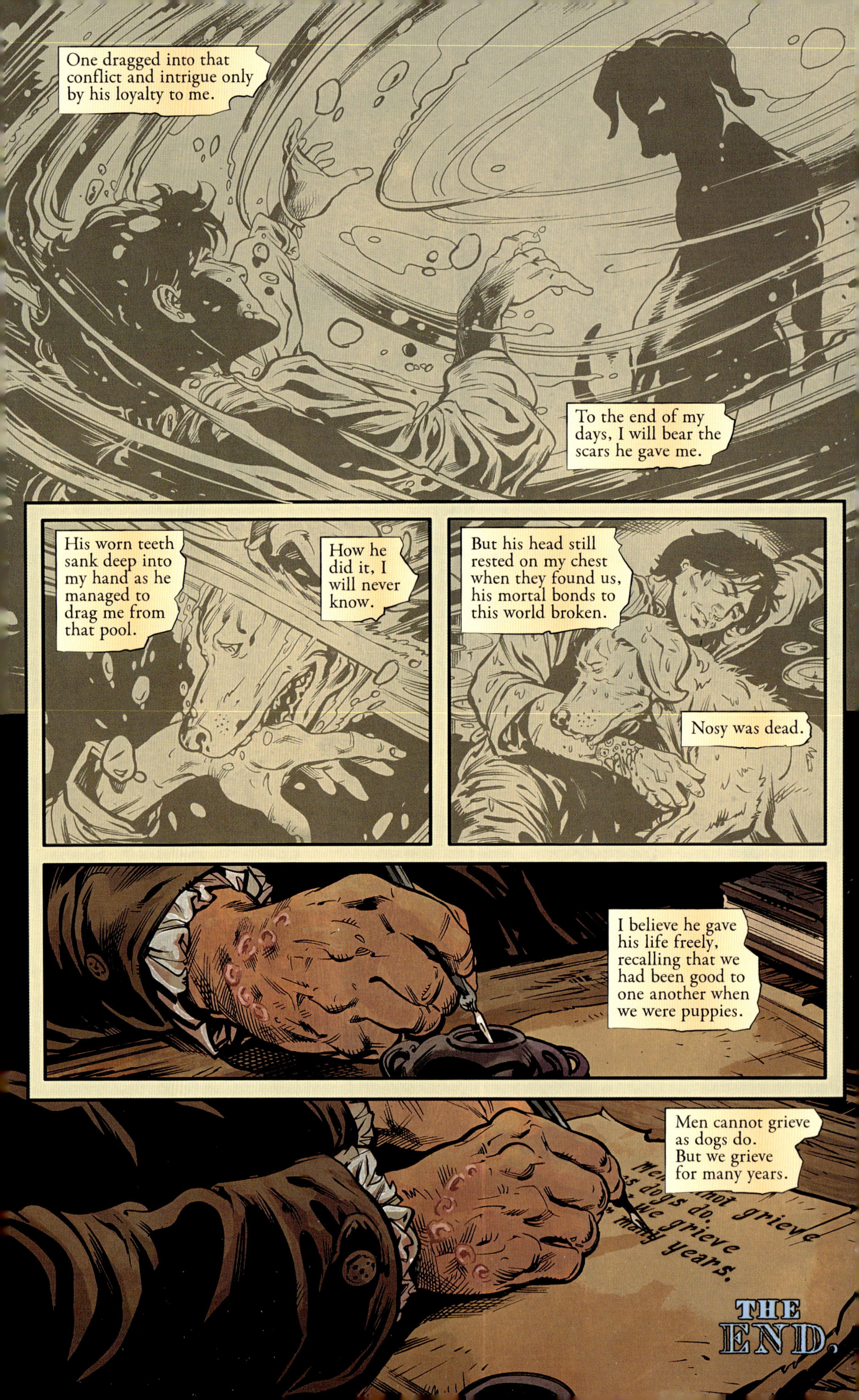
One dragged into that conflict and intrigue only by his loyalty to me.
To the end of my days, I will bear the scars he gave me.
His worn teeth sank deep into my hand as he managed to drag me from that pool.
How he did it, I will never know.
But his head still rested on my chest when they found us, his mortal bonds to this world broken.
Nosy was dead.
I believe he gave his life freely, recalling that we had been good to one another when we were puppies.
Men cannot grieve as dogs do. But we grieve for many years.
THE END.

Assassin's Apprentice III

Sketchbook By Ryan Kelly

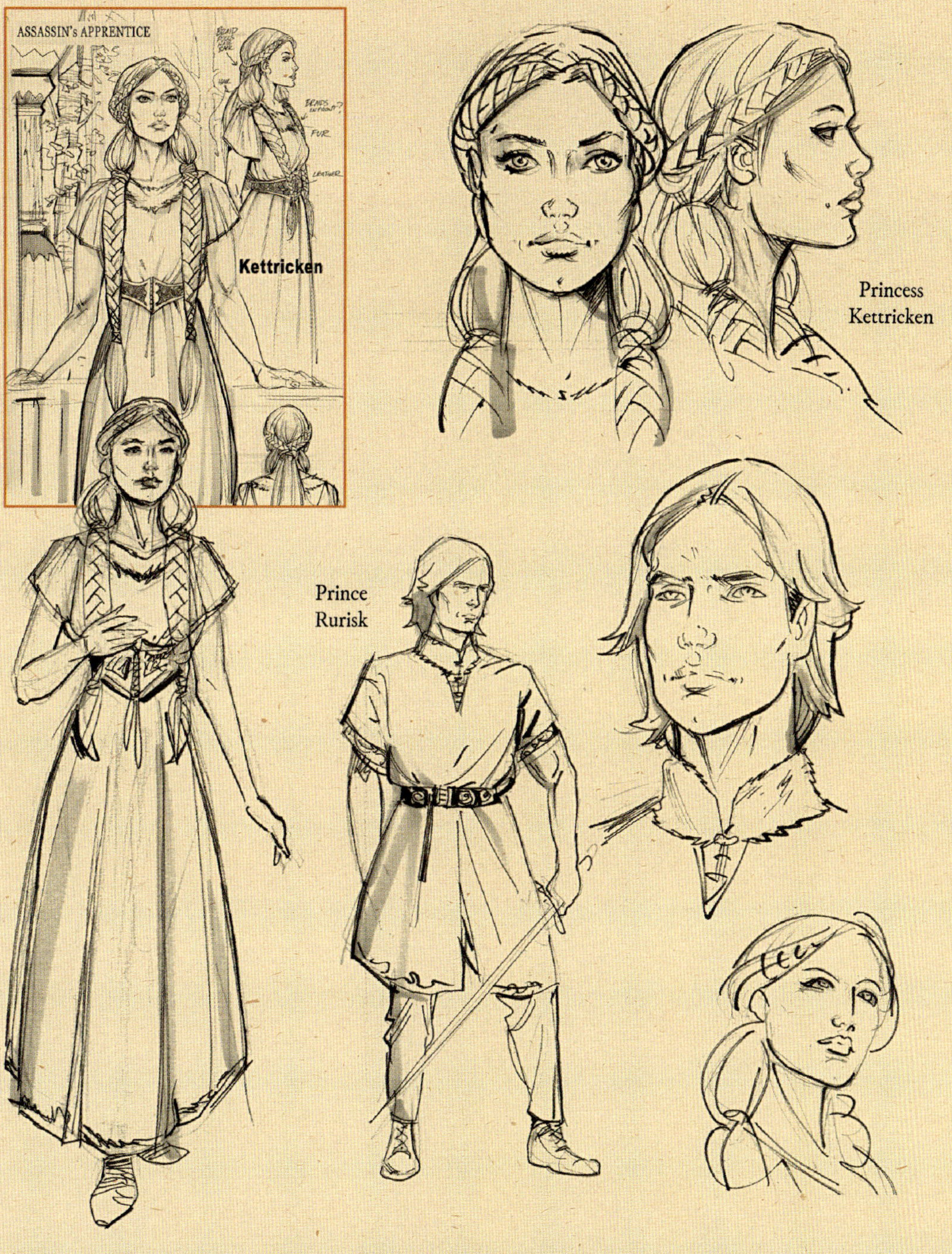
ASSASSIN's APPRENTICE
Kettricken
Princess
Kettricken
Prince
Rurisk

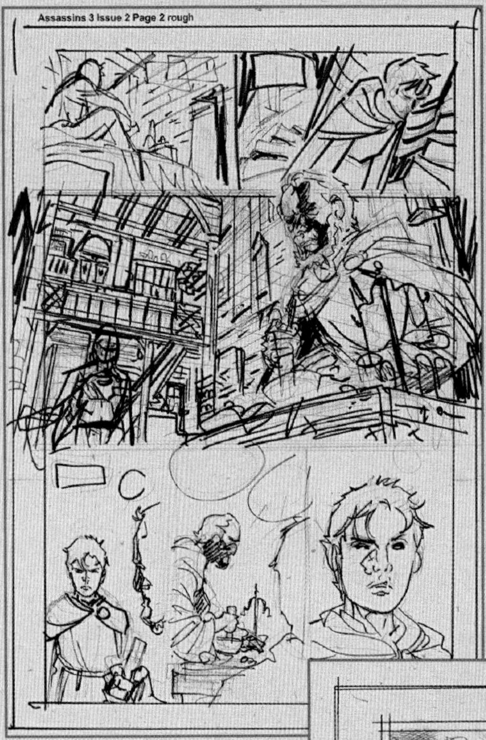
Assassins 3 Issue 2 Page 2 rough

When I work from the script, I "thumbnail" each page. A thumbnail sketch is a small drawing the size of a baseball card. It can take me almost a week to thumbnail a whole issue. After that, I do a layout, then pencils, then the final inks. Therefore, I draw every single page in the book a total of four times! I would not recommend this method to artists. It's a bit taxing and time consuming. But it was my chosen approach for *Assassin's Apprentice*. Here is a rare look at one of my intermediate layout stages. This is drawn quickly with pencil and markers on 11 x 17–inch copy paper. I spend no more than an hour on this stage.

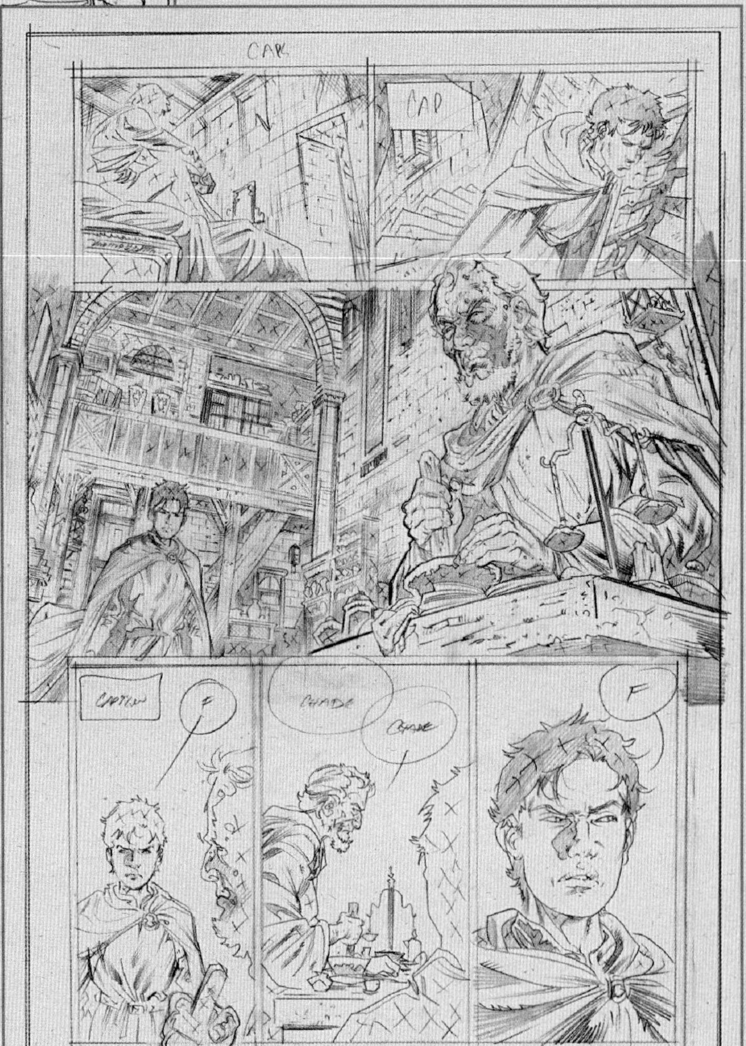
CAP
CAP
CHADE
CHADE

I take my marker layout and lay a large sheet of translucent vellum paper over it. On the vellum, I work the page over in pencil, creating a more refined representation of the page. This is what I normally present to my editor for approval. On the layout, I work with gestural shapes and basic graphic elements, but on the pencils, I work in exact detail and think about depth, space, and lighting.

These are the final inks. One could say there is not much strategy and creativity left at this stage, but that would be a failure to recognize the value of inking. First, there is the danger that I will lose all the energy and spontaneity of the original layout, so I try to bring that back in the inking, keeping the ink lines fresh and loose. There is also the danger of "killing" your pencils with a lot of bad inking: using uniform line weights, inking clunky lines where they should be smooth, over-rendering areas that should be bold and open. Things like that. Even at this stage, I make some bold decisions, such as coloring a whole shape in black silhouette even after previously penciling it in bright detail.

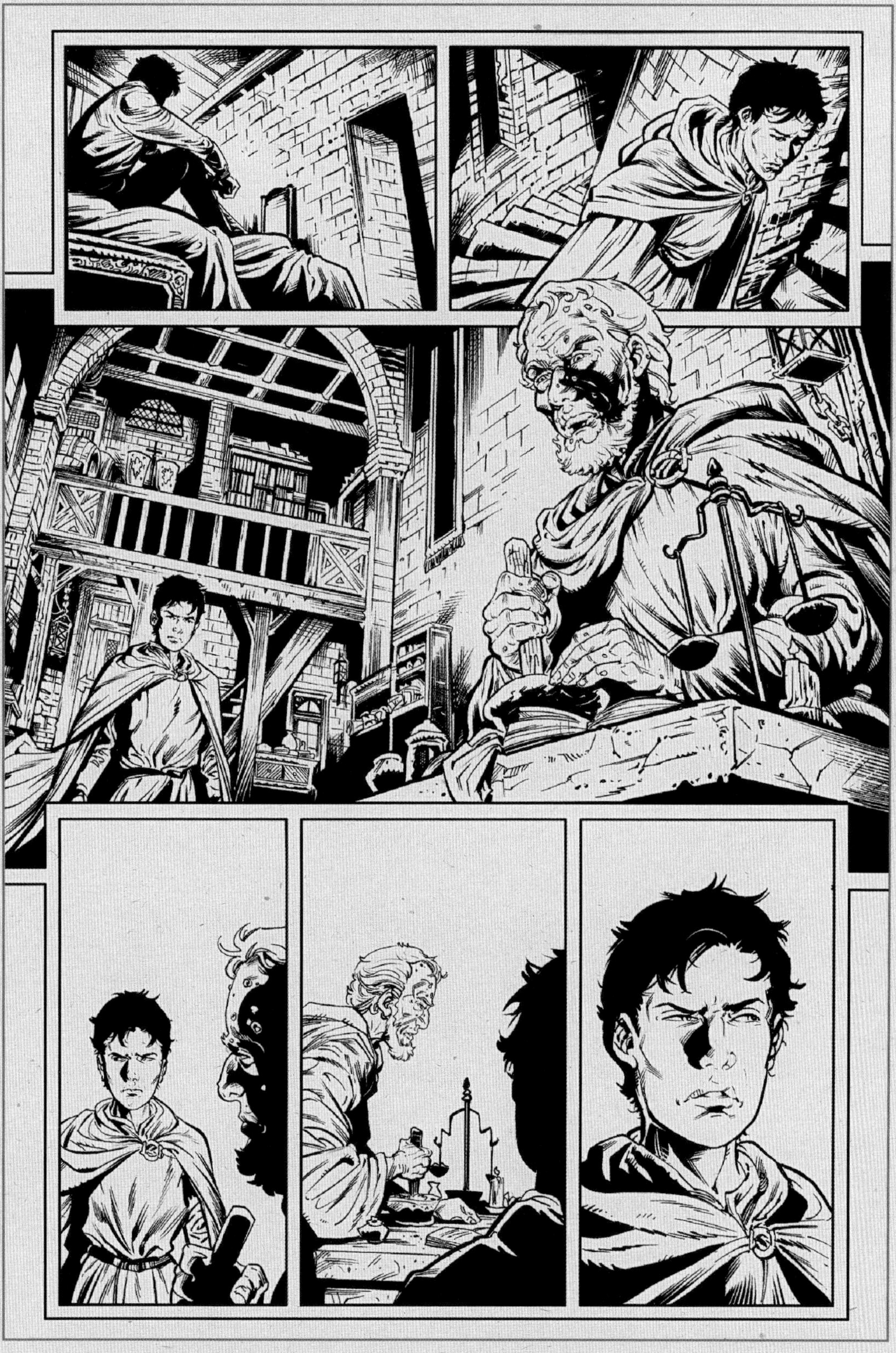

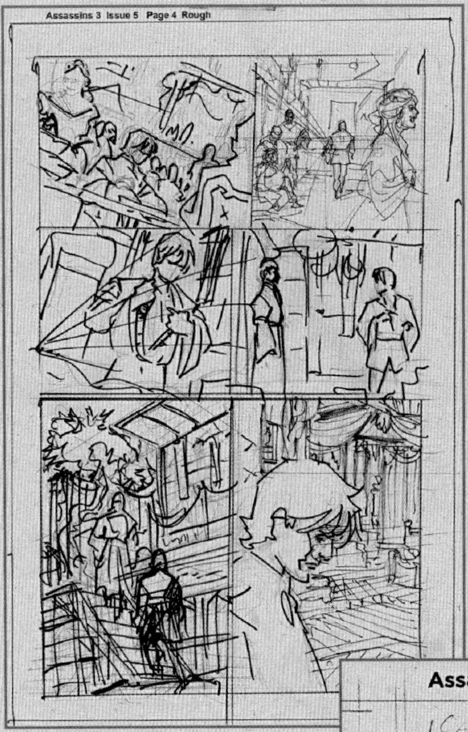
Assassins 3 Issue 5 Page 4 Rough

As you can see in my rough layout, I put little care into "drawing well." I can do that later. In this stage, I just draw right through shapes, work in quick gestural marks, and allow horizon lines and perspective grids to sit freely on the design. It's the scaffolding of the comic page. I plan out my angles and camera shots in this quick marker sketch. I even physically draw in the balloons and caption boxes, making sure to allocate enough room for them.

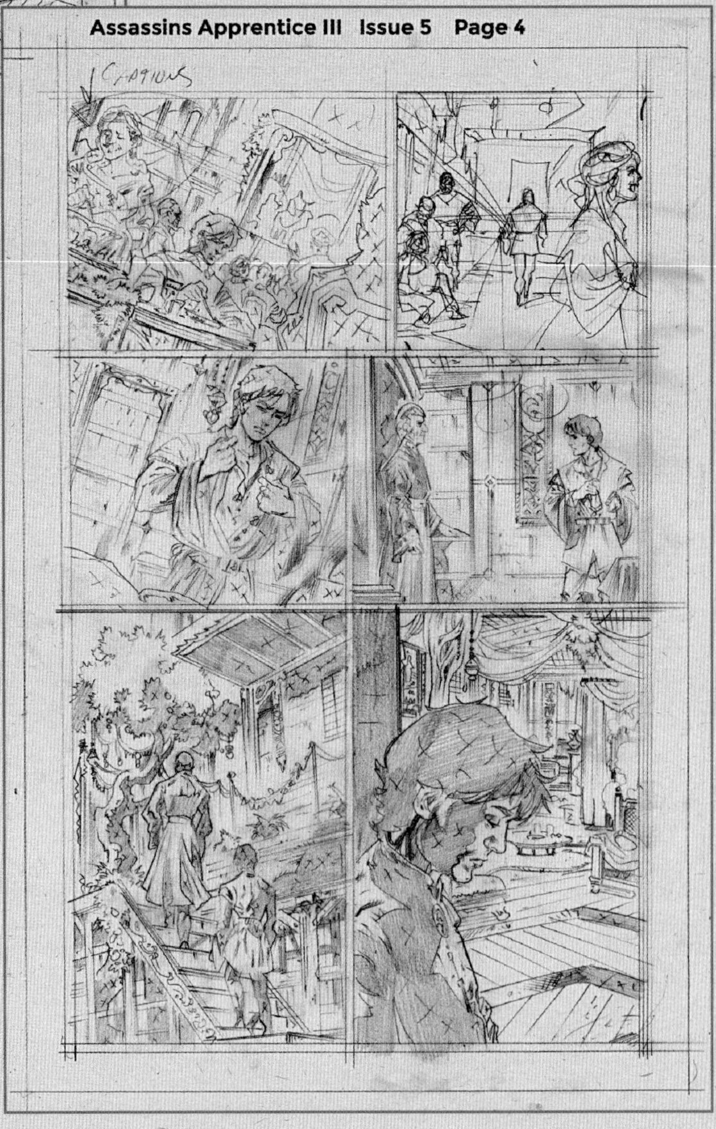
Assassins Apprentice III Issue 5 Page 4
CAPTIONS

The final page begins to take form in the pencils. This is where I create a sense of atmosphere and make sure the facial expressions are clear and, hopefully, matching the dialogue. I do my best to vary my shots and angles. Variety is the spice of comics! After working in this storytelling medium for a long time, one can catch oneself using the same shot or panel arrangement too much, creating a monotonous reading experience.

In the final inks, I do my level best to control the reader's eye using the tools I have: shadows, line weight, textural details. As you can see, there is a lot of movement and activity in these scenes, and I try to make it flow using different camera angles. I make an effort to include a few "down shots" in every issue, even though they are a pain to do. A "down shot" is when the "camera" or "eye line" is high up and looking down on a scene. Those are not fun to draw. But I try to sprinkle in a few when I can!

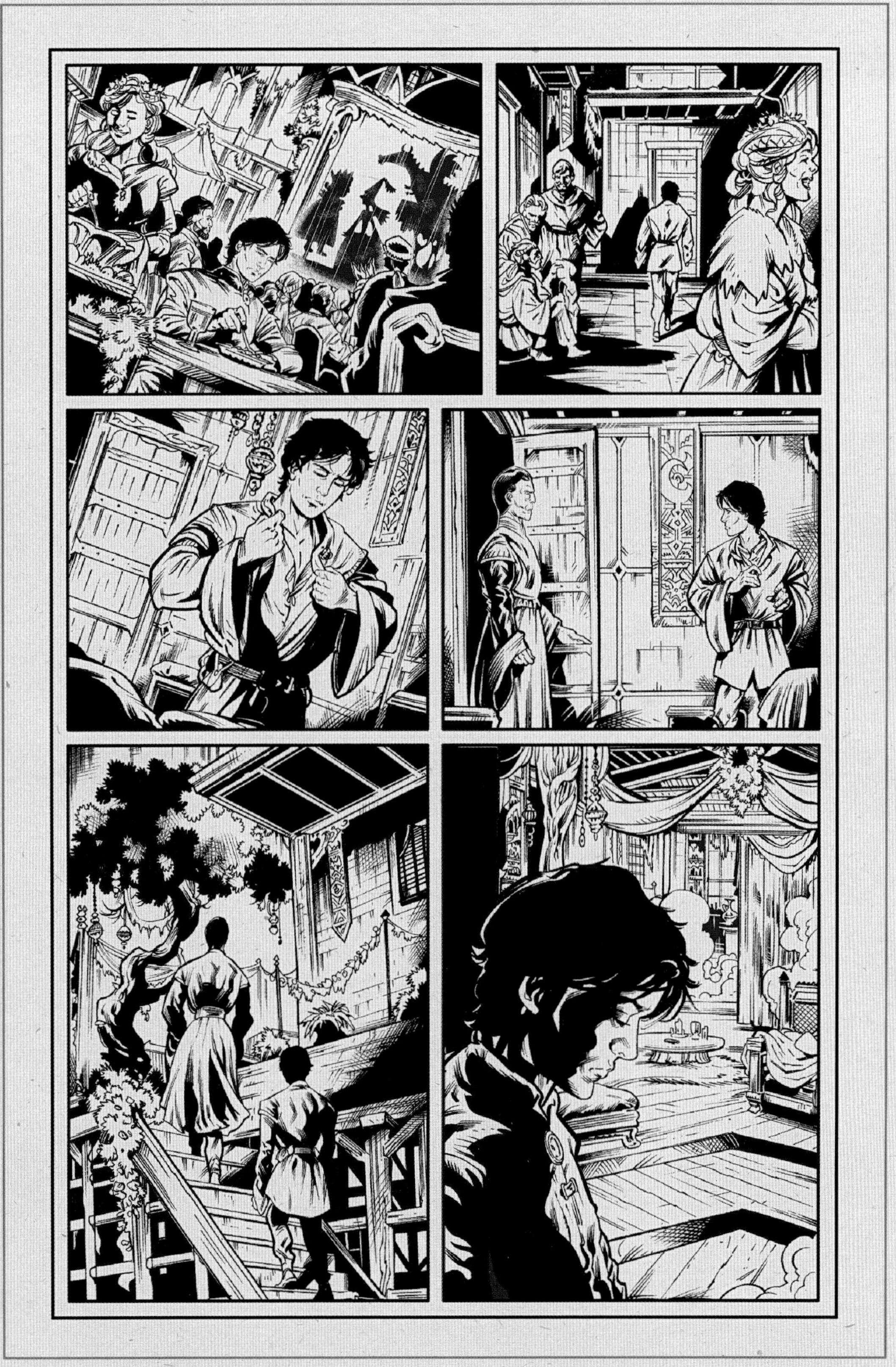

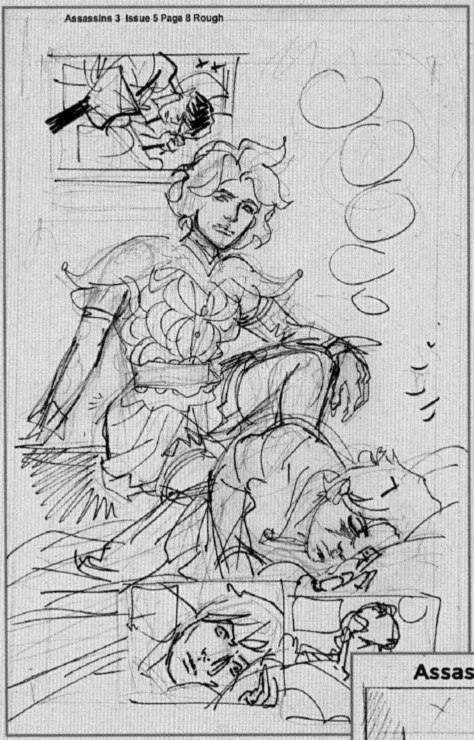
Assassins 3 Issue 5 Page 8 Rough

This page was a breath of fresh air! It's nice to get a big, open page to draw in between the denser story pages. We're fitting much of the original source material in each issue, so sometimes the pages are populated with a lot of caption boxes and narration. I really value some of these more personal and emotional character moments where the creative team can slow down and really illustrate what the characters are feeling—in this case, Fitz and the Fool.

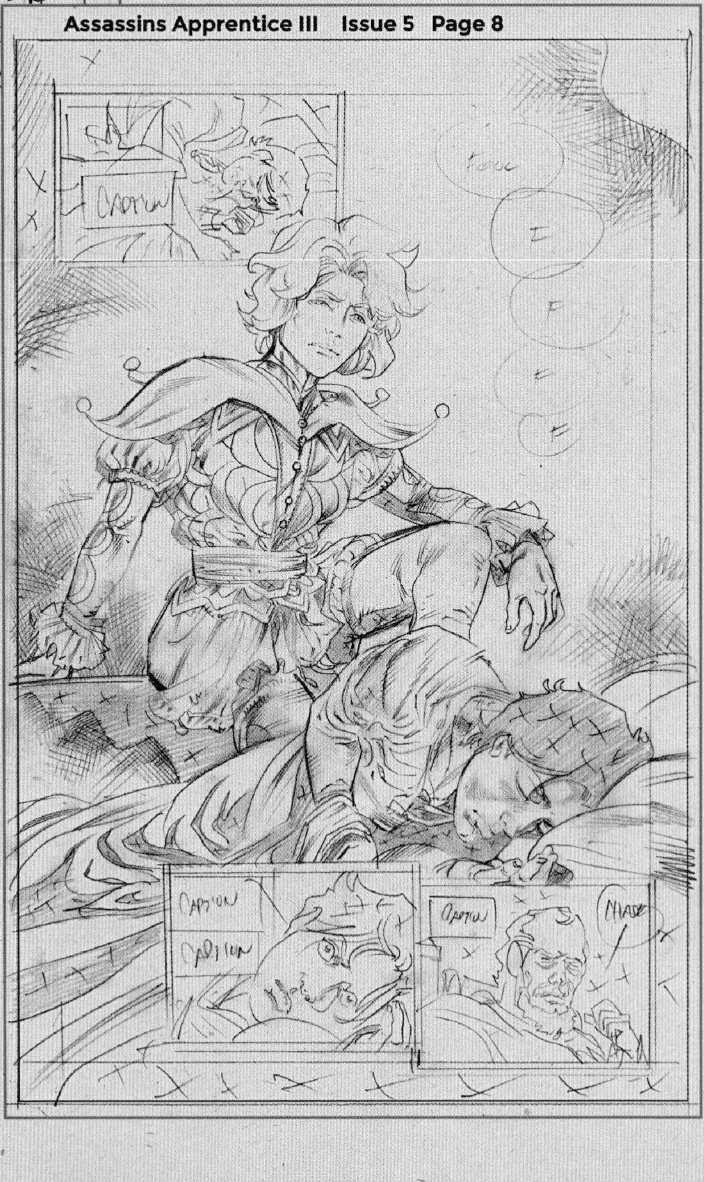
Assassins Apprentice III Issue 5 Page 8
CAPTION
CAPTION
CAPTION
CAPTION
CAPTION

It was important for me to make the art on this page look dreamy and atmospheric, matching the Fool's free-flowing word balloons. I tried using more shadowy shapes and relied less on background lines and details. I think it worked to establish a more magical and spiritual space among the very sharp and real conflicts Fitz was dealing with.

This is essentially the final shot of the Fool in the series, so I tried to make it count. At this point in the series, I was becoming acutely aware that these were my final moments with the people of the world of *Assassin's Apprentice*. My last time drawing them. That finality was beginning to hit me in a stark way as an artist. When you spend every day drawing these characters for three years—and I work alone—they become your sole personal companions . . . almost literally.

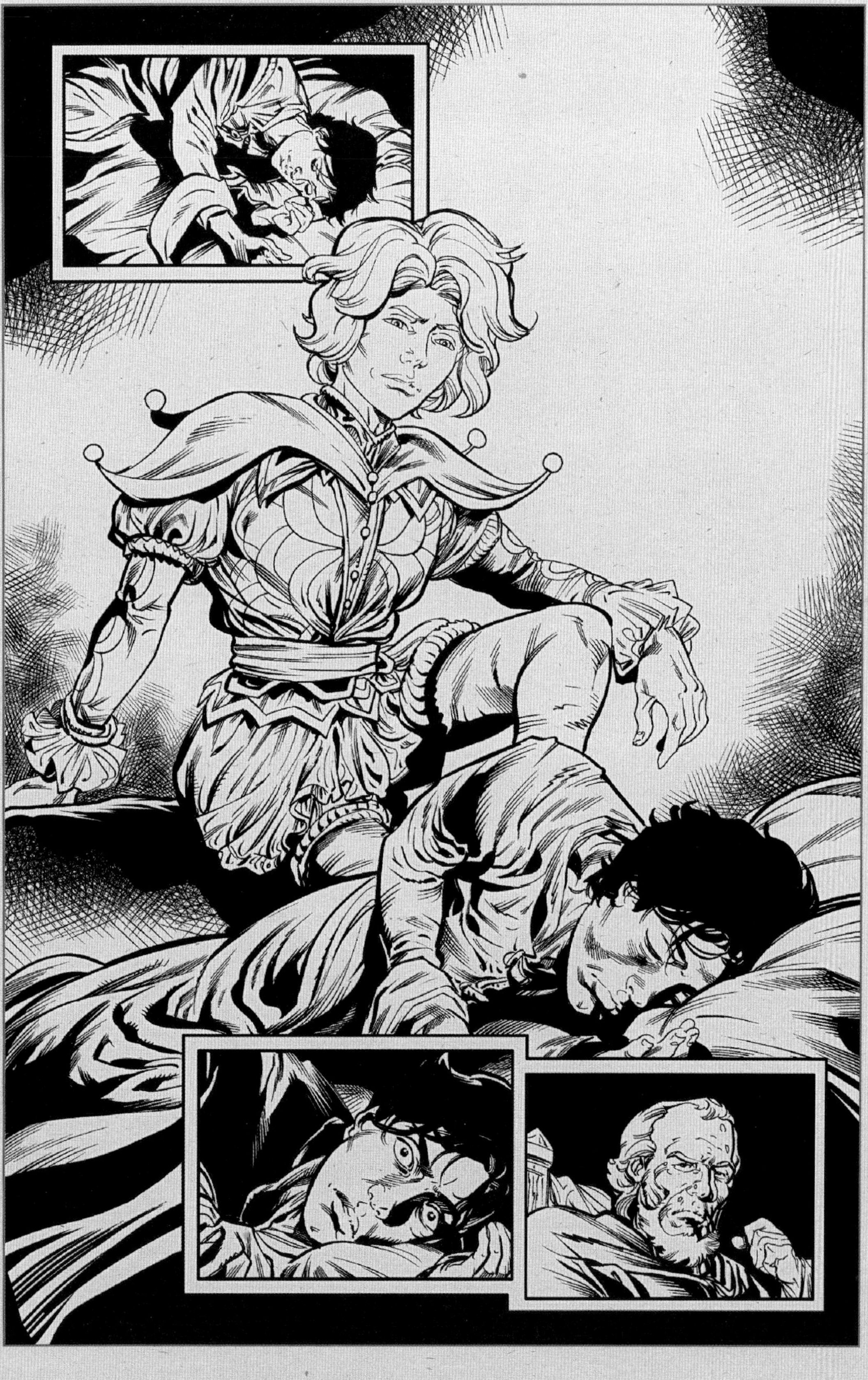

Assassin's Apprentice 6 Breaks
17
AUGUST
AUGUST + REGAL
WITHYWOODS
GALEN
KETTRICKEN
18
BUCK KEEP
SHIP
19
20
NOSY
NOSY FITZ
HAND BITE MARKS
SCRIPT
FITZ VERITY
VERITY
SLEEP
HAND?
THE END

Assassins 3 Issue 6 Page 19
SKILL
VERITY SKILL
CAP

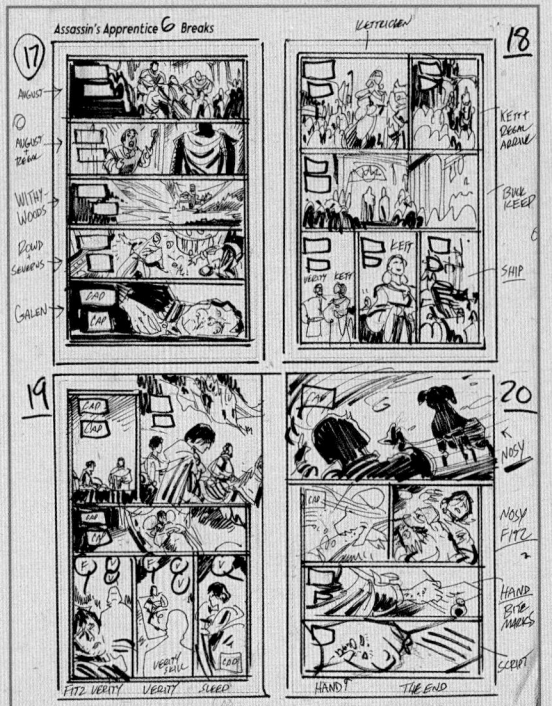

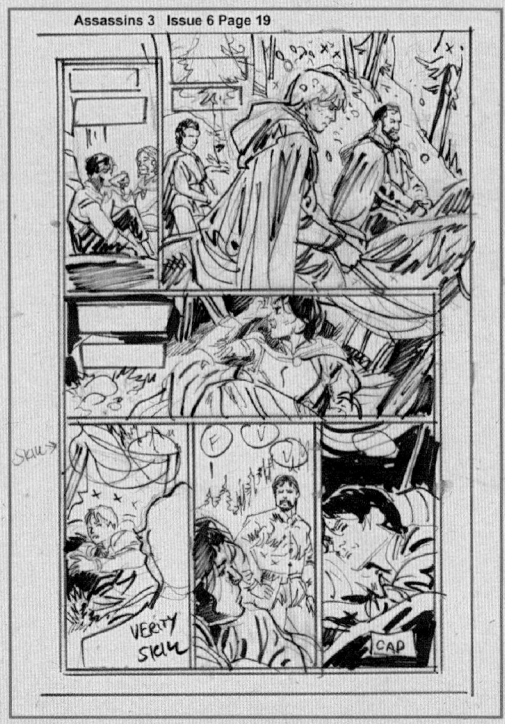

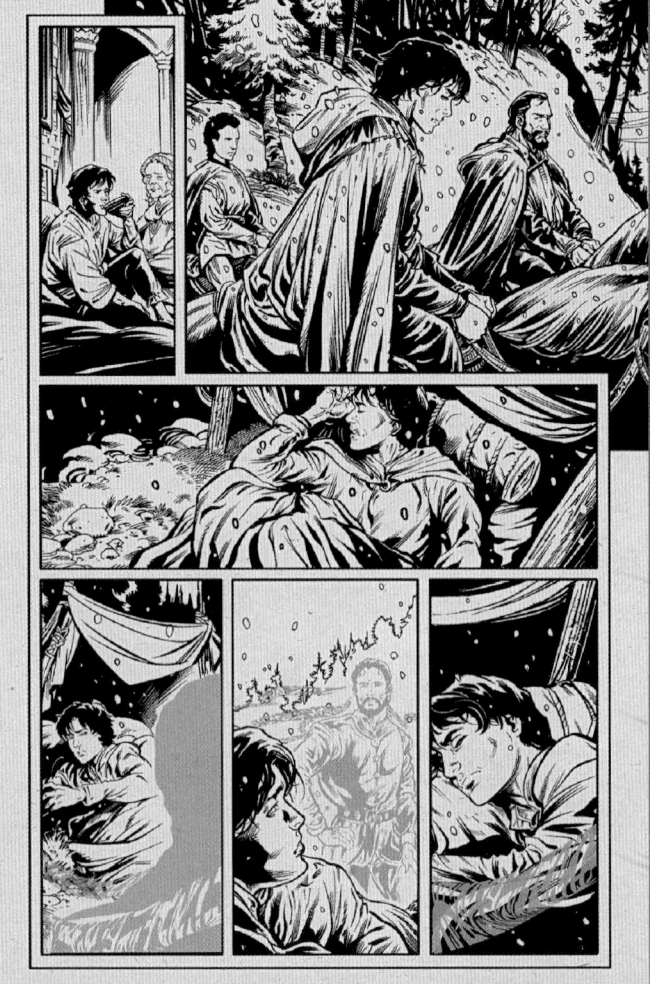

Drawing the final pages of the series felt momentous even though the moments themselves are very somber and quiet. I like that Fitz very much looks the same way I drew him in issue 1, even though he is much older here, and I wanted the art to echo that and resonate with readers. I appreciate the whole creative team lifting me up on this project. I couldn't have done it without them, not even close. And most of all, I hope we created something that honors the book and the fans of *Assassin's Apprentice*.

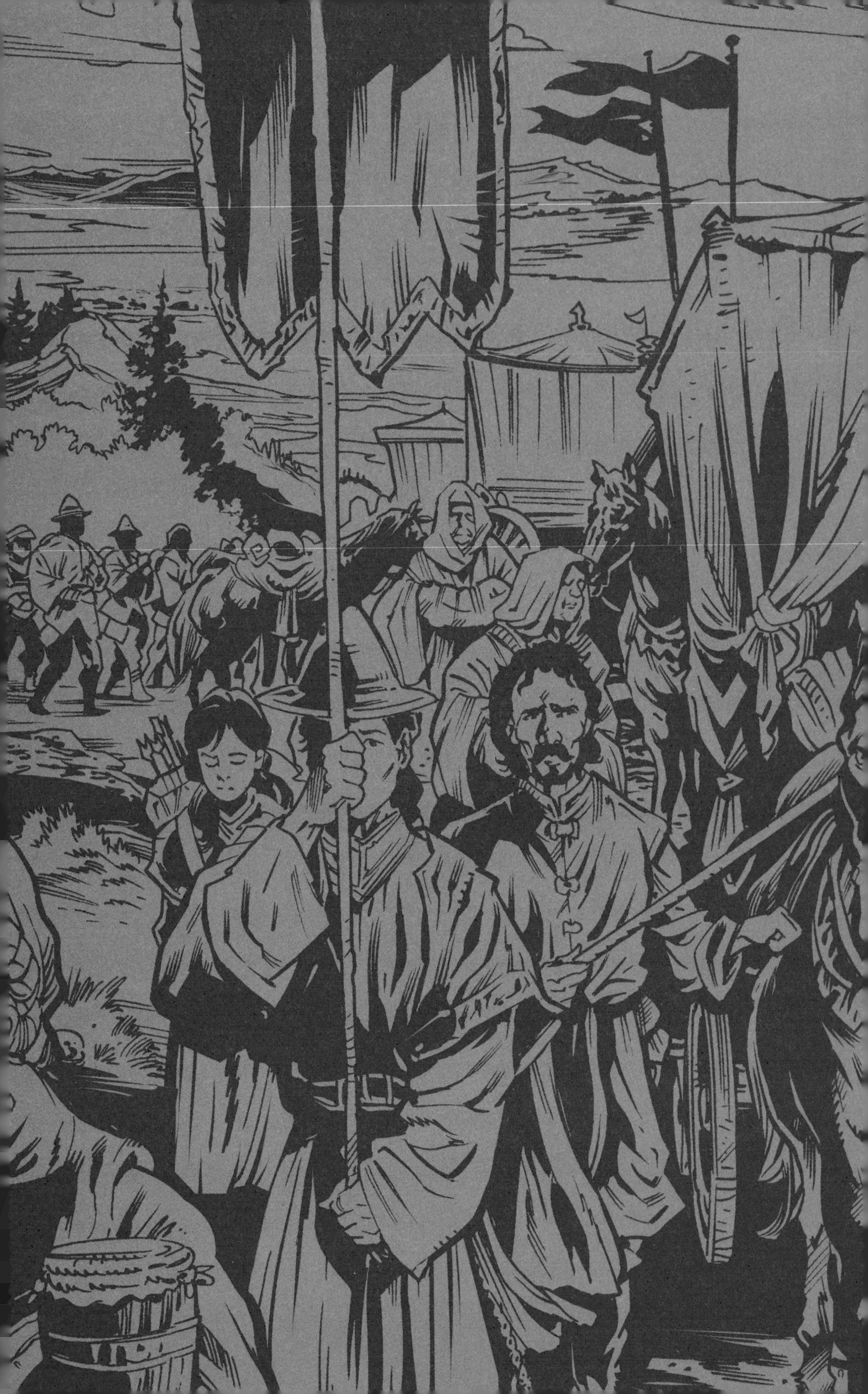